MR. SECOND BEST

LM FOX

MR. SECOND BEST

Editor: Kelly Allenby, Readers Together

Proofreader: Cheree Castellanos, For Love of Books4 Editing

Formatter: Shari Ryan, MadHat Studios

Cover/Graphic Artist: Hang Le

Cover Photographer: (Front) Michelle Lancaster Instagram:@lanefotograf, (Rear) Wander Aguiar |Cover Model: (Front) Heath Hutchins (Rear) Adrea McNulty

*Hardback Discrete Cover Design: KateDecidedToDesign

To all of the brave firefighters and their families who put their lives on the line, day in and day out, in service to others.

Ask, believe, receive, and be immensely thankful,
for all is possible when we live in gratitude and joy.

PROLOGUE

TWO YEARS EARLIER

MELANIE

"Great. So I guess it's just the kids and me. Again. People are going to become suspicious you don't actually exist." After all the years we've been together, you'd think this wouldn't set me off. But I've grown tired of attending every social function alone. Is it asking that much that my husband spends a little quality time with his family once in a while?

"Melanie, you aren't being fair. I'm exhausted. I just finished working seven days straight in the ER. And you know I don't sleep well. Especially when these shifts bounce between days and overnights. I just want to chill here at home," Jake answers in a huff. "And trust me, everyone knows I exist. You post enough on social media."

Was that a dig? I'm irritable and don't know if it's that time of the month or if he's canceled on me so often my patience has run out.

I know this man loves me. He'd do anything for us. But he's *always* exhausted. It's starting to feel like the hospital is the priority, and we're just here when he decides to call it a day.

"I get tired of going to everything alone. This is no life, Jake. Spending all of your time at work. We deserve to see you too."

"I get it, Mel. But you have a heavy social calendar. I don't mind that you like to attend as many things as possible. Entertaining our friends, going to parties and concerts, impromptu drinks... I just can't keep up when I'm running on empty. Work is crushing me right now."

Turning to face him, I put my balled fists on my hips. "Last I recall, you make the schedule." I know I sound testy.

'Cause I am.

"Why aren't you getting the others to pick up some shifts? This has gone on for years. You can't continue to do it all. I don't want the kids looking back and feeling like they had an absent dad."

"That's a low blow. Thanks, Melanie. Way to pile on the guilt."

Ugh. Maybe I went too far. My frustration at feeling like a single parent most days is catching up with me.

My friends seem to think being married to an ER doctor is glamorous. They only see the posts where we're attending hospital galas or out on the water enjoying a rare day together away from work. I think the recent photo of us on the boat I put online may have happened a year ago. He's right. Social media is a smoke screen. But when I saw the picture on my phone, it made me smile. I only wanted to share it, not paint a picture of something we're not.

Walking over to me, he wraps his arms around my waist and pulls me close. "You know you mean everything to me. It's you, me, and the kids. I *am* making a conscious effort to get better about the schedule. I'm trying not to keep picking up the shifts no one else wants. But it isn't easy, honey. I can't afford to have anyone else leave our practice because they aren't happy. Our job is stressful enough. When they quit, that leaves even more shifts to fill until we can get someone new credentialed. And that can take months."

Burying my face in his neck, I try to remember how lucky I am. How lucky our family is. I have this incredible man by my side who works so hard. Undoubtedly, he'd be going to this cookout with us if he weren't so drained.

Jake has been the life of the party since the day we met all those years ago. Kissing his throat, his jaw covered in day-old stubble, I murmur against his skin, "Do you remember that cookout we went to?" Kiss. "When we were in our early twenties at the rescue squad?" I place another kiss on his Adam's apple before continuing, "Munish said, 'Hey, you two come by on Saturday. Bring a few friends if you want.' Then we showed up with half the squad because you mentioned it to everyone you knew." I laugh. Those were definitely the days. We may have worked hard to get where we are now, but we lived life to its fullest.

"Poor Munish. When everyone walked into his backyard, he looked like a deer in headlights." He chuckles. "I didn't think I told *that* many people. And I never thought they'd all show up."

"Ah, Jake. You are the party. Everyone just wanted to be where you were. It's still that way." Squeezing my handsome husband around his chest, I continue. "I'm sorry I'm making things harder for you, asking you to join us when you're worn out." I stop for a moment, biting the inside of my cheek to rein in my emotions. "I just miss you."

"Ah, Mel." He sighs before kissing my temple, his large, warm hands caressing my back. "I'm sorry, hon."

I'm startled to feel tears in my eyes. Why am I getting so weepy? Maybe this *is* PMS. "No, I'm sorry. I shouldn't have said what I did. You're doing so much. Maybe, we'll come back from the cookout a little early and have a movie night with you."

"I'd like that. I just need a few hours of sleep." I feel a pat on my backside as he pulls away and heads for the shower. The long hours in the hospital are bad enough, but when he works the late shift, we're like two ships passing in the night. I know we aren't unique in this. Millions of people make it happen for their families by working late into the night. It just gets to me sometimes. The desire for normalcy. To enjoy time with friends and relish the life we have. Instead, those few moments we spend together outside our home often feel forced. Because I know Jake's spent, and he doesn't want to be there.

I admit, there were times I'd contemplated whether my husband was bipolar. He never displayed any mood swings. Yet he'd vacillate between his party animal persona and a couch potato, all in one week. Surviving on little sleep between work, studies, and partying. You can get away with that kind of behavior in your twenties. But it catches up to you.

Eventually, I reasoned it was merely his personality. Jake lives life large, giving one hundred fifty percent to anyone and anything in his orbit. He goes full steam ahead until he hits a wall, then crashes for a few days before returning to his old self again. I need to remember that when I'm feeling left out. He's only human.

Walking to the hall closet, I grab my large tote bag and gather what I'll need for spending a day with friends outdoors. Placing it on the kitchen counter, I also retrieve the insulated bag I'll use to transport water and the side dishes I prepared for the cookout.

The evening will be low-key. Simply a few friends from my college sorority and their families that I haven't seen in ages. We'll probably laugh over margaritas while the kids play cornhole or kick the soccer ball. There's a good possibility Jake not coming has as much to do with Kelly and the girls as his current fatigue. I probably would've had a better chance of getting him to join me at a social function with our close friends Nick, Kat, and his best friend, Huggie. *Let's get real.*

"Hey, Mom. When are we leaving?" my nine-year-old, Seth, asks.

"In about thirty minutes. Can you grab the sunscreen and some bug spray?" I tend to get eaten alive at these types of functions.

"Sure."

"Oh, and let Ruby know to grab a light jacket, just in case it gets chilly. We might not need it since we're leaving early."

"Why are we leaving early?" my beautiful raven-haired seven-year-old questions as she skips into the kitchen.

"Dad's exhausted from the last week. He's going to get a few hours of sleep while we're gone. We've all been missing him, so I told him we'd come back and have a movie night with him."

"Yay!" Ruby shouts before Seth quickly covers her mouth with his hand. "Oops. I didn't wake him up, did I?"

"No, baby. He's in the shower."

"I was just excited. I've really missed him," she says, coming in for a hug.

"I know. We all have. He works very hard. But he does it to give us a great life and because he loves taking care of people in the ER. It's hard for him to be everything to everyone. We need to accept his job is part of who he is." I kiss her on the top of her head, pulling her into my side, hoping I can convince her *and myself* that what I'm saying is true. When selfishly, I still want him with us more. "Asking him to work less would make him unhappy. He thrives on it. So we need to be supportive."

"And you are," his reassuring voice interrupts our conversation from the hallway. He's leaning against the doorframe, arms crossed over his chest, and his dark hair still damp with a bit of a curl at the ends. There's a look of pride on his handsome face. It warms my heart to know we've gotten past our earlier conversation.

"Daddy!" Ruby squeals and collides with him before he can get his arms open for her.

"Umph. Hi, princess." He chuckles, giving her a bear hug. "It's been a rough week. We were already short with Donovan on vacation, and then someone called out sick. I'm going to try really hard not to work that many days in a row anymore. I miss you guys too."

"It's okay, Dad. I understand," Seth says as he embraces his father. "We'll see you tonight after you get some sleep."

"Thanks. You guys have fun," he says, bending to kiss Ruby on the nose before walking over to the fridge to fill a glass with water. Turning to me, he gives me a quick peck on the cheek. "Not too much fun, Mel. Call me if you've had too many drinks."

"Oh, that won't happen." My party days aren't what they once were. Since having kids, I practically fall asleep before getting that intoxicated. And definitely not at a family function. "I want to make it through the movie with you guys tonight before I start snoring."

"Well, it is loud." Jake teases with a wink. "The three of us won't be able to hear over you."

"Mommy, you snore?" Ruby cackles as I swat Jake with a kitchen towel.

I'd like to rib him about wanting to save my energy for more intimate activities later, but there's no point. That's an area that's been lacking for a long while. Again, probably more of a result of getting older, exhaustion from raising kids, and familiarity. When you've been married to the only man you've ever been intimate with... well, familiarity doesn't always prove to be a great aphrodisiac.

"I'm going to hit the sack. Hoping I'll be tired enough that I won't need the sleeping pills. I'll see you when you get home." And with a quick peck, he strolls out of the room.

~

"I'm sorry Jake couldn't make it," Jim says as he pops off the bottle cap of his lager.

"Yeah, the hours in the ER are grueling. He tried, but this was a tough week. Unfortunately, everyone can't work nine to five." I hope I don't sound as bitter as I feel.

Kelly comes out of her back door carrying a tray of appetizers and places them on the picnic table in front of us. She and Jim have been married for four years. Their three-year-old son, Maddox, is chasing Seth and Ruby around the backyard, squealing with fits of laughter when they pretend to let him catch them. "I bet you don't get to see much of him, huh?"

"Not really. But I knew what I was getting into." Sadly, knowing it didn't make it any easier.

"Yeah, I'm glad we both work normal hours. I don't adjust well to change." The two other girls from my sorority laugh, knowing she's spot on. Kelly is a control freak. This life wouldn't bode well for her. My eyes drift over to the kids and notice they're now playing peek-a-boo with Maddox from behind a large old oak tree. It seems like just yesterday Seth was doing that in our yard with Rub—

"Mel?"

I look back and notice everyone staring as if waiting for an answer.

"Oh, I'm sorry. What was that?"

"I said, I think you guys are overdue for a vacation."

"You know, you're right. We are." That's it. Jake's been promising to take the kids on a Disney cruise forever. We're blessed to be able to afford such a luxurious trip. It's time we can't seem to come up with. Maybe I'll broach the subject tonight during the movie. If we plan this out far enough, perhaps the schedule won't be an issue.

Hours later, we enter the house gingerly in case Jake's still sleeping. He's had issues with falling asleep for as long as I can remember. When we rode the rescue squad together as teens, I'd fall asleep in the bunk room while he'd study or watch television hours into the night. It wasn't until he was in medical school that I noticed he'd started taking zolpidem.

The sleeping pill seemed to help, but he's never taken it regularly, to my knowledge. So if he didn't admit defeat and take one until this afternoon, he could be down awhile.

Placing our things in the kitchen, I remove the items from the cooler and rinse the serving dishes before placing them in the dishwasher. Wiping my hands on a hand towel, I turn and head for our room. Yet all I find there is an empty messy bed. I walk to the bathroom, but the lights are off. Had he managed a few hours of sleep until work called him back in?

"Dad's car isn't here," Seth states as he comes in from the garage. I'd parked in the drive on autopilot to carry everything into the house, never considering he wasn't here.

"I'll text him. Hopefully, he just ran out for popcorn."

But my gut says we aren't that lucky.

The metallic sound of keys causes me to wake. Rolling onto my back, I notice Jake standing by the dresser. He's dressed in dark scrubs and looks freshly showered.

"Are you coming or going?"

"Going. I have to work the early shift," he says with nonchalance.

"What, you just came home to shower?"

"Mel, please don't start in again."

"Is it even safe for you to work back-to-back like this?"

Jake gives me a quizzical look before walking to my side of the bed. "I'll see you tonight."

"Please try to come home before the kids go to bed. They were really heartbroken movie night didn't happen. We need to make up for last night."

Again with the quizzical look. "Okay," he answers before leaving without another word.

"Daddy," Ruby yells, jumping from the couch to greet her dad. Thank goodness he made it home at a decent hour. "And you brought pizza?"

"I did. Your favorite. Cheese with extra cheese."

"Yay!"

"What're we watching tonight, Seth?" he asks.

"We were waiting for you to help us pick."

"How about The Incredibles?"

"Oh, I love that one." Seth grins.

I pull out plates and cups for everyone and we settle in for an overdue family night. It feels like ages since we've done this. But as soon as the movie begins and I see the smiles on my children's faces, I feel content. I admit, wanting to talk to Jake about a cruise is distracting me. I'm antsy to get him out of the kids' earshot long enough to question him about it. It's been well over a year since the last time the four of us had a whole week together.

"We should dress up like these guys for Halloween," Jake says.

"Yeah!" Ruby claps.

"That would be awesome," Seth joins in.

"You want to put on that bright red Lycra one-piece?" I ask, more than a little stunned at his suggestion.

"If I get to see you wearing one, it'll be worth it." He snuggles up with me as the movie plays and it reminds me just how much I love him. The way I feel cared for and safe when he's here. Even after all of these years.

"I'm heading to bed," Jake says as he stretches his arms overhead.

"Awe, the movie is almost over," Ruby pleads.

"I'm sorry, Rubs. I tried to make it, but I've been forcing my eyes open for the last thirty minutes." Jake stands and walks over to where the kids are lying on the sectional. Kissing them each on the head, he comes over to give me a chaste peck before heading up the stairs.

The movie credits begin rolling within minutes of Jake's departure, and I gather up the drink cups and ask the kids to carry the popcorn bowl and napkins into the kitchen before heading to bed. They have school in the morning, so I'm thankful they bathed and changed into jammies before the movie began. Their spirits appear brighter after tonight, which makes me one happy mama.

After tucking them in, I make my way toward our bedroom. It's obvious Jake's out cold by the way he's sprawled across the bed. Maybe he *was* too tired to last that extra few minutes.

Deciding a hot shower might settle me to sleep, I turn on the spray and step in. As I lather my hair, I can't help reflect on the last few months. Tonight was a treat. Yet between Jake's long hours at work and our poor sex life, the thought suddenly hits me.

Is he having an affair?

We've been together since we were teens. I'd joined the local rescue squad, and a few weeks later, Jake was assigned to my crew. Looking back, I recall thinking he was a true force of nature. Even as a young man, he was confident and made things happen. It didn't matter if it was getting accepted into medical school or planning a last-minute get-together. He accomplished whatever he set his mind to.

I guess that included me.

He was only a year older than I was, but Jake completely swept me away with his outgoing personality. Anyone who met him felt they'd known him forever. He never met a stranger, as the old saying goes.

Our friendship quickly morphed into more. As I rinse the suds from my hair, I recall the red roses he'd leave for me to find. There was never a card or deep discussion about his feelings for me. He's never been the romantic sort. But I knew early on that we belonged together, and his reassurance of that was all the romance I needed.

Stepping out of the shower to towel dry, I look in the mirror. *There's no way on earth Jake Harris would cheat on me. He has more integrity than anyone I know.* I can't even entertain that the man I've known and loved for twenty years would do anything dishonest where our relationship was concerned. Nodding my head in solidarity with the woman staring back at me, I toss those questions aside.

I drop my towel onto the counter and notice Jake's prescription bottle of zolpidem. I can't help but wonder if he took one this evening before the movie began. Turning the small amber colored bottle of pills in my hand, I read the multiple warnings on the label. My thoughts instantly go to my friend, Kat, who was experiencing sleep walking with a similar medication. Funny, you don't see *that* warning written on here.

I return the bottle to the counter, hang up my towel, and pad quietly into the bedroom.

Deciding to get a good night's sleep and face the morning with a better disposition, I crawl into bed and gaze lovingly at my husband. He's a good man, Melanie. Things will get better.

~

Awakening with a jolt, my skin covered in a sheen of perspiration, I turn and find Jake still sleeping soundly beside me. My heart is thrumming wildly in my chest. That nightmare seemed so real.

It took forever to fall asleep last night, and once I did, I recall replaying a conversation I'd had with Kat over dinner some months back.

"Jake mentioned when he uses zolpidem, occasionally weird shit happens. Is that true?" she'd asked.

"Yeah. Sometimes he gets completely turned on, and the sex is incredible. Is that what you mean?" I remember thinking it was odd he'd share that with her.

"Well, more the fact he said he doesn't remember a thing about it the next day."

I remember feeling I'd been struck by lightning at her statement. *"God, I thought he was pulling my leg about that. Hell. That's some sleeping pill."*

"Now you know why I decided to stop taking them. I'm starting to wonder what is real. I question what I could've been doing when I wake up wearing strange clothing," she'd added, looking humiliated.

"Maybe I should pay a lot more attention at home. When he's taking those."

I recall talking to him about my conversation with Kat after I'd returned home that night. He assured me everything was fine. Jake said he'd noticed some things seemed off if he'd mixed alcohol with the sleeping pill, but he's cut his drinking way back. He'd tended to go overboard in college on more than one occasion, but luckily it never went too far. Could the zolpidem be to blame for his erratic behavior?

"You okay?"

Looking over, I notice he's awake. "Yeah, why?"

"Because you're sitting up in bed, and you look like you've run a mile. Did you have a bad dream?"

"I think so. I don't remember much except chasing after you."

"Oh, honey, come here," he says, pulling me to him. "I'm sorry about the way things have been lately."

"Jake?"

"Yeah?"

"Where were you the other night?"

"When?"

"The night you were supposed to be waiting for us to come home and have a movie night? The three of us got here, and you were gone. I assumed you got called into work. When you didn't return my calls or texts, I went to bed. But the next day, you acted like you didn't know what I was talking about."

The room grows quiet, and I can't hold back any longer. "I'm worried you're doing weird things on the sleeping pills. Do you even remember where you were?"

Again, silence. I know I'm right. Something isn't adding up. "Jake?"

"I don't know what to say, Mel. I can't stop taking them. I'll never sleep."

"But it isn't safe. You were driving around like that. There has to be another way."

"I know." I can feel him exhale a puff of warm air against my clammy skin. "I'll try to stop. And if I use them, I'll make sure you're aware first, okay?"

"Okay." I guess it'll have to do. How long has this been happening? What if he'd hurt someone?

~

"I have a busy day today," I yell over the white noise of the blow dryer. "I'm going to run some errands until I meet up with the sitter later. Don't forget. You promised to go to Seth's school for career day. It's really important to him."

"I know, Melanie. It's important to me too. I'll be there." The sound of his voice grows louder with each word, and I look up to see him standing in the doorway with his black scrubs on. "You're beautiful."

Turning toward the mirror, I take in just how beautiful I am. My face is avocado green, courtesy of my new organic mask, and my toothbrush is sticking out of the corner of my mouth as I blow dry my unruly hair, which desperately needs a trim. "Really?"

"Yes. Really," he tosses back with a smile as he comes closer and carefully places a chaste kiss on the corner of my mouth not inhabited by a toothbrush.

"That's talent," I joke, noticing he only has a small trace of pea-green lotion under his lip. Wiping it off, I return to drying my hair.

"I'll meet you back here tonight. I'll text if I'm running late."

"No. No running late. You have to be at Seth's school on time, and then you're coming here. I want today to be a good day, Jake." I've no sooner lectured him that this will not fly today when the thought of seeing my bestie overtakes me. "Oh, I can't wait to see Kat. I want to hear all about her honeymoon." I dance in place in sheer joy that my friend is home. I must look like a cartoon character hopping from foot to foot in my current state.

"Bye," he bellows from down the hall. I hadn't even seen him walk away.

∽

"Hey, babe. What's up?" I ask, juggling the phone on my shoulder as I attempt to place my groceries into the car.

"Dad didn't come." I can hear the heartbreak in Seth's voice, and my stomach drops. It's enough for me to want to drive to that damn ER and strangle Jake.

"Seth, I'm so so sorry. I'm sure something bad must've happened for him to miss it. He knew how important this was to you."

"I know. But I'm pretty mad. He didn't even call. We all just kept sitting there, waiting for him."

I can feel my blood start to boil. It's one thing when he disappoints me, but the kids. He said he had it covered. That it wouldn't be a problem. "Seth, I'm on my way home. I'll talk to your dad."

"What's the point?" He huffs. I wonder if he's right.

Hanging up the call, I'm tempted to call Jake right now, but this conversation needs to happen in person. And I don't want it in earshot of the kids. So for now, a text will have to do.

3:45 p.m.
Melanie: I'm headed home from the store. The rest of my errands will have to wait. We need to talk. You not making it to Seth's school really upset him. This isn't okay anymore. I know you have a lot on you at work, but you could've at least called the school.

Thirty minutes pass, and there's no response. I don't know if he's ignoring me until tonight or if he's too busy to answer. His shift was over hours ago. Seth is sulking in his room. Poor Ruby is watching television, trying to act as if everything is okay. But I know she's hurting, too, as she's squeezing her stuffed bear, Boo, under her arm like a life preserver.

My cell phone dances across the marble kitchen countertop, and I jump at the intrusion. Grabbing it quickly, I'm shocked at the female voice on the other end of the line.

"Melanie? Are you there?"

"Oh, yes. I'm sorry. I was expecting Jake."

"I'm sorry to have to call you, dear. I'm afraid Stacy isn't going to be able to sit with the kids tonight. She's come down with a wicked cough and a low-grade fever."

"Oh. I'm sorry to hear that." Well, this day has gone to hell. "I hope she feels better. Thank you for calling, Vicky." The line goes silent, and I contemplate if I should simply bail on tonight's plans and see Kat some other time.

"Who was that?" Seth asks from the doorway.

"Ms. Beazley. She said Stacy is sick and can't come tonight."

"I bet Ms. Jones next door would watch us for a little while," Ruby chimes in. "She's always inviting us to come over and have cookies when she bakes them."

Hmmm. Maybe. Truth be told, I'm not as excited about this evening as I once was. It'll be evident Jake and I are fighting, and we don't need an inquisition. My emotions are too raw. Maybe this will give me the excuse I need to give a quick hello to my friends and come back here to the kids. I need to find a way to keep a clear head so I can have this conversation with Jake once and for all.

"Oh my gosh, married life looks good on you!" I shout as I squeeze my dear friend, Kat.

"It feels good too." She giggles.

"I hate to do this, but can we plan a lunch or something so I can hear all of the dirty details?" I laugh. "The sitter wasn't well, so I had to leave Seth and Ruby with the neighbor. I couldn't wait to see you and Nick. Oh my gosh, you're so tan!" I pull back to take her in. "I want to hear all about your romantic honeymoon when I'm not distracted by thoughts of getting back home to them."

"I completely understand, Mel. Of course," Kat reassures me. "Give them a big hug from me."

I give her another squeeze. Not only because I've missed her, but I secretly think I'm using her like Ruby needed Boo the bear earlier today. She doesn't realize she's comforting me any more than that stuffed bear knew his role with Ruby. Looking over Kat's shoulder, I see Jake looking in my direction. His expression is unreadable.

"Okay, I'll call you tomorrow, and we'll figure out when we can make lunch or drinks happen."

"You've got it," she sings back. Kat is literally glowing. I'm tickled for her. This girl has waited her whole life to find happiness. I hope, being married to a surgeon, they can keep some balance before they end up like our current mess.

Walking over to my husband, I don't pretend to be the dutiful wife. "I'm heading home. Thanks for calling and letting me know what happened," I add with venom. I watch as Jake drops his head in shame. I, on the other hand, am keeping my head held high. This is on him, not me. Had he come here early after receiving my text to start drowning his troubles?

"I can't win, Mel. I was in a code. We worked on that poor patient for hours before I had to break the news to his family that we couldn't save him. I'll apologize to Seth. I shouldn't have agreed to go to career day. I just couldn't say no when he asked, and now I've fucked up everything. Again."

That part of me that wants to fix everything is dying to make this okay. But it's not okay. I know Jake had an awful day, but a phone call could've gone a long way. Recalling the sound of Seth's voice cracking under the strain of his disappointment has my Mama Bear in full force.

"Jake, I understand your job is demanding. But you hurt your son. And when you hurt the kids, you hurt me. I'm not going to make a spectacle. I need to get the kids from Ms. Jones's house before they eat their weight in cookies. But if you can't make us a priority, maybe you shouldn't come home."

"Mel—"

I walk briskly past him to the exit doors. This isn't okay anymore. I don't want to give him an ultimatum, but our family needs to come first.

∼

Knock, knock.

"What?" I mumble, rousing from where I've fallen asleep on the couch, and look at my watch.

1:30 a.m.

Knock, knock.

The banging has me fully awake now. Wiping the sleep from my eyes, I head to the door. Why would Jake be causing all of this ruckus, knowing he could wake the kids? Unless he's drunk. He's probably had one too many after what I said to him, and he's come home ready to fight. Grabbing the door handle, I crack the door and peer out to prepare myself.

"Huggie? What are you doing here? Did you have to drive Jake home again?" Folding my arms across my chest in disgust, I feel my ire start to rise. This wouldn't be the first time this has happened.

"No. Can I come in?" This guy. He's been my husband's right-hand man from the moment they met. Jake probably sent him to do his dirty work.

"Sure." I extend my arm in a cynical invitation. "Do you know where he is?"

He walks past me, allowing me to shut the door before he stands before me and takes my hands.

Holy crap. Did I go too far? He's sent Huggie to tell me it's over. That he doesn't want a life with our family anymore.

"Melanie, can we sit down?"

"Just say it, Huggie. Say it. Where is he?" I shout, completely forgetting I have two young children asleep upstairs.

He looks at me with a mixture of pity and confusion. "He's gone, Mel."

Ripping my hands from his, I slump onto my couch. I feel like I'm going to be sick.

Twenty years we've been together.

We have two beautiful children. And he's throwing it all away.

He chose the job over me.

"Is he staying with you?" I choke out. It would only stand to reason he'd move in with his best friend. Now everyone will take sides. We've always had the same friends, and now there will be a divide.

"Melanie," Huggie interrupts.

I turn to look at him, so overwhelmed by what's happening that I'm unsure if I've missed what he's said.

"Melanie, there was an accident. The roads were bad and he..." He takes a steely breath. "Mel, Jake's gone."

CHAPTER ONE

TWO YEARS EARLIER

MELANIE

"Has she said anything?" I overhear faint voices drifting down the hallway from behind me.

"No. But to be honest, she's barely uttered a word since the night I told her." The unmistakable timbre of Huggie's voice breaks through my gloom. "She just nodded when I asked if I could tell the kids. I'm sure she was in shock. There's no way she could've done it."

"Oh, Huggie," Kat cries. "How could this have happened? It's been over a week and I can't get that image of his car out of my head. I keep reliving rolling up onto that accident that night over and over."

"Kat, I'm so sorry. How's Nick holding up? I'm sure finding Jake like that hasn't left his thoughts either."

"We don't really talk about it. It's like living in a tomb."

Lying here, I absorb Kat's words. That's exactly how this feels. Like I've died with Jake, yet I'm stuck here, in this lifeless vault.

I don't know how I managed to get through the funeral. I'd like to say I did it for my kids. But that would be a lie. I'm a far worse parent than I accused Jake of being. I can barely manage myself. Thank heaven for my friends, or my kids would starve to death. I don't have the physical or emotional strength to want to lift my head from this pillow, much less comfort my children who've lost their father.

What is wrong with me? Who does this?

Looking back, it's all a blur. I couldn't tell you anything that was said at the service. There were no tears. I remember feeling like it was an out-of-body experience. I was there, but I wasn't.

The shock of it all must've overtaken me. Or maybe I was merely empty by that point. I forced myself to go through the motions. To get it over with. I'm just worried I'll spend the rest of my days doing the same. Feeling heartbroken and alone. He's all I've known for so long.

～

"I hate leaving her like this," my mother says.

Day after day, I hear conversations swirling around me as if I'm not here.

Because I don't want to be here. Without him.

"I know. Thank goodness she has such great friends. But I can't take any more time off from work," my sister adds.

"I wish there was another option. If I wasn't your full-time sitter, I could stay here with her a little longer."

"Oh, Mom. Please don't make me feel any worse. I feel terrible about this. But my job's pushing me to come back, and I don't have any other arrangements for the kids. Ed's boss has been understanding. But he's worked from home as long as they'll allow." Morgan sounds torn up about going home. I should get up and thank them. Reassure my sister it's okay that she's returning to her life.

Life. What does that even mean anymore?

But I don't have it in me. I don't even have the strength to cry anymore. If only I could force myself to get up and be the mother my children need.

Tomorrow. Maybe tomorrow.

～

"Please try and eat something, Mel. I know this is hard," Kat says above me. "We're here if you need anything."

The only thing I need is sleep. So I cry, knowing that usually sleep will follow.

Lying on my side, I face the wall of windows opposite my bedroom door. I can't handle looking at anyone yet, all of their pitiful glances. I certainly don't have the energy to eat anything. It takes all I can muster to get to and from the bathroom.

A few rays of sunlight sneak through the heavy drapes into the otherwise dark room. It's enough to allow me to see several bouquets of bright red roses I hadn't realized were there before. My eyes trail from one sitting atop the dresser to another on the corner table by my reading chair. I've cried so much my nose is too swollen to have smelled them.

From what Kat shared, the rest of the house looks the same. *Like a funeral home.* All of them generously sent by coworkers, friends, and family. They express their condolences through foliage that will meet a similar fate to Jake's. Who thought sending flowers to someone after death was a good idea?

They'll only die too.

I'm so bitter at life. I've started to despise things that once brought happiness. I used to love how flowers brighten up a space. Bring joy to a room. But I don't deserve to feel joy. I'm not worthy of feeling loved. I stole that from Jake. Sent him to his grave, thinking he had to choose between his job and us.

A sob escapes me as I recall the tortured echo of his voice. The last sound I heard fall from his lips.

Mel...

My heart died on that highway with Jake. And the last words I said to him cause guilt I'll take to my grave.

Today has been brutal—one of the toughest by far. I'm surprised I don't have bed sores from lying in this same position, staring out into space.

I barely had the strength to shower. Then the overwhelm of my last few moments with my broken husband overtook me. I'm not sure how long I crouched on the shower floor. My body shivering from the harsh cold spray hitting my skin was the only thing that brought me back to the present. It took sheer will to stand and turn off the water before practically crawling back to bed.

Drifting in and out of awareness, I'm barely conscious of the soft drag of a brush through my hair. Kat's so good to me. I'd hate to think how my family would've survived without her.

What's left of my family.

~

"Get your things, Ruby. I'm taking you and Seth to our house for a few days, okay?"

I can hear Kat reassuring my heartbroken daughter. This would push any normal mother to get up and comfort her. What kind of parent am I? That I can't force my way through this for my children? Just one more layer of guilt piled on high.

"Is Mommy okay?"

"Yes, baby. She just needs some alone time. She'll be all right. We all miss your daddy, but this is hitting her pretty hard. We need to be strong for her, okay?"

Tears tumble down my cheeks. I need to get my shit together. Another couple of days to wallow in my sorrow. Then I need to put one foot in front of the other. If only for my kids.

~

"I'm getting worried about her, Huggie."

"I know. She's tough. Give her more time, Kat. Those two were thick as thieves for decades. It's going to take her a while. Thanks for taking the kids to the lake with you guys. I think they could use a change in scenery. I'll look out for her."

Silence envelopes the room, and I don't know if they've left or if I've succumbed to sleep again. How do people survive this type of depression?

I take this quiet time to say goodbye. To try to let this go so I can be the kind of mother my children deserve when they return. It's as if my brain is encouraging this unrealistic plan by sending me flashbacks of the happy times with my husband.

Memories of Jake proposing to me in a row boat at Smith Mountain lake bring back a time I'd almost forgotten. He could be romantic when he wanted, when he wasn't beaten down from his work, having nothing left to give. I became so caught up in the day-to-day I'd let my relationship with him become routine. Only focused on the negative when we were so blessed. We had it all.

It's odd. But occasionally, I feel his presence. The sensation of him spooned against my back and his arms wrapped tightly around me.

Is he trying to tell me he forgives me?

When I wake, I'm shocked at the unfamiliar sensation of a smile on my face. Jake's spirit seems so real. My hand instinctively reaches to touch my cheek to reassure me it's there. The feeling is so odd. Then my eyes land on the flowers, and I remember.

He's gone.

CHAPTER TWO

ONE AND A HALF YEARS EARLIER

MELANIE

"I'd almost forgotten what you smelled like," I say to the gray sports coat draped across my lap. The subtle aroma of Jake's favorite cologne still lingers upon the expensive material. Looking up and about the small space, I take in my husband's clothes. I rarely saw him dressed in a suit unless it was for a work function. What a waste. That man knew how to rock a suit.

It's taken me six months to get here. The few short feet from my closet to his. Six months since he left us. But I wasn't ready. Truthfully, I'm still not. But I'm trying to force myself to take baby steps.

The next thing to go is the bed. The frequent washing of linens has removed Jake's once lingering scent. Now it's simply the torture chamber where I lay my head as I try to sleep. It's time I donate this and try to reclaim restful slumber.

I'm careful not to remove too much of Jake too quickly. My children need the comfort of his things around them. And to a certain extent, I do too. But there's a fine line where it's almost painful. It's a constant reminder of all we've lost. Then it doesn't take long before the guilt settles back in. And I can't keep feeding that. My kids deserve more from me.

Try as I might, I haven't been able to make peace with how it happened. That senseless accident resulted from bad weather and road rage. Losing Jake was hard enough, but the bitterness that he died arguing with an ex-friend before taking to the road is the glue that won't let me move on. That and the shame at what I'd said to him.

I'm mad at everyone involved. Including him. How could he have put himself in that situation? In any situation, that would've taken him from his family.

"Mel, you here?" I jump at Huggie's voice bellowing from downstairs. He's had a key for years but is usually very respectful about using it. Jake may have just given it to him since he was here so often. It comforts me that Huggie can be here at a moment's notice to help if something happens.

"I'm upstairs."

Moments later, my sweet friend looks down at me as I sit on the floor of Jake's closet, several of my husband's things folded and stacked next to me. "Here you are. What're you doing?"

"It was time." I shrug.

The six-foot-two muscled firefighter lowers himself onto the closet floor and mimics my stance as I sit crisscross applesauce, almost making me smile. "You need any help?"

This man has been my rock. The night he came to my door will permanently be etched in my mind. I was already reeling from the day's events. Angry that Jake had disappointed Seth. Mad he hadn't called. Then anxious about confronting him at the bar. So my mind instantly jumped to what I thought was the worst-case scenario. What I'd give to trade our current situation for the possibility of a marital separation.

I can still hear Huggie pleading with me to understand what happened.

"Mel. He was in an accident. I'm so sorry."

"What? What are you saying?"

"I don't know all of the details. But Kat and Nick were leaving The Sports Page, and the weather was bad. They came upon an accident.

When they identified the drivers, it was Mark Snow and Jake. Nick found him. There was nothing they could do."

I remember his body engulfing me as I sobbed. Utterly speechless. I didn't ask many questions about what had happened until later, too overcome by grief. It wasn't until right before the funeral that I discovered that Jake and Mark had been arguing, and road rage played a part.

Mark had been a friend for years until his actions caused a split from the rest of our group. Why he chose to be there that night, I'll never know. He knew his presence wasn't wanted. He'd done too much to shatter friendships, and we'd all kept our distance.

I don't understand where the case against Mark is these many months later. While he'd survived the accident, he's been in and out of rehabilitation due to a spinal cord injury he suffered because of it. I try to make regular visits to our friend Munish's office. He's been looking into the case pro bono. However, if it becomes a civil case, that will change. For now, I'm simply grateful for his input. He loved Jake too. And I trust him.

Some days I'm filled with rage at how my life has changed. I want Mark to pay for what he's done to our family. Other times, I'm so filled with self-loathing over my behavior that fateful day that I feel the only guilty party is me.

"What are you planning to do with all of this?" Huggie asks, interrupting my thoughts.

"Donate it." I immediately regret being so insensitive. "Huggie, I'm sorry. I never thought to ask before. Was there anything you wanted?" His eyes flash to meet mine, and I witness an odd grimace.

"No, Mel. Jake was my best friend." He stops speaking and runs his hand along the sleeve of the sports coat draped across my lap. "What I want, I can't have."

I get it. I want him back, too.

"I dropped by because the station is having a pancake dinner tonight. It's the yearly fundraiser. I wanted to see if you and the kids wanted to come."

"Oh, that's right. The kids would love that. Pancakes for dinner would be enough on its own, but add eating them at the fire station..." I force a laugh. Looking at the oversized closet, I know I'll never put a dent in this if I go.

"I can take Seth and Ruby. Give you some time to take care of this without them."

"Oh, Huggie, really? Now that I've started, I don't want to drag this out. And honestly, I don't want them to see what I'm doing. This is hard enough on me."

"Mel. I get it. I'll pick them up from school and take them to the station to help set up for tonight."

"Oh my gosh. Seth will be happier than a pig in slop." I actually giggle. The sound surprises me as it passes my lips.

"I've missed that," he says, staring down at his hands.

"What?"

"Hearing you laugh." Huggie wraps his large, warm hand over mine. He possesses a unique warmth I don't feel from others. Probably because he's still grieving too. "We'll get through this, Melanie."

Flipping my hand over, I give him a gentle squeeze. "I don't know what I would've done... between planning the funeral and helping with the kids, I wouldn't have survived without you."

"Mel. You guys mean everything to me. After my mom died, and I became estranged from my dad... well, I think I adopted you guys as my family whether you liked it or not." Lifting my hand to his mouth, he gently kisses my knuckles before rubbing the area with his left hand. An odd current remains, like a tiny synapse gathering energy beneath my skin. My eyes snap up to meet his, finding he's still looking at my hand. Had he felt it too?

"Okay, I better head out if I'm going to get the kids. Good luck with this. Leave everything here once you've packed it. I'll take it wherever you want it to go."

"Thanks," I respond, feeling a little off-kilter. I'm sure it's the impending doom of what lies before me. This isn't going to be easy.

"I should be back with the kids around eight."

"Okay."

And with that, he stands and gives me a kind smile before walking away.

HUGGIE

"Uncle Huggie, what're you doing here?" Ruby shrieks as she charges at me from down the school hallway.

I'd decided to pick the kids up from school so Melanie could have as much time as needed. Nothing about packing away Jake's things can be easy. Hell, planning the funeral was hard enough. I can't imagine how difficult it'd be to sort through his belongings.

"I have a surprise for you. But let's wait for Seth—"

I've no sooner uttered his name when I see him round the corner. He smiles wide as soon as he makes eye contact with Ruby and me. It softens my battered heart to know I can make these two happy. Even if only for a few hours.

"Hey, what're you doing here?"

"Well, I wanted to see if you'd be interested in having pancakes for dinner."

"Wow, really? And Mom's okay with it?" Ruby blurts.

"Okay with it. It was partly her idea." *So it's a little white lie. She was on board once I mentioned it.* "It's our annual pancake dinner fundraiser at the station."

"We get to eat pancakes for dinner at the firehouse?" Seth beams. Melanie was right. Happier than a pig in slop.

"Yes."

The two of them start jumping up and down, and I suddenly feel like Santa Claus.

"Is Mommy meeting us there?" Ruby asks.

"No, Rubs. Your mom's doing some things at the house." My heart squeezes as a look of disappointment crosses her previously happy face. I'm sure she's worried her mom is regressing.

Melanie had a tough time pulling through after Jake's death. I've never seen a case of clinical depression up close and personal, but that had to be it. It took some work shielding the kids from the worst moments of her despair. She still has a way to go, yet she's getting better every day. A sense of pride fills my chest at the thought.

Bending down, I lift Ruby's chin. "I told her you'd make a pancake stack for her to go."

"Oh, yes. I will." She claps, returning to the vicarious child I adore.

Dropping an arm around their shoulders and steering them toward my truck, I add, "I hope you don't mind, Seth. I told the guys you'd help us in the kitchen."

His look of pure adoration makes me feel ten feet tall. I've given up on the idea of having kids of my own one day. But I don't mind renting these two from time to time if it can make me feel like this.

~

"Seth, we need more pancakes. Can you get Jamie to slap some on a serving tray and bring 'em over here?" I yell.

"I'm on it," he shouts back with a huge smile. That kid. His cheeks are going to hurt tomorrow.

"It's really good what you're doing, kiddo," Wilson says as he pats me on the back.

"What? Chopping fruit?" I snicker.

"You know exactly what I mean." Wilson is one of the older firefighters at our station.

"Well, they're practically my godchildren. If any of us was catholic." I chuckle.

Wilson simply shakes his head.

"Besides, I've started training him early to be a future fire fighter. I'm pretty sure we knew his career choice once he had his fourth birthday party in a row here. And we can use all of the recruits we can get."

As I finish my statement, I notice Ruby standing before me, her face appearing downtrodden. "What's the matter, Rubs? That's not the look I saw a few minutes ago. Do you have a tummy ache?"

"No. It was something you said."

Holy shit. What on earth did I say? Had she overheard me saying something to Wilson that she could've taken the wrong way? Darting around the counter, I scoop her up and carry her into a quieter area of the fire station. "Don't be sad, Rubs. What did I say that made you upset?"

"Stephanie invited me to a birthday party."

I look at her in confusion. How is this something to be sad about?

"It's at the petting zoo."

I try to prod her gently for answers. "Are you afraid of the animals?"

"No," she answers with a bit of a giggle. Well, at least that's an improvement.

"Are you allergic to animals?"

"No."

"Do you secretly want to be one of the animals?" I ask with my voice low.

"No!" She laughs out loud this time.

"Then what is it? That party sounds like loads of fun."

"I've never been to a petting zoo without Daddy."

It's as if someone rammed that cutting knife I'd been using on the cantaloupe straight through my chest. This poor kid. "Ruby, I wish I could tell you why bad things happen, why we had to lose your dad. But I know he'd be disappointed if you didn't go to that petting zoo party."

"I feel like it would hurt his feelings to go without him." Her little pout is killing me. But at least there aren't any tears.

Sitting down, I place her in my lap and continue carefully. "I bet it *is* hard to think of going without your dad when your memories are so special. But I don't think you're going without him."

She looks at me as if I've lost my marbles. Maybe I have. I'm not sure that I'm cut out for these conversations.

"I feel your dad's spirit around me all the time. Especially when I'm doing something we liked to do together."

"Really?"

"Yeah. I believe he's still here with us. He'd be sad if you didn't go because he couldn't be here. Let him enjoy watching you."

"Huggie? Can I ask you something?"

"Anything."

"Will you come with me?"

"If I'm not working. I'd love to come," I say, pulling her in for a big squeeze. "Thank you."

Her smile returns for only a moment before looking up at me with a serious expression. "Can I ask you something else?"

"Hit me," I say, tickling her ribs.

"Why did your parents name you Huggie?"

I can't help but snort. "They didn't. My name is George."

Her face scrunches up adorably, and I can't stop laughing.

"My name is George Hughes. Everyone at the rescue squad started calling me Huggie instead of Hughes. You know, I think your dad probably gave me the name, now that I think about it." I return to tickling her and am relieved when she lets out a full-on belly laugh that melts my heart. "I better stop this before I'm wearing your pancakes. Speaking of which, have you made the stack to take home to your mom?" Looking down at my watch, I realize we'll have to head out soon so they will have time for baths before bed.

"No. I'll make it right now," she answers, jumping from my lap and pulling my arm toward the kitchen.

Suddenly, it hits me. "Did you two have any homework tonight?"

"Nah. I have a class project coming up soon, but my teacher doesn't give a lot of homework."

That's a relief.

"But you might want to ask Seth. He got 'Homework Hildegard' this year."

I can't help but chuckle. "Who's Homework Hildegard?"

"She's the toughest teacher in the whole world. And she gives out the most homework. No one ever wants to get her."

Uh oh.

~

"Seth, Ruby is making your mom's pancake stack. Any chance you can make her one too?"

He gives me a questioning look, wondering why they both need to make them.

"Just trust me on this," I add.

"Okay."

"Oh, and did you have homework tonight you should've been doing? I don't want you to get into trouble at school because I picked you up and brought you here instead of doing your assignments. Ruby told me about Hildegard."

Seth laughs. "No. I try to start all of my assignments during lunch, so I don't have as much to do when I get home. So I can help Mom out."

This kid.

"I think Miss Hooker gets a bad rap. I like her. She's a good teacher, and her assignments aren't hard. I've learned a lot in there."

"Your teacher's name is Hildegard Hooker?"

"Yeah." He snickers.

"Who names their kid that?" I ask, flabbergasted. That's probably what Ruby was thinking about my parents earlier.

"I just call her hot." My mouth drops open as he waggles his brows at me. *Holy shit.*

I give him a playful shove. "That's why you don't mind doing the assignments. Because she's Hot Homework Hildegard."

His cheeks turn rosy, and I know I've nailed it.

"Ha!" I guffaw.

"Uncle Huggie, I've got Mom's pancakes. Are you ready to go?"

I look at Ruby, who's holding a white box. "Your brother's going to make a stack for her too. Can I see yours?"

Seth and I are greeted with an immense look of pride as she opens the takeaway container. Inside is a meal worthy of a diabetic coma. Four large slapjacks topped with whipped cream, sprinkles, and chocolate syrup dripping down their edges lie within the box.

"What, no butter?" I tease.

She starts to close the lid and turn when I grab her arm. "I'm teasing, Rub. She's going to love it. Grab your stack, Seth," I say, turning my head so only he can see me mouth the words, *only pancakes.*

A smile crosses his face, but he loves his sister too much to give us away.

"We'll meet you at the car," I say, grabbing some fruit from the countertop.

∼

"We're here!" Seth shouts from the front door.

"And we brought a surprise for you," Ruby adds in a sing-song voice.

I place the takeout containers on the kitchen island as the kids search for their mother.

"She's in the shower," Seth says.

"Not a bad idea," I answer, looking at the clock on the microwave. "It's getting late. Why don't you two go get showered, and we can show Mom what you brought for her after you guys are all done?"

"Okay," they answer before scurrying up the steps. "Seth, can you help run Ruby's bath for her?"

"I do that almost every night," he belts from the top of the stairs.

I shake my head, full of pride. Proud of how these two have handled all life's thrown at them. Jake would be proud too. Reaching for the refrigerator door, I open it and look for a drink to go with Melanie's meal. I'm tempted to grab the Pinot Grigio and chuckle.

"What's so funny?"

I close the refrigerator door, and the smile instantly falls from my face. Her eyes are pink and puffy, and I know she's been crying. "Mel," I say, wanting desperately to hold her. "You okay?"

"Yeah. It was just a lot. Thank you for taking the kids."

"We had a great time. They're getting cleaned up for bed. Don't peek in the containers until they get back, or they'll be disappointed."

She walks over to where I've started unpacking the sack containing her meal options along with a side of fruit. I have to temper my reaction when she wraps her arms around my chest.

It's been twenty years.

Twenty years of loving her from afar.

Twenty years of wanting her to touch me.

And twenty long years of knowing it will never happen for us.

Other than losing my mother, Jake's death is the hardest thing I've ever experienced in my life. Beyond grieving the death of my best friend, having to break the news to Melanie and the kids nearly broke me. Yet as gut wrenching as it was, there was no way I was allowing some police officer to tell her Jake was gone.

Planning his funeral was tough. However, watching the woman I adored slip into a depression I couldn't rescue her from was worse. I wanted to comfort her, but needed to constantly remind myself to respect the boundaries of our friendship.

Melanie belongs to Jake. Whether he's still here or not. And once she's ready to move on, I can't disrespect my best friend by making a play for his wife. What's more, I can't risk ruining our friendship or causing anything to change for those kids. They've lost enough.

So, I stay trapped. I can't move on, but I can't have her. I'm stuck in my own private hell, trying to enjoy the moments she'll give me.

CHAPTER THREE

ONE YEAR EARLIER

MELANIE

"Melanie, come in, come in," Lori greets as I'm shown to her office. "Please, take a seat."

I can't believe how nervous I am. This isn't my first interview. I worked before the kids came and have stayed active in volunteer jobs or as-needed positions to keep my license current. Fortunately, in Virginia, the need for nurse practitioners has remained high. Plus, I can always fall back on my nursing degree if needed. But this job isn't about paying the bills.

"So, this meeting is unceremonious," Lori begins. "You've already met with Marcus, the Advanced Practice Provider lead for the practice, and had the formal interview. My part of the process is to answer any questions you may have and explain the administrative side of our practice."

I try to relax a bit. This sounds positive. They wouldn't have called me in for this portion of the process if they weren't at least a little interested, right?

"I looked over your CV and didn't see where you'd worked in

cardiology before. You were in family practice previously, is that correct?"

"Yes. I worked in an office in Radford. My husband and I were living there while he finished medical school. Once we started having children, I focused on volunteer work at the clinic. It was more flexible. I've cut my hours back significantly, but I'd like to continue volunteering when possible. It's a great organization." It suddenly dawns on me that I haven't answered her question. I must be more nervous than I thought. Interviews used to be so easy for me. "But I've always wanted to work in cardiology. It fascinates me. And I'm a quick study." *Gah, I hope I'm not screwing this up.*

"Oh, I don't doubt that. Your references all speak very highly of you."

A sense of relief washes over me. And a bit of pride, quite honestly. Knowing my work has garnered praise when it took a backseat to my children. It was a tough choice. I'd worked hard to get my master's degree. But with Jake's erratic schedule, I felt it was necessary to work part-time and focus on the kids during their early years. I'll never regret the time I had with them. Men will never understand the impact of being a working mother. It's expected they work outside the home.

"What field is your husband in? If you don't mind my asking?"

Caught off guard by the question, I freeze. I knew there was the possibility this could come up, but I still feel ill-prepared.

"It's okay, Melanie. You don't have to answer if you don't feel comfortable. It has no relevance to your interview."

My expression must've given me away. "No, it's okay. My husband was an emergency room attending. Here at St. Luke's, actually." I observe the exact moment when she digests the word 'was' and matches my last name to Jake. It's predictable watching her expression change.

"Oh, Melanie. I'm sorry for your loss. Everyone in this office thought very highly of your husband."

"Thank you," I acknowledge with a bit of a bite. It was kind of her to say, but I still grow irritated with these conversations. It's always awkward. No one ever knows the right thing to say. I need to push past the morbid part of this exchange. "I wondered if you could tell me how the orientation process works with your group. Since I haven't worked in cardiology before, I want to make sure I'm prepared."

"Oh, of course." She readjusts herself in her chair at our conversation's change in direction. "I'll introduce you to the attendings in the practice, and then we can meet with Marcus about the specifics."

We continue to review topics like the rotation of an on-call schedule, rounding in the hospital, and taking paid personal time off before Lori stands from her chair.

"Let me give you a tour and see who's in the office, so you won't have so many people to meet once you come aboard."

Now, this sounds *quite* promising.

"Ah, Dr. Hart, I'd like you to meet Melanie. She's interviewing for the APP position we have open. Melanie, this is Dr. Hart."

I shake hands with a very attractive man who stands about three inches taller than I am. He has dark hair and eyes with a twinkle that instantly puts me at ease. He appears a few years older than I am, with the slightest hint of silver at his temples. Yet the scruff along his square jaw remains dark. I'm surprised I'm taking inventory in this way. I mean, I'm going to be working with him.

"As it so happens, you'll be partnered with Dr. Hart for most of your work week. Each physician has a primary Advanced Practice Provider, but Dr. Hart's physician assistant recently took a travel assignment."

Well, that's an unexpected benefit Lori left out of the human resources packet. If he's as easy to work for as he is on the eyes, this will be a win-win.

"It's very nice to meet you, Melanie," he finally interjects. His voice is as smooth as silk.

"Thank you. Likewise."

Lori continues to point out various offices that I'm sure I'll forget. As we turn toward the breakroom, I notice Dr. Hart smiling in my direction. *Dr. Hart?* What are the odds of a name like that in a cardiology practice? I can't help but grin inwardly. And it feels nice.

～

"Oh, it's so good to see you, Mel," Kat greets as I approach her table. "I was so excited when you called to do lunch. I feel like it's been ages."

"I know. I've had some big things happening, and I wanted to talk to you and Huggie about one of them."

"Speak of the devil," Kat says, jumping up from her seat to greet him with an embrace. "Hey, Huggie. How are you?"

"I'm good. Better after I got an invite to have lunch with my two favorite girls."

"Awe. Have a seat. When I got here, I ordered water for each of us but wasn't sure what else you'd want."

As if on cue, the server arrives with our water and quickly takes our orders.

"Okay, Mel. Huggie's here now, so spill the beans."

"Wait, what'd I miss?" he asks.

"You didn't miss anything. I told Kat I wanted to talk with you both for a couple of reasons. The first is to thank you." I stop to gather myself. I want to say this without getting overly emotional. "It's long overdue. I wouldn't have survived without the two of you over the last year. I'd never been depressed before losing Jake. How people live with that, I have no idea. I still struggle. But you took care of the kids and allowed me to grieve how I needed. I'll never be able to repay you."

"Melanie. You would've done the very same for either one of us. I know it," Kat interrupts. "There's no need to thank us. Right, Huggie?"

"I don't know. I could use a new truck."

I cover my mouth to stifle a laugh at the appalled expression Kat's currently wearing.

"So what's the other thing?" Kat asks while still giving Huggie the side eye.

"I interviewed for a job. And it sounds promising."

"Oh, that's great, Mel. Congratulations."

"You sure you're ready for that?" Huggie asks. "I mean, financially, you don't need to go back right now, do you?" He seems flustered as if he's unsure he should've gone there. "I'm sorry, Mel—"

"No. We're friends. It's okay. That's why I wanted to talk to you guys. To bounce all of the pros and cons off of you. We're okay financially. This is to get myself back out there and set an example for the kids."

"Well, I think it's great," Kat says, extending her arm over the table to grab my hand.

"I do too. I just don't want you to take on too much," Huggie says with a look of concern.

"I've spoken with a neighborhood teen who can help in the afternoons on the days I work. The only issue I'm concerned with is when I'm on-call."

"I'm happy to look at my schedule and take the kids to the lake whenever you're on-call, and I'm off."

"Are you sure, Kat? Your daughter's still so small. That seems like a lot."

"Oh, you won't be on-call that often. And Nick would love to take Seth and Ruby to soccer on Saturdays. He used to love spending the afternoons with your kids on the field."

This brings a mixed feeling of joy and melancholy as Jake would always take them to play with Nick. "They'd love that."

"Well, you know you can count on me, Mel. Whatever you or the kids need. So long as I'm not on duty at the fire department, I'm there."

"Thank you, guys. I feel like it's the right time to get back out there. I wasn't ready before. But this could be good for me."

The server returns with our meals, and we dig in. I'm blessed to have known these two for so long. I know they'll help me. Facing life as a one-parent family requires preparation. I was kidding myself when I thought I was functioning as a single parent when Jake was alive. I didn't give him enough credit. He did so much more than I realized until I was forced to do it alone.

"You okay, Mel?"

Looking up into my dear friend's caring silver-blue orbs, I nod and try to keep my emotions in check. I was blessed to have Jake for twenty glorious years. I don't understand it, but I've never seen Huggie with anyone special. Some people simply never find *the one*. I need to count my blessings and focus on all the good in my life. "I'm getting there. One day at a time, right?"

"So, tell me about the job. Where would you be working?" Kat asks.

"It's with Old Dominion Cardiology."

"Oh, I know that group," Kat says around a bite of pasta. "The docs all seem super nice."

"I've only met a couple. I'd be working with Dr. Hart."

Suddenly, I hear the clink of metal against ceramic and look up to see Kat beaming at me in shock.

"What?" Huggie and I ask in unison.

"He's smoking hot, Mel."

I shake my head at her ridiculousness as I scoop another fork full of quiche into my mouth, stopping short when I see the look of disdain on Huggie's face.

"What?"

"I think it's appalling how you're objectifying her soon-to-be boss," he grumbles at Kat. *Is he for real?*

"Oh, for fucks sake, Huggie." Kat laughs.

"I don't know what the policy is on interoffice relationships, but I'd assume it's frowned upon," I add. This conversation is absurd. Like I'd ever consider taking up with a work colleague. Some men are fine to look at but off-limits for anything more.

"Well, that's a darn shame." Kat does a double-take when she sees Huggie's stern expression. "What?" she blurts, her mouth still full of noodles. "They're both widowed. And they're both hot. What's the problem?" She twirls her fork through her fettucini again. "Is widowed even a word?"

"He lost his wife?" I blurt.

"Yeah. It was sad. She was the sweetest thing. A nurse at Mary Immaculate. She died of leukemia about two years ago."

"Oh, wow." What a coincidence. I slowly pick at my food and realize Huggie has grown quiet. "You okay, Huggie?"

"Sure. I'm just trying to figure out how we went from a logical conversation on how to support you if you go back to work to 'they're both widowed, and they're both hot.' Is that how women make career decisions?"

Is he joking?

"Huggie, you really need to get some. You're getting a little too testy," Kat says as she makes a face and eats another forkful of fettucini.

"You're probably right," he adds before reaching for his wallet. "I've got to go. I'll settle the check on my way out."

"Oh, don't go," I whine. Is he really upset? And why did the thought of him *getting some* give me heartburn? Maybe we aren't as close as I'd like to believe if I don't like hearing about his exploits. He's always felt like family. Perhaps that's it.

"Awe, come on, Huggie. You know I'm playing," Kat tries to backtrack.

He shakes his head and strolls toward the register at the front of the restaurant.

"What's gotten into him?" I ask. He seems a lot more on edge today.

Kat looks back at me with a knowing expression. Replaying her parting shot about needing to *get some,* I can't help but look back at him. I've never understood why someone as attractive as Huggie doesn't have dates galore. Maybe he does and simply chooses to keep his private life private.

But I can say with certainty that the girl Huggie eventually chooses will be one lucky woman. He's kind, devoted to a fault, attentive, and very attractive. It feels odd considering my friend that way, but a fact's a fact. He's tall with blond hair and silver-blue eyes. He's built but lean, not overly muscular like so many of his firefighter brothers. He looks equally handsome in glasses or contacts. He's like the boy next door but inked.

Now that I think about it, I'm pretty sure I've never seen him without a shirt. It's surprising, considering how long we've known each other. Given his fair hair and complexion, I assume his skin is overly sensitive to the sun. He's always worn a swim shirt when we've gone tubing or been on the boat. But when he's wearing a short sleeve shirt, the winding vines of deep red flowers and barbed wire along his right arm are mesmerizing—

"Earth to Melanie."

"Oh, I'm sorry. I was stuck in my own head."

"I saw that."

"What did you ask me?"

"I asked when you start?"

"The job? Ha! I haven't actually been offered a position yet. But they made it seem like it was a formality when I was getting the tour today."

"Well, I hope it works out. I think it could be perfect for you."

"I do too," I answer. "I just hope they don't wait too long to call. I'm excited to start a new chapter."

Huggie

"Huggie," Ruby yells, sitting on a stool at the kitchen island. She immediately jumps down and rushes for me. I admit I've grown accustomed to her lively reception. "What're you doing here? Is that for me?"

"What?"

"The soccer ball, silly."

"Oh, that. It was taking up too much space in my garage, so I thought I'd bring it here."

"Funny, it looks brand new." Melanie points out my sorry excuse to join them as she walks barefoot down the hallway. She's wearing tight-fitting yoga pants and a light cotton T-shirt that rides up, exposing her navel as she walks. "Hi, Hugs."

"Okay, you got me. But it's beautiful outside, and I thought it might be a great day to go to the sports park and kick the ball around."

"That'd be awesome," Seth chimes in.

"But only if you've finished Hilde's homework." I wink.

Seth's cheeks turn a light shade of crimson, and I have to stifle a laugh. I notice Mel watching us closely with a curious expression.

"Don't worry. I did hers first."

Coming around the counter, I give his hair a toss, and he quickly bats my hand away. Guess he's getting too grown up for my shenanigans anymore.

Melanie opens the refrigerator door and retrieves some lunch meat and cheese. "Why don't Ruby and I make some sandwiches? We can eat dinner there."

"You're coming, Mom?" Ruby asks excitedly.

Instantly, I witness Mel's facial expression change. It's almost imperceptible, but it's there. She harbors so much guilt for how she handled Jake's death when it came to the kids. Everyone handles grief differently. I wish there was a way to convince her that she's a great mother. Her depression was at a 9.5 on the Richter scale. It's incredible how well she's doing, considering how debilitating that time was. Applying for jobs. Getting her kids where they need to be. I know she still has a ways to go, but I'm proud of her.

There are times when I notice Melanie exhibit a degree of self-loathing regarding Jake's passing. I don't understand it. At first, I thought it was part of the five stages of grief. But subtle comments she's made have me speculating there's more to it. It's been a year and a half, but I still don't feel comfortable confronting her about it. Yet, seeing her react to Ruby this way pulls at my heart.

"Ruby, I—"

Melanie's response is quickly interrupted as her phone dances across the kitchen counter. Dropping the cold cuts and cheese on the counter, she mouths to Ruby to *grab the bread* as she answers the incoming call.

"Hello." Mel remains silent as she listens intently, her face expressionless. *It's probably someone wanting to talk to her about her car's extended warranty.* I laugh to myself. "Thank you. I'm looking forward to it."

I look at Seth and Ruby standing at the island, fixed on their mother. The anticipation is killing them too.

"Okay. I'll see you then. Thank you so much for calling. Bye."

"Who was that?" Ruby blurts. I don't know if she's excited to get the intel or worried something could derail her mother from coming to our little picnic.

"Remember I sat you two down and said I'd wanted to try going back to work? That I'd need your help to manage if it worked out?"

"Yes," they both answer excitedly.

"Well, I got the job. I start working with Dr. Hart on Monday!"

"Yay!" They both cheer excitedly.

I stand watching all three of them entangled in one another, jumping excitedly. It's probably the first time in years I've witnessed it. I should be happy for Melanie. This is a big deal. But my mind keeps replaying those words from earlier.

They're both widowed. And they're both hot.

CHAPTER FOUR

SIX MONTHS EARLIER

HUGGIE

"Man, I needed this," I tell Nate.

"Me too. It's been ages since we were all able to get out." He looks over the dance floor as if looking for someone in particular.

"You expecting anyone?" I ask, taking a swig of my beer.

"Nah. I met someone here a while back. Just keeping my eyes peeled in case they turn back up—"

I turn to see what's caught his attention when I see Tate and Tanner.

"If it isn't the Manning boys," Nate says.

"Hey, grab a seat." I motion to the chairs to my right. "How've you been?"

"Good. Our nephew's been keeping us busy," Tanner says.

"What? When did that happen?"

"Our little brother knocked up a girl a few years ago. Caleb will turn two just before Christmas."

"No way. He live with his mom?"

"No, with Tucker."

"Wow," Nate reacts, not bothering to hide his shock.

"Yeah. That kid had to grow up quickly. I mean, he's only a few years younger than we are, but Tucker has always been the most immature of the lot," Tate adds.

Tate and Tanner Manning are twins I've known for years. They both work for the police department, and although they're fraternal twins, no one can tell them apart. It does a number on some of the intoxicated folks we've seen them arrest.

There are six Manning boys. Tate and Tanner have an older brother, and then there's Tucker, followed by two younger brothers. I love Seth and Ruby, but the *two* of them can wear me out on the occasions we're together. I cannot fathom six kids.

"I can't picture it," I say, given what a reckless playboy I recall Tucker being.

"Mom helps him out. But she's been good about putting her foot down." Tate chuckles. "She told him, 'You make 'em, you raise 'em.'"

"Your mom's amazing. I don't know how she survived the six of you." I laugh, finishing my beer.

"You can't relate because you were an only child," Nate says. "But six *is* a lot."

"Yeah, and we were a handful," Tanner says, flagging down a cocktail waitress.

"Hey, get me another, will ya? I'm hitting the head," I tell him.

As is typical, I walk past the long line of ladies waiting to gain entrance to the restroom while I walk unencumbered into the men's room. I quickly take care of my business. Heading back to our table, I notice a young woman staring at me from the back of the washroom line. She must be celebrating something as she's wearing a crown and a sash.

"Don't I know you?" she asks, her voice sounding thick. If she's not already intoxicated, I'm sure she's well on her way.

"I don't think so," I rebuff as I continue walking to my table. By her appearance, I have to admit it's quite possible. She's my usual type, minus the inebriation. Tall with long dark hair and brown eyes. Acknowledging my anxiety that I could, in fact, *know her*, I try to brush it off and return to an overdue evening with friends.

I slide back into my seat and discover Nate's on the dance floor with Brandon, the newest addition to our station, and a girl I don't recognize. From what I can see between people dancing around her, she's short, with blonde hair and big tits.

The club is jumping tonight. Or perhaps it's been so long since I've gone out that it merely feels that way. I believe this is the first time I've been out to a club since Jake died. Not that clubbing has ever been my scene. But occasionally, it's nice to go somewhere other than a sports bar. That's usually my go-to for a few beers, but I'm feeling the need to drown my frustrations, and this place is less conspicuous if I attempt to sneak out without being seen.

"Hey, Huggie. This is Brandi," Brandon introduces.

"Wow, really? Brandon and Brandi?" I snicker. "That's cute." I think that fifth beer might be kicking in.

No sooner have I finished making light of their names and Brandi's climbing over me to sit in the seat Nate had vacated.

"Well, drop in anytime." I guffaw. *Not really.* This girl is not my type.

"It's Brandi, with an i," she clarifies.

I laugh. Thanks for the spell check. *As if I'm going to write her a letter.*

"Why is that funny?"

"Why is what funny?"

"You just snorted," Brandi says, looking crestfallen.

Leaning in, I tell her, "I'm just high on life, Brandi, with an i. No offense intended." I'm not that intoxicated. But if she continues to sit here, I might need to be.

"Oh, good. 'Cause, you're cute." She giggles, dragging her finger along the red and black ink on my arm.

Oh, brother. Where the fuck did Brandon go? Looking to my left, I see him coming to our table carrying two cocktails. He seems irritated. Trust me, I'd know. Sitting here with Brandi touching me is making me prickly.

"Dirty martini for the lady," he says as he slides the cocktail across the table to Brandi.

I immediately start scanning the room for any excuse to get up and let Brandon have the hot seat. I guess the bar it is. I down the remainder of my Guinness and make eye contact with Nate as he returns from the dance floor. "Hey, I'm heading to the bar for a refill. You want anything?"

"You finished that already?" he asks, seeming shocked.

Shrugging my shoulders, hoping I can downplay my stealthy exit, I hear Jamie's laugh rumble from across the table. I give him the stink eye, hoping he won't cause a scene as I try to escape this overly aggressive girl's clutches. "Come on, Jamie. I'll buy you a drink."

He shakes his head, confirming he's well aware of what I'm doing. I don't like causing a scene, but I don't want to continue giving this girl the slightest idea I'm interested. Especially when Brandon has his eyes on her.

"Now that was fun."

"Oh, shut it, man. You almost outed my escape plan."

"I'm just saying. She could've been fun," Jamie adds.

"Not my type."

"Hey, fellas. What can I getcha?" the pretty redhead asks from behind the bar.

"I'd like the most expensive scotch on the menu," Jamie tells her.

"The fuck?" I blurt.

"You're welcome. Or maybe you want to head back to Bran—

"No."

"Besides, I know you're good for it."

He's right. "Make it two," I tell the pretty barkeep as a megawatt smile crosses her face. "Hell, redheads aren't usually my thing, but she's hot."

"Yeah. I'm sure it's your witty personality she's into." I look up at him in question until I see him nod at the platinum card in my hand. "Not the almost one hundred dollar pours you just ordered two of."

"Whatever." I know he's right.

She delivers two fingers of overpriced scotch to each of us with a side of heavy flirting, and I again hear a familiar rumble next to me. *Jesus.*

I shake my head as we head back to our table. "Fuck, man. I've had such a dry spell that I almost fell for that."

"Yeah. You've had your hands full."

I glance up at him and see a knowing look in his eyes.

"Doing the right thing comes with sacrifice," he says.

"Hell, man. Right thing or not, it's been so long. I just want my dick sucked."

No sooner have the words left my mouth than we're standing in front of Brandi, who's now wearing a shit-eating grin.

Uh, no.

"Hey, I was just looking for you," she says, giving an extra bat of her eyelashes. Fuck, where is Brandon? She starts to trail her sharp, hot pink manicured nails along the ink of my right forearm again, just as another female's voice interrupts.

"He's not interested."

I almost thank the woman until I realize it's the brunette from earlier. She's still wearing the sash, but the crown has slipped. It's barely hanging onto her head by a few tangled strands. And to think I had the nerve to believe this situation couldn't get much worse.

"He only likes brunettes. Tall, brown-eyed brunettes." She attempts to enunciate each word clearly around her thick alcohol-soaked tongue.

What fresh hell is this?

Grabbing Jamie's arm, encouraging him to move along, we barely take two steps before my jaw tightens with her next words.

"Isn't that right, Nath—"

"Pam, there you are. Where'd you go?" the blonde next to her blurts while teetering on four-inch heels. She seems similarly affected by one too many cosmos. "I'm going to tell your hot fiancé you were flirting with a—" She stops momentarily for a closer look in our direction. A huge smile crosses her face, and she wobbles toward us. She lifts her hand as if about to put it on Jamie's chest when a growl emerges.

"I know you're not putting your hands on me." Hell, he's not even speaking to me, and I'm a little anxious.

"Sorry," she utters quickly and steps away. I'm glad she was sober enough to catch that loud and clear.

Hell, that was close. Luckily, this happened while I was with Jamie. I don't think he'd pressure me about what just happened, as private as he is.

"Anything you want to tell me?"

Fuck. So much for that.

"Not really. How 'bout you?"

"Nothing comes to mind."

Returning to our table, we slide in as Brandon drops down beside us.

"Man, I thought I'd scored tonight with that one too."

"Who? Brandi?" Nate asks.

Jamie and I immediately look at each other. Why couldn't she sink her claws into Brandon? He's not a bad-looking kid. Maybe she's one of those girls who sets her sights on the one guy she thinks has no interest. Or, as I was reminded earlier, perhaps she saw the Ralph Lauren Steel Skeleton sitting on my wrist. That thing is almost worth more than my car.

Bzzz. Bzzz.

Looking down at my phone, I see a text from Melanie. But when I open the messaging app, there's an image of Seth and Ruby sitting at the kitchen island with banana splits in front of them. They're peeking over the mound of whipped cream piled high atop each sundae. I can practically see the smiles radiating from their eyes.

"Hey, look at this." I show Nate and Jamie.

"Ha! That's awesome," Nate shouts over the music.

I feel Jamie's hand on my upper back and almost jolt in surprise. He is *not* someone who communicates through touch.

"You did good," he says.

"I didn't do anything. This is all her. I'm proud of her." Looking back down at the two imps staring back at me, I can't contain my smile. "She's come a long way."

I have to admit I haven't done myself any favors by allowing myself to get so close to them. It's not healthy the way I feel about her. I've always had a fondness for those kids. With their father gone, it felt natural to be the one to step up and be the male presence they need. But it's only a matter of time before she meets someone, and I'm pushed aside. I need to start backing away before I get in any deeper.

Turning my head, I connect with Jamie's soulful brown eyes. I appreciate the gesture. I know he would've done the same for any one of us.

Leaning toward me, he keeps his voice low. "If that's true, then maybe it's time your limp dick got some action."

He's right. She doesn't need me anymore. It's time I get back to my old life.

As fucked up as it was.

CHAPTER FIVE

PRESENT DAY

HUGGIE

"Oh, god. Nathan," the overly dramatic brunette cries out.

Grabbing a fistful of hair, I wrap her tresses around my hand and tug. "I thought I made it clear you weren't supposed to speak," I bark out.

I was close this time. Thought I was finally going to make it across the finish line before another one ruined it for me. Still buried inside her, I try to chase this much-needed orgasm. One that's eluded me for too long. Pounding into her from behind, I try to regain my rhythm.

So close. I was so fucking close.

Closing my eyes, I picture the one thing I know will push me over the edge. The one *person* that is. I visualize her delicious curvy figure splayed out before me. Her creamy skin is begging me to take a bite. My mouth almost waters at the thought. The image of her small waist tapering out to a shapely, round ass has my climax within reach. I grab ahold of my current companion's hips and begin to thrust into her relentlessly.

There it is. I'm right there. But as my gaze travels down to my willing partner, I find her imploring brown eyes staring back at me from over her shoulder. It's as if connecting with her in this way has deflated this overblown balloon, ready to pop. I'm immediately brought back to the here and now and feel my orgasm dissolve.

The tight thread of restraint I've been holding on to suddenly snaps. "I know I made it clear you weren't supposed to look at me," I growl.

"Yes, sir," she whines apologetically.

Withdrawing from her, I remove the condom and immediately turn to look for a trash bin.

"What? Please, don't go. I promise I'll stay quiet and face forward. Nathan, you get me so turned on I just lost control for a—"

"We're done here," I reply, cutting her off before the incessant begging can persist. I rarely remove my clothing anymore, almost anticipating complete and utter disappointment. Thus, it doesn't take long to tuck everything back where it belongs and exit the room.

With determined strides, I make my way to Annalise's office. I've had enough of this shit.

Pound, pound, pound.

"Mr. Mars. I'm afraid Annalise is on a call. Is there something—"

"Let her know I'll be canceling my membership," I spit.

As if on cue, Annalise's door swings wide, and a look of relief washes over her assistant's face.

"Mr. Mars. Is there something I can do for you?" she asks with a look of genuine concern.

"Yes. I felt I owed it to you to let you know in person that I'll be canceling my membership. I know you try to accommodate my requests, but the last few visits have been beyond unsatisfactory."

The tall brunette gives her assistant a curt nod, dismissing her from this conversation before looking up at me. "I'm very sorry to hear that. Would you mind stepping into my office before you go? I'd like to understand more so we can learn from any disappointment we may have caused."

My anger continues to simmer, but I'm not as raw as when I first pummeled her door. "Okay, but just for a moment. Then I need to leave." I huff. I sound like a pouty kindergartener sulking over not getting his way on the playground. *Fuck, maybe I am.*

Irritated or not, it doesn't stop me from watching the sway of her hips as she sashays in front of me. Annalise is a beautiful woman. She's only two years older than my thirty-six but has the poise of a fortune 500 CEO. She's managed the inner workings of The Rox for as many years as I've been coming here.

The Rox is a members-only sex club located in Rockville, MD. It's a stone's throw from Washington D.C. and caters to clients with bank accounts large enough to afford this level of extravagance and discretion. The members of this club seek what they can't find elsewhere. Unique encounters with beautiful women in a completely private setting. These experiences vary from simple fetishes, voyeurism, to any type of BDSM or kink you can imagine. Its members are assured of the utmost respect and confidentiality regarding their requests. *I should know.*

I learned about this club from a firefighter I worked with years ago who grew up in neighboring Bethesda. When volunteering, he'd responded to a call and had gotten an eyeful. Having preferences of my own, I decided to try them out when visiting his hometown and have remained a member for over a decade.

In the beginning, my needs were basic. I simply wanted an evening with a pretty brown-eyed, dark-haired girl who wasn't looking for more than one night. Someone I didn't need to worry about bumping into in the produce aisle or making excuses when they wondered why I hadn't called. But as the years passed, my requests became more specific.

"Mr. Mars?" Annalise's soft voice breaks through my reverie, and I notice her extend her arm toward one of the two expensive black leather seats beside her desk.

I'm beyond frustrated, but in all the time I've come here, she's been nothing but polite and accommodating, and I need to be the same. Taking a seat, I try to relax as she gracefully lowers herself into the matching chair beside me.

"I hope you know how much your business means to us. I'm sorry you've been unhappy enough to consider leaving us after all these years."

This is humiliating. I feel like I'm in the hot seat. And being put on the spot is making me feel defensive. "While I'm here, I should tell you I bumped into one of the girls in Hanover about six months ago. I'm assuming she's no longer with your club, but she had no problem outing me to anyone within earshot."

Annalise adjusts herself higher in her chair. "I'm sorry to hear that. You know we go to great lengths to protect your privacy. Do you recall her name?"

"I don't typically ask their names, not that their club name would be real anyway."

"You're correct. However, it may make it easier for me to identify who confronted you so I can issue a cease and desist letter. All of the girls sign a legally binding nondisclosure agreement at the beginning of their employment. Whether she has left us or not, she needs to be aware of the implications of violating such a contract."

I have to admit that this makes me feel more at ease. Annalise has always run a tight ship. I've never had any concerns regarding confidentiality. "Her name was Pam. I didn't get the last name."

"Was she tall, brunette?"

My eyes connect with hers, and I can feel my ire build again. Being called out regarding my specific type has me feeling more annoyed, not less. "Yes," I mutter, pulling at my collar.

"It will be handled. Now, may I ask which girl you were with tonight?" she probes, returning us to the main reason I'm here.

"It was Rebecca. But it isn't just her. The last few girls I've been with have left me frustrated." *More* frustrated than when I arrived at The Rox. I'd driven two hours north of my home in Hanover, hoping to sate this ache. Now it feels like I've just poured gasoline on this infuriating fire.

"Can you give me any more detail? I'd like to know how we can better accommodate your needs. Not to mention that retraining of my staff is in order."

I'm such as asshole. I can't believe I'm having this conversation. "I pay a lot of money to be a member here. I know my requests are not typical, but I'm not asking them to do anything unreasonable." I huff. "I just want to get what I'm paying for."

While most firefighters don't have an income worthy of this lavish lifestyle, I'm fortunate to be in a different class. I've run a side hustle since graduating from the fire academy and have made quite a name for myself.

In recent years, more and more film crews have descended on Hanover, Richmond, and the surrounding areas. The region is rich with photogenic architecture and river views that are attractive to movie producers. And neighboring Williamsburg, Jamestown, Yorktown, and Charlottesville offer historical backdrops for films. The business has been far more successful than I anticipated, with production companies willing to pay top dollar for the ease and convenience of having us on set. I manage a crew of twenty off-duty firefighters who provide EMS and fire services on location while filming. The guys trust my vision, and it's become a profitable off-duty job for all of us.

"You're absolutely right. You've never asked for anything questionable. I'm sorry the girls on your recent visits have let you down. Would you mind telling me what has occurred to cause your disappointment with them? And us?"

Taking a fortifying breath, I attempt to share my recent encounters without sounding like a complete buffoon. I lower my voice, given the delicate nature of our conversation. "I expected the girls could get upset if things got out of hand, and I was a little rough," my voice trails off.

How the fuck have I turned into this man? Someone who'd need to be rough with a woman at all, much less pay women to allow me to be an asshole and then complain when they aren't obedient enough.

I admit my sex life has changed. The older I've gotten, the rougher I've enjoyed my encounters with women. I'm not a Dominant. I don't enjoy making women submit to me. However, I find I'm more relaxed after an evening of vigorous, no-holds-barred sexual activity. It's always consensual. If tonight with Rebecca taught me anything, it's that the women I've been with seem to enjoy it.

"Yet they don't appear to mind that. It's abiding by the rules of no speaking or making eye contact during sex that they can't seem to handle." I cannot help but shake my head at my ridiculous needs as I voice them out loud.

What the hell has happened to me?

"I'm not sure why this has become an issue. In the past, it didn't seem to be a problem."

"If I may be so blunt..." Annalise pauses until our eyes meet, and then she continues. "You're quite the attraction when you arrive, Mr. Mars. The girls compete to be the one who gets to spend the evening with you when you enter The Rox. I even have several blondes who've died their hair and others who've obtained colored contacts hoping they'll have a chance to be considered. I'm afraid their fierce admiration may have caused the slips to occur."

I look at her dumbfounded. Sure, I'm no ogre. Working in the fire department amongst my incredibly fit brotherhood has motivated me to stay on top of my fitness routine. But I certainly don't think I'm worthy of this degree of admiration. Hell, I'm no Chris Hemsworth.

"If you oblige, I'd like to review your requirements," Annalise says.

Still caught off guard by her earlier comments, I simply give her a curt nod.

"My understanding is that you prefer women in their mid-twenties to thirties with long, dark hair and brown eyes, who are tall and thin?"

"Not thin," I interrupt. "Hourglass."

She gives me a bright smile, and I try to swallow down my embarrassment. Again, I nod. This conversation is beyond irritating, but if there's a chance they're going to get this turned around so I don't have to start over somewhere else, I guess the discomfort is a necessary evil.

"They should be without tattoos or significant marks on the skin and piercings limited to the ears," she continues.

God, this sounds ridiculous when she's reading this shit back to me. I like what I like. "While those are my physical preferences, the things I need most are the ones I've been unable to rely on. And without them, satisfaction is not achievable," I add, confident she's aware of my unspoken meaning.

I can't come without this.

"They should remain silent, even if I'm speaking. No words. And I cannot make eye contact with them. Their eyes need to be fixated anywhere but my face. Preferably looking down." Jesus, I sound like a first-class prick. *Fuck, I probably am.* But it's either this or my hand for the rest of my damn life. And I've practically got blisters from that shit now.

There's no use denying I have a specific type. I've been attracted to tall, confident brunettes since high school. Meeting and falling for Melanie only amplified this. I've gone out with a few blondes and redheads, but they've never really done it for me. In my twenties, I slept with a variety of women and enjoyed them all. What twenty-year-old can't get off with a hot body beneath them?

Yet, now that I'm in my thirties, many of the women I meet are interested in a relationship. Even if they initially agree on a one-night stand, they push for more. I've tried more, and it simply doesn't work for me. There's no sense in starting a relationship when I know it won't end well. If someone comes along that makes me feel otherwise, I'm not opposed to giving it a shot. But my heart belongs to Melanie, whether I like it or not. And seeing or hearing anyone different causes me to feel I'm being unfaithful. Even if I'm the only one aware we're in a relationship.

Some may think I'm psychotic, fixated on a girl I can't have. But I'm tired of trying to force a square peg into a round hole. Being able to play out my fantasies is why I come to The Rox. It's my one source of sexual release with another person. This isn't hurting anyone if I'm not in a relationship and we're consenting adults.

Well, except me, when they won't play along.

"Rest assured, you will not have to engage with anyone who has provided less than satisfactory service in the past. And future companions will be educated regarding your requirements before joining you. I'll make it clear if they cannot perform as requested, they'll be terminated."

The room grows quiet, and I'm struck with guilt at the thought that any of these girls could lose their jobs because of me. But I remind myself that I'm paying for a service. It's merely a job requirement.

Do I really want to chance this again? Maybe this is a sign that I need to deal with my demons rather than put them on someone else.

As if sensing my apprehension, she breaks the silence between us. "I'd even go so far as to offer *my* services. If that would make you feel more confident that your wishes were being honored."

My head snaps up, taking in her look of sincerity. I'm shocked. I didn't realize Annalise entertained men in the club. I've always assumed her position was purely administrative. She's definitely my type. She's the right height, with big brown eyes, long, straight dark hair, and legs that go on for days. And I'm sure if she's offering, she'll do whatever it takes to make me happy. My dick twitches for the first time in months at the thought.

"That's a generous offer, Annalise. One I don't take lightly. Is it okay if I think about all of this?"

If I accept her invitation and it doesn't go well, that could make things all sorts of awkward. I'm not sure I want to add that stress to what already feels like a pressure cooker returning here.

"Please do. We'd hate to lose you as a member here, Mr. Mars."

I can't help but cringe as I hear her use my name after extending such a personal offer. Well, not *my* name. But my friend Nate's name.

I couldn't take the chance of getting caught when I joined this gentleman's club all those years ago. So instead of using my name when I filled out the membership form, I used my friend Nate's. I figured if anyone heard a rumor Nate Mars had been to The Rox, they'd quickly determine they had the wrong guy, as my friend Nate is openly gay. The Rox primarily caters to heterosexual men, although I'm sure some members are into group kink. But using his name was still a shit move. I recall how anxious I was about all of it. When I went to fill out the form, I couldn't think on the fly, yet I was clear I didn't want to be another Mr. Smith. And there was no way I was advertising George "Huggie" Hughes was a member. But after all of these years, it's too late to change it now.

Unless I leave The Rox.

～

"Hey, man. What'd you do this weekend?" Nate greets.

I cringe at the question. Just as I always do when I return from a trip where I've stolen his identity to protect my ridiculous life choices. Life choices that have again left me annoyed and dissatisfied. "Nothing worth reliving," I answer honestly, dropping my gear onto my bed in the bunk room.

I haven't slept well since Saturday. Even the lousy hand job when I finally got in the shower did nothing to soothe this ache. It's sadly become a part of my life that I've learned to accept, being lonely and frustrated. But time doesn't make it any easier. "How 'bout you, playa? Meet anyone new this weekend?"

"As a matter of fact, I did." He beams. His expression catches me off guard. Nate is a good-looking guy. I'm only interested in women, but I'm man enough to admit he's unfairly attractive. It's not just physical. Nate Mars is a tall, fit, light-skinned Black man with an infectious smile. He has a personality that is larger than life but not campy. You'd never know this man was gay unless you were in his inner circle of friends, and even then, he keeps his relationships close to the vest. Well, not as close as I keep mine. But close.

But then again, fucking nameless women who aren't allowed to speak or look at you isn't really a relationship, now is it?

"I sense this is more than just a hot guy in a club," I tease.

"You sensed right." He chuckles. "I can't explain it. I met this guy Friday night and haven't stopped thinking about him. I can't believe he's gotten under my skin like that. It feels a little maddening."

"Yeah. I get it." I laugh.

You have no idea how much I get it.

"I'm happy for you, man."

"Well, don't get too happy yet. Anything could happen," he scolds.

Reaching over to my friend, I grab ahold of his upper arm. "You're right. Anything could happen. I have a good feeling about this." I wink. "You deserve it."

"Thanks, Huggie. That means a lot, man."

"And if that guy does you wrong, I'll kick his ass."

"Yeah, right. You're the fucking nicest guy I know. You wouldn't hurt a fly," Nate guffaws.

If he only knew. I appear to save my pent-up frustration for the girls at The Rox. While I'm not into sadism or BDSM, I've clearly taken my irritation out on them lately. Anger from years of pushing down my feelings, unable to move on.

"You know..."

"What?"

"You know you deserve it too, right?"

It's rare any of my friends bring up dating with me anymore. I've shut the conversation down too many times to count. I simply shake my head in response.

"I'm just sayin'... sex is a lot more fun with two people."

Fuck. Don't I know it?

"Don't worry about me. Just because I'm not interested in the same thing you're looking for doesn't mean I'm not getting any." Well, it doesn't mean I am, either.

"What is it I'm looking for?" Nate chuckles.

"You know, happily ever after and all that shit. And you deserve it. It's just not in the cards for me."

Nate gives me a knowing glance. I'm sure he's heard this enough to know there's no point in pursuing this.

Reaching into my sack, I grab my laptop and water bottle before heading to the main room. I always arrive a bit early to get my things situated so I can be as flexible as possible. One never knows when the screeching tones of the firehouse will go off, and we'll have to jump into gear. We each develop a bit of a routine. I have my boots and turnout gear sitting next to the engine, ready to go at a moment's notice. Occasionally, I'm assigned to ride the ambulance with Jamie 'The Hammer' Sherman. I always ride shotgun on those days, as I'm the paramedic, and The Hammer drives and assists with the heavy lifting.

Jamie's a veteran at the firehouse. He showed me the ropes when I was a rookie, and I still look up to him. Hell, everyone looks up to him. The dark-skinned Black man is six foot five and built like a tank. With his imposing size, shiny bald head, and reserved personality, he gives off an air of authority to those who don't know him. His mere presence demands respect, like the squad leader of a S.W.A.T team. But that guy would do anything for those of us in the brotherhood. Even ex-firefighters with questionable pasts. Hell, who am I kidding? I think the guy would give his last dime to a homeless guy on the street.

Speak of the devil. "Hey, I'm starving. Any chance of hitting the store early and making breakfast?" Jamie asks as he drops his gear on the bunk next to mine.

"You cooking?" Nate chuckles.

"C'mon, man. You know if I made breakfast, either no one would eat it, or I'd set off the station's fire alarm in the process. That'd be embarrassing as hell."

"So, you want us to go to the store and make you breakfast? Is that what you're saying?" I jab.

"Yeah. Basically." There's a slight curl to his lip. I could count on one hand how many times I've seen him smile over the years, so this is jovial for him.

"As soon as we check the engine and make sure we've got all our gear on board, we'll head to the store. I know it takes a lot of effort to keep that body fed and watered." I laugh.

"You're damn right," he says, flexing his arms like The Hulk. Hell, I don't think The Hulk has anything on The Hammer.

~

"Hey, I'll meet you at checkout if we don't get a call first," Nate says as he heads for the dairy aisle.

"I'll get the rest," I holler back. There's no sense asking Jamie to grab anything. He really is a terrible cook. He'd probably just stand in the middle of the store looking confused. I don't know how he does it at home. He's so private. After all this time, I've still never heard mention of a live-in girlfriend. Or even a roommate, for that matter. Unless his mom cooks his meals for him at age forty, he must have one hell of an Uber Eats bill.

"Uncle Huggie!" I spin on my heel just before Ruby plows into me. At nine, I still get the celebrity treatment whenever I see her.

"Hey, Rubs. Did you drive up here?"

"I'm not old enough to drive." She giggles.

"Hi, Hugs."

My body instantly becomes electric at the sound of the soft, feminine voice lilting my way. It's as if her very presence has flipped a switch. "Hi, Mel."

She's wearing a light blue chambray button-down blouse with long sleeves and a short khaki skirt. Her sandals expose her dark red toenails, and I fight to keep from staring. I try to return my gaze to hers without giving away my ogling. After all of these years, you'd think I'd have perfected it. Her dark hair is piled high in a messy bun today. Over the last few years, I've noticed she rarely wears it down. While her clothes were once form-fitting and chosen to grab attention, she now gravitates toward articles that let her blend in with the crowd.

My eyes meet hers momentarily. They're void of any spark. I know the only spark she ever had was for Jake. But that torch has been extinguished for years now. The luminous smiles and twinkling bright eyes of days gone by are almost nonexistent. Now she seems to wear the brave face of someone who's decided to make the best of it. She's not truly living.

My heart aches for the girl that once was, now trapped beneath her endless grief. But despite all of the heartache life has brought her way, she's still the most beautiful woman I've ever met.

"Hey, Huggie," Seth greets.

"What? Were you parking the car?" I joke.

"You're too young for dad jokes," Nate says as he approaches with an armful of eggs, cheese, and yogurt. He's barely finished the jab before I notice everyone's faces fall. "Oh, Mel. I didn't mean—"

"Nate, it's okay. I know you didn't."

"You guys making something?" Ruby asks.

"Jamie forgot to eat before he came to work." I laugh looking at Nate's single carton of a dozen eggs. "You might need to get another one of those."

We look over to Jamie, who simply nods.

"Be right back."

"I can't wait until I'm old enough to hang out in the firehouse with you guys," Seth says.

"You're eleven. It's not too much longer now."

Nate returns with his arms full just as the tones go off on our radios, alerting us of a call.

"Damn," Jamie utters under his breath.

"Seth, Ruby, grab Nate's things," Melanie urgently instructs. Sprinting over to me, she reaches into my arms for the plastic bag of peppers, onions, and the sack of potatoes I'm carrying. As her hands skim my forearms, I feel a charge ripple through my nerve endings as if I've been struck by a defibrillator.

"We'll drop these off at the station on our way home," Melanie adds.

My eyes meet hers, and it steals my breath.

Fuck, this woman.

CHAPTER SIX

MELANIE

I observe my son's intense gaze as he watches Huggie, Jamie, and Nate run to the engine from the front of the grocery store. He's wanted to be a firefighter since the first time Huggie put him on his shoulders and carried him into the fire station years ago. Try as he might, Jake couldn't compete with the allure of the fire department. Seth's father was merely an emergency room physician. He'd given up hope of changing Seth's mind when he'd asked to spend his birthday with Huggie and the boys year after year. I inwardly laugh at the memory of the dejected expression on Jake's face. It's a wonder Seth even asked him to do career day.

My heart immediately drops into my stomach at the thought.

That horrible, awful day.

"Mom, this doesn't look like a lot of food for all those big guys," Ruby says as she looks into the shopping cart. She's been my little helper when I've hosted parties in the past.

We'd only come to the store for a few staples before running into Huggie and the boys. Looking down into the metal cart, I have to agree with Ruby. Their purchases are a mish-mash of breakfast items. While just the three of them were here shopping, several more were usually back at the station assigned to the truck and the ambulance.

"Hey, why don't we grab a few more things, and if they still aren't back from their call, we can make breakfast for them," I suggest to the kids.

"Yeah," Seth chimes in. "Let's do it."

"I'm grabbing some cinnamon rolls," Ruby squeals.

"Okay, meet me at the front in ten minutes," I tell them. An odd sensation reminiscent of a smile inhabits my face. I feel this so rarely I barely recognize anything joyful. I need to try to force myself to express happiness more often, if only for the kids. They say time heals all wounds...

But whoever *they* are, lied.

"Hey, Mel. To what do we owe this surprise?" Wilson greets us at the door to station twelve with a smile.

"Hi. We bumped into the boys at the store, and they got a call before they could check out. We thought we'd bring their things," I say, glancing at my kids, who nod in agreement with big grins on their faces.

"That's so nice. Here, let me help you with those."

"Have they made it back?" Seth asks.

"No. I think they responded with a volunteer EMS unit on a possible hip fracture. Sometimes those can take a bit of time to get into the ambulance."

Hip fractures are terribly painful and, in my experience, occur in elderly patients riddled with weak bones or arthritis. They don't fare well after a fall. Getting them onto the stretcher and in the back of the ambulance can take great finesse to prevent making them more miserable than they already are.

"Would you mind if we started working on breakfast? It could be lunch before they get to it."

"Are you kidding? We'd be thrilled. We all take turns with meals, but I'm sure none of us can whip up anything close to your cooking."

I bite into my cheek, hoping not to let the memories of yesteryear pull me under. Before losing Jake, I was quite the social hostess amongst our friends. We'd host parties and have people over for Friendsgiving. We'd occasionally make food trays and deliver them to the guys at the station or bring them to the ER where Jake worked. These hard-working folks in EMS, fire, law enforcement, and the medical field don't take meals for granted. They often work long hours without eating.

Unpacking the sacks of food items, I take inventory as I lay them out on the kitchen counter—eggs, cheese, bacon and sausage, potatoes, peppers, and onions. I place the fruit and yogurt in the refrigerator and begin familiarizing myself with the utensils and cookware. I notice Seth walking around, opening doors like he's at an open house, and Ruby sitting in the main room in front of the television.

"I'm sorry, Mel. I hope I didn't upset you. It's been a long time, but..."

Reaching for his arm, I try to reassure him. "Wilson, it's okay. It's been years. I don't want my friends walking on eggshells around me. This is my issue, not yours. Now, where's the cutting board?"

Wilson gives me a quick tour of the galley-style kitchen and excuses himself when the phone rings in the other room. I get to work on cleaning and chopping the potatoes and vegetables to sauté before starting on the eggs and sausage. I might as well crack all two dozen eggs.

You'd think I wouldn't feel so out of sorts here. I've worked in this kitchen many times in the past. Spaghetti dinners and pancake suppers to raise money for the fire department. Yet I was in a much different place mentally back then. I was surrounded by friends and strangers, all working together toward a common goal. These days I feel like I'm floating alone in a lifeboat with a hole in the bottom, watching the world thrive around me.

Everything seems so abrasive. As if I'm forcing myself to be a part of the living. Was that how Jake felt when I pushed him to join me at social gatherings? I thought he was merely tired, but maybe working in the emergency room for so long had taken its toll.

He'd witnessed so many tragic things during his career. Overdoses in young people, families grieving for patients he tried so diligently to save, domestic violence, trauma, suicide attempts, or having to diagnose someone with cancer. Dispensing bad news to patients day after day catches up with you.

"Mommy? Are you crying?"

"No, no. It's the onions," I say, doubtful it's true. "Ruby, can you put these cinnamon rolls in the pan so I can put them in the oven?"

"Sure, Mom," she answers excitedly. She loves helping me in the kitchen. I haven't done much cooking in the last few years, instead opting for prepared meals I can heat with little fuss. I need to get better about returning to healthy cooking and bringing Ruby in to help out. If nothing else, it's a convenient way to check in on her and how she's feeling.

"Holy shit, what's that smell?" I hear an unidentified voice from the doors leading to the bay where the fire engine and EMS units are parked. Nate turns a corner and I instantly realize the words must've come from him as he grimaces when he sees Seth and Ruby. "Sorry for the language, Mel. We were cursing ourselves for not grabbing a sweet roll on the way back from that call. We're starving."

I give his huge bicep a reassuring squeeze.

"What a great surprise," Huggie says behind me. But as I turn to answer him, I realize he's speaking to someone else. That long-lost smile of mine reappears as I see his arms around each of the kids beaming back at him.

Huggie has always felt like more of a family member than a friend. I met him the day I joined the volunteer rescue squad when I was sixteen and wide-eyed at all the new experiences I was about to face. I trained as an EMT and was prepared for the various emergencies we could be transporting to the nearest ER. I'd dreamed of a career in nursing since I was a child and knew this would give me the foundation to excel in school. Huggie and I were assigned to the same crew every Wednesday night at the rescue squad, and later, Jake joined our team. While Huggie and I have always been close, he and Jake became fast friends. I'd go so far as to say, Huggie was Jake's best friend.

My kids think 'Uncle Huggie' walks on water. Heck, maybe he does.

The man is a saint. He's been by our side from the moment we lost Jake. I discovered months after the accident that Huggie insisted he was the one to tell me, not allowing the police or anyone else to do it. And then he broke the news to my kids when I was in no shape to say the words out loud. I'll never be able to repay what he's done for our family. But then again, *he's* more a part of their lives than several biological aunts and uncles who live states away. He's attended soccer games and dance recitals over the years without batting an eye. Frequently stepping in when Jake wasn't able to attend.

I can't help but wonder why he hasn't found his own family. The man is everything any woman would want. It's more than his handsome face and dreamy smile. Huggie's thoughtful and supportive. He's such a positive presence in my children's lives.

I admit there was a time I thought he was gay, but Jake assured me that wasn't the case. I never pushed for more, as much as I would've loved to have heard the dirty details. Yet Huggie never brought girls to dinner. I've never seen him with a date to any of the rescue squad banquets, always electing to go stag. He's pretty closed-lipped about his immediate family. Perhaps an issue with his mom and dad caused him to choose the single life.

Heck, he may simply prefer to date without commitment. But that doesn't match his personality. He's the epitome of the boy next door.

You'd think I could just ask him as close as we are. But after I tried, not so subtly, to set him up with our friend, Kat, and that went nowhere fast, I've just stayed out of it.

I feel a sizzle against my arm and quickly pull away, assuming it's a small splatter of grease from the bacon, until I remember I've already put those on a plate. My eyes spring upward, and I notice Huggie's troubled expression.

"I'm sorry, Mel," he tries to reassure me. "I was just trying to say thank you. I didn't mean to—"

"No, no. Don't apologize. I thought it was something else."

Huggie looks down at me with a puzzled countenance. It mimics the way I'm feeling right now. What was with that heated feeling from his touch? Static electricity? And why am I suddenly feeling so flushed? *Am I coming down with something?*

CHAPTER SEVEN

HUGGIE

"Hell, it's hotter than Satan's ballsack out here," Nate whispers in my direction.

"Yeah. It had just started to cool off, and now we get this hot and humid day on set." You never know what you're going to get in September in Virginia. "At least we don't need the full suit unless something catches fire."

We all rotate shifts on the set of the revolutionary war drama that's being filmed in the area. We've primarily been on location in Richmond and Petersburg, but today we're a bit closer to home in Scotchtown.

It's wild living so close to such historic landmarks. You take them for granted when you grow up around them. I've spent many years in Hanover, but my only visit to Scotchtown was years ago when I chaperoned Seth's class during a field trip to Patrick Henry's home. Poor Jake tried to go but had to attend some mandatory thing at work. I think the kids enjoyed running around at the picnic grounds afterward much more than the historical portion of the trip, but I'm glad I have that memory with Seth.

"My nuts are about to catch fire," Nate reminds me.

"Ah, it's like the Christmas carol."

"These are not chestnuts," Nate corrects, seeming offended.

"Chestnuts are big nuts, man. That was a compliment."

"What the hell are you two talking about?" Jamie interrupts. Luckily, his arrival signals the end of Nate's shift.

"Never mind. Let's just say your timing is perfect. Nate's a delicate flower." He's getting a little too whiny, even if it does feel like walking through soup out here.

"C'mon, man. We've been sitting here watching them shoot the same dumbass scene all day. If it got any hotter or stickier, I'd have to start taking things off that should be left on."

"Why did you get The Hammer to split the shift with you? Got a hot date?"

Suddenly, I realize it's grown quiet and look over at Nate. "I'm meeting the parents."

"Holy shit, Nate. No wonder you're sweating."

"Yeah. This could be the real deal. I stopped waiting for the other shoe to fall, you know?"

No. I don't know what that feels like. But I'm happy for him all the same. "I'm glad, bud. You deserve it. When do we get to meet him?"

"Nah, not ready yet," he says, his voice low.

"I get it." I try to give him a reassuring glance. I want him to know his friends are supportive, but this is a big deal. He's never brought anyone to a function with all of us. It has to happen when he feels it's the right time.

"Well, if anyone should, it would be you," Nate adds.

"What's that mean?" I know full well what he means. I need to change the subject.

"There's no one more secretive on the planet when it comes to who they're seeing. Fuck, I know more about The Hammer than I do you." We both look at Jamie and chuckle. Yeah, I doubt that. He doesn't tell anybody anything. "At least Adam won't have to have an anxiety attack meeting mine."

My heart breaks for Nate. He's honestly the nicest guy I know. The fact that his parents have shunned him for being gay makes me livid. "You don't think your sister would come around?"

"I think if anyone would, Lyla would. She's not a bad egg. She's just trapped beneath Mom and Dad's thumb. She doesn't really think for herself. It's a shame because she's wicked smart."

If she got Nate's DNA, she's probably a looker, too.

"I'd think staying in this sauna would beat meeting the parents," Jamie says.

"Probably. But Adam's a good guy, and I'm excited things are going in this direction." Nate smiles. All nervousness is gone.

"Just be yourself. They're going to love you," I tell him with a slap on the back.

Jamie and I sit mindlessly scrolling on our phones when we suddenly hear a thud followed by screaming. I grab my medic bag as Jamie bolts toward where a group of actors and extras gather at the base of some scaffolding.

"Excuse us," Jamie belts out. I've learned to let him lead. There's no one standing in our way when Jamie's yelling to clear the area.

"It looks like a piece of the floorboard broke," a male dressed in colonial garb advises as he points toward the scaffolding. He's standing next to a middle-aged man who is sprawled on the ground. I'm not exactly sure of his role here, but he's clutching a camera as he lies in the grass, staring up at us.

"I'm fine. I think the fall just knocked the wind out of me." He begins to sit up, and Jamie quickly pushes him back down to the ground.

"Sir, let us check things out before you move. It looks like you fell at least ten feet."

"Jamie's right. We can't force you to be evaluated, but you really should go to a trauma center." I'm not sure we can convince him to go anywhere, but St. Luke's is closer if he's willing. They can always transfer him if they find something.

"This seems like overkill," he blurts.

Luckily, someone from the production team arrives and advises the patient he'll need to get medical clearance before he returns to the set.

He stands and walks unassisted to the ambulance, refusing to go downtown.

It looks like we're heading to St. Luke's.

"Hey, Huggie," Kat greets at the ambulance bay doors.

"Hey, Kat."

"I missed the report you radioed in. Who have you got here?"

"This is Mr. Donaldson. He works for the paper and was taking pictures on the set of the new TV series they're shooting in Scotchtown. He fell approximately ten to twelve feet from scaffolding when a floorboard broke. He landed on his back and insisted he walk to the ambulance. He denied striking his head or loss of consciousness, but given the mechanism of injury, the production team insisted he get checked out before he's allowed to return."

"I think you must be made of Teflon, sir," Kat jokes.

"Come with me, Mr. Donaldson. I'll take you to triage so we can get you checked in," a pretty young nurse says.

"Take care, sir." I wave.

"Thanks for the report, Huggie. That guy looks like he got lucky, or else has a super high pain tolerance."

"Well, I hope you don't find anything bad. He flat-out refused to go downtown to the trauma center. I wasn't sure we could convince him to get checked out at all. He must really want to come back tomorrow."

"Have you been pulling a lot of shifts with the movie crew? That must be exciting."

"Nah. It sounds better than it is. It's a lot of sitting in the heat, is what it is."

"But the pay ain't bad," Jamie adds.

"There's that. So many of the guys' kids are doing fall sports that I've been working every weekend. How've you been? I haven't seen anyone in a month of Sundays."

"We're good. We've been busy too. Nick's been taking Seth and Ruby to soccer to give Melanie a break."

Hearing her name gets my pulse beating a bit faster. I've been trying to put a little more distance between Melanie and me. She knows she can count on me if she needs anything. But I was starting to feel like I was outstaying my welcome. I didn't want to crowd her now that she seems to be doing better. But honestly, it's self-preservation. I can't allow myself to get any more attached.

"I need to try and catch a game. Thanks for the reminder. How's Mel?"

Kat gives me a surprised look. "She's good. Usually, you know better than I do." We both stand in silence for a moment. It's as if she's sizing me up. Looking at her watch, she adds, "I think she's with Munish right about now."

"Lawyer's office stuff?"

"It could be these visits are to learn about Jake's case, but I wonder if it could be more."

"What do you mean, more?"

"Secretly, I think Mel's always had a thing for Munish," she whispers.

What the hell?

My blood instantly starts to simmer, and I try to ignore the odd expression on Kat's face. This is too much. I knew it was a matter of time, but Munish?

I really need to get laid.

$$\sim$$

"Annalise, I've given it a lot of thought. You've been nothing but accommodating. I was frustrated but had no right taking it out on you."

"I understand completely. There's no need to apologize. We fell short, and I assure you that will not happen again. I hope this means you'll be staying with us."

"Yes. For the time being," I say dryly.

Several moments of silence cross the line, and I'm sure she's wondering if there's more to this phone call than an apology. *Hell, I'm second-guessing why I picked up the phone.*

"If I may, Mr. Mars. I have a new girl. I think she'd be perfect for you. I think she'll be a little more reliable than the girls you've been paired with recently. She's twenty-nine and meets all of your criteria. I've advised her that I have a client with specific needs and reviewed your requirements with her. She's assured me she can give you what you're looking for."

This news is unexpected. I merely called to apologize to Annalise for my neanderthal behavior the last time I visited. But I have to confess, this is tantalizing.

"Is she available this weekend?"

"Yes, sir. That can be arranged."

There's no sense in walking away now. Starting over somewhere new would be exhausting, and there's no guarantee I'll have a better outcome. Plus, it's not like there are ultra-private clubs of this nature on every street corner.

"Good evening, Mr. Mars," an unfamiliar blonde greets as she opens the door to The Rox. The club is located within an in-descript brownstone tucked alongside residential dwellings of similar style. Annalise had shared that the club owned many of the homes on either side of The Rox. She resides in one, as do the club's owners. One is used by security, and a few others belong to billionaire members who've been with the club for some time.

"Do you have plans this evening?" she asks, her big blue eyes appearing hopeful.

I almost shake my head at my recent conversation with Annalise. Suddenly, I'm entertaining the thought they all want me. Good lord. *Can I be any more ridiculous?*

"I believe Annalise has scheduled something."

"Oh, that's too bad." She winks playfully.

So, maybe not that ridiculous.

"Have a good evening. I'll let Annalise know you've arrived."

Pacing about the corridor, I shove my hands in my pant pockets and head to the bar in the front room to order a scotch. Finding a deep red wing-back chair in the corner of the room, I take a seat and await the delivery of my drink and Annalise's arrival. On occasion, my companion for the evening will greet me here, but more often than not, Annalise will escort me and make introductions.

This isn't your typical sex club. There aren't members coming and going. Most preschedule their visits to minimize spending time in the main rooms, thus protecting their privacy. Sure, there's a strict nondisclosure agreement in place. But I don't come here to mingle. I have no interest in seeing any of the other members. From what Annalise has shared, the owners of The Rox have a few affiliated locations with a more private nightclub feel. Yet my membership only provides access to this location. Which, until recently, has suited me just fine.

"Mr. Mars. I'm so happy to see you've returned," Annalise greets with her hand extended.

I want to correct her and tell her to use my first name, but given that I stole it from Nate, that feels awkward as hell. *I wonder how many Mr. Smiths there are here.* "Thank you for trying to be so accommodating," I say as the bartender approaches with my scotch.

"If you're ready, I'll escort you to your room."

I give her a nod and try to take a few cleansing breaths as we walk the dark wooden floors of the hallway. As past encounters have shown, I can't let my hopes exceed my expectations here.

The light gray walls have beautiful white moldings and are artfully decorated with colorful paintings in gilded frames. There are ornate chandeliers in the main rooms and tastefully appointed furnishings throughout. We approach a door at the end of the hall, and Annalise turns to me as she rotates the glass doorknob. "Please, relax. Enjoy your drink. You know to pick up the phone and let us know when you're ready for company."

Closing the door behind me, I take another sip of my drink before familiarizing myself with the room. There's a king four poster bed along one wall, an antique dresser along the opposite wall, and a plush white chair with a teal throw tossed over the back in the far corner. I've not seen these accommodations before. Surprising, given how many times I've been here over the last ten years.

The bathroom is quite opulent, with white marble counters and a tiled shower. I notice a second door that I know opens to the hallway, based on other rooms with a similar design in this building. Thick white towels and luxurious toiletries are on a darker marble dressing table. I've never shared the lush bath amenities with any of my companions. It's more intimate than I wish to allow. My needs are basic. *I want to fucking come with another person in the room. That's it.*

I take another sip of my scotch and turn to face the bathroom mirror. What the hell has become of my life?

My gaze returns to the bed, and I try to get my thoughts back on my main objective. Most men would be excited about having their desires played out with a beautiful stranger. But I'm merely here looking for some relief. I have to acknowledge this isn't about the disappointment I've had here recently. Getting my needs met this way is starting to bother me. But what other choice do I have? Walking toward the dresser, I finish off my scotch and pick up the receiver.

"Yes, Mr. Mars?"

"Hi. I'm ready."

Moments later, there's a knock at the door, and a familiar rush of adrenalin instantly courses through my body. I just hope the night ends better than evenings of late.

Opening the door, I immediately sense this encounter will be different. A tall brunette stands before me with her long, glossy locks tumbling over her shoulders. She's wearing a black satin, flowing gown held on by delicate spaghetti straps. Her nails are painted a deep red which matches her lipstick. I have no doubt she has brown eyes, but they're trained on the floor.

"Please, come in," I direct, waving my hand toward the room low enough that she can see it.

She practically glides into the room, her posture rivaling an angel from a Victoria's Secret fashion show. Her hands are clasped in front of her, but she doesn't appear nervous. This is thanks to Annalise.

"You're stunning."

A blush stains her cheeks, but otherwise, she remains quiet. I've never asked for their silence from start to finish, just not during sex. But I'm an asshole. I'm more than willing to take what she's offering.

I step forward and brush her hair over her shoulders so it falls behind her back. I usually know the girls' names, but no introductions were given, and again, I'm going with it. Would it really matter anyway? *I mean, mine doesn't belong to me.*

Placing my lips against the shell of her ear, I can't help but take in the slight smell of eucalyptus. "Would you do something for me?"

I feel a curt nod before I can pull back to see it.

"Would you wear this for me?" I dangle the black silk blindfold I've retrieved from my pocket in front of her. I'm not taking any chances this time. I'm relieved to note a hint of a smile as she again nods her agreement. Carefully tying the blindfold around her, I stand back to take her in. I hadn't noticed until now. But it's apparent she's not wearing a bra as her nipples are now poking through the soft, smooth fabric of her dress. There's some contentment in knowing she's aroused, even if I'm using her this way.

I reach for her hand and walk her over to the edge of the bed. Her compliance, combined with her undeniable attractiveness, has made my dick ready to play. I'm well aware I've paid for the opportunity, but I always ask for permission. "May I touch you?"

She again grants permission with a simple nod. I honestly didn't think Annalise could find a girl like this. But it's still early. I'm getting ahead of myself.

I reach for the thin straps of her dress and gently lower it until it pools at her feet. Taking her hand, I help her to step out of the garment so I can lay it over the end of the bed. As I return to my place in front of her, I cannot help but take a few steps back to study her. She's wearing four-inch black heels and a tiny black lace thong. Her perky tits are full, at least a C cup, and her tight pink nipples confirm she's ready to play.

Dropping my lips, so they hover just above the nape of her neck, I again ask permission. "May I kiss you?"

This time I'm met with two succinct nods and a slightly larger smile that raises her cheeks. I place my lips on the nape of her neck and trail chaste kisses down to her collarbone. Once there, I give it a quick swipe of my tongue before returning my lips to her sweet, warm skin.

I cup the soft swell of her breasts and pull back to give her nipples a firm pinch before dropping my mouth down to give each a suck and a tight pull with my teeth. As I tease them with my tongue, I look up to see she's biting down on her lip to the point she could break through the tender flesh.

I stand to my full height and remove my charcoal gray suit jacket because, let's face it, it's getting hot in here. Unbuttoning the top two buttons of my starched white shirt, I roll up my sleeves to mid-forearm. A dark vine from my tattoo escapes my right sleeve, but with the blindfold in place, there will be no need to entertain questions regarding its origin.

Sliding my hand down her alabaster skin, I touch her core and notice her legs are shaking. Hell, standing on these heels has to be difficult enough. Balancing on them while my fingers tease her relentlessly is just plain unfair.

Standing, I scoop her up and carry her to the bed, where I lie her back to finish what I started. Returning to my knees, I make it my mission to finger her until she can't hold back any longer. I'm a large man. Even the girls here deserve to be warmed up beforehand. I'm not looking to hurt anyone. My only kink is wanting a warm body that can get the job done without allowing thoughts of *her* to derail me.

It's clear she's close as her fingers dig into the bedding. "I need you to come for me." With two fingers buried inside her, I reach up with the other hand to pinch her nipple. "That's it," I encourage her as her body starts to quake beneath me. "Such a good girl."

Looking down at her, I note her flushed skin and the smile that is no longer hidden. There's a sick satisfaction in knowing this encounter isn't completely one-sided. Even if giving her pleasure is only a convenient result of trying to avoid ripping her in two.

I reach into my pocket to retrieve a condom and drop it onto the bed. Grabbing hold of her legs, I pull her body toward the edge. "On your knees, pretty girl."

She gracefully sits up and perches on her knees before me, but instead of turning away as I'd pictured, she's facing me. I'm instantly drawn to her pouty crimson lips and change gears.

"It's not going to take much for me, I'm afraid. You're beautiful, and it's been a very long time," I say. I stroke her cheek before cupping her chin. "I'm not going to fuck you tonight. But, could I ask..." *Fuck. What the hell has happened to me?* This is completely absurd.

Before I can further chastise myself, she climbs off of the bed and situates herself at my feet. The temptress opens her mouth and drops out her tongue in invitation. I can't help but observe her subservient posture. She's now sitting back on her heels, creamy thighs spread wide, with her hands clasped in her lap as I assume a submissive might. Is that where this girl came from?

My thoughts about her past are distracting. I don't want to dominate her in that way. "Touch me, pretty girl. I don't want to fuck your face. I want *you* to make me come."

"Thank you," I say quietly as I untie her blindfold. The release brings a sense of relief and satisfaction that's been long overdue—nothing more, nothing less. But for a few short moments, I'm grateful to feel alive.

She stays in character, a demure smile on her lips as she keeps her eyes trained on the floor. Standing, she gathers her things and heads to the washroom.

I'll refrain from dressing until I hear her exit the bathroom. Then I'll shower and head back home. It's late and a few hours' drive, but I'm feeling more invigorated than I've felt in months. It'll be good to get home and start tomorrow on a better foot.

It's biological, really—my need for this club. Try as I might, I've had very little success with any other scenario. I'm clearly not cut out to live my life as a monk. I need some degree of physical interaction, even if it's cold and controlling. Who knows how long I'll feel this way? But for now, this is my only option. Because the one woman I want, I cannot have.

My attraction to my best friend's widow is like a second skin. I couldn't act on it when Jake was alive, and I certainly can't disrespect his memory or risk ruining the relationship with the one person who means most to me by pushing for more. I've tried dating, but it's not fair to other women when my mind is on someone else. I ruined the one relationship I tried with a woman when I was finally able to achieve an orgasm and called out Mel's name.

I might as well embrace my situation. Living a lonely bachelor life where the only stand-in for my hand is the occasional hookup at The Rox. Where I pay a nameless, voiceless, random brunette, who could be Melanie's doppelganger, to give me what I need.

Such is the life of a man possessed.

CHAPTER EIGHT

"Melanie. Any chance you have room in your schedule to join me for lunch today?" Dr. Hart asks from the doorway.

"Sure. I was going to get caught up on my charts with a salad. This sounds much more appealing." Ugh, did that sound overly flirtatious? I think my nerves got the best of me when he asked me to join him. Usually, when your boss wants to meet with you, it's because there's a reason.

"I was planning on ordering take-out from Luigi's. You okay with that?"

"Wow. Of course. That salad can wait 'til tomorrow." I giggle.

"Good. I'll just order a few things and take home whatever we don't eat. I still haven't quite managed food for one."

The statement makes my chest squeeze. Dr. Hart doesn't speak of his private life often. I'm sure, much like me, he's still raw, even after all these years. You can't help but stay guarded, careful not to open the door to unwanted topics when discussing your new normal. His knowledge that I live with a similar heartache probably makes him more comfortable with me than with others who simply don't understand.

"My office at one o'clock, okay?"

"That's perfect. My last patient is scheduled at noon."

~

"Come on in," Dr. Hart greets, my hand still raised mid-air, about to knock on his office door.

I have to admit, I'm a bit uneasy, not knowing why he wants to speak to me. But he wouldn't order take-out from Luigi's before firing me, right?

Dr. Hart walks over to my side of his desk and grabs a paper plate and plastic utensils. Handing them to me, he says, "Please, have whatever you like." He turns and retrieves a plate for himself before opening several containers to look inside.

"Oh my gosh, it looks and smells amazing. I might need a nap after this." I immediately regret my words. What if he's called me in here to discuss my poor performance, and this lunch is just a way to soften the blow?

"Me too. I'm not sure what I was thinking ordering this heavy food mid-day?" His chuckle brings instant relief.

I glance in his direction and take in the faint lines at the corners of his eyes. How can men rock crows' feet? I use high-priced eye creams to keep them at bay as long as possible, but on a distinguished man, they're quite sexy.

"Melanie?"

Holy crap. Was I staring? "I'm sorry, I zoned out for a minute. This isn't a good sign if I'm like this before I've even taken the first bite." I laugh nervously.

He gives me a sweet smile and repeats, "I asked if you wanted a roll?"

"Oh, yes, please. Luigi told me long ago that none of the carbs in his restaurant count."

"Sounds like him." He says with a grin. I notice him inspect my plate containing a small salad, a roll, and two squares of ravioli, and he frowns. "You aren't hungry?"

"Can I be frank, Dr. Hart?"

I watch as he promptly places his plate down and sits down beside me. "Of course. And please call me Derek. You've worked here for months."

"I'm sorry. It's a hard habit to break."

"What were you going to say? You just had Luigi's for dinner?" He jokes, attempting to lighten the mood.

"Not last night." I laugh. "But we do get our fair share from there."

A broad smile crosses his handsome face, and he leans back in his chair. "Well, that's a relief. I thought you were going to tell me you were gluten intolerant."

"No." I tear off a piece of my fluffy yeast roll and bring it to my mouth. I may be uneasy about this conversation, but I'm still well aware we only get forty-five minutes for lunch, and then it's back to work. So I try to force a few bites until my nerves settle.

"I'm honestly too tense to eat. Would you mind jumping to the chase? I'm a little worried as to why you wanted to meet today?"

"I'm sorry, Melanie. I didn't mean to make you feel that way."

"I was preparing myself for an uncomfortable talk about my performance," I say looking in his direction.

"Hell, no. You've just been on my mind lately."

The roll stops at my lips, and my tongue suddenly feels like sandpaper. *What was that?*

He stands to retrieve his plate, and I contemplate why he could've been thinking about me. My nervousness eases a bit when he sits behind his desk to eat after filling it with salad and a variety of pasta.

"Why on earth would you think I'd have anything negative to say about your work? You're efficient, give great care, and the patients love you. I couldn't have asked for anyone better."

My cheeks warm at the compliments. I wasn't expecting this. I've tried so hard to learn this specialty and worried I wasn't keeping up with the other Advanced Practice Providers who've worked in cardiology for a while. I reach for my water to clear my throat as I nudge this conversation onward. "Why have I been on your mind lately?"

My shoulders draw up as he places his fork down and makes direct eye contact with me. "I think it's beyond coincidence that we're working together after being dealt similar situations in our personal lives."

I try to push down the food that now feels lodged in my esophagus. Where is he going with this?

"I don't presume to know what your private life is like. I can only speak for myself that it's been the most difficult thing I've ever confronted. A heartache beyond anything I imagined possible. I feel guilty at the thought of even considering someone new."

I feel frozen in my chair. His words are heavy with emotion, a sentiment I couldn't have expressed better myself. But is he—

"I guess I just wanted to check in. Given our shared circumstances, it felt odd that I'd never reached out to let you know I'm here if you need anything. I mean, if anyone understands what you're going through, it's me."

This kind man. My heart aches for him as much as for me.

"Are you okay? Please pretend we don't work together for a moment. I'd like to be your friend if you need me. If you don't, you can tell me to shove it, and I'll get back to my patients and pretend this awkward lunch never happened."

Sitting here, I try to come up with a poignant response. Something that will relay my appreciation for what he's trying to do. But before I can find the words, he continues.

"I know working with someone can make anything outside of the nine to five feel off limits. And I respect your privacy. Don't feel obligated to talk about anything. I only want you to know if you ever need to talk, you can. I get it. We're a part of a club no one wants to join. Even after all of this time, I feel guilty if I laugh at something someone says or if I enjoy a glass of wine, knowing she can't." The lost look in his eyes reveals his continued anguish. It's like I can almost feel his pain hanging in the air between us.

"Yes. That's exactly how it feels." Reaching for my water bottle, I take another sip, hoping it will keep my emotions from tumbling onto my plate. "Do you have kids?" I ask, pointing to what I already know is his daughter's photo on the desk beside him.

"Yeah. Katie is away at school. Losing Margaret hit her pretty hard. She's a smart girl and had expressed interest in an international exchange student opportunity in Spain after her mother died. She's in Barcelona now. I miss her, but I'm excited she has this chance to focus on something great after all we suffered over the last few years."

"Wow, that's such a wonderful opportunity for her." *But lonely for you*, I immediately think. I've had Kat, Huggie, and my kids. I hope he's had someone. "I hate to pry. But do you have any family or friends checking on you? I've been surrounded by them, whether I wanted them nearby or not." I laugh half-heartedly.

"Yeah, I get that too. My wife's family has stopped by. Mine aren't local, but they've checked in a fair amount. It was pretty lonely the first year, but I didn't want anyone around anyway. Luckily, I've found a support group and that's helped a lot. It's nice to have people there if you need them, but don't push you to 'get back on the horse,' so to speak. You're welcome to join me—"

Knock, knock.

I look over my shoulder as Phylis, the receptionist, slowly opens his office door. "Dr. Hart, I'm so sorry to interrupt. You're usually alone, and I didn't think—"

"It's okay. Just a work lunch. What can I help you with?" His voice is so reassuring.

"Mr. Stanley is here. He doesn't have an appointment. He's been having chest pain but wouldn't let his wife take him to the emergency room, insisting you'd see him. I don't think he looks very good."

Derek instantly leaps from his chair and pushes past Phylis on the way to the front desk. I'm hot on his heels, worried Mr. Stanley has delayed treatment of a heart attack.

I've only seen this gentleman once. It was in follow-up of an ER visit for angina. His stress test was inconclusive, but he declined to have a cardiac cath procedure, saying 'he'd rather take a pill' for it. I recall Derek mentioning Mr. Stanley's risk factors. He said he was very direct with the patient that his obesity, high cholesterol, smoking, and family history put him at great risk of a heart attack. The catheterization would allow for visualization of the arteries and intervention to prevent any further damage to the heart. However, Mr. Stanley wanted no part of this.

"Mr. Stanley, when did you start feeling so badly?" Derek addresses as soon as he reaches him. "Phylis, call the ER and tell them we're on the way."

Suddenly, his wife appears as gray as Mr. Stanley. "It started yesterday," she advises.

"We need to get an EKG, but I don't want to delay getting you downstairs so they can place an IV and get everything we need in case we're headed to the cath lab."

In case? This guy looks dead on a doornail. "I'll get him downstairs. I can help them get the EKG and start the IV once we're there," I tell them.

~

Over the next fifteen minutes, Mr. Stanley is the eye of this cardiac storm. Multiple ER nurses and patient care technicians hover obtaining an EKG and lab work. His EKG confirms changes consistent with a heart attack. Derek works with Donovan, the ER physician, to get all of the medications Mr. Stanley will need before heading to the cath lab, where a blockage can be identified and hopefully repaired without needing open heart surgery.

"Hey, what's going on?" Kat asks from behind me.

"A patient from our office didn't want to come to the ER. See what that got him?"

"Yeah. We get that a lot. I take it he's headed to the cath lab?"

"We tried to get him there a month ago. Just hope it goes well." I watch as Derek talks to Mrs. Stanley, reassuring her we're doing everything possible as they quickly wheel her husband toward the elevators. "We probably would've gone straight to the lab from his office, but everyone was at lunch, and Derek wanted to get an IV and medications onboard while the cath team assembled."

"Derek, huh?" She pokes my back with a giggle.

"It's not like that. We only work together."

"Still hot." I hear over my shoulder just as Derek comes closer.

"Thanks, Melanie. Sorry about lunch. I'll see you upstairs later."

"Of course. I'll cover as best I can until you get back."

He's barely made it ten steps before the beam of light radiating from Kat's overimaginative grin blinds me.

"Stop," I scold. "I don't think I'm ready for a relationship. If I was and we didn't work together, maybe I'd consider him. He's very nice. But I don't think he's ready to date either. So stop worrying about my love life. You're wasting brain cells that could be used for more important things. Like treating your patients with emergencies."

"Joke's on you. You're the only one treating emergencies today. The most stressful thing I've managed was someone whose work note was only for two days instead of three."

I don't know how Kat works with these people. She has to juggle serious medical conditions and trauma among people who use the emergency room for things that could be handled at their primary care office. "Were they seriously ill?"

"She came to the ER for a pregnancy test. Which was negative."

"Maybe she anticipated needing to grieve," I say, shrugging my shoulders in question. You honestly cannot make up the stuff you see here. "I need to run. I've now got my patients plus Dr. Hart's."

"You mean Derek's." She teases as she walks back to her workstation.

Oh, good grief.

~

"Melanie, your first patient, and Dr. Hart's first patient are in rooms. We explained there'd be a delay as you both had to tend to a critical situation," Phylis says from the hallway as I make my way down the corridor toward my office.

"Thank you. It'll be just a minute and I'll go see them." Heading for my office to retrieve my lab coat, I catch a glimpse of Derek's desk out of the corner of my eye. I'm surprised Phylis hadn't put his food away. Maybe she assumed he'd be back and would want to finish eating before clinic resumed. Instantly, his words come back to taunt me: *I'll take home whatever we don't eat. I still haven't quite managed food for one.* I can't leave this out. Gathering the leftovers, I dart to the office fridge and place them inside. I return to the office to cover his plate with another and take it to the refrigerator as well, hoping he'll have time to eat something when he returns. There. That feels better.

Once I've donned my lab coat, I make my way to the waiting patients, hoping I can keep up and provide adequate care in Derek's absence. I admit I feel much more prepared for this juggling act after his kind words earlier about my performance so far.

◠

"Thank you for holding down the fort," Derek says as he pops his head around the door frame.

"Oh, you're back. I was about to see Mr. Richter. How is Mr. Stanley doing?"

"Lucky. That's how he's doing. He's going to need a bypass, but we were able to stabilize him. It was touch and go for a while there. I was shaking in my boots for a bit," he says with a nervous chuckle.

My immediate thought is how in awe I am of what people like Derek and Jake do every day.

Did. Did every day.

Remembering the man in front of me, I quickly get back on track. I don't have time for morose thoughts of the man I miss. "I put your food in the employee lounge fridge. Please go eat something. I'll see the next two, and we can catch up before the next patients arrive."

"No, you've done—"

"Stop. That's what you pay me to do. While you were saving a man's life, I'm here checking lab results and blood pressure readings. I'm fine. Eat."

"Thank you. And you were worried I had concerns about your work." He laughs.

◠

"Mommy," Ruby yells as I walk through the door. I feel good. It was an exhausting day, but I managed to stop and get a few things to cook dinner for a change. This take-out routine I've started needs to stop. Other people work and manage to feed their families. I never realized how tiring it would be to work full-time and care for them. Single parents are rock stars.

"Hi, baby. Sorry, I'm late. I had to stop by the store." Walking over to the island to place the groceries, I greet Stacy, who's doing homework sitting atop one of the barstools. "Thanks, Stacy. See you tomorrow?"

"Sure. It won't be this late tomorrow, will it? I have a big test on Friday, and I need to be able to study."

"Oh. I'm glad you said something," I say, hoping I haven't caused her stress. She's a teenager juggling life and a challenging curriculum. If this is too much for her, I'll have to scramble to make other arrangements. "I'll make a point of getting here earlier. This trip to the store took a lot longer than I expected."

"I know. My project is due on Friday, and you said you were getting the supplies. I'm so excited. What did you get?" Ruby squeals jumping up and down by my side.

Suddenly, my stomach is doing the backstroke. *Holy crap. How had I completely forgotten her project?* Looking at my watch, I have to concede there's no way I can get dinner finished and make it to the craft supply store in time. "Ruby. I'm so sorry. I completely forgot. We still have one more night. I promise to go get everything tomorrow, and we can order pizza and spend the entire night putting it together." So much for avoiding take-out.

Ruby's face immediately falls. "I've been waiting all day to do this with you. It's too much for one night." It's clear she's trying to be strong. In the past, this would have brought on a torrent of tears. But the obvious disappointment in her eyes is gutting me.

"Bye, Mrs. Harris," Stacy says as she gives me a look similar to Ruby's. I certainly can't ask her to help tomorrow. And how am I supposed to pick this stuff up after work and simultaneously be here so she can get home to study? My eyes return to the tear-filled ones of my dejected daughter.

"Is there any part of it we can start on tonight?"

"I have to put a bunch of math problems on index cards for the players to answer when it's their turn. But I don't have any index cards. And the game board is going to take a long time to get perfect." A lone tear tumbles down her cheek, and I feel like the worst mother on the planet.

"Do you have all of the math problems written out?"

"No. I was going to write them on the cards."

"Why don't you start thinking of the problems and write them out on a piece of notebook paper? I'll put them into the computer and print them out, so all you have to do is glue them on the back of the cards."

Wiping her tear, another two join the party. I pull her into my arms to try to comfort her. "I'm sorry, Ruby. We'll get it done in time. I promise."

"What's going on?" Seth asks, looking alarmed, as he walks into the kitchen. After all we've endured, I'm sure even seeing something as innocent as this can evoke serious concern.

"Hey, bud. Ruby has a big project to do, and I've let her down. I was so tired from work and getting groceries I forgot to pick up the supplies she needs. Do you have any index cards in your room we can borrow until I get more tomorrow?"

"I might. I'll look."

Explaining to Seth the plan for Ruby's project, he offers to help her print the math problems off the computer after she writes them out. It's essential she complete as much of the assignment herself as possible, but if she's doing the work, that's the important part. Well, that and figuring out how to get all of this done in time.

Seth and Ruby head to his room, and I quickly set about putting away the grocery items and starting dinner. I get emotional thinking about how I've let my daughter down and put us in this predicament, so I try to focus all of my attention on the task at hand. There's nothing else I can do right now. And I'm done letting my children see me cry all the time.

"Goodnight, Mommy. You'll get the rest of the things tomorrow, right?"

"Yes, Ruby. I'm sorry. Now get some sleep. It's going to be a long day tomorrow."

After checking in on Seth and thanking him for his help, I head to my room. I want a good cry in the shower to allow me to rest without feeling like a failure. But, sadly, the tears start to pour before I can make it further than my bed. Burying my face in my hands, I try to let out enough of this emotional burden to get myself to the bathroom. Even there, I know I need to be cautious of letting my emotions take over. The walls in this house are thin, and I don't want my children to hear me upset.

"Mellie?"

CHAPTER NINE

HUGGIE

"Mellie?"

Instantly, she jolts at the sound of my voice.

"Hey, hey." I rush to her side. "I'm so sorry. I didn't mean to startle you." Wrapping my arms around her, I pull her against my chest. "Don't cry." I'm trying to keep a grip on my cover, that we're just really close friends and nothing more. But I can't stand watching her suffer. She's come so far. Wrapping my arms tighter around her, I feel her body start to shake as she sobs into my shirt. My chest is wet, I'm assuming from her crying, but it could be my broken heart bleeding into her tears.

She adjusts a bit, lying her soaked face against my neck. The sniffles sound as if they are slowing. "Why are you here? Not that I ever mind. I'm just surprised."

"Seth called. He said you might need a hand. What's the matter? Talk to me."

"I'm such a failure at everything. My kids. My—"

She stops short as if she is going to admit to more, but she's in no position at the moment for me to push her.

"I got home late with groceries, and now I'm worried the sitter won't hang in there with me because she's taking a demanding course load in high school. I was proud I was finally going to feed my children a home-cooked meal instead of take-out, then Ruby reminded me I'd forgotten the items she needed to complete her school project. It's due Friday." Another sob escapes as she continues describing how her evening has gone. "Now I can't pick them up because Stacy has to get home immediately after work tomorrow to cram for an exam."

I grab her arms and hold her steady until her eyes meet mine. "Take a breath. We've got this."

"Huggie, I don't know how single parents do this." She sniffles.

"I don't either. But you're the strongest person I know. This is just a speed bump."

"But, I—"

"All of the supplies are downstairs."

Suddenly, her eyes spring wide. "What? But how?"

"Seth called me."

All of a sudden, her tears are back.

"What's the matter? No more tears," I try to reassure her. "I'm off tomorrow. I'll pick up a few finger foods for dinner and make sure Stacy gets out the door on time. You take your time coming home. We will all attack this together."

Melanie wraps her arms around my chest and squeezes me tight. I can feel the relief washing over her.

"You know I'd do anything to help you. My fire rotation limits me, but we just need to make a plan. But I want it on the record."

She pulls back to look at me, her red-rimmed eyes pulling at my heart again.

"I wouldn't brave Walmart for just anyone." I chuckle.

As she rests her cheek on my chest, I notice her breathing has slowed.

"Mel?"

"Yeah?"

"I've never asked before. Do you have a counselor or a support group you go to? It's been years, but you've handled so much of your grief on your own. I wonder if it wouldn't help to have someone to talk to."

She remains quiet, and I'm nervous I've crossed a line. I'm sure she knows I'm only asking because I care about her. But I'm well aware after losing my mother that everyone handles grief in their own way. Therapy wasn't for me. I managed to recover by putting all of my attention on the girl I loved. Whether she was dating my best friend at the time or not.

"Derek said he's been going to a support group. I'm sure I could ask him about it."

My body immediately stiffens. *Who the fuck is Derek? Try to keep it together, George.* Taking a fortifying breath, I try to contain my growing unease. You knew this could happen one day. "Who's Derek? I don't recall you mentioning him before."

"My boss. Dr. Hart. It feels odd calling him Derek. But he insisted."

I just bet he did. Wonder how long it took Derek, the hot widower, to suggest they console each other at group therapy?

"I don't think talking about my situation in a group of other people who've lost their spouses is going to help me." She's silent for a moment. "It might make things worse. Hearing their grief, knowing..."

Knowing what? Why do I feel like she's talking in code when it comes to losing Jake?

"Kat saw a counselor she liked. I might ask her for his information."

"I think that's a perfect idea," I add. Let's hope this counselor doesn't look like the hot widower.

She looks at me skeptically, and I realize I've probably been a little overzealous with that recommendation. *Shit.* You'd think I'd be better about keeping my feelings hidden after all these years. The thought of her with other men, the struggle not to blurt out 'I love you' when she's hurting.

Unable to control myself, I stroke her hair. She leans back to look at me, and I find her eyes are still puffy but not as red as before. "You're still wearing your work clothes, aren't you?"

"Yeah." She sniffles.

"Go. Get a hot shower. I'll make you some tea and leave it here before I go." I lean down to kiss her head. "Get some sleep. We've got a big day tomorrow."

"Mommy, look," Ruby squeals in delight as she holds up the large foam posterboard with pencil markings all along the edges as Melanie walks through the door. "Huggie is drawing all of the spaces, and then I'm going to use the pretty tape you bought to make the squares look pretty.

She drops her things in the foyer and rushes over to Ruby's side. "That's fantastic. Did you guys ever finish the cards with all of the math problems on them?"

I point to the kitchen table covered in wet index cards. The kids used entirely too much glue. I hope they aren't all stuck to the furniture once they're dry.

Melanie walks over and inspects them, attempting to lift one and discovering the soppy mess. She gives me a weary smile, and I just grin and shake my head. I try to mouth to Melanie over Ruby's head so she won't see. "We can re-do them tonight."

"Thank you for getting me all of this, Mommy."

Melanie's eyes meet mine, and I quickly shake my head, directing her not to correct my little white lie to Ruby.

"And you got these cute bunny stickers too. I'm going to call my game The Bunny Hop." She beams. "They have to answer the questions and hop to the next spot."

"That's so clever," Melanie says as she hugs her daughter.

"Why don't you go change? We've got this. I've got grilled cheese and chicken noodle soup on the stove. As soon as I get the squares drawn, Rub is going to decorate the board. That's where you'll come in to oversee that part of the project. I'm not so good with the frilly stuff."

"I don't know, Hugs. Something tells me there is little you aren't good at," she says, walking toward her room.

I'd like to show you what I'm good at.

Ugh. Just as I suspected. I should've supervised this better. I'm not cut out for parenting.

"What's that look for?" Melanie says from across the room. Lifting my face to try to beg forgiveness for ruining her kitchen table, I'm instantly speechless when I see her walking toward me in sleep shorts and a thin cotton T-shirt that hugs her tits in the most delicious way.

"What?" is all I can get out. *Fuck.* The slight sway of her generous breasts as she walks makes me think she's not wearing a bra. Now my dick is trying to sit higher to get a better look.

She stands right in front of me with her hands on her hips. "I said, what's that look for."

I somehow think the look I'm currently sporting is not the one she's referring to. Attempting to get my breathing under control, I answer her. "I think we may have a problem."

Her eyes follow mine to the card I'm trying to lift that's stuck to her beautifully stained, natural wood kitchen table. Melanie reaches over to the one closest to her and meets a similar fate. "Oh, no." Suddenly, she's shifted from jovial to devastated.

"I'm sorry about the table."

"It's not the furniture I'm worried about. There are fifty cards here that I'll have to do over for Ruby's project in the morning."

"No."

"Yes. Well, no. You're right. I can't wait until the morning. This project needs to be finished by the morning, so I can drive her to school."

"Uh, Mel. That wasn't why I said no." She looks at me with concern as I continue. "There are one hundred cards."

"Oh, god," she bellows, dropping her head into her hands.

"It's okay. We've got this. Go reprint the sheets we cut the math problems from. If you can start cutting them apart, I'll try to get the rest of this sticky mess off of the table. Then we'll start gluing."

"Okay," she says, sounding worried.

"We've got this."

Forty-five minutes later, we're ready to start assembling the cards. The table will need to be sanded and restained, but I'll fix that over the weekend. Luckily, they usually eat at the kitchen island anyway.

We slide the bottle of glue back and forth between us as we adhere the paper to the index cards. Thank goodness I bought two stacks. I look down at my hands. I can barely feel my fingertips for all of the dried glue covering them. "Mel, I'm sorry. I don't think I'm cut out for this kind of stuff."

"What? Why would you say that?"

"Why? We're re-doing everything, and your table's a hot mess. I'll fix it this weekend. I promise."

Melanie reaches over and cups my cheek in her hand. The gesture sends my heart racing. "You're the best, Hugs."

"Nah. Jake was the best. He would've never let this happen." The words are out of my mouth before I realize I've said them. *Fuck. I hope I haven't upset her.*

Melanie squirts glue onto another card and carefully adheres it to the paper containing the math problem. "You're right."

Hell. I guess I had that coming. I wasn't fishing for compliments. I meant what I said. *But why did her answer sting?*

"He wouldn't have let this happen because he never would've helped. If he was home at all, he'd be too tired or distracted." I'm surprised by her answer. She's normally so quick to defend him. "But he did his best, and I should've seen that more clearly when he was still here."

Melanie turns to me, and I start to apologize for bringing him into this conversation when she starts to giggle. "You've got glue on your face." Looking at her fingers, she gasps. "Oh, no. I think I did that to you."

"It's only glue. It isn't that bad, is it?"

"Hugs, it looks like I did a fingerprint test on your face. I had no idea I had so much on my hands."

"It's okay." I chuckle. "It's only fair after what I did to your table."

We both laugh quietly, trying not to wake the kids. Placing my latest index card on the counter, I drop my head. "Only seventy more to go. I need a drink. I bought some Sangria at the store. Want any?"

"I'd love some," she says, continuing her assembly line: squirt, apply paper, and smooth. Squirt, apply paper, and smooth.

I'm about to hand her a glass when I stop. "Check your hands. I don't want you getting stuck to the stem of your goblet." I chuckle. "Maybe we need straws."

"Good call." She giggles, reaching into a drawer and retrieving multicolored straws for each of our glasses.

As we continue to move through the stack of cards for Ruby's homework, I try to keep my eyes on my own paper. I want desperately to gaze over at her supple rack, pressed against that clingy little shirt. Does she have no idea the effect she has on men? Or is she just clueless when it comes to me?

"Oh, no."

Looking over, I see Mel staring down at a card that's landed on the floor. She bends to pick it up, and I can't help but gaze longingly at her soft, smooth legs and perfect ass. What I'd give to run my tongue up the back of her calf.

Think she'd notice?

As she stands to her full height, her giggling has me concerned she's read my mind.

"What?"

"Stand up and turn around."

"What?"

"Your butt. Let me see it."

Holy hell. Is she getting frisky with me? I turn, biting the inside of my cheek to stifle a groan as I feel her hand on my backside. This continued torture isn't helping my dick get the message this isn't the time to say hello.

Looking over my shoulder, I see Melanie waving a card at me.

"I saw it peeking out between your butt and the stool. It was stuck on your ass."

Hell. I knew it was too good to be true.

It's approaching midnight as we manage to complete the last card. I reach over to lift several to ensure none are sticking to her kitchen island when my fingers get stuck to the card. *Good lord.* I carefully peel the corner off of the pad of my finger.

"Oh my god. We did it," she whisper-shouts, jumping in place. Her glorious tits bounce underneath that barely-there shirt, and my cock springs back to life. Before I can look away, she's thrust herself at me, engulfing me in a tight embrace.

I can feel her warm hands on my back and try to ignore the knowledge those gorgeous mounds of flesh that have been teasing me all night are currently pressed into my chest.

"I couldn't have managed any of this without you."

I want to correct her, but all of the blood has rushed from my brain to my damn dick. I can't find words.

She grows quiet, still clutching me. I take a deep inhale of her hair. *What is that? Watermelon?*

"Huggie?"

"Huh?"

Her voice suddenly sounds timid. "Can you stay here?"

CHAPTER TEN

HUGGIE

"Uh, what?" I take a step back to attempt to clear my head. "You mean tonight?"

"Well, yes. It's late." She hesitates for a moment. "But, is there any way you could stay with us? Just for a little while until I figure out how to manage better."

"Um..." *I should've known.* I mean, what the hell did I think she was asking me? *Stay the night, Huggie. I want to thank you for your help by fucking you all night long, Huggie.* "Mel, I'm not sure I can. You know I'd do anything for you and the kids..."

God, I don't want to hurt her. But I'm not sure I could handle that. Spending tonight with her in her tiny sleep shorts and tempting top has already made me a wreck. Not to mention I'm going to have blue balls. How would I survive staying here?

Yet, I'm proud she asked for help. She's so independent and strong; she normally just tries to push through and do everything on her own. I'm positive she wouldn't have asked me to do this if she wasn't struggling. How can I say no? Maybe just a few days every now and then? The thought has no sooner come to mind than I feel her wriggling against my chest, and I remember why this is a very bad idea.

"I could pay you. I don't expect you to give up your life for free."

"Hell, Melanie. Why would you say that?" I attempt to pull away, but she brings me in tighter. I'm offended, but looking into her hopeful eyes, I still want to kiss her. Hold her like this for as long as she'll let me. "Those kids are the closest things I'll ever have to my own children. I'd never let you pay me to help with them."

"I don't understand. Why can't you have your own kids? Is that why you're never in a relationship?" She whispers. "You've got infertility issues?"

"What? No. My sperm count is just fine."

"Then why—"

"I just meant I'm never getting married, so it stands to reason there'd be no kids." I exhale, trying to rein in my emotions. "Mel, it's been a long day. I really don't want to talk about me."

"I'm sorry," she mutters. "I didn't mean to pry. And it was wrong of me to ask you to stay." Melanie grows quiet. "You have your own life. I'll figure it out. Maybe I could hire a live-in nanny. Or an Au Pair. The Jensens have one and love him."

Max, the Jensen's Au Pair, is a twenty-something heartthrob from Spain who's fucking half of the coeds at VCU while he's here earning money as their live-in nanny. I have no doubt he'd be screwing Mrs. Jensen, too, if that was on the table. *Fuck no!*

I feel a familiar wet spot against my chest and worry I've upset her. "Mel?"

"I'm making a mess of everything. Again."

I want to reassure her, but I decide to pull back and see if she needs to get something off her chest.

"It feels like it's taking too long to recover from all of this. This doesn't feel normal. I thought I was finally turning a corner, you know? I'd started to forgive myself for not being a better mother to my kids until this happened. In the beginning, I was so overwhelmed by grief that I had to let others parent my children for me. I wanted to be strong for them, make cookies, and take them on trips somewhere to replace their bad memories with good ones. They deserved better. But it's been years, and... Huggie, I'm starting to wonder if I can do this."

Holding her to me, I can tell she's not overly emotional as she's been in the past when speaking of this awful time. She's come such a long way. The last few days were simply a minor setback.

"You couldn't help how you reacted. You were clinically depressed, as anyone in your situation would've been. You taught Seth and Ruby it's normal to grieve and ask for help when they need it." I smile as I gaze at her beautiful face. "There's no timetable. Do you think it's taking too long to grieve, or is it getting used to your new normal?"

She pauses to consider my question. "I'm not sure. It's hard to see the difference some days. I feel like I've been having more good than bad lately." She pauses again, dropping her forehead to my chest. "But I feel like that's because of you."

God, I love this woman. I look down at her until her eyes connect with mine. "I can do it."

"What?"

"I won't be able to help much when I'm on at the fire department, and I've picked up a lot of shifts with the movie production crew since we're short." And I might need an occasional trip out of town to work off the sexual frustration I'm about to torment myself with.

She buries herself in my shirt, squeezing me tightly before she looks up at me with the most beautiful smile. "Huggie, are you sure? It won't be for long. I feel terrible asking, but everything goes so much better when you're here. It'll allow me to figure out how to make this work on my own."

I stare down into her big brown eyes. I've never realized it before. The dark brown hue from this angle makes them look almost violet. She looks so happy right now—such a 180-degree change from last night. And I was able to do that for her. Hell, I'd paint her nails if she asked me to.

There's no point denying it. I'm pussy whipped without the pussy.

"I'm happy to help."

Burying her face into my chest, she gives me another tight squeeze before attempting to pull away from me. Yet as her arms drop to her sides, I realize mine aren't moving from where they've rested for the last ten minutes.

"Uh, Mel."

"Yeah."

"I think we have another problem."

Gazing up at me curiously, I pull my hands back, causing her shirt to go with them, and notice the moment she's figured out why I can't move.

"I'm stuck."

"Oh, god." She giggles. "Hold on, it can't be that bad."

I pull and rotate my fingers, attempting to break free without success. I don't want to rip her top. Melanie tries to reach her hands behind her back to help free them, but the position is too awkward.

"I think the only solution is for you to take my shirt off."

Holy shit. I might come in my pants just thinking about seeing her sweet tits up close and personal. And how do I look and not touch? Well, that can't happen without squeezing them through her shirt once it's off.

"Close your eyes."

I'm trapped at the corner of respect for the woman I love and horny perv. The spank bank material I'd have from just a two-second peek—

"Hugs?"

"Oh, sorry. They're closed."

"Okay, I'm lifting my arms overhead so you can slide the shirt off."

Maybe I should've asked her to close hers too. She's about to get an eyeful when she sees my cock is as hard as a brick. Lifting the shirt overhead, I feel my heart thudding against my chest. I can't get the vision of suckling one of them out of my head.

"Mel?"

"I'm going to grab something to wear. I'd soak your fingers in dish soap and see if the shirt will come off."

Opening my eyes, I see her standing in the hallway, her arms crossed over her beautiful breasts, pushing the mounds up higher. She's a fucking wet dream standing there topless in her tiny sleep shorts. Who am I kidding? She's a wet dream, fully clothed. I immediately close my eyes again, not wanting to ogle. Plus, hoping she'll get the hint to go find a shirt because once I put my hands and her discarded shirt in the sink, there will be nothing masking the size of my dick.

I turn on the water and try to get it to warm up, hoping the dish soap and some aggressive scrubbing will get this shirt off my fingers. I'm shocked at how well the shirt adhered to my fingers with regular glue. It's not like we were using superglue or anything. But her top feels like it's made of tissue paper it's so damn thin. If she walks around the house wearing clothes like this while I'm here, this will be utter torture.

"Any luck?"

"Yeah, I think it's working. But I don't think I'll have fingerprints left when I'm done."

I hear her gasp and chuckle. Melanie now wears a much less revealing T-shirt, but she's no less appealing.

"I'm kidding. I've got four fingers free already."

"Thank goodness. I feel terrible."

I glance at the clock on the wall and realize it's almost 1:00 a.m. "Hell, Melanie. You need to get to bed. It's so late."

"I want to show you where everything is," she says, returning to stand beside me.

I'm torn. Do I tell her I had to figure that shit out real quick right after Jake died? I practically moved in here then. She just doesn't realize it because she was so out of it. Me, Kat, her mother, and sister took turns after it happened. She was in such a bad way I don't think she has any idea what went down. But these last forty-eight hours have been so stressful. I'm not bringing that up now.

"Voila!" I yell before Melanie quickly slaps her hand over my mouth. "Sorry. I'm free." I hold my hands up for inspection and watch as she giggles back at me.

All of a sudden, it dawns on me. This collection of little moments I'm about to experience with her and the kids will break me when they're over. Laughing over homework, cheering them on at soccer when I'm off, and the evenings with the four of us here together. This is a huge mistake, staying here any more than absolutely necessary. I just keep getting deeper and deeper into this rabbit hole. What the hell am I thinking?

My thoughts are interrupted as I feel Melanie drying my hands with a hand towel. "Come on. Let's get you to bed."

Jesus, take the wheel.

"Okay, so that's pretty much the grand tour of the more private parts of our house," Melanie whispers as we stand inside the guest room door. "I'm sorry it doesn't have its own bathroom. We'd planned to have one with an en suite, but Jake took that as his study."

"It's okay. This is fine. The bathroom isn't far."

"And you know I'm just across the hall if you need anything."

Fuck. I needed you not to tell me that. How the hell am I going to get any sleep here?

"The kids don't get up once they're down for the night. But I like to keep it quiet, just in case. I tend to stay up later than I should, trying to enjoy the silence. Even if it's just reading a book or soaking in a bubble bath."

Shit. Now I'm going to have that image stuck in my head.

"It's terrible saying it, but once they're asleep, it's the one time of the day that's just for me. Sometimes, it's hard to turn it off and go to bed."

"Don't feel terrible. You deserve it. I'll try to keep to myself if I'm here after the two of them are in bed. Or I could go home."

"Oh, no," she says, grabbing my arm. "I'm looking forward to having some company. Please don't shut away in the guest room." She pauses to give me a serious glance. "But if you want to go home, I understand."

Trust me, if I had what I wanted...

Looking at her hand draped over the red rose tattoo on my arm, I have to fight not pinning her arms overhead and kissing her right here and now. My restraint has taken a serious beating tonight.

"Huggie. I have to say this. Earlier, when we were talking..." She pauses momentarily and comes closer, laying her hand on my chest. "I don't want to pry into your private life. But I don't understand why you're so set against getting married and having kids. You'd be a great dad. I don't recall you having a serious relationship in all the years we've known each other."

I feel my hands start to sweat and wonder if she'll buy interrupting her with a yawn or saying I need to take a leak. This is getting more uncomfortable than I'm ready for.

Looking deep into my eyes, she continues. "I'm sure you have your reasons. But other than Kat, you're my best friend. I wish you'd share more of your life with me."

I'm not sure you're ready for that, Mel.

CHAPTER ELEVEN

MELANIE

"Hi. I have an appointment with Dr. Miller."

The striking blonde receptionist looks at her computer and acknowledges my scheduled time before handing me a clipboard. "I just need you to fill this out for me."

"Oh, I thought I filled out the psychological questionnaire beforehand." That thing was terribly long. There's no way I want to repeat that torture. "Did you not get it?"

"No, we received it. This is the patient privacy information."

Whew. That's a relief. Turning, I sit down to sign the form. The reception area is small but well-appointed. I'm not sure what I was expecting when I came here. One thing I've had to acknowledge during the last two years is how incredibly lucky I've been until now. I've certainly never experienced anything worthy of a counselor before.

My dear friend, Kat, has had to endure so much. Years of heartache. Hence why I chose to see Dr. Miller over group therapy. She'd spoken highly of his care, stating he was kind and professional. And if I don't get anywhere with counseling, at least my visits will be easy on the eyes. Kat had said he was a dead ringer for—

"Ms. Harris. Dr. Miller will see you now."

Grabbing my purse, I hand the clipboard to the receptionist, who escorts me down the hallway. The pictures hung in both the lobby and the hallways look museum-worthy. Most have an Ansel Adams look about them. Magnificent black-and-white shots of majestic mountains, waterfalls, and foliage are combined with similar images in color. Both equally capture the splendor of mother nature.

The designer of this office deserves a lot of credit. I'm not typically into minimalist décor, but it allows the artwork to shine. The color palette chosen as the backdrop for the walls within the office only intensifies the photography.

As I reach Dr. Miller's office and see him rise from his desk to meet me, I have to fight to keep my mouth from hanging open. Holy crap. Kat wasn't kidding. This guy looks like he could easily be Matthew McConaughey's twin.

"Hello. Should I call you Melanie or Mrs. Harris?" he greets with an outstretched hand. I have to admit that I'm a little starstruck. I honestly thought Kat was exaggerating. Even his voice sounds the same. All of a sudden, I realize he's just standing here, staring at me.

"Oh. I'm sorry. Melanie is fine," I blurt out. I'm so embarrassed. He's got to be used to this, right? I mean, he has to know people are stunned by the resemblance.

I follow his outstretched arm in the direction of a modern-looking hunter-green chair and take a seat. It's not comfortable, but again, it's in keeping with the modern minimalist décor of the office.

"I'm sorry. I have to apologize. I'm more than a little nervous. I've never been to see a therapist before."

He takes a seat behind his desk and gives me a comforting smile. "There's no need to be nervous. Just try to think of me as a new friend you've met. I'd like to hear whatever is on your mind and possibly give you a different perspective. There's no wrong or right here."

That actually sounds pretty good. Maybe this won't be so bad after all. So long as I can ignore the fact my new friend is hot as hell.

"How about you start from the beginning? How did I end up fortunate enough to meet you today?"

Oh. Hot as hell *and* charming. How does any female remember why they even came here? I wouldn't put it past a few to make up something, simply to have an hour with this guy entirely focused on them.

Again, I sense how quiet the room has become and glance over to see him patiently looking in my direction. Hells bells, he asked me something, didn't he? Oh, that's right. "Well, I lost my husband two years ago. I went through a terrible bout of depression. I've never been clinically depressed before, but this hit me hard." I blurt out the information rapid-fire. I sound like a robot. I take a deep breath and try to collect myself before diving back in.

"I barely left my bed for months. My friends cared for my kids and basically force-fed me until I had the will to live." I stop briefly and think. "I take that back. They forced me to eat and drink until, one day, the guilt of being such a horrible mother took over and propelled me to put one foot in front of the other."

I stop to give myself an invisible pat on the back for coming so far. Huggie's right, I should be proud of how strong I was. I don't know how I forced myself to rejoin the living, especially when I still felt so dead inside.

"Your desire to be there for your children despite your overwhelming grief says a lot about you."

"In what way? I was a horrible mother. Lying in that bed, knowing they had lost their father. I should have comforted them. Forced myself to focus on them, not my own misery."

"Depression of that magnitude doesn't work that way, Melanie. That type of overpowering grief is debilitating. The fact this is the first time in two years you are speaking with a therapist about all you've dealt with is remarkable. It sounds like you have a great support system. That, coupled with your undeniable tenacity, is the only explanation I can come up with."

I can't help but stare blankly at him. "Dr. Miller, while I appreciate the compliment, I don't see it that way. People lose spouses all the time and still manage to be there for their children. They don't practically become vegetative as I did. I honestly think something is wrong with me that I could've behaved that way. Thank God my kids are so tough."

Dr. Miller sits up taller in his chair, his facial expression appearing much more serious than when he first greeted me. "Aside from the fact that no two people grieve the same way, I think other forces were in play."

"I'm sorry. What does that mean?"

"Well, in my experience, when someone has such a severe grief reaction without a known history of depression, it's because there are things that contributed to the situation."

My head immediately drops. I never considered the guilt over what I did to Jake had added to my grief in such a way. I have to acknowledge that my behavior not only sent my husband to his grave but also robbed my children of the support they needed.

"If I may, could I ask how your husband died?" His voice is low and soothing. I know he's here to help me. I can't continue to avoid talking about this. It's been years. That's why I'm here.

"My husband died in a car accident. It was a rainy night. But I found out it was possibly road rage that led to the accident. Our ex-friend was stirring up trouble at the bar he was at just before the accident. I'm working with a lawyer to stay abreast of any charges that may be filed against him, but..."

I peer over to Dr. Miller, sitting patiently, hands steepled in front of him.

"My husband and I argued earlier in the day. The disagreement had actually gone on for several days, but we'd gotten past it until that afternoon. He worked as an ER physician, and his hours had been causing a lot of strife in the family. I'd put up with it for years, but he'd missed a commitment with our nine-year-old son for career day at school. Seth was devastated."

All of the familiar feelings from that day start to rush back, and my limbs start to shake. Why am I putting myself through this? Can anything good come from rehashing this?

Suddenly, Dr. Miller is by my side, holding out tissues. As I reach for them, he lowers himself into the chair beside me, giving me his full attention. "It's okay," he encourages.

I've come this far. I might as well soldier on. "My son was so upset. Jake hadn't called the school to tell them he couldn't make it. He wouldn't return my messages, but I was angry, and I'm sure he was avoiding speaking with me."

My lips start to tremble, and I will myself to go on without crying. "We were supposed to meet at a bar to welcome my friend home from her honeymoon, but I was only there a few moments before I had to leave to get back to the kids."

Pausing for a moment, I reach for a tissue. I know there's no way I'm getting through this without one. "But before I left, I basically gave him an ultimatum. The job or us." A sob breaks free as I replay the sound of Jake calling my name as I walked away. "I told him if he couldn't get his priorities straight, maybe he shouldn't come home."

That did it. The dam has broken. I reach for several more tissues and pray I can get myself together before I have to drive home.

It feels like an eternity sitting here with no one saying anything. But I have nothing more to add. He's the only person I've shared this with. My unforgivable behavior.

"That was the last time you saw or spoke to him?"

I simply nod as I sop up the downpour of tears.

"Thank you," Dr. Miller says quietly.

I look in his direction, unsure of what to say. I'm wrecked. Was this supposed to make me feel better? Coming here? I'm going to leave here feeling like I did all those years ago.

"It took incredible courage to share that with me." Pause. "Have you told anyone else about your conversation before the accident?"

"No." I sniffle.

"It explains a lot, Melanie. Be kind to yourself. This amount of guilt can be insurmountable. You should be proud of pulling through the way you have."

Wiping my eyes, I take a fortifying breath. He's right. I have come a long way. I've still got a ways to go. "I've been blessed. I have amazing people in my life who've been incredibly supportive."

"That's great. It can make a big difference. So you don't feel as if you have to manage everything on your own."

"I have been feeling that way. That's probably why I'm here." I give a half-hearted laugh. "But I have someone moving in with me. He's been great with the kids."

Dr. Miller straightens in his seat. "Oh, so you've been able to start a new relationship, despite all the guilt you've been carrying?"

"Oh, no! Huggie's just a friend. We've been friends for years. He's lost a lot too. He was my husband's best friend."

Dr. Miller grows quiet. After a few moments of silence, I start to grow uncomfortable. Looking down at my watch, I find we still have a few more minutes left. I was starting to think we'd run out of time, and he didn't have the heart to tell me.

"I think it's great you have a support system in place. Especially people who you and your children already have a healthy relationship with. But... be careful."

My head jerks up at his warning, surprised by his tone. "I don't understand."

"It can be fairly common, after the loss of a loved one, to experience transference. When some of your feelings can be transferred to someone new."

"Oh, no. Huggie and I have been friends for years. It's not like that."

"I understand. But grief can be tricky. Just be aware, so when you do begin a relationship with someone, it starts from a healthy place."

"Thank you, Dr. Miller. I appreciate meeting with you today. I think this will be helpful," I say, extending my hand to shake his before saying goodbye.

"I'm glad, Melanie. Feel free to make another appointment so we can talk about how things are going. And if you're struggling with something, don't wait. We'll find a way to accommodate you. You've done this on your own for far too long."

As I exit his office and head to my car, I reflect on how things went. It felt good to get things off of my chest to someone impartial. Pulling my keys from my purse, I open the door and slide inside. "Everything felt right on the money until the end. There's no way I'd develop feelings for Huggie. He's like family."

I play back recent memories of Huggie at the house. Comforting me, spending time with the kids. I have to acknowledge there *is* something there.

And it's not brotherly.

CHAPTER TWELVE

HUGGIE

Looking over my planner, I wince. I'm finally on my ten-day break from the fire department, but over half of those dates, I'm working on the movie set.

One of the great perks of the fire department is the schedule. We have a permanent rotating schedule that allows time to work a side job or travel each month. During the third week of each rotation, we get a ten-day break, and we all look forward to it. This life can be tough for the guys with a family, as the shifts are twenty-four hours starting at 6:00 a.m. But that break is hard to beat.

There was a time I could work both jobs and not bat an eye. But I'm exhausted. I think my old age is catching up with me. Looking over at my bed at the suitcase I've opened, I shake my head. What the hell am I thinking with this?

When Melanie asked if I could stay with her and the kids, I immediately knew it was a bad idea. I've been feeling the tattered edges of my self-control fraying for a while now. But after the other night in her kitchen, my willpower is clearly falling apart. It took everything I had not to make a move once her shirt came off.

She's not asking for much. Another adult she trusts to help her out while she tries to maneuver her current circumstance. She only asked me because she knows I'm not in a committed relationship. She'd never want to put someone out in that way.

She's come so far, the job and being more active with the kids. I know she's still grieving, but I'm hoping she's gradually rejoining the living. Well, as much as I am, anyway.

I have to live with my life choices. I could seek counseling or force myself to move on and date other women. But honestly, I'm just not interested. I'm tired of coming home disappointed. I'd rather spend my time with people I care about and go to The Rox if I need an itch scratched.

And after all of these years, if I'd tried to force a relationship with someone else to work, how would that go? Would my significant other take to my looking out for Mel and the kids? Probably not. But I have no doubt this is where I'm supposed to be. I've never been more certain of anything.

I grab several pairs of socks and boxers and place them in my suitcase. I planned on 'moving in' to Melanie's guest room this weekend, so I might as well have a bag ready. I walk into my bathroom to retrieve a toiletry bag when my phone buzzes.

"Hello," I answer blindly as I juggle my phone, razor, and body wash.

"Hi, Hugs." Melanie's soft voice comes across the phone line, instantly causing me to smile.

"Hey. What're you doing?"

"Well, I took your advice."

Stopping dead in my tracks, I have to think for a moment. *What the hell did I advise her to do?* "Do me a favor, Mel. Remind this old man what I encouraged you to do."

Her giggle comes through and travels from the phone straight to my heart. "You asked me whether I'd seen a counselor the other night. I was surprised he had an opening, but I saw Dr. Miller today. Kat recommended him."

"Oh, Mel. That's great. I'm proud of you. I know it had to be intimidating."

"It was. In the beginning, I kept wanting to run for the door."

Ugh. I'd probably feel the same. "How did it go after you got past that part?"

"It was good. Getting it all out there felt freeing. I'm still pretty emotional about the whole thing. Is there any chance you could come by later?"

Taking a deep breath, I look over at my suitcase and sweat a little. I don't have any plans and want to help her in any way I can, but I'm not sure I can handle comforting her like I did the other night and then trying to sleep there afterward.

"Sure. I wasn't planning to bring my things until tomorrow, but I packed a bag, so I can stay if you need me to. It's the first day of my ten-day break."

"Oh, thank you. The kids will be thrilled to see you. I wanted to ask Kat if she'd meet me for dinner so I could tell her how it went. Since she's familiar with Dr. Miller."

That's a change in direction I wasn't expecting. "That sounds great. I'll head that way in a little while."

"Thank you. I left baked spaghetti and salad in the fridge for dinner. I shouldn't be too late. Kat usually has to drive to the lake house, and I don't like to keep her where she'll be driving those back roads in the dark."

"Take your time. I'll get the kids started on their homework, so they'll have their weekend free."

"You're the best. I promise to make it up to you." I can picture her grinning as she says it. Knowing I've made her smile is all the payment I need.

"Huggie, what are you doing here?" Ruby asks as she walks in the front door.

"Your mom is meeting up with Kat for a 'girl's night' tonight." I tease. "She asked if I could watch out for you two until she gets home."

"Yay!"

Seth comes in the front door, a big toothy grin covering his face once he sees me. "Hi, Huggie."

"Hi. Got much homework?"

"Nah. I'm all caught up. Where's Mom?"

"With Kat. Hey, can I talk to the two of you for a sec?"

They both look anxious, giving me their full attention as they come to the kitchen island where I'm standing.

"So your mom's been trying to manage the house, your schedule, and her new job. It's a lot for one person. You two have been trying to help her, but I wanted to do my part too."

"You have been helping," Ruby says. "You helped me with my project."

"I know. But there will be more things like that, and I don't want your mom to stress about trying to juggle it all. So, I brought a calendar we can put on the fridge." Reaching down, I retrieve it from my bag. "I thought we could write down when projects are due and when you have soccer, so we can have a plan in place. Your mom may already be doing that, but this one will stay in the kitchen so I can see it and help out. I've already put my work schedule on there."

"That's a great idea," Seth says. "Let me get my planner out of my backpack."

"Me too," Ruby shouts.

They run to and from their backpacks, sitting on the entryway bench, back to the kitchen island

"I'm going to stay here some nights, so it's easier on your mom," I add. I've barely completed the sentence before Ruby runs around the island to engulf me in her version of a bear hug. I don't have to wait long for Seth to join her.

"Thank you," Seth says quietly.

My heart is in my throat—these two. "I know the two of you have had to grow up quickly over the last few years without your dad, especially given how hard this was for your mom in the beginning. But I'm so proud of you. Whether I'm staying here or not, know I'll always be here for you if you need me. I promise."

I owe it to their dad to look out for them.

"Now, let's fill this calendar out and go kick the soccer ball around before dinner."

~

We've managed to straighten up the kitchen after dinner, and the kids are cleaning up and changing into their pajamas when my phone buzzes.

Melanie
7:55 p.m.
Mel: Kat's staying at her bungalow in town tonight. Nick's there with Grace. Is it okay if I stay a little longer with her and have a drink?

7:57 p.m.
Huggie: Of course. Enjoy yourself. We're having a Friday night house party.

Melanie
8:00 p.m.
Mel: Don't let me find out the neighbors called the cops.

Chuckling, I put down the phone. I'm glad she's finally able to let her guard down and spend time with Kat without worrying about the kids. This makes me smile.

"Can we make popcorn?" Ruby asks as she pads into the kitchen in her Avengers pajamas.

"Sure. Your mom sent a text. I think she's going to be a little longer with Kat."

I expect to hear disappointment at this. Instead, she carries a barstool into the pantry, climbs on, and attempts to reach a box of microwave popcorn on a shelf too high for her to grasp.

"Rubs, be careful," I scold. "I can get it."

"She's always doing that," Seth says as he enters the kitchen. "I keep telling her if she falls, a broken bone hurts like heck."

"He's right. Please ask us from now on. I don't want anything bad to happen to you."

"I'm sorry. I'm just excited."

"About what?"

"Having popcorn, game night, and a sleepover with you."

This kid.

~

"One more game, Huggie?" Ruby pleads.

How on earth did I let this little imp con me into this? Looking over at Seth, he just shakes his head. "Come on, man. Play with us?" I beg.

"No way. I'm reading my book." He chuckles. "It's getting late. I might watch a little television before I fall asleep," he adds with a big yawn. "I don't think I can concentrate on this book with only one eye open."

"Your turn, Huggie," Ruby says after setting up the game board. "Okay, but this is the last one."

What have I gotten myself into?

MELANIE

"Oh, I'm so glad to see you," Kat squeals from her table in the corner of Luigi's.

"You too. Have you ordered?"

"Yes. I got us two glasses of water and our usual pasta choices. Is that okay?"

"Of course. I know you have a long drive to the lake. So I don't want to keep you too late."

"It's okay. I'm staying in town for the night. Nick is on call until the morning. He's watching Grace, so if he gets called in, I'll have to leave and meet them at the hospital."

The server arrives with our water and a basket of fresh bread. "Can I have a glass of Pinot Grigio?"

"Certainly."

"That bad?" Kat asks with concern.

"What do you mean?"

"The appointment with Dr. Miller. Was it bad enough to cause you to drink?"

"No. I can't explain how I feel. I'm a little edgy. I don't know what I was expecting, but for the most part, it was good. It took me a while to relax enough to share anything deep."

"Yeah, I get it. You need to develop a comfort level."

"And it didn't help that I felt like I was sharing my innermost secrets with a Hollywood celebrity. Jesus, Kat. You weren't kidding. He even sounds like Matthew McConaughey. I thought I was sitting with Jake Brigance from *A Time to Kill.*"

Kat nearly chokes on her water. "I know, right?" She wipes her mouth before continuing, "I was fixated on him saying "alright, alright, alright," like his David Wooderson character in *Dazed and Confused.*" She laughs. "Jeez, he's so hot with those glasses."

"Everything about that place was pleasing on the eyes. The art, the doctor..."

"Even Barbie."

"Who?"

"His receptionist. I call her Barbie. I secretly think they get it on when no one's around. You notice there isn't one personal photo anywhere? He's wearing a ring. But you'd think if he was happily married, there would be a photo or something."

"Maybe he's just protective," I muse.

"Clearly, my mind wanders when I'm there," Kat adds as she tears off a piece of bread from her roll. "I don't want to pry. But did you have any big breakthroughs?"

Taking a sip of my water, I reflect on the appointment. I'm not ready to discuss how my last day with Jake ended. Kat will only try to reassure me that it didn't matter. That Jake knew I loved him. I'm not ready to hear any of that noise. "I think so. He was very reassuring."

The server arrives at our table with our main courses, and we dig into our food. The session today must have gone better than I thought. I feel ravenous. I haven't had an appetite for much in years.

As we eat in silence, my mind wanders back to the end of our session today. "There was something Dr. Miller said that I found odd."

"What was that?"

"Well, he tried to warn me about transference. I'd always learned that term in reference to a patient-provider relationship. I think it was in a psych lecture during nurse practitioner school. You know, when a person is grieving, they have the potential to transpose their feelings onto someone.

Kat immediately starts giggling.

"What?"

"God, Mel. How bad were you drooling when you were sitting there?"

"Ha! No, not me and him. He meant Huggie and me." I shake my head and take another bite of pasta.

"What?"

I can barely make out the one-syllable word as Kat's mouth is full of chicken marsala.

Kat wipes her mouth, takes a drink from her water, and then looks me straight in the eye. "Um, how did that come up?"

"Well, I told him Huggie was moving in—"

"He's what?"

"Oh, calm down. It's not like that. I had a bit of a breakdown the other night when I forgot to pick up supplies for Ruby's class project. In true Huggie style, he came through for us. But I think I was so relieved, I asked him if he could stay with us for a little bit. So I could figure out how to manage single parenting and work. It's been more of a challenge than I expected."

I take another bite of my food, and as I bring the fork to my lips, I notice Kat blankly staring at me.

"So, just like that. He's moving in?"

"I misspoke. Huggie is only staying with us a few nights a week around his work schedule to help out."

Kat grows quiet. All I can hear is the wheels spinning in her head. "Where's he sleeping?"

"The guest room. Where do you think he's sleeping? What is wrong with you?"

She again is more quiet than usual, which worries me. "Mel?"

"Yeah?"

"I think Dr. Miller might be on to something."

"Oh, for God's sake, Kat. It's Huggie. What do you think is going to happen?"

She merely raises an eyebrow as if to mock me. Perhaps her mouth is full again. "Melanie, you haven't even once considered Huggie? I mean, I know he's our friend and all... but he's the nicest guy I know and... well, he's hot."

Now I nearly spit out my water. "What? No. He's like my brother."

"Then I condone incest."

"You've lost your marbles. If he's so hot, why didn't the two of you work out when I tried to set you up years ago when we rode rescue together?"

She gives me a look as if I should know the answer to this already. "That wasn't because I wasn't interested."

"Oh, I'm sorry, Kat."

She reaches across the table and takes a gulp of my wine, and I suddenly feel terrible. Kat had a terrible dating history when we were younger. It all worked out for the best, as she's married to the perfect man. But I'm sure my reminding her of that time, and Huggie rejecting her, isn't her favorite topic of conversation.

"Just be careful with him, Mel."

Why does that sound so cryptic? I mean, it's Huggie. Did he do something to her? He couldn't have. She just said he was the nicest guy she knew and was condoning an incestual relationship between us. None of this makes sense.

"So, is he at the house with the kids now?"

"Yes. They adore him."

Now she looks deadly serious as she puts her utensils down and clasps her hands in front of her.

"What? You're making me nervous."

"Melanie, I love you. But you need to be careful when it comes to the kids."

"Okay, what on earth?" I put my napkin down in haste. "Is there something about Huggie I need to know?"

"No, honey. It's not that. But your kids could get really attached. How is that going to work when a new relationship starts, and he has to move out?"

Slumping back in my seat, I fan myself with my napkin for dramatic effect. "Whew. Well, that's a relief. I wasn't sure what you were getting at. He's only doing this until I can get my head above water. And Huggie assures me he's never going to have a relationship with anyone."

"I meant you," she murmurs.

I gaze at her, deadpan.

"Melanie. I know it still seems too early. But eventually, you *will* fall in love again. Your heart is too big to survive on this earth without a mate. And when that day comes, it's going to be tough for them to bond with your children when they already have a father figure in the game."

All of a sudden, I'm completely dumbfounded. I could easily tell her she's wrong and that I'll never remarry. But as much as I can't imagine ever trusting myself to be a better partner to someone than I was to Jake, the idea of spending the rest of my years alone is heartbreaking. She's right. I don't want that either.

Yet I've never seriously contemplated what bringing someone new into my life would do to the kids. Ruby and Seth are intelligent and kind-hearted. I'm sure whomever I fell for, they'd grow to love too. And Huggie will always be in our lives. I'll just have to make sure anyone I consider dating knows he's a package deal.

If only he'd be okay with moving in for real. We could both 'not do relationships' together. *Wonder if he'd go for it.* I have to bite my lip to keep from laughing. I doubt he'd get much action hanging around with the kids and me all the time. He'd have to rent a hotel room or go to their place. Or join one of those sex clubs you read about in romance novels. I can't help but laugh out loud at that one.

"What's so funny?"

"I think I'm getting used to having too much time alone with my thoughts. Sometimes random ones pop into my head at the strangest times." Looking at my watch, I realize it's 9:30. "Holy cow, Kat. When does Luigi's close? I had no idea how late it was."

We both look around and realize we are the only two seated in the restaurant.

Kat flags down our server. "I'm so sorry. Are you guys closed? The time just got away from us."

"No. It's a slow night. We're open for thirty more minutes."

I smile as I realize both of our shoulders are starting to relax in unison. "Can we go ahead and get the check? I really should get home."

"Yeah, I can't believe we managed to get through the evening without Nick getting called into work. We need to do this again soon. Now that you have a live-in Manny."

Rolling my eyes, I give her a firm glare. "Please don't ever let Huggie hear you say that!"

Walking in the front door, I try to keep sound to a minimum. I can't remember the last time I came home this late, and the kids were already down. As I come around the foyer to the den, I notice they're down all right.

The television is still on a Disney movie, and popcorn and drinks are on the coffee table. Seth has fallen asleep in the reclining chair, and Ruby is out cold on the floor in her sleeping bag. Huggie wouldn't have left them like this and gone to bed. Would he?

Coming closer, I notice he's fallen asleep on the couch, and I stop dead in my tracks. I have to cover my mouth to prevent waking everyone with my laughter.

Huggie is wearing a princess crown, a purple necklace, and a little purple plastic ring on his pinky. But the clip-on dangly plastic purple earrings steal the show. Seeing the game board on the table beside him, I realize Ruby conned him into playing Pretty, Pretty Princess with her.

Trying to compose myself, I get the kids to shuffle off to bed in record time. Returning to the den, I put away the drink cups and popcorn before coming to stand by the couch. I don't want to startle him. I'd love to take a picture of this, but I'd never want to embarrass him after he's been so good to them.

To us.

Carefully lifting the plastic crown from his head, I can't resist brushing the loose golden strands of hair away from his forehead. He really is handsome, even with the earrings. I giggle.

My laughter must've startled him as his eyes fly wide, and he grabs my wrist in alarm.

"Shhh. I'm sorry," I say quietly. Pulling my wrist down so my hand can rest on his cheek. "I didn't want you to have a sore back tomorrow from sleeping on this couch all night."

I can tell he's still out of it as he quietly processes what's happening. "I must've fallen asleep."

"Any wonder? You had a big night," I add, nodding my chin toward the game board.

"Yeah. I feel like you should've warned me about that."

"What fun would there be in that?" I laugh, pulling off the earring that's closest to my hand.

Realizing what he's wearing, he sits up in a rush. "For fuck's sake."

Suddenly we're nose to nose, and my breath catches. I could drown in those deep blue eyes. How had I never noticed how mesmerizing they were? His warm breath coats my face with each exhale, and I can't help closing my eyes and absorbing the odd comfort in it. Yet when I reopen them, I get a little flushed by the intensity of those tranquil orbs staring back at me. My gaze drops to his lips—his full, kissable lips.

Holy crap. What has Kat done to me?

CHAPTER THIRTEEN

HUGGIE

What the hell is happening? Am I dreaming? If this is a test, give me the fucking F and just let me kiss her.

Her eyes are on my mouth. Do I have popcorn stuck there from earlier? Her breath smells of fruit. Did she have wine with dinner, or is it the watermelon scent I assume she showers with? There's barely any space between us. I could just lean in and—

Pop

Melanie giggles as she holds the remaining earring in her other hand. *Good lord.* "Unless you want to wear them to bed." This laugh causes her to cover her mouth. The one I was one hot second away from tasting.

"No. I'm good," I mutter.

Her giggling has changed to a look of dejection. "I'm sorry I was so late getting back. We honestly lost track of time." Hell. None of this disappointment is her fault.

"No, it's fine. They were great."

She reaches for the plastic necklace I'm still wearing and gives me a questioning look.

"Nah, it was all in fun. After your session this morning, I'm hoping that the 'lost track of time' was a good thing and not rehashing something that was bothering you."

A quizzical look crosses her face for only a few seconds before she forces a smile in its place. "No. It was good."

Why do I feel like she's hiding something? I know I'm being a little short with her. But in my defense, my dream girl woke me, and I thought she was going to lay one on me. *Okay, so hoping she was going to.*

All of a sudden, it hits me. "Mel, did the kids put themselves to bed? I feel terrible. I must've fallen asleep during the movie. You sure that you want my help?" Jeez. First night here, and I've already dropped the ball.

"I got them settled. The kids had a great night. They probably felt like they were having a sleepover with you."

"Pretty much. I'll do better next time."

"Stop. I uprooted you from your bachelor life to come here and help me out. My kids went to sleep happy and safe. That's a far cry from what I've done for them the last few years."

"Now you stop. You're a great mother. I won't listen to you beat yourself up about this anymore," I say, grabbing her arms for full effect. "You have the biggest heart of anyone I know. If this had happened to Kat, would you talk about her this way?"

It appears I may have finally gotten through to her, as she pauses for a moment to let the question sink in. "You're right. I wouldn't."

"Then start treating yourself better." I almost add *because it hurts to see you criticizing the woman I love* but think better of it.

Grabbing her hands, I want her to really hear me. "You were allowed a pass to feel guilty in the beginning, but time's up. Upward and onward. Those kids are damn lucky to have you." Checking to make sure she isn't about to show me the door, I continue. "And you haven't said it, but whatever you're thinking about Jake's death, knock that shit off."

Her eyes fly open at the statement, and I realize I may have overstepped. But I know Melanie. There are enough things she's said in the past to realize she's blaming herself for something.

"I'm not going to make you tell me what you're thinking. You have this counselor for that now. But let me make it very clear to you... you did nothing wrong."

Her eyes drop to our conjoined hands, and I know I've hit the mark. I release her, so she won't feel trapped. The heaviness of my words is enough. But she needs to hear it. "Thanks, Huggie. I'm trying. I think Dr. Miller will be a huge help. I'm not sure I would've been ready before now. The grief was suffocating then."

Pulling her into me, I kiss her head. "I know. But you're doing great. And asking for help is a big step."

She gives me a reassuring smile, and I feel better for voicing my concerns.

"Now the help needs to go to bed." I chuckle. "I'm going to take the kids to soccer tomorrow. I've missed it, and it's the only Saturday I'll have off for a while."

"Are you sure? I'm not on-call, so I'm going to take them. Nick often offers if something comes up, but I'm off. You just spent all night with them. Why not enjoy your day?"

"I will be. I love hanging out with those two." And it's true. This bachelor had the best Friday night he's had in ages. Pretty sad that I'd rather play Pretty, Pretty Princess with Ruby than look for a queen of my own. Reaching down for my shoes, I ask, "Will it bother you or the kids if I shower this late?"

Noticing the room has grown silent, I look over to Melanie and find her staring blankly at me. What is she thinking? Is she still perseverating on what I said earlier? I did change the subject quickly.

"No," she finally answers. "So long as you don't sing off-key."

Stripping out of my clothes, I adjust the temperature of the water before stepping in. It always takes me a while to get used to someone else's home. Particularly their bathroom. Like where to find things and remembering to bring my change of clothes, so I'm not prancing around with just a towel.

This is not my bachelor pad where I can let everything hang out.

Literally. And I'll have to sleep in a shirt or at least keep one nearby, as I don't need any questions about my tattoos from her or the kids.

The warm spray hits my back, and I let out an exhale. I think falling asleep on that couch must've done a number on my neck and back. Or it could've been the way I woke up.

Usually, I'd work out the stress with a little one-handed action, but I don't want to do that here. The last thing I need is one of the kids darting in here to pee, and I've got my hand wrapped around my dick to thoughts of their mother.

I towel off, grab my flannel sleep pants and a shirt, and head to 'my room' for the night.

Lying here on the guest room bed feels awkward. The uneasy feeling isn't from spending time with the kids. Despite the crazy kid jewelry, I had more fun with them than I expected. Plus, we have the calendar done for their mom. Yet now that everything is quiet, all I can think about is her.

I lift up to rest on my elbows and take inventory of my new digs. The room is a light gray, making the white trim pop, and a couple of expensive paintings are hanging on the walls to bring pops of color. It's all I need, really.

The queen-sized bed is centered along the back wall, with dark-stained nightstands to either side. The bed is draped in a light gray comforter and white sheets. Nothing overly feminine, thank goodness. There's a tall black dresser next to the door.

I only plan on staying here once in a while when I can help her out. Anything more will feel like playing house. That's more torture than I can handle. I already know this is probably a big mistake. Getting any closer to the three of them will make this hurt like hell when it's time to go.

I slump back down into the pillows and take a deep breath. There's a light, clean scent on the sheets, but thankfully, they don't smell like her. I'd never fall asleep, wanting to jack off all night.

But with her so close, I doubt I'll get any sleep anyway.

～

Stretching my arms, I rise to the smell of bacon and coffee. Am I still asleep? Taking another whiff, I can't help but grin. Now, this is what I call living. I spring from the bed to brush my teeth and wash my face before checking to see if they've left me anything. Knowing Mel, there's a spread fit for a king. And if there are any perks to this situation, enjoying her meals is one I'm allowed to partake in.

"Good morning, troops," I greet. "What's that incredible smell?" Rubbing my palms together in anticipation, I can't wipe the broad smile from my face. This guy is lucky to find a protein bar on a Saturday morning.

"Huggie," Ruby yells. "Mom made eggs and bacons."

I chuckle. This kid. "Ah, more than one, eh?"

"There's plenty," Mel adds. "Help yourself to coffee." I walk over to the coffee pot just to her left and take her in. She's still wearing her sleep shorts and a T-shirt, and her hair is piled in a sexy messy bun. I watch her scoop scrambled eggs and several pieces of bacon onto a plate and then point to a tray with toast and bagels. "What would you like?"

You. Don't even need butter or jam.

"A slice of toast would be great. Thanks."

She hands me my plate with a sweet smile, and I beam back at her. Hell, I hadn't even considered this. The meals with them will make it even more brutal when I have to return to my place alone. But I'm going to enjoy every calorie I can until it ends.

"Nice hustle, Seth," Melanie yells from the folding chair beside mine. I can't believe it's been so long since I came to one of their games.

"Hugs, can you hand me the sunscreen out of that bag over there? I can't believe how hot it is for September."

Reaching into the bag to retrieve the lotion, I start to agree but notice someone speaking to her.

"Hey, I heard you were working with Dr. Hart at St. Luke's. How's it going?"

Yeah, Mel. How's that going?

"It's been great. He's a fantastic boss. I hadn't worked in cardiology before, but the whole office has helped get me up to speed. And they've been so accommodating about working around my schedule with the kids or appointments."

"That's great," the unknown soccer mom responds. "He's not hard on the eyes either."

Here we go.

"Yeah." Melanie smiles back at her.

Well, that told me nothing. Is she interested in the hot widower?

"Barb, will you get me a bottle of water from the concession stand?" an unknown soccer dad yells in our direction. I'm assuming this is Barb since no introductions were made. I'm about to jump in when a thought dawns on me. Is Melanie embarrassed to be sitting here with me? Wondering if people will assume she's moved on from Jake to me? Maybe that's why she said I didn't need to come today.

"Oh, Barb, this is Huggie. Well, George, but everyone calls him Huggie." Melanie turns to me and simultaneously points to the goal keeper.

"He's a mess. He loves playing keeper but will goof around down there until the ball comes his way and nearly give me a heart attack. Sometimes, I have to go for water or a snack simply to have a reason to pace." She laughs.

"He's good," I tell her. "I've enjoyed watching him." Well, that's a relief. I feel stupid overanalyzing things, but I don't want to do anything that'll make Melanie uncomfortable.

"Okay, I'm off to get water. I might see you at the hospital Monday. I have to get my dad there for a stress test in the afternoon."

"Oh, I'm sorry. I'm afraid I won't be there in the afternoon. But I hope your dad does okay."

As Barb walks off, I decide to go all in. "Hey, I'm off Monday. You need me at the house? Have an appointment or something?"

"Oh, Huggie, that would be great. I was going to see if Stacy could do it because I'm certain I'll be home by five. I'm meeting Munish."

I'm getting whiplash from all the hot men she bounces between. Munish is a lawyer. He used to volunteer with us at the rescue squad when contemplating a medical career. All of the girls drooled over him. He's attractive, charismatic, and confident—the trifecta. He's been keeping Melanie updated on the case against Mark Snow, the other vehicle's driver in Jake's accident. There's been a lot of speculation over the years that Mark incited an argument at the bar and then took it to the street afterward. But no one knows for sure. Mark is certainly not talking, and there were no witnesses on the highway. It doesn't look like alcohol was a factor. Thank God.

"Run, Seth. Get in there," Melanie yells beside me, bringing me back from the past.

I watch Seth run over to where the ball is tossed around and try to get his foot in the mix. He's a natural. "Ruby, you ready for your game? You're up next."

"Yeah. I'm ready," she answers, looking very serious. She's wearing her team's green and black striped jersey with her hair tied back in a braid. "They're going down!"

I toss my head back in laughter. The wind blowing across my sweaty face feels good. Turning to my left, I catch Melanie looking at me. She's been doing that more often lately. And this time, I know there's no plastic jewelry or popcorn in my teeth.

"Thanks for being here, Hugs. It means a lot to the kids," she says.

Ah. The kids. Glad we cleared that up.

CHAPTER FOURTEEN

MELANIE

"How've you been, Mel? You look good," Munish says as he meets me at his office door.

"Thanks. I feel better than I have in a while, actually."

"Anything in particular to attribute this to?" he asks, sitting down in his office chair.

"A combination of things, really. I started seeing a counselor. I don't know why I put it off for so long, but after one visit, I already feel lighter. And work is good, so it keeps me busy. I'm trying to get myself back out there."

"And the kids. How are they doing?"

"They're both playing soccer and love it. And they're excelling in school, despite me."

"What does that mean?" he asks, a teasing expression on his face. He's always been easy to talk to.

"I got overwhelmed with managing everything and trying to get home to the sitter and forgot about Ruby's class project. If it weren't for Huggie saving the day, she probably would've failed."

He gives me a comforting smile. "First. You would've found a way. I know you. And second, I'd expect nothing less of your kids than excelling. But I'm glad Huggie was able to help. From what you've mentioned, it sounds like he's been there for you guys since the day it happened."

"Yes. I'm so grateful for all of my friends, but Huggie especially. He's practically given up his freedom to help us out."

"Mel, that guy would do anything for you."

"Yeah. He's just that kinda guy," I answer, finding his statement has caused an odd sensation in my chest. I mean, Huggie's the kind of man that would help anyone in need. I'm simply fortunate to be such good friends with him.

"So catch me up, Munish. How do things stand currently?"

"Well, not much has changed, really. I don't think the police have enough conclusive evidence to go after Mark. They've looked into everything, but there's simply no proof Mark is at fault."

"What about all of the people at The Sports Page who witnessed the argument and the way they left?"

"None of that is proof of who caused the accident. The weather was terrible, and either one of them could have been the aggressor. No witnesses have come forward from the highway that night. But we can still file a civil case and get formal statements from witnesses at the bar if you want to pursue this."

These conversations always tear me apart. I don't want Jake's death to be in vain. But Mark is in his own private hell, confined to rehab centers, unable to walk. Not sure how much different jail would be than his current situation. And there are no guarantees anything good would come of this. It may just be a long and drawn-out case costing a lot of time and money to no avail. And one thing's for sure. It's not bringing my husband back.

"Is it okay if I think about it and let you know? After all this time, I need to be sure that if we move ahead with this, it'll be worth it, win or lose."

"Absolutely. And I'll support your decision, whichever direction you choose."

～

The drive home from Munish's office is quiet. My tattered soul seems even more fragmented after these meetings. The desire for vindication doesn't match the yearning for peace. But does one ever really feel peace after something like this?

What had Huggie called it the other night? *My new normal.*

While I'd never imagined I could be a single, working mother of two children at thirty-three, I need to focus on the good things in my life. I have my health, my children's health, and a safe home. And we don't have to worry about our next meal. Jake provided for us, and the friends in our lives make us all the richer.

Pulling into the driveway, I see Huggie's car and smile. Munish was right. He would do anything for us. I couldn't ask for a better friend to get us through.

Walking into the house, I try to recall if there's anything in the kitchen to make for dinner. Maybe there's mac n' cheese or something. I should've done that on the way home, but I never think clearly after discussing Jake.

"Mommy," Ruby yells as she clomps over to me in her soccer cleats. Seth is behind her, carrying a soccer ball. "Huggie is taking us to practice."

Looking up at him apologetically, I ask, "Did you have a chance to eat anything?"

"Yeah, he made PB and Js. He said it's the dinner of champions."

"I'm so—"

"Take a warm soak in the bath. I've got this," he says as the kids bound out the front door toward his truck. "And if you tell me you're sorry one more time, I'm taking you over my knee."

A gasp comes out before I can stop it, but Huggie's already out the door. I should laugh, but I'm a little alarmed at my response.

Why do I feel so hot and tingly all of a sudden?

～

Forty minutes later, when I can't relax enough to run a hot bath, I find myself here. The one place I can speak openly and don't feel judged.

Walking through the tall grass, I gaze over the area. They must not have had time to cut it lately. There are a few random bouquets of artificial flowers lying about. Probably from the recent blustery days. I wouldn't want to place them in the wrong spot, so I decide to leave them be.

As I approach the familiar gravestone, my heart is a mixture of sadness and pride. The pride I always felt standing with my husband. That this man chose me.

Coming close, I find a stray deep scarlet rose lying beside the granite, and my heart skips a beat. It's identical to the ones he used to leave me when we were dating.

There's no note.

Really, Mel? Like there'd be a note.

I gaze about the area and notice a bouquet of similar roses a row over. I'm sure the wind carried it here. It's only a coincidence, even if, for a moment, it felt like Jake wanted me to find it.

Bending to my knees, I sit and trace his name with my fingertip. "I miss you," I tell the stone in front of me. "I don't like being here without you. But I'm trying to find my way."

Reaching into my pocket, I grab a tissue. I'm sure to place them in all of my pockets now, never knowing when tears will come. How long do you feel like this after your spouse dies? Maybe I should ask Dr. Miller what's considered normal.

"The kids are doing great in school. They're at soccer. Huggie took them. He's been a really great friend, Jake." My heart squeezes, and I stop to gather my thoughts.

"I'm trying to forgive myself for what I said to you... I know you've already forgiven me. That's just who you are." I pause again to wipe my eyes and take a fortifying breath. "I don't know how to do this. It's been years, and I still feel guilty. That I'm here, and you're not. You did so much, and I took you for granted."

Sniffling into my tissue, I know getting this out is important. So I can move forward. My therapist seems like a thoughtful, compassionate man. But I'm not ready to cry like this in front of him. I feel safe with Jake.

"I'm also feeling guilty for another reason." I feel a shudder at the heaviness of what I'm about to say. "I don't want to spend the rest of my days alone. After the way I treated you, I shouldn't deserve another chance with someone. But I'm trying to start treating myself as I would others. And I'd tell them their spouse would want them to be happy."

Wiping my tears, I continue. "I'm starting to notice all of the people around me enjoying life. I don't want to fake it anymore. Our kids are smart. They'll see right through me. I have too much time ahead of me to spend it all alone.

I take a deep breath and nervously look around, ensuring no one is watching. "There are wonderful men all around me. But I don't want to feel guilty about considering a life with someone else." Sniffle. "I don't know why I'm feeling the need to tell you this. Like I need to ask for your permission. But you're all I've ever known, Jake. It feels as if I'm cheating on you. How do I get past this? The grieving is getting better. Day by day. Yet this is where I feel stuck."

Bowing my head down, I acknowledge my disappointment. What did I think was going to happen? I was going to hear him speak to me?

I'm an intelligent woman. I know it's completely normal to have these feelings. The fear of moving forward is hard. But there's no other choice. And having Huggie around the house has shown me that I find great comfort in having male company. Not that he'd ever think about me in that way. Having him near has sparked a desire to have more in my life. That's all.

I stand, acknowledging this is a one-sided conversation, and turn for the car. I think I've avoided the need for counseling all of this time because I've been able to carve out time to sit and talk to Jake. In some small way, it's as if he's still here. If I were to meet someone, would they understand and be supportive? Or would they resent this desire I have to spend time with my deceased husband?

Climbing into the car, I let myself contemplate a relationship with someone new. How it might go. I've never really dated. When Jake and I were teens, it seemed predestined we'd be together. There weren't the butterflies I'd heard others speak of. Would I experience that with someone after all of these years? Or would I simply compare everyone to Jake?

Pulling into the drive, I notice Huggie and the kids haven't returned. Maybe I'll go have that soak after all.

HUGGIE

"Why don't you guys wash up, and I'll get the plates."

"Thanks for picking up a pizza on the way home, Huggie. My PB & J wore off a while ago," Ruby says.

"You worked up an appetite out there."

"Where's Mom?" Seth asks. "Should I go and get her for dinner?"

"Yeah. Just go quietly in case she decided to rest. She's had a long day."

I wash up and reach for the plates and grab a few cups for the kids.

Practice seems to fluctuate based on the coach. When Nick is there, he helps run drills and get the kids organized on the field, pairing them off with players of similar talent. Tonight, on the other hand, was a mess. They did a lot of running up and down the field, but I don't think any of that was legal soccer play. I chuckle, remembering the coach yelling at Ruby and her friend as one chased the other from goalpost to goalpost, carrying the soccer ball in their hands.

"She wasn't in her room," Seth says.

That's odd. Her car is parked outside. "Hey, you guys dig in. Let me go check on something."

Heading up to her bedroom, I peek inside and notice the bed looks neatly made. No nap while we were gone, I surmise. I turn to see if she could be in the laundry room when I hear water splashing.

Walking back to the doorway, I peek my head in and notice light shining from where her bathroom door is ajar. I feel guilty entering her private space, and I start to turn until I hear the familiar sound of her crying. *Fuck. What happened? She seemed good when I left.*

Standing frozen in place, I worry about how to proceed. Do I go downstairs to the kids and pretend I didn't hear anything?

My need to comfort her wins out, and I carefully walk to her bathroom door, standing to the side so she doesn't think I'm creeping on her since it's open. Tapping lightly, I pray she won't be unnerved that I've intruded. "Mel? You okay?"

The abrupt sound of water splashing has me regretting this. "Yes."

"I just wanted to let you know we're back. There's pizza downstairs if you want some."

"Okay."

I start to walk away, but she stops me.

"Hugs?"

"Yeah."

"Thank you." She again sounds as if she's sniffling.

"Mellie, are you decent?"

I hear more splashing. "Yeah, the bubbles are covering all of the important stuff."

Shit. This really isn't a good idea. I slowly push the door open, just enough so I can confirm she's okay, when I see her swollen eyes. "What happened?"

"I've had a lot on my heart lately. Stuff I'm not ready to talk to Dr. Miller about. So I went to see Jake."

That was the last thing I was expecting. "You want to talk later? After the kids are down?"

"Sure. I'd like that. I won't be long. I'm getting all pruney anyway." She giggles, wiggling her fingertips at me. Bringing her hands out of the water shifts the bubbles enough so I can clearly make out what appears to be a rosy nipple, and my mouth instantly goes dry.

Changing gears with little finesse, I say, "Okay, I'll save you a slice. See you downstairs." Spinning on my heel, I make a hasty exit and head toward the kitchen. Hopefully, Ruby and Seth's antics will distract me from replaying that sight over and over, or else I'll have

"How was practice?" Mel says from behind me. Turning to answer her, I see her in her sleep clothes, hair damp, kissing Ruby on the head.

"It was good. Me and Maria had fun doing drills."

"That wasn't a drill, Ruby. That was a game of keep away," Seth interjects, not bothering to hide his indignation.

Deciding to let Melanie have some alone time with her kids, I wish them goodnight and make my way to the shower.

Lying on my bed, I look at the bedside clock and notice it's 9:15 p.m. The kids should be down by now, but I'm still feeling a bit guilty about intruding on her in the bath, so I'm not sure I want to invade her privacy again. But hearing her cry rips my heart in two. Luckily, it doesn't happen that often anymore. But I hate that she's still suffering.

Knock, knock.

The door is open, so Melanie just looks at me as if waiting for permission to enter. "I wasn't sure if you decided to head on to bed. I'm sorry I interrupted your bath earlier," I tell her.

She comes closer and motions to the bed with her chin, and I nod. I'm so worried about where her mental state is right now that I'm not concerned about anything else.

"I'm okay."

"Do you want to talk about it?"

"It's hard to explain. In the beginning, I'd spend time with Jake often." She stops abruptly, and I know she's taking inventory of what she feels comfortable sharing.

"You don't have to tell me, Mel. I was just concerned. Things seemed to be going better, but if—"

"Things are better, Hugs. Especially because you're here." She lies back on the bed beside me, the enchanting watermelon scent of her dark hair teasing my senses.

Wrapping my arm around her, I pull her toward me. I can't not do it. It just feels necessary to have her close right now.

"I think I'm at a point where I'm considering my options. I can't say I'm moving on. I'll never be able to *move on* from Jake. But I don't want to live my life feeling I'm barely getting through each day." She pauses for a moment, and I try to give her space to share whatever is on her heart.

Lying here, I stroke her arm in encouragement and wait.

"I felt like I needed his permission. I know it's silly."

I tighten my grasp on her and give her a squeeze. "You know he'd want you to be happy. But I understand what you're saying. I talked to my mom a lot after she passed away. Asked her advice, knowing I couldn't hear her answer. Just hoping for a sign."

She bolts upright, startling me a little. "That's it! Exactly." We stare at each other briefly before she lies back down, this time placing her head on my chest.

"I miss him too," I say, stroking her hair. It's times like this I feel torn. Trapped between wanting to tell her I love her, and my immense guilt for the way I feel about my best friend's wife.

After a few moments of silence, I strain my neck to ensure she hasn't started crying again and notice she's fallen asleep. I'm comforted that she's given way to rest until I realize...

She's asleep on top of me.

On my bed.

CHAPTER FIFTEEN

HUGGIE

"Man, this sucks," Nate says, sitting in almost the same spot we were in the last time we were on the set of this movie. "I'm thinking historical movies aren't my jam."

"Nah. I think it's going to be great. Just sitting here doing nothing for hours gets to you."

"There's only so much TikTok and social media I can handle for hours at a time," Nate grumbles.

"Yeah, sucks getting paid to watch TikTok." I chuckle, slapping him on the knee.

It's been tough staying awake, sitting here all day. And not because historical movies 'aren't my jam.' I haven't caught up on my sleep since the other night in Melanie's guestroom. I doubt I got more than five hours that night. I struggled with what to do once Melanie fell asleep, grappling between leaving her there to rest or taking her to her bed. But worrying if the kids found us like that propelled me to carry her back to her room. I let her sleep for a few hours. *Okay, so I got to hold her for a few hours before I returned her to her room.*

Bzzz. Bzzz.

Swiping on my phone, I see a text from Melanie.

Melanie
8:45 p.m.
Mel: The kids miss you. Think you could talk to them for a minute or two?

8:48 p.m.
Huggie: Sure.

"Hey. I'm just stepping out of earshot of the director," I tell Nate pointing to a tree nearby.

He nods and returns his gaze to some ridiculous stunt he's watching on TikTok.

I hit the green button on the phone that enables video chat and wait for Melanie's face to fill the screen. Instead, the call opens to three smiling faces. Ruby waves and it pulls at my heart. I've worked all weekend and have to return to the fire department tomorrow since Wilson is out with the flu.

"Hi, Huggie. Anything cool happening there?" Seth jumps in before Ruby can get a word in. Her scowl is hilarious, and I fight the urge to laugh.

"No, it's been a long day of doing a whole lot of nothin'." I joke.

"Well, it beats someone getting hurt," Melanie adds.

"You're right. How did your game go yesterday, Ruby?"

"We lost. I don't know what they're feeding the kids on that team. They're huge."

I chuckle, knowing she must've overheard one of the parents making such a comment. She's like a little sponge. This thought reminds me I need to be very cognizant of what I say around these two.

"How about you, Seth? How did your team do?"

"Same. But we were short a couple of players. So all of us played the whole game without breaks. I loved it at first, but by the end, I was outta gas."

"Will you be here tomorrow?" Ruby blurts.

"No, Rubs. I'm going to be at the fire department tomorrow."

"Awe. I miss you."

I completely get it. I didn't realize just how much I missed them until this call.

"I wanted to show you our Halloween costumes," she exclaims.

Holy crap. It is almost Halloween.

"You aren't working on Halloween, are you?"

"No, Rubs. I have it off." I've been trick-or-treating with the kids almost every year since they were born. Jake rarely had the day off, and on the rare occasion he did, we went all out. "What are you and Seth dressing up like this year?"

"No, it's all of us. We're going to be Marvel characters. I'm going to dress like Spider-man, Seth is Thor, Mom is going to dress like Natasha Romanoff, the Black Widow."

My dick twitches at the thought of Melanie wearing that tight black leather one-piece.

"And you're going to be Dr. Strange."

Uh. What? "You guys want me to dress up?"

"Yes!" The two of them shout. This was never part of the deal before. My eyes connect with Melanie's, and I can't keep from smiling back at her. She's practically glowing with joy. Hell, she's never dressed up before, either. Is she trying to be all in for the kids?

"Okay. But just for you two. And I better get premium chocolate from your candy bag for this."

"No way! Get your own candy." Ruby giggles.

"All right, let Huggie get back to work," Melanie encourages.

"I thought he said he was doing a whole lotta nothin'?" Ruby says, arms crossed over her chest.

"Isn't it past your bedtime?" I prod.

"Why are y'all there so late?" Seth finally gets a word in. "I didn't know they filmed at nighttime."

"Sometimes. They plan out their scenes according to the weather and sunlight. It jumps around."

"Cool."

"You guys hit the sack. I'll see you on Tuesday."

"Bye, Huggie," the three shout into the phone, and my heart swells in my chest. I stroll back to my chair and stop when I find Nate staring.

"What?"

"You're screwed, man."

"What? Did something happen while I was gone?"

Nate shakes his head. It's as if he's in on some private joke. Sitting down, I continue to look at him, awaiting some explanation.

"How long have we been friends?" he asks.

"I don't know. Fifteen years, plus or minus."

"In all that time, have I truly pressured you about your lifestyle?"

Sitting up in my seat, I wonder where he's going with this. Has he gotten mail from The Rox? "What lifestyle?"

"Cut the crap, Huggie. You've been in love with that girl for years. Do you honestly think this is a good idea, staying with them?"

My stomach flips right before I feel all the blood drain from my face. "What—"

"And before you say one more word, do not insult me by pretending you don't know what I'm talking about."

Shit. If he knows, who else does?

Dropping my head into my hands, I try to let it sink in. "Does everyone know?"

"Nah, man. I think there are a few people who have their suspicions."

"Like who?"

"Well, Kat's the one that mentioned it to me back before Mel and Jake got married."

Fuck. Dragging my hand over my face, I realize I must be the worst actor on the planet.

"Does *she* know?"

"Mel? No. I don't think so."

Lifting my head, I look at him, stunned.

"I'm just worried this could be your tipping point. I honestly don't know how you've managed this long. Any other man would've left town if he couldn't get past it."

"Don't think I haven't considered it. But Jake was my best friend. And out of respect for him, I'll always be there for her and the kids."

The concerned expression on Nate's face is telling.

"Spill it."

Shifting in his chair, so he's facing me, he takes a visible deep breath, and my shoulders stiffen. "Let's just play Devil's advocate. I know you think you're helping, but what if you being there gets them attached? What if it keeps her from moving on, playing house with you like this?"

He has a valid point. I replay how I felt, missing the kids, during the phone call earlier. Even if I don't want to consider the thought of her moving on with someone else.

"There's no chance you could just tell her how you feel?"

"What? No. Jake was my best friend, man. I can't disrespect him by moving in on his girl now that he's no longer here. Fuck, if other people know, that makes it even worse. They'll all think I was lying in wait, just planning my attack."

"Come on, Huggie. We know you. No one's going to think that."

Well, I'll know. And the guilt will eat me alive.

"Okay, Nate. My turn. How about I play Devil's advocate? Say I did tell her. And by some stroke of luck, she hasn't permanently friend-zoned me and gives us a chance. What if it didn't work? Then not only do I lose her, but I lose the kids."

Nate grows quiet, and I assume I've made my point until he surprises me.

"I think Adam and I are going to give this a go."

"What? I thought you already were."

"No. Yes. I mean, we're going to give this marriage thing a go."

Jumping to my feet, I grab him into a bear hug. "Holy shit, Nate. That's awesome."

"Why?"

I pull back from him, astonished. "What do you mean, why? I'm excited for you. You deserve this."

"So do you, Huggie. You've loved her for more than half of your damn life. Sometimes, the things you want most require risk. Don't wait too long to take yours."

Sitting back in my chair, I try to get my head straight. This is a lot to take in during the last hour of our shift.

"Besides..."

Rotating my head in his direction, I listen with my eyes trained on the ground.

"If you keep living this way, you're going to end up one of those old rich guys who has to go to a sex club to get laid."

"Trick or treat!"

This is ridiculous. I'm wearing the most absurd getup right now. I'm not the type to dress up for adult costume parties, either now or in college. How on earth I got swindled into—

"I just love Halloween. I'm going to be sad when they outgrow this," Melanie says, looking melancholy before the night's even over. My eyes drop down from her head to her toes, and I'm glad this costume has a few layers to mask just how much I admire her. She's wearing a black skin-tight one-piece that hugs all of her curves in the very best places. Scarlett Johansson has nothing on Mel. God, this girl's a stunner and has no idea.

"Want one?"

"Um, what?" All of a sudden, I notice the wrapped lollipop in her hand. "No, that's okay." On the other hand, maybe I should. Might help how parched my mouth has gotten, looking at her in that outfit.

"Your loss." She laughs, unwrapping the crinkly paper and popping the Tootsie Roll pop in her mouth. *Shit. This isn't helping.* "How many licks do you think?"

"What?"

"You remember that commercial, right? How many licks does it take to get to the center of a Tootsie Roll pop?"

That's not what I'm picturing licking. I'd like to show you how many it would take for you to—

"Huggie, look! They were giving out whole candy bars!" Ruby squeals.

"Think they'll remember us if we come back here again?" Seth asks her.

"I think they might," Mel says, giving them a playful shove toward the next house. We barely make it to the end of the driveway before they dart toward the next one.

"Be careful," I yell.

Melanie gives me a sweet smile, and I can feel my face warm. This is so fucking dangerous. Nate was right. What the hell am I doing.?

"I wanted to ask you something."

"Sure. Anything."

"I'm trying hard to return to the things I loved. There are times I wonder if it's still too soon, but I don't want to live like a hermit anymore."

I stop walking, turning to give her my full attention.

"I'm thinking about doing Friendsgiving again this year," she says, scrunching up her face.

"That's fantastic, Mel. What's the face about?"

"I'm not sure I'm prepared for what it'll be like without him."

Hell. I hadn't considered that. Beyond his making the day go off without a hitch year in and year out, there's the emotional element. Him not being there.

"Will you help me?"

"Of course." *Jesus, George. You just got done saying how dangerous this was, and then you dig yourself in a little deeper.* "We all will."

The kids come down the driveway and have odd looks on their faces.

"What's the matter?"

Ruby flicks her treat up with a look of disgust. "They were handing out toothbrushes."

I can't stop laughing. "The nerve."

"Huggie!" Ruby yells as she runs into the house, flinging her overstuffed backpack onto the barstool by the kitchen island.

"Hey, Rubs. What have you got in that thing?"

"Stuffed animals," Seth says from the doorway.

I raise a brow at her in question.

"They're emotional stress relief dolls." The room goes quiet at her shocking answer. "What? School is hard," she adds before sticking her tongue out at Seth. "I'm so glad you're here."

"Really?" Why does this feel like a setup?

"Yes. I have to make a pie for the Fall Festival. It's for the bake sale."

I stare at her deadpan. "And where do I come in?"

"You're helping me."

"Oh, no, Rubs. I don't bake. I can barely manage the meals we've thrown together here. What makes you think I'd know how to make a pie?"

"'Cause you're good at everything," she answers matter of factly. "Just ask Mom."

Well, that has me standing a little straighter.

"I think this is Mom's fault, actually," Seth adds.

"What do you mean?"

"When Ruby mentioned it to her, she muttered something like I wish Huggie could handle this project like he does all the rest."

I look at Seth, trying to understand the context.

"I think she's just tired. Mom works hard, and these school-related projects are a lot when you're the only parent."

This kid is wise beyond his years. "Well, I'm happy to help. But I think the pie may need to come with a 'eat at your own risk' sign, so I don't know how much money it'll raise.

Several days later, the kids arrive to find the kitchen island covered in apples, flour, sugar, cinnamon, and the like. I've looked endlessly through my phone and have what appears to be the easiest recipe I can find. I plan to convince Ruby to let us use this store-bought pie dough to make the crust because there's no way I'm figuring that shit out.

"What's all this?" Seth asks as the front door closes behind him.

"Are we making the pie?" Ruby bounces up and down with a hopeful look on her face.

"We're going to try. Seth, I'm begging you. Man to man. Will you please help us out with this thing?"

He laughs. "Well, after I left you alone to play Pretty, Pretty Princess with her, I think this is the least I can do."

The kids wash up, and I give Seth the chore of peeling the apples and chopping. I tell Ruby we're in charge of the pie crust. Lord, help us.

She's apparently baked with Melanie enough times she knows how to spread out the flour and lay out the dough for the top of the pie.

"Oh, wait!" Ruby yells.

Seth and I stop dead in our tracks as she runs to grab a stool, drags it into the pantry, and starts to climb up.

"Woah, woah, woah. I thought we talked about this."

"Sorry. Can you get that green box up there?" Ruby points to what looks like some type of Tupperware container on the top shelf of the pantry. Hell, she would've broken her neck trying to reach that thing.

Pulling it down, she grabs it and returns to the kitchen table to retrieve the items.

"Found it!" Ruby runs over and holds up a cookie cutter shaped like an apple.

"I thought we were making pie, not cookies, Rubs."

"It's for the top. I saw it on a cooking show once."

Bending down, I smile at her. "That's all you. You are way past my kitchen skills on this one."

"No! You have to help." She pouts. Hell. This little imp has me almost as wrapped around her finger as her mother.

"Okay." I huff.

"Come here," she says, pulling my arm with her to the kitchen island. "Move all this stuff over there, and we can spread out the dough."

"Bossy much?" I tease her.

Ruby gives me that look. The one she no doubt inherited from Melanie. She carefully places the first layer of pie crust in the bottom of the pan and tries to mold it without tearing the pastry. I'm pretty impressed. She seems to have a grip on this. She spreads a liberal amount of flour onto the countertop and unrolls the second layer of pie dough. "Now you start making a few apples," she directs, pointing at the cookie cutter.

Okay, this can't be that hard. "Seth, you doing okay over there?" It's gotten quiet, and I was starting to get concerned until I realized he's eating as he peels. I place the metal-shaped instrument in the center of the dough, and a replica of an apple easily comes out. Moving lower, I repeat the process several more times.

"Huggie."

"Yeah?" I'm expecting her to tell me what a great job I'm doing like her mother might do until...

"If you keep spreading them out like that, we'll be here all day."

What the hell?

Ruby shoves me to the side and gathers up the remaining dough, squeezing it into a ball before spreading more flour. "You need to cut them close together to get the most apples out of it, so we don't have to keep rolling it out." She pulls out the roller and pushes back and forth over the ball of dough until she has it spread back out. Reaching for the cookie cutter, she artfully arranges the shapes so she uses up almost the entire thing.

"Show off," I tease.

"I think we can get a few more."

"How many do you think we need? The pie isn't that big."

No, but we could put butter on them and sprinkle them with cinnamon and sugar," she says like a pro.

"That's what mom does," Seth adds, mouth still full of apples.

As Ruby dumps more flour onto the marble surface, it flies everywhere. "Oops."

Looking down, I notice that I'm covered in it. So is the floor.

"Okay, but this is the last of it. The kitchen looks like it's the middle of winter."

The kids laugh.

"Laugh all you want. You're helping clean this up."

Ruby places the apples on top of the pie after Seth pours in the pie filling. I melt a little butter for the remainder of the dough that Ruby's turning into cookies. Once it's ready, I swing back around to retrieve the sheet pan with Ruby's remaining apples and hear the door fly open. In a flash, Ruby shrieks and runs toward the door while the room goes topsy-turvy.

Thud!

Instantly, I slam into the floor in a cloud of smoke. No, a cloud of flour. The pain from the impact of hitting solid travertine causes a sharp stabbing sensation. Fuck, I'm too young to break a hip.

"Huggie!" I hear Melanie shout before all three of them are

crouched around me in the small space between the kitchen island and the stove. "Where do you hurt?"

"I think I broke my ass!"

"Hugs!" Mel rolls her eyes and pinches my side as the kids cover their mouths and guffaw.

"You asked," I tell her incredulously.

"Let me see."

"My ass?" I blurt. "Ow!" Melanie pinches me again, making the kids howl with laughter.

"Do you think you broke anything?" she whispers.

"My pride." I chuckle. "Ow. Why does laughing hurt my—"

Mel quickly covers my mouth with her hand. Her beautiful dark hair cascades down, enveloping either side of my face like a tent. Looking up at her, I just want to pull her down on top of me, kids or no kids.

"Is the pie okay?" Ruby suddenly interjects.

"Rubs. I'm sorry. It was your little apple cookies. I think there was too much flour on the floor."

"Yeah. It's not 'cause you're old or anything."

What? "Old? I'll show you old." I attempt to get up off the floor and tickle her but don't make it far before realizing I might be older than I'd like to admit. It's taking an effort to get up.

Melanie and Seth come to my side, and I'm able to get myself upright between them and the use of the kitchen island.

"Thanks," I say. Looking about the kitchen, it looks like a flour tornado hit it. "Oh, Mel. I'm sorry—"

"Stop! Are you kidding? You managed to get this pie done. Cleaning up is the least of my worries."

My gaze drops to my clothes, which are completely covered in flour, sugar, and who knows what else. "I'm going to get a shower."

"Do you need help?" Melanie asks.

My eyes widen, and it's all I can do to ask if she's offering before she realizes where my mind has gone.

"Getting to the bathroom?"

"No. I'll be okay. Might just take me a day or two."

"Okay." She laughs. "I'm going to start dinner." She steps away for a moment, going to her purse to retrieve something. Walking briskly back to the kitchen, she fills a glass with water and hands me the tablets in her palm. "Ibuprofen. Please yell if you need something." She gives me a light tap on the ass as she walks away.

"Hey!"

~

Well, that took me forever. I was able to drag my sorry ass, no pun intended, up the stairs and strip everything off. It just took me a while to prevent having her bathroom also covered in flour. I think showering has taken me an hour.

Stepping over the bathtub into the steamy room, I try to see if there's a big bruise on my backside, but I can't see it from this angle. Not to mention the mirror is fogged up.

Scanning the bathroom, it hits me. I didn't bring a change of clothes. I attempt to dry off as best I can before wrapping a towel around my waist. Gazing down, I note my tattoos are on full display. So, I drape a second one around my neck until I reach my room.

I open the door, hoping to make a dash for my room when I crash into Melanie. I breathe in relief that it wasn't the kids until I realize my towel is lying on the floor. And not the one that's hanging from behind my neck.

Bending quickly, I attempt to retrieve it when a sharp, searing pain stabs through my right ass cheek. "Fuck!"

"Are you okay?"

Pushing through the pain, I quickly cover myself. I notice Melanie staring at my ass out of the corner of my eye, and I stand to my full height. Well, I guess it beats what she could've been looking at. I can't discern her expression. But she doesn't look shocked or embarrassed.

Then, what?

CHAPTER SIXTEEN

MELANIE

Beep, Beep, Beep, Beep

Gah, that alarm! I feel like I just fell asleep. There's no denying it. After seeing Huggie's granite ass on display last night, I thought of little else while trying to go to bed. What the hell is wrong with me?

This dear friend practically moves in, at my request, and I'm ogling him in a towel. Okay, so I can't help it if he wasn't looking where he was going and ran straight into me. Thank goodness we didn't both end up on the floor. Then who'd take care of the kids? Most likely, it would be him. Because after seeing his ass and those abs up close and personal, there's no doubt who is in better shape.

I should feel bad, admiring him that way. He's been such a good friend for so long. And he and Jake were closer than any two guys I'd ever known. I'm sure he doesn't think of me in that way. But all night, my mind kept wandering to places it shouldn't.

I'm probably just hormonal. Who knows if my cycle is coming? When you haven't had sex in years, there's not much point of keeping up with it. But even though my heart didn't seem ready to consider another man, my body apparently has other ideas.

Sitting up and sliding my legs over the edge of the bed, I stretch my arms to try and get myself going. I have to get the kids up and ready. We're delivering the pie to school today since the festival is tonight. I'll meet them back at the school for that, but I know Ruby wants to turn this masterpiece in. Oh, the pride on her face when that thing came out of the oven. It's a shame Huggie couldn't see it.

He'd retreated to the guest room after his shower. I think that fall really did a number on him. After I figured out he wasn't coming down for dinner, I sent Seth up to his room with a bag of frozen corn. Poor Ruby thought *that* was his supper. I told her it was probably the best thing for his bruising since it would mold around him.

As much as anything could mold itself around a piece of chiseled stone. But I refrained from sharing that part with her.

I head to the shower to prepare for my day, stopping long enough to look in the mirror. Expecting to see shame mirrored back at me, I proceed to turn on the water. I haven't so much as touched myself, much less allowed my head to think of anything but how much I miss Jake in years. So when I finally gave in to the thoughts Huggie had stirred, I didn't fight it. I decided to enjoy it and face the guilt of it in the morning.

Yet I don't feel guilty. Maybe I should. But it has been so long since I've allowed myself to let go... for my heart to race, chasing something purely physical. I've never been a screamer. Not that our sex life was really anything to scream about lately. But so long as no one heard me, and I'm not hurting anyone, I'm giving myself a pass.

"Good morning, Seth," I greet as I turn the corner into the kitchen. He's eating a bowl of cereal, as I find him most mornings. "How'd you sleep?"

"Good," he says, slurping another spoonful.

"I'm worried we might have to check on Huggie."

"He's at the fire station."

"What?"

"He had to work today."

"Oh. He told you that last night?"

"No. It's on the calendar."

I completely forgot about that thing. Well, I guess he won't be joining us tonight. "I wonder if he got to see the pie before he left."

"Oh, he saw it."

I spin on my heel at this statement. "Were you up?"

"No." He chuckles as milk dribbles down his chin. He points to the pie with the hand not being used to shovel in Cheerios.

Walking over to the pie, I see a folded piece of paper lying next to it.

Rubs,

It looks perfect. I'll think about it every time I sit down.

Love,
Huggie

Covering my mouth, I can't help but laugh. He's honestly the sweetest thing ever.

∾

"Kat, I'm so glad you were off today."

"Me too. How'd you manage a weekday off?"

"Dr. Hart is away at a conference. So he asked the office to schedule light this week. Since I primarily see his patients in follow-up, they asked if I could just be on-call today after I finished rounding in the hospital. So I started the minute I got the kids on the bus." I laugh.

"No doubt. You probably don't get any time to yourself these days."

"On the contrary. I feel like I get tons. Huggie has been so helpful. He even tried to help Ruby make a pie for the Fall Festival."

"What? How'd that go? Is the kitchen still standing?"

"Yeah, but he wasn't." I giggle.

Noticing her shocked expression, I quickly explain what happened, so her mind doesn't conjure up something ridiculous.

"I wanted to talk to you about Thanksgiving."

She gets quiet, giving me her full attention.

"I'm thinking of having Friendsgiving at the house this year. The Saturday before."

"Wow." She puts her water glass down and looks at me in total shock. "Are you sure you're ready for that?"

"I don't know, honestly. But there's part of me that thinks if I keep waiting 'til I feel like I'm ready, it'll never happen."

"What can I do?"

"Are you free to help? I'll try to plan things out like before, but I'm worried I could get a little emotional... doing it without Jake. I need someone to step in and tell me to snap out of it."

"Awe, Mel. You're allowed to feel emotional."

"I know. But I've allowed that long enough. I want to get back the things I loved." The statement instantly pulls at my heart. Some things you just can't get back.

"Well, I can't cook like you. But I can slice cheese and open a box of crackers." She laughs.

"I think between you and Ruby, we will be good. I'll probably get the sympathy card from everyone, so I doubt they'll expect much."

Kat reaches her hand across the table to squeeze mine, her eyes demonstrating her understanding of my statement. I don't want anyone's pity. But on occasion, I'll just accept it.

"You just tell us what you need, and I'll be there with bells on."

It's a week before Thanksgiving, and now that the kids are in bed, I'm sitting at the table surrounded by cookbooks and my iPad in an attempt to come up with a menu. It's only three days away. I knew it'd be tough planning and carrying out the meal prep without Jake, but I never considered the impact of being at work full-time now.

"Hey, what's this?" Huggie asks as he steps into the kitchen and reaches into the cabinet for a glass.

"I've got the day off tomorrow to prepare, so I'm trying to come up with a menu so I can make a grocery list."

"Good thinking, waiting for Ruby to go to bed first."

I laugh. "Yeah, no one wants PB & J with a side of candy corn for dinner."

Huggie picks up a piece of paper that is tucked under my iPad and grimaces. "Is this the guest list?"

"Yeah, why?"

"You invited Derek?"

"Is that a problem?"

"Didn't realize you two were that tight."

Turning to look at him, I'm a little shocked he's questioning me on this. "He lost his wife. I just wanted to offer so he had people to spend the day with if he didn't have other plans."

"Why wouldn't he spend it with his family?"

Now I'm irritated. "His daughter is an exchange student in Spain. I don't think he really has a lot of other family. I would think you'd know how that is. You've spent all of your holidays with our family."

He stands abruptly, muttering under his breath. "Didn't realize I was putting you out."

What the heck?

~

I've got the menu planned and the grocery list made. Now I just need to make sure the house is ready for all of these folks to descend on us. In the past, we've had nearly fifty people attend. I tried to keep the guest list down in case this all catches up with me, and I have a breakdown. I don't expect it to happen. I feel better than I've felt since the accident happened. Yet, if I've learned anything, it's to expect the unexpected.

"Hey, Mom. What's all that?" Seth asks with Ruby hot on his tail.

"Oh, I was just about to put this away. I'm getting organized for our Friendsgiving dinner on Saturday."

"Yay!" Ruby squeals.

"I wouldn't get too excited. I'm putting you to work." I laugh. "I'm headed to the grocery store as soon as you guys leave for school. But I could use your help cleaning up tonight and pulling out the tables and chairs from storage."

Seth gives me a weary look.

"Do you have too much homework?"

"No. I think it's going to be a lot of work. Is Huggie here? He can carry a lot more than me."

I grimace. "No. He left earlier." I'm not sure what it was I said. He couldn't possibly be upset that I invited Derek to dinner. But it isn't like him to leave and not even say goodbye.

"Is he coming back?" Seth pushes.

"I don't know. Listen. Huggie has been staying here when he can to help us out, but he still has a life. We have to respect that he can't drop everything whenever we need him for something." Their faces look glum, but I know they understand. And they're good kids.

"I'll make a deal with you. If you help me set everything up tonight, I'll go get pizza for dinner."

"Deal," they both blurt.

It's late. The kids are down for the night, the house looks good, and the tables and chairs are all set. So why do I feel so off? I know why. He hasn't come back. Why does this bother me? I shouldn't care that he's upset about Derek coming. Why wouldn't I invite him? Did Huggie think he was a charity case, being invited to spend family holidays with me, Jake, and the kids every year?

Turning out the light, I head upstairs to go to bed. It's going to be a long day tomorrow, getting ready for Saturday. Thank heavens Kat is coming over to help. We will save a few tasks for Ruby when she gets home. But I should probably try to get a good night's sleep.

After washing my face and brushing my teeth, I change into sleep clothes and climb into bed. Closing my eyes, I already know this isn't going to be easy. It's unsettling the way Huggie left. Even though I didn't do anything wrong, I don't like feeling he's cross with me.

A door shuts across the hall, and I sit up. He's back. I assumed he'd decided to stay at his house tonight. Slumping down into the pillows, I'm relieved he's back. But I hate how tense this feels. It's the opposite of everything Huggie.

"I can't take this anymore," I mumble and get up and trudge across the room. As I near his door, I lift my hand to knock when I hear him.

"Hey, I made it okay. Thanks for tonight." Pause. "No, you're right. I know you're right. It was a mistake." Pause. "I just need to get through the weekend. Then I'll fix it." Pause. "I was trying to do them a favor, and it backfired."

"Oh." My heart sinks. He's leaving us. Is there a way to say I'm sorry? I don't even understand what I did. I turn to make my way back to my room and hear the door fling open behind me. My first thought is to keep walking and shut the door. I don't think I'm up for this tonight. But I don't want to enter into the 'Friendsgiving' event with him upset with me. Maybe I simply tell him 'thank you for all you've done,' so hopefully, we can stay friends once he leaves.

Why does this hurt? I knew he'd leave eventually.

"Mel?"

I stop in my tracks. I can feel I'm getting a little emotional and don't want to look at him. Why does everything make me feel so raw these days? I know I'm still the same strong, confident woman I used to be. Why should I care if he's throwing a temper tantrum?

"Yeah?"

"You okay?"

With my back still to him, I simply reply, "Sure." Deciding to call it a night. Hopefully, whatever this is will pass. He can't be that upset if he's checking on me. And even though I know he's leaving, that was always part of the plan. Right?

Friday morning greets me like a sledgehammer. I didn't sleep well, so the rude screech of the alarm clock is more irritating than usual. I manage to get the kids out the door to the school bus by the skin of my teeth. But as I return to the house, I see Huggie's car in the driveway.

That's odd. I thought he was at the fire department today. Returning inside, I check the calendar, and sure enough, he's supposed to be working 6:00 a.m. today to 6:00 a.m. tomorrow.

My stomach lurches at the thought he's somehow overslept. I take the steps two at a time and lightly knock on the door before cracking it, so I don't scare him half to death or see something I shouldn't.

However, the room is empty. That's strange. As I turn to make my way to verify the bathroom is unoccupied, I notice something on the floor by the dresser. I might need to get my eyes checked as I thought it was a stain, but as I kneel, I realize it's a petal.

Standing up, my heart does a weird somersault. The only reason he'd have this in here... is if he gave it to someone. Curling my hand around it, I quickly leave his room.

It's clear, as close as we are, I don't know him at all. Is that what is so unsettling? Men typically don't buy flowers for women unless they're special. Does he have someone he feels that way about while he's staying here? He'd been clear that he wasn't looking for a serious relationship with anyone. Like ever. So who...

Heading to my bathroom, I splash some water on my face and look in the mirror. None of this is any of your business, Melanie. You shouldn't have gone in his room. He's your friend. It's wrong to violate his privacy in that way. Looking back at the woman in the mirror, I have to admit that this isn't the way you feel when you discover your friend could be dating someone special. I should be ecstatic.

It's simply all the secrecy. That's all. I've completely opened my world to him. Sure, he's kind enough to move in here and help me with the kids. But still. We've known each other for twenty years. Why can't he share things with me?

But then again, do I really want to hear it?

Shaking my head, I chastise myself. I don't have time for this. Focus on your to-do list, Melanie. He's leaving after the weekend. You heard him.

~

"Okay, how many people did you say were coming? There's enough food for an army here," Kat blurts.

"Hi. Come on in."

She steps over to where I'm standing and gives me a side hug. "You doing okay?"

"Yeah. If I stay busy and don't think about it."

"Awe, baby, he's here."

Twirling around, I look at her in shock. "Who?"

"Jake, of course. Who did you think I meant?"

I continue cleaning the vegetables I'm about to chop. "I don't know. I think that's why I was confused," I lie. Why, when I was so worried about getting through this without getting emotional about my dead husband, am I instead fixated on a friend who wants to return home? A friend with a girlfriend, apparently.

"What do you need me to do?"

"How about start working on the dips on that list over there? I've made them all before, so I'm sure you helped."

"Mel, my help is usually limited to taste testing."

I laugh. She's probably right. I think Ruby tends to be a bigger help in the kitchen than Kat.

"The recipe cards are right there. They're all super easy. I just need them in the fridge overnight." I need to stay busy. I have a lot to get done before tomorrow, I can't let my mood swings play havoc. I refuse to go backward.

"So you never said. Who's coming tomorrow?"

"Mostly the usual suspects." I force a laugh. Who am I kidding? I want a glass of wine and a bubble bath. How had my week turned on a dime? "Tate and Tanner Manning, Nate and Adam—"

"Oh. My. God. No way. He's bringing Adam?"

"Yes." Okay, this giggle is genuine.

"I've been dying to meet him," Kat gushes.

"I know. Me too."

"If anyone deserves a happily ever after, it's Nate." Kat dances in place as she opens the refrigerator looking for something. As she closes it, she returns to stand beside me. "And you. You deserve it too."

"Thanks. But I'm starting to wonder if it isn't greedy to want it twice."

"No. It's not. You have a lot to give some lucky guy. And I think you'll be surprised by how things turn out. When you're ready to let someone in."

"Thanks," I say, kissing her on the cheek. "Now, get to work."

~

"Oh my gosh, something smells incredible." Tate Manning bends in for a hug, and his brother gives me a wink from behind him. "Is it wrong that we were so excited you were doing this?"

"No. That makes me happy."

"Hell, we'd prefer this to our family's Thanksgiving."

"I don't know. I'd love to be a fly on the wall for that. Six brothers and their dates all in one house."

"Yeah, well, only the truly brave bring their girlfriends."

"Go help yourself to appetizers and drinks." I leave out 'because the bartender is no longer here.' *Chin up, Melanie. This is a good thing. You're moving forward. Remember?*

As I start to shut the door, I spot Huggie walking up the driveway with Nate and a guy I don't know. This must be Adam. Focusing on the excitement of meeting Nate's mystery man, I try to tamp down my concerns over Huggie's behavior over the last few days. It won't change anything anyway. Right?

"Oh my gosh," I say, running out to meet them. "Hey." I give Nate a big hug and await introductions.

"Melanie. Thanks for having us. This is Adam."

I cannot stop the huge smile crossing my face as I take in Nate's attractive boyfriend. He's a tall, well-built Black man whose complexion is a little darker than Nate's, but their radiant smiles are identical.

"Is it okay if I hug you?" I ask, knowing some folks, like Jamie, don't appreciate physical gestures.

"Oh, I'm a hugger." Adam laughs, lifting me off of the ground with his. "Thanks for making me feel at home so quickly."

"Well, we've all been waiting a long time for this." I give Nate a wink and see his smile broaden. I don't want to embarrass either one, so I'll leave it at that. "Go on in. Nate, you know how this works. Fix yourselves a drink and get your nibble on. We won't have the big meal for a while."

"I know. Sorry we came so early. Huggie will explain."

"Don't apologize. But now it's fair game if I decide to put you to work."

"Bring it. I love to cook," Adam says.

Clapping my hands and grinning, I look directly at Nate. "You may not see much of him today."

Nate grabs Adam's arm as if in a possessive gesture, chuckles, and heads for the door.

As Huggie comes closer, I remind myself to stay focused on the joy those two have already brought to my day. "Hi." The sarcastic part of me wants to say, 'thanks for showing up,' given I would've expected he would come by early to help.

"Hey. Sorry I'm so late. It was a rough night at the firehouse. Nate was going to drop me off earlier but took me back to his place to crash for a few hours since we knew it would be Grand Central Station here." His expression looks off. It's more than when he left here the other day. Is he merely apologetic, or is this something more? Is it because he's preparing to tell me he's leaving?

"I'm sorry you had a bad night. Just a lot of late calls?"

"No, only one. But it was tough." From his tone, I don't gather he wants to elaborate. After riding rescue for so many years and knowing Huggie the way I do, I suspect this was really bad.

I can't take it anymore and reach out for his arms. "You dressed up? I thought I told you we were going casual this year. T-shirts and jeans."

"It's all I had at the station. I'm not that dressed up." He's wearing a white collared dress shirt and khakis. My skin feels like a bundle of nerves. Is it the way things have been between us lately, the fact that I'm noticing him differently after all these years, or that I used him to get myself off the other night?

"Mellie, I—"

"Mel, I don't know what to do with this stuff. I told you I'm horrible in the kitchen. And Ruby told me to ask you, so I don't screw it all up." Kat laughs.

"Sorry. I have to run."

"What can I help with?" he says from behind me.

"We've had these for years. Just jump in wherever."

~

Looking about the kitchen, it looks like Martha Stewart everywhere. The appetizers have been flowing, the turkey is carved, and all sides are warming in the oven. Thank goodness Huggie took over bartending. It gives me something nice to see when I look over, versus the absence of our regular barkeep.

"Mom, someone is here asking for you," Seth says as he steals a piece of turkey off of the platter.

"Who?"

"I don't know."

"What do you mean? You know everyone here."

"Not this guy."

Wiping my hands on a kitchen towel, I walk into the main room and see Derek. He looks lost—poor thing. I make my way over, determined to have him feeling like one of the gang before he leaves today. "Oh, I'm so glad you came." I lean in for a hug and notice his expression soften.

"Thanks for having me. Holy cow, this is quite the setup."

I giggle. "Yeah, it seems to get bigger every year." I bite my cheek at the statement, knowing it *had* gotten bigger every year. Now it feels a little hollow.

"These are for you," he says. Derek hands me a beautiful collection of fall flowers with a large sunflower at the center. I notice a familiar gold ribbon with Cygnature Blooms printed on it. It's my favorite flower shop in town. The arrangement is tucked in a ceramic pumpkin, and his genuine thoughtfulness almost makes me tear up. I instantly know this is a kind gesture from a man I work with, nothing romantic. No flowers to a grieving woman. Simply considerate.

"These are beautiful. Thank you. I know just where to put them." I turn to find Kat staring at me wide-eyed from the kitchen doorway. "Kat, come here," I shout.

As she strolls over, she gives Derek a hug. "Hey, it's so nice to see you outside of the hospital. I'm so glad you're here."

"I'm honored to have been invited."

"Kat, do you mind introducing him to a few folks and showing him where we have the drinks?" I spin on my heel to point toward our makeshift bar when my eyes connect to a very grumpy-looking Huggie.

What is with him and Derek? Does he know him outside of the hospital? *Maybe it's not a good idea that Huggie makes his drink.*

"Mom, do the green beans need to go in the oven? They're cold."

"Oh, Ruby. What would I do without you?"

"Well, this would have turned into a pizza party with your other helper. Kat can't cook."

I giggle. She's probably right. "The oven is full, so I'll sauté the beans. Can you start asking if anyone wants water with dinner?"

"Sure. I can't wait to hand out the special cups," Ruby squeals. I was looking for clear plastic drinkware to limit the cleanup, yet I gave in to plastic Marvel cups.

As I turn back to the stove, I stir the beans and mentally go down my to-do list to ensure I haven't forgotten something. But my mind goes blank as I feel warmth across my back. A masculine arm reaches over my right shoulder to the glass cabinet as electricity shoots through my left hip at the touch of a warm hand. My nerves are quivering beneath my skin. Although I'm almost certain I know who's behind me, I'm dying to turn and verify the source until their warm breath dances across the back of my neck. There's no way I'm moving a muscle if it'll break this spell. I haven't felt anything so electrifying in... well, I can't ever remember anything this tantalizing.

"Hmmm. I'm starving." Huggie's recognizable voice hits my ear and the delicious words are not helping my situation. The kitchen could catch fire, but there's no way I'm moving now. He places his glass down on the counter beside me, and his other hand drops to my right hip. I'm frozen in place, completely distracted by the hunger in my lower belly. And this craving is not for anything I've prepared for today's meal. As I nervously turn to look at him, I see he's already walking away.

What was that? I almost miss the fact the beans are sizzling a little louder than they should, so I start stirring and remove them from the heat to prevent them from burning. Did I misinterpret that? Am I suddenly so ready for physical contact I'm imagining things?

"Hey, Mel. Is it time? The troops are getting anxious for the main course, and I think all of the appetizers are almost gone."

Nick comes up behind Kat and gives her a squeeze. "What can I help with?"

"Well, how about we start putting everything out on that long buffet table so people can help themselves? Can you grab that platter of turkey?" I've barely finished my question when my eyes focus more clearly on what the two of them are wearing. Nick is wearing a khaki green shirt that says *She's my sweet potato.* Kat's shirt is orange and says *I Yam.* "Oh, my gosh, you two." I cover my mouth to contain my grin. They're so sweet. "I'm going to get diabetes looking at you."

Kat giggles as Nick buries his face in her neck. Gah... I need to let go of thinking I'll ever have that again. Well, honestly... I've never had that. I was blessed to have Jake, but he was never one for gushy romantic gestures or public displays of affection. But I wouldn't change a thing.

"Hey, Melanie. What can I do to help?" Derek asks. I try to focus on a task to give him and ignore Kat's goofy gestures behind him. I all but lose it when Nick turns to grab the platter, and she mimics grabbing Derek's ass.

"Could you help Nick and Kat take things to the buffet table? We usually all serve ourselves. I've got to get these beans on a serving platter."

"This is amazing. Are you sure you're in the right line of work?" he teases.

"Yeah, I think she'd be better running her own catering business or a restaurant," Huggie declares. And that scowl is back. *Wait 'til he sees Derek is sitting next to me.*

~

Everyone is seated with plates piled high. Huggie is further down the table from us, sitting between the kids. There was no way they were allowing anyone else there. I ignore the occasional stern glances from his direction and focus on the day. This is made easier by having Nick, Kat, Nate, and Adam seated closest to me.

I take a deep breath and slowly stand from my chair once the last guest has taken their seat. *You've got this, Melanie.* "I wanted to thank you all for coming. It means the world to the kids and me to have you here." I swallow down my nerves and take a look at the empty plate, highball glass, and candle sitting on a library table by the bar area. "He may be gone but not forgotten. Thank you for loving us until we could get to the place where we are now." Forcing myself to look anywhere but the faces of my guests, I lower myself to my chair and pray the tears will stay put for now.

"To Jake," Huggie says proudly. I look down the table to see him and my kids with their glasses raised, and there's no use trying to hide my emotions.

Nate places a hand on my shoulder and leans in. "He'd be so proud of you."

Dabbing my eyes, I just smile my thanks. As much as I would've liked to have gotten through the day without crying, it's simply not realistic. But these almost feel like happy tears. He is here, surrounded by the people who love him.

I notice Huggie whispering something to Ruby with a grin just before she blurts, "Let's eat!"

The low hum of constant chatter about the room soothes my soul. This is a good day—a huge milestone for my family and me. To truly celebrate *with* Jake instead of feeling every occasion is marked by his absence.

"Hey, you holding up okay?" I overhear Adam asking Nate. His voice is hushed, and I feel guilty having heard their private conversation.

"Yeah. I'm more worried about Huggie."

Wait. What?

Perhaps I'm getting bolder in my old age or tired of having my emotions tested twenty-four-seven, but I charge in where I wasn't invited. "Nate, did something happen?"

He looks about to make sure only the people sitting immediately around us can hear. "We got a late call. It was a lady on hospice. She'd passed away, and the daughter was having such a hard time dealing with it that she called 911 instead of the hospice nurse. Huggie tried to comfort her until the nurse arrived."

My potatoes suddenly feel as if they're lodged in my throat.

"I think it took him back to when he lost his mom. He didn't sleep at all after we got back." Nate places his fork in his roasted vegetables and starts to lift it to his mouth before deciding against it. "He's had a rough week."

Now I don't want to eat. Is this related to the conversation I heard? Had the new girl he'd been seeing given him an ultimatum? My mind is ping-ponging from one possible scenario to another.

"Is he okay?" I ask warily.

In an instant, I notice Nate, Adam, Kat, and Nick all staring at me. God, was I completely insensitive asking in front of everyone? But the curiosity would've eaten me alive.

"He's Huggie. How would anyone know? He keeps everything important under wraps," Nate says.

"That guy. His heart's too big," Adam adds.

Now I'm really a mess.

"He was having car trouble. And instead of taking it to his regular shop, he let one of the guys from station eight take a look at it. The guy just started a side business, and you know Huggie. He wanted to support his brotherhood. But we'd heard the guy was kind of a mess. Like several of the guys were shocked he'd managed to get a business up and running because he's so unreliable. Long story short, the truck is worse, not better. He's going to try to break it to the guy that he needs to get his act together because Huggie's not going to lie to anyone who asks about taking their car there."

Sitting up taller in my seat, it hits me. Is that the conversation he was having with someone on the phone? Is he breaking up with them and not me?

Breaking up? Mel, cracking up is more like it. He's only staying here to help you out. What kind of relationship are you creating in your head?

This still doesn't explain the flower petal, but I'm only going to be so nosey here. Clearly, my emotions are too on edge for anything else. I look down the table toward Huggie and the kids. All three of them have a dollop of mashed potato on their nose. My heart starts to swell.

Do they make them any better than this guy?

～

"Wow. What a mess," Kat says. "You know I'll help, but any chance I could trade you?"

"Trade me what?" I ask, confused.

"If we get the food put away, could I take your kids home to give you some quiet time and leave Nick here to clean up the rest?"

"Hey! What?" Nick belts out.

I can't help but laugh out loud.

"It's okay, Nick. I've got it. I didn't help with anything before the party. The least I can do is help clean this up and put everything away," Huggie says.

"You sure?" Nick asks.

"Yeah. It'll keep my mind busy."

My heart aches at the statement. He has had a rough week. He rarely lets anyone know when he's struggling.

We all set to work bringing the leftovers into the kitchen, and I grab storage containers. "Anyone want anything for the road?"

"I'll look through the fridge when I drop the kids off tomorrow. My stomach is too full to even think about food right now." Kat rubs her flat belly and groans.

"Well, help yourself."

The items get packed away faster than I anticipated, and Nick and Kat head off with Seth and Ruby after they prepare overnight bags. I walk back into the house feeling proud of all I accomplished today until I see the shape of my dining room and den. *Ugh. I need a drink.*

The thought has barely left me before a margarita is placed in my hands. "You're a mind reader," I tell Huggie.

"You haven't had a drink all day. You need to relax. You've earned it."

"Thanks. But there's no time for relaxing. Look at this place."

"You've got the food taken care of, put your feet up."

"Huggie, if I do that, I'll probably fall asleep. I'm going to enjoy this and attack the kitchen," I say, knowing it's the truth. I haven't recovered from the poor night's sleep and all the questions hovering about him. I could nap straight through until Monday, but I don't get many opportunities without the kids to get things done.

Returning to the kitchen, I find a small, uncluttered surface to place my drink and start rinsing dishes to place in the dishwasher. My energy is fed by the replaying of the feel of him against my back when I was in here earlier. *Don't let your mind go there, Melanie.*

All of a sudden, his arms slide under mine as he places a few stray glasses into the sink. The electric current is back. But this time, it doesn't start at my back and fan out as before. It's much lower.

"You're amazing, Mel. Today was perfect." His voice reverberates against the shell of my ear. It's only fueling this fire.

"Thanks. I'm pretty proud of myself. This feels like a turning point for me." The sensation of his mouth placing a chaste kiss on my ear is flaming whatever this is between us. My legs are shaking, and I have to hold on to the side of the sink to steady myself.

Turning around, I look at him. He looks alarmed.

What the hell is happening?

CHAPTER SEVENTEEN

HUGGIE

Looking into Melanie's eyes, I realize I better step away or I'm going to lose control after all of these years. I'm not sure what's happening right now, but if I don't put some space between us, I might snap and take her right next to the leftover macaroni and cheese.

There's been an odd shift in the energy here since everyone departed. I assume it's simply the day catching up with us. I always feel that pull when I'm near her, but this is somehow different. The little looks she's sending. The subtle way she moves her hair over her shoulder as if she knows I'm watching. I read too much into her actions, always hoping there's more to it. But her coy glances and biting of her lower lip tonight seem different.

She's been working on the dishes in the kitchen for over an hour. I feel like I've barely put a dent in the cleanup of the main rooms. Bringing several more highball glasses into the kitchen, I again come up behind her and slide my arms to either side to place them in the soapy water. I know this is dangerous. But I can't stop myself.

God, she smells good. The scent of her shampoo combined with the lingering aroma of dessert in the air is delicious. I again realize this is like putting a kid in a candy store and quickly move away.

"You want another glass?" I ask, pointing to her empty goblet.

"Yeah, that would be nice." Her voice is low. It doesn't appear sad. I'm trying to prepare myself that the enormity of the day could hit her at any moment.

"Another margarita?"

"No. Maybe I'll switch to a glass of wine."

Reaching into the fridge, I find her favorite Pinot Grigio. I slide the glass beside where she's washing and place another kiss on her temple. Not sure why I keep doing this, really. I just feel the need to comfort her today.

Back and forth from the den to the kitchen, I bring assorted stemware and dishes to be cleaned. It'll take several runs of the dishwasher and hand washing to get this mess under control. With each trip, we do this silent dance. Both of us giggling as we make room for the other. Whenever our eyes meet, I sense a crackle in the air. Is this only me, as usual? Or does she somehow feel it, too?

Managing your thoughts when you've felt this way for as long as I have is difficult. I question everything. And I have to remain on guard to prevent anyone from seeing what I'm feeling. Reflecting on my discussion with Nate, I realize I've done a poor job of that.

But interpreting her emotions is even more challenging. She still struggles with loss. As is normal, I'm sure. Yet, it can be tough to know if I need to push her to open up, so she doesn't struggle in silence or leave things be.

I look at the clock and realize it's after ten. It's been a long day for me but an even longer one for her. "Hey, why don't you go relax? Take your glass and have a soak. I'll work on this. You've been going at this for days. I only stepped up to help tonight."

Spinning on her heel, she gives me a tired smile. "I think I might actually take you up on that. I won't be long, or I'm afraid I'll fall asleep in there." She laughs.

"Well, don't do that." I chuckle. Why do I suddenly feel so nervous talking to her? What is going on?

She gives me a little wave and walks to the stairs. Her expression is unreadable. Is she simply tired? Emotional? Whatever it is, I need to put on my headphones and think about something else while she's up there. Because if I walk in on her in the tub this time, I'm likely to join her.

~

About forty-five minutes later, I hear Melanie coming down the steps and turn to assess how she's doing when I freeze.

She's gliding down the stairs in a rose-colored silk nightgown with spaghetti straps. Her hair is down around her shoulders, the ends a little damp. She looks like a dream. Her nipples are poking through the material like beacons. I have to force a swallow, hoping it'll bring some moisture to my parched mouth.

She slowly walks my direction, and I'm spellbound. Standing before me, she places her hands on my chest. The immediate sizzle that follows has my adrenalin pumping. "You're not leaving, are you?"

"What do you mean? Tonight?" My voice squeaks.

What is happening right now?

"No. I overheard you on the phone the other night. I didn't mean to eavesdrop. You were upset and had left, and I was so relieved you came back. I went to talk to you and heard you telling someone you made a mistake and were fixing it after the weekend was over. Earlier, Nate said you'd had car trouble." She pauses. "But I thought you meant us."

Her beautiful violet eyes look sorrowfully at me, and it's taking every ounce of restraint not to kiss her. "No, Mel. I meant the car. I'd talk to you before I left. I'm sorry I got upset."

"Why does Derek have that effect on you? Do you know him?"

"No. I... I don't like thinking about how close you two are getting." Why on earth have I told her this?

"We only work together. I didn't want him to be alone today if he could be among friends. But it's nothing more than a working relationship. It's not like with us."

Us? What does that mean?

An hour ago, I would've brushed that off. But now she's standing in front of me with this gown on and—

"Huggie?"

"Yeah?"

And with that, she pulls my head down to hers and places her soft, beautiful lips over mine. It's nervous and sweet, and holy hell. Am I awake right now? Is this really happening? I don't know where this kiss is coming from, but I'm all in. She starts to pull away much too soon. I'll worry about why she did this later. There's no way it's ending this fast, not after all of these years.

Cupping her cheeks, I hold her face to mine. My mouth parts so my tongue can slide in, tasting her. It's a heady mix of sweet, minty warmth. The sensation of her hands on my chest draws my attention away long enough to realize I'm gripping her hair like a madman. Loosening my hold, I nibble on her lower lip before pulling back, praying she isn't a mirage.

"Huggie," she moans. I've never heard a more beautiful sound. "I..." She looks around as if lost. All of a sudden, she grips my shirt, and a look of seriousness takes over. "Please help me?"

"Mel, you don't have to kiss me to help you clean up." I force a chuckle. I'm more than a little anxious about what's happening here.

"No. I..." She appears to be struggling. Has she had too much to drink? I don't want to take advantage if this emotional day has caught up with her, and she's searching for an escape.

"What's happening? Talk to me," I coax, stroking her hair.

"I want you to... I..."

"Mel, have you been drinking more today than I thought?"

"No."

"You're not upset about anything?"

"No."

"Then talk to me. What—"

"I want you to have sex with me," she blurts.

My entire body stills, startled by her statement. Stepping away from her for a moment, I take a deep breath. I don't understand what's happening. *Fuck. I'd give anything if this was real.*

"Hugs?"

I turn back to her and find her eyes appear to be pleading with me. "Please?"

"Mel, I don't understand." I'm not sure how to best get to the bottom of this without upsetting her... *or me* if I talk her out of it.

Slowly, she comes closer, her trembling hands holding onto my arms as if to steady herself. "I want to feel alive again."

Her words hit me like a sledgehammer. *Shit. This is real.* But how can I do this?

"I've never felt this way with anyone but..." Her head drops down, and I know immediately I can't let her go there.

Lifting her chin with my thumb, I make direct eye contact. "What are you saying, Melanie? I need you to spell this out for me because I don't want to do anything that'll come back to harm either of us. You mean too much to me."

"It's been so long, Huggie. I want to be surrounded by something powerful, electric... anything but sadness. Please?"

Jesus. What the fuck do I do now? As if being so close to her and the kids isn't dangerous enough. "Mel, what if this goes sideways? I can't lose you."

"It won't. It's just physical. Nothing more."

Her answer is like a punch to the gut. I'm not sure why I'm surprised. I know she doesn't have feelings for me. Only him. And I couldn't act on them even if she did. Just considering this request feels like I'm stabbing my friend in the back. But she's pleading for help. And I don't think there's a man alive that could withstand this temptation. Let alone me.

"Mel, I—"

"I understand. I can't believe after you've been kind enough to move in here, I'd put you in this position."

I grab her by the back of the neck, pull her into me, and cover her mouth with mine. This kiss is hard, unrelenting. I pour every second of longing into it. *Into her.* There's no room for reason here. I've waited too damn long for this moment. I can't possibly walk away from her when she's asking for this.

Backing her up against the kitchen island, I push my pelvis into her. The moment she realizes I'm hard, her breath catches around my tongue, and I start to become unglued.

"Do you want me to fuck you, Mellie?"

"Yes." She pants.

"I need you to be real sure about this. Because I don't want any doubts when I'm making you come for me."

"Oh, my god. I... Please?" she begs. *I've got to be fucking dreaming now.*

Squeezing her ass tightly in my hands, I scoop her up until her legs wrap around me and try to make it up the steps without stumbling. I've never wanted anything so damn much in my life. I'm practically shaking.

Listing to the right and left, I eagerly carry her down the hallway. I'm just trying to remain upright. I'm lost in her, licking her collarbone and biting the side of her neck. It's impossible to stop now that she's given me the green light. But I realize I need to take a moment to get my thoughts together once we're in there. I need some ground rules. Everything about this is fraught with danger. There has to be a way to minimize the damage.

Placing her down on the end of the bed, I straighten and look down at her. Even with the limited light from the hallway, I can see her face is flushed. "Are you nervous?"

"Yes. I've only ever..."

Hell. How had I not once considered this? Not only had she gone years without sex, but it had only been with one man.

Don't think about him, you asshole. You can pretend you're helping Mel with this request, but you know the truth. You're simply going to have to ask for forgiveness and not permission from him. Because we both know you're too weak to walk away.

Ground rules. I need ground rules.

These guidelines will keep me focused on the fact this is for *her.*

One: Distract yourself whenever you link the physical with your feelings. Picture yourself wearing those stupid plastic earrings. Whatever it takes.

Two: Make this about her. Only her. Please her.

Three: Keep this between the two of you. Don't let anyone think we're in a relationship. *Or you might start believing it too.*

Four: Do not come inside her. Or on her. You'll never get that out of your head. *Why make your hand jealous after all these years?*

And lastly, Five: This is the only time. One night.

"I'll try to be careful. But I need you to talk to me. If you want to stop or if you're too in your head. Nothing can come between us, Mel."

"Yes. You're right." She sounds more eager than anxious.

I close my eyes, take a cleansing breath, and force myself to stick to the rules. But as I glance down at her, I give myself permission to enjoy every. Fucking. Moment.

"Lie back for me, Mellie."

Her eyes widen in confusion before she falls back onto the bed, her legs still draped over the edge. Dropping to one knee, I slide my hands from her ankles to her knees and stop to reassess her before continuing. It feels as though she's shaking, *but that could be me.* As my hands glide up her soft skin toward her hips, I dart soft kisses along the inside of her thighs. This proves difficult because they're clamped shut.

I know she's nervous. But she's made it clear what she wants, so I reach up for her panties and am reassured when she lifts her hips for me. Continuing to kiss her soft skin, I discard her lacy panties on the floor by my feet and move my hands to caress her thighs. Now I know my hands are trembling.

My ears are trained on the sound of her heavy exhales, hoping any change will be a clue to check in on her. As I lift her gown up over her hips, her breathing quickens. *Or is that mine?* She's just as I dreamt she'd be. Soft, swollen, pink, and bare. I've eaten enough today to feed an army, but I could feast on this meal for hours.

Stroking her sweet center with my fingers, she starts to wriggle. I'm so turned on right now I'm afraid my dick is going to tear through my pants. Unable to hold back any longer, I slide the flat of my tongue through her wet folds and quickly place a hand on her pelvis to keep her still as she cries out. I've barely licked her once, and I already feel ten feet tall.

I tease her clit with the tip of my tongue and try not to moan. This is about her, remember. Out of the corner of my eye, I see her fists balled around the bed linens. It's as if this is the flag signaling the beginning of this race to the finish line. My pace picks up, licking and sucking until I slide one finger inside her. She's so tight. I have to palm myself, inwardly groaning as I imagine her wrapped around my needy cock.

Once I've subdued the ache a bit, I clamp my hands around her creamy thighs and spread her wide as I use my tongue to make small circles around her swollen clit before diving into her sweet pussy. The years of fantasies come to life as I practically hear Harry Styles singing "Watermelon Sugar" around me like it's the long-awaited scene from a movie.

"Oh, god," she pleads, spurring me on. I place two fingers inside her and glide them in and out as I suck on her bundle of nerves. She's close. I'm certain of it. Her thighs are shaking, but she continues to clamp her legs down against me, and I get the feeling she's steeling herself.

"Mellie, you're right there. Why are you holding back?"

The room grows quiet. Has the enormity of what we're doing hit her? I stop and climb onto the bed so I'm straddling her. "What's going on, baby?"

"I don't want it to end too soon," she says, looking embarrassed.

"Mellie, you have me all night. I'll make you come until you can't walk. Don't fight it."

Her eyes appear to roll back in her head before her lids close, and I take this as my signal to continue.

Dropping back down, I bury my face in her delectable pussy and tongue fuck her like I've imagined doing for decades. One night, right. I'm going to smell her sweet scent for weeks, replaying this fantastic fucking moment. Rubbing her clit with my fingers as I eat her, my theme music begins to play again as her body starts to shake beneath me.

"Oh, god," she yells, burying her hands in my hair.

Withdrawing my tongue, I slide two fingers inside her and curl them forward as I give her clit another firm suck. Her moans are unintelligible now. I feel like the king of the world.

Her breathing slows, and I place tender kisses on her lower belly before wiping my mouth. I climb onto the bed beside her, waiting for her to look at me. As her lids slowly open, her eyes are glassy and unfocused. But the bright smile on her face nearly does me in. Jesus. I'm never forgetting this night. Ever.

"You liked that?"

She doesn't answer, but she doesn't have to. Reaching across her, I lower one strap of her gown before moving to do the same with the other. It takes great effort to contain my reaction. I've waited so long. I want to bury my face in her chest, but I'm afraid I'll cry like a baby. She has the most beautiful tits I've ever seen. More than a handful, creamy, soft, and with tight rosy nipples, just as I'd envisioned after seeing her in the bath.

Dipping my head, I tease one with my tongue before sucking, repeating the action with the other. I want to spend hours suckling from them, but I need to make her come again.

As I reach back down to stroke her pussy, she reaches for me.

"No."

"What? But I want to touch you."

"This is about you tonight," I tell her.

"But I want it."

It. Not me.

"Please?"

"You're not ready yet."

Propping herself up on her elbows, she begins to question me until she stops short. "Why are you still dressed?"

Trying to think quickly on my feet, I say, "I told you. Tonight's about you." Clearly, I haven't thought this through. Trained for disappointment by The Rox, it's more likely force of habit I've left them on. That and worries about having to shut down any conversation about my tattoos.

Reaching for me again, I move her hand away. "You're not ready yet." I get up from the bed and decide to lock the door. We were in a rush earlier and shouldn't take any chances. Plus, this will darken the room more, so I'm less likely to get an inquisition about my ink. "We can't be too careful."

Climbing back on the bed, I push her down with the palm of my hand before removing my shirt and dropping down for seconds. This time, I alternate teasing her swollen wet folds with reaching up to massage her tits.

"Please? I swear I'm ready," she pleads.

I don't think I can hold out much longer. Her soft skin, her scent, and her taste have caused my balls to ache. Removing my pants, I place them on the chair after retrieving my wallet. I have one condom. One. Now to pray I last more than mere minutes once I'm inside her.

"Can I touch you?" she asks nervously.

"No."

"But—"

"Mel." What do I tell her? That the minute her hand touches my cock, it's game over? I haven't waited my whole adult life for this moment, just to come in her hand. Opening the condom, I sheath myself. "Do you want me to fuck you? Or stick to third base?" I know I sound harsh, but I'm in self-preservation mode here.

"I want you to fuck me."

Shit. Hearing those words will make me empty into this condom before I'm inside her anyway.

I return to the bed and resume stroking her. My dick is long and thick. The very last thing I want is to hurt her. I bend down to kiss her. The reality this is actually happening is doing a number on my head. She accepts my tongue as it slides between her lips, and I fight for control as she whimpers against my mouth.

As I pull back, I withdraw my fingers from her sweet pussy and enjoy the taste of her arousal on my tongue. Her eyes widen at the act, and she squirms beside me. Taking her hand, I wrap it around my cock before settling between her thighs.

Melanie gasps, and I quickly change positions. "I told you. You weren't ready." As I climb over her, my limbs start to tremble. This moment is so surreal. I can't believe this is finally happening. I'll need to look away, so I don't either beat her to the finish line or succumb to my emotions.

Dipping my head down, I give her a slow chaste kiss. "Are you sure about this?" Please, Lord, don't say no.

"Yes."

She barely gets the whole three-letter word out of her mouth before I nudge the tip of my cock into her entrance. Her hot, wet pussy feels even better than I imagined, and I have to bite my lip to prevent groaning.

Her whimpers sound a little more strained now.

"Mellie, am I hurting you?"

"No. It just burns a little."

I try to rotate my hips back and forth, encouraging her body to relax enough to take me all the way. Fuck, the sensation of her wrapped around me is almost too much.

Suddenly, I sense her walls relax as I inch forward and can push further in. I have to bury my face in her neck. This moment is so intense. It's more than physical. If this is all I have with her, I'll cherish every second.

I'm brought back to reality when I feel her wrap her thighs around me and grind her pelvis against mine. Fuck. This isn't going to last long.

"Baby? You, okay?"

"Yes. Better than okay." Her nails dig into my ass, and I know neither of us will make it much longer.

"Tell me if I hurt you."

"Okay."

With that, I adjust the angle of my hips and begin to rock in and out of her. She's so wet. The sounds of our connection pair with the drag of my heavy cock inside her, and something detonates. My pace picks up, almost on its own. As if I'm merely along for the ride. I can sense the crescendo building, and it's all I can do to hold on until she comes for me.

"Oh, please," she whimpers, her nails clawing into my skin.

That's it. The chains are off, and I pound into her. All the years of waiting are pushing me closer and closer to the finish line. Making the mistake of looking at her, I turn away, trying to think of anything else. "I can't look at you." She needs to get there quickly. I'll never live this down if I finish before she does.

My heart is thudding in my chest, the sounds of our arousal the only soundtrack to this long-awaited moment. Oh, please let me hang on.

"Fuck."

CHAPTER EIGHTEEN

MELANIE

"I can't look at you."

I barely make out the words as he continues to hammer into me, striking my clit with each delicious thrust. The climax building within me is almost scary. I've never felt anything like this.

"Fuck!"

His words should alarm me. He sounds as if he's pained, doing this for me. But it's so good I wouldn't ask him to stop, even if I could right now. I can't form words. The only thing coming out is unrecognizable, even to me. I had no idea my body could feel this way.

The force of his thrusts gets harder, faster. He turns his head, his mouth resting on the shell of my ear as he repeatedly rams into me. "That's it. I need you to give it to me." His pounding is sending me over the edge. I hope I can withstand this orgasm without fainting. "Fucking come all over my fat cock."

His words are like striking a match. My body starts to quake, the intensity overpowering. I dig my nails further into his rock-hard ass and hold on as the orgasm rips through me. The sounds of screaming bounce against the four walls of this room, and it's not until my breathing begins to slow that I realize that echo is me.

"Oh, thank fuck."

Barely able to catch my breath, I open my eyes to see Huggie withdrawing from me. He raises up and grabs ahold of his heavy cock before growling as he empties into the condom.

My head drops back, and I try to will my heart rate to slow down. I don't think I knew what I was in for when I started this. I'd yearned to feel the adrenaline coursing through my body. I wanted the rush. Boy, did I get it!

As Huggie grabs his pants and steps out of the room—I assume to go to the bathroom—I let what just happened reel back through my head again. It's not a matter of comparison. My sex life with Jake was different for a number of reasons. We were childhood sweethearts. We didn't really know anything other than what we had. It was an expression of what we felt for the other.

But this... I had no idea sex could be like this. I've seen scenes like this play out in the movies, but I never imagined anything this explosive occurred in real life.

But one thing was odd. We used a condom, but he still pulled out. And he seemed pained at times. He even said he couldn't look at me. Was this too much to ask of him? *Of course, it was, Melanie.* The man has literally been there for me anytime I've asked something of him. This crossed the line.

Yet I don't have it in me to say I regret it.

Attempting to change my position, I'm barely able to move. I manage to roll onto my side and tuck my hands under my cheek. I'd question needing to go to the gym, but the last twenty-four to forty-eight hours have been exhausting. Both physically and emotionally. What time is it anyway? I yawn.

Trying to roll over in my sleep, I wake when I realize there's a warm, heavy arm draped over my midsection. *What the?* Enough light filters through the heavy drapes that I can make out the distinct image of a vine of thorns and barbed wire on the arm's surface, and I'm immediately transported to last night. I must've fallen asleep waiting for Huggie to return to the room.

As if the tattoo and the delicious memory of the night before weren't confirmation enough, a large protrusion nudges my back. I couldn't see much last night, but who knew this boy next door had quite the package?

Everything about Huggie is unexpected. He's the kindest, sweetest friend I've ever known. I mean, I trust him with my kids. But instead of what I predicted would be an awkward night, two friends fumbling under the sheets, it was anything but.

He took control and let me simply feel. There was no uneasiness. Granted, there were moments I was concerned he was forcing himself to do this for me. But there wasn't an issue with the plumbing. And holy cow, his dirty talk alone would've given me the release I was craving.

I have a long day ahead of me. We didn't clean that much last night, and the kids will be back this afternoon. I should try to get a few more hours of sleep. Yet, as I close my eyes, the pad of Huggie's thumb continues to dust over my nipple until it's furled into a tight peak. My belly starts to quiver with the familiar feeling of lust from last night as he thrums my nipple and nudges his hardness into my backside. He's got to be awake. Right?

I push my hips back, forcing my ass into his massive erection, and try not to giggle. If he's able to sleep like that, I don't want to wake him. At least I shouldn't want to wake him.

Suddenly, the thrumming against my nipple turns into a firm pinch. "Ouch."

Now there's no mistaking that all of him is awake as he ruts his dick between my ass cheeks and slides his hand down between my legs.

"Mornin', Mellie." His voice is deep and gravelly. While hearing it had never elicited a sexual response before, after what I've learned about his hidden traits, it's certainly doing that now.

"Good morning," I answer. And it is. I haven't woken up feeling this light in years. Of course, after the pounding he gave me last night, I might not be able to walk once I get up. But these are minor technicalities. "Oh." The sensation of his muscular finger against my clit is driving me crazy.

"You need more?"

Okay, this is reassuring. I mean, even if he woke up with morning wood, he wouldn't initiate this unless he wanted me. Would he?

"Yes." I pant out.

I feel him roll away from me and am unsure what he has in mind until his warmth returns to my back and his fingers caress my most sensitive flesh.

"I had to go out last night to get another condom."

"What?"

"I only had one in my wallet."

"You went out while I was asleep?"

"Yeah. I promised all night. Didn't want to go back on my word."

I'm about to answer him with some snarky comment when I feel him lift my leg, pulling it toward him to wrap it around his hip. His fingers dance over my sex just as he slowly glides back in.

"Oh, god," I moan. He must have a lot of experience with women because he knows exactly the right places to touch. And don't get me started on his talented mouth.

It doesn't take long before I arch my back in ecstasy, the tingle in my lower belly signaling the climax is already close. He moves his hands, holding me still as he drills into me from behind.

"Touch yourself," he growls. "I want to feel you milking me."

I drop my hand down, circling my clit, knowing I'm mere seconds away from coming completely undone.

"Ah, Mellie. Does that feel good?" He grunts. "Playing with your pretty pink pussy while my dick is buried in your sweet little snatch?"

Turning my face into my pillow, I let out a scream as another powerful orgasm crashes into me. It's clear I can't withstand his dirty talk.

There is similar heavy breathing behind me. Until he again pulls out and, I assume, finishes inside the condom. I have to admit that it bothers me. It shouldn't. He doesn't want to get me pregnant. He's made it clear he's not interested in a long-term relationship or kids. And he's given me multiple orgasms. I should simply be grateful for the night he's given me.

"I'm going to slip out and take a quick shower," he says.

"Okay."

I hear him shuffling and assume he's getting dressed. This is so awkward. He gave me what I asked for. I shouldn't want to push for more. Besides, it's bad enough I'll be replaying last night over and over in my head. It's better I don't know what he looks like naked in the daylight. I'd never be able to look him straight in the face.

I try to close my eyes and get another hour of sleep, but the events of the last twenty-four hours are distracting. I fade in and out, exhausted. I can't stop yawning. I mean, it was a workout from start to finish.

"I brought you some water." Huggie's voice awakens me just as he slides back into bed behind me. His hand trails down over my hip and makes me smile. I can tell he's doing everything he can to make this less uncomfortable. If only I could blame my asking him for this on alcohol. Instead, I have to accept I was only desperate for someone's touch.

"I should take a quick shower myself."

"Lie with me for a while," he says into my hair. "Morning is getting here fast enough."

Tracing my nail over the intricate art of his tattoo, it's clear morning is here. The sun has risen, and I can see more clearly now. I've never really looked at this up close before. The artwork is impressive. Near his wrist, there's a vine with only a few leaves and thorns intermingled with barbed wire. It almost looks like a helix. Similar to a strand of DNA. As it travels up his arm, I notice several dark roses appear. There aren't many, but they're there.

As I lie here, his breaths feel heavier, and I suspect he's fallen back asleep. Maybe I will take a few more moments of shut-eye before I have to put this incredible night behind me and face the day.

As I drift off, visions of my happy moments with Huggie over the years dance beneath my heavy lids—both past and present. While I'm closer to him than almost anyone, he's still such an enigma. I remember what Kat said as we sat in the restaurant recently. That I had too big of a heart to spend my future alone. The same could be said for Huggie. I'll never force my opinion on him, but it'd be a travesty for him to remain on his own. He has one of the biggest hearts of anyone I know. And hopefully, some lucky girl will land him.

This thought brings an ache to my chest. Which is surprising given

I'm the one wishing for him to reconsider his lifelong bachelor status. It dawns on me that if Dr. Miller knew how I was feeling right now, particularly after last night... he'd say his warnings were on point.

And perhaps he's right.

CHAPTER NINETEEN

MELANIE

Knock, knock.

"Huggie, you in there?"

My eyes fly open right before I'm catapulted to the floor. I bite down hard on my lip, so I don't cry out, but it probably won't matter once they hear my heart thudding against my chest. I hear what I believe is Huggie walking over to the door.

"Hey, guys. What's up?"

"We can't find Mom," Ruby shouts.

"But her car is here," Seth adds.

"Oh, she probably hasn't made it back yet. She was so tired last night we didn't finish cleaning up. So she said she was going to take a walk to get in gear for the rest of the dishes."

Wow. That's thinking on your feet.

"I was waiting for her to come back too. But now that you're here, why don't we go downstairs and come up with a plan to help her?"

"Okay," Ruby says.

"I'm going to grab some socks and shoes, and I'll be right down. Wouldn't want to slip and fall again."

Seth and Ruby laugh briefly before it gets quiet.

"Hey."

"Oh, god. You scared me," I whisper.

Coming to my side, he scoops me up. "I'm so sorry. I didn't mean to toss you over the side of the bed. I was trying to get you to climb down and hide. I couldn't remember if I locked the door after my shower."

"Heck, at least you got one."

"Well, I'm going to go down and keep them busy. Try and grab a quick one and meet us downstairs."

"Okay."

I follow him out of the guest room and dart over to my bedroom as he heads for the stairs. I guess I'll need to use dry shampoo, or they'll wonder why I went for a walk with soaking wet hair. What on earth has become of me? Lying to my kids.

The thought quickly disappears as I step into the spray and the overused muscles of the last eight hours taunt me. No time to replay that, Melanie. You can save that for later.

"Hey, you're back earlier than I expected," I say, trying to sound winded.

"Mommy," Ruby yells. "You didn't clean very much after we left."

My inclination is to look at Huggie, but I keep my eyes trained on Ruby. "I think the day caught up with me. I got super tired."

"Hmmm. I bet," Kat says from behind me.

"Oh, I didn't see you there."

"Well, I felt bad leaving once I saw the shape the den and kitchen were still in." Kat gives me a skeptical look, and I quickly turn to Seth.

"Did you guys get breakfast?"

"No, Kat made them come home hungry." She says sarcastically. I roll my eyes and try not to consider we've already been caught red-handed.

"Seth and I are going to finish up in the den. Ruby is going to help you in the kitchen," Huggie volunteers. I'm sure he's trying to deflect.

"Okay, let's roll, Ruby."

"What should I do?" Kat asks.

Ugh. This awkward situation isn't her fault. But the sinister way she's acting is making me anxious.

"We've got this. You were awesome to take the kids. Why don't you, Nick, and Grace enjoy your day together?" I finally turn to look in her direction, and she's giving me the once over.

"Okay. If you say so," she throws back with a mischievous grin.

Oh, good, lord.

～

"Sorry," I tell Huggie. We've nearly collided on multiple occasions as he's come into the kitchen with stray dishware and glasses. I can't believe after last night, he's still finding more. The back and forth between us as we clean up has been awkward. I can't even look at him. What must he think of me after the way I begged him to sleep with me? And I know if I make eye contact, I'll only blush. How on earth did I think I could pretend last night didn't happen?

Keeping my back to him, I focus on the dishes in the sink. I just need to finish this up and then focus on the kids. Yet each time he returns with something, I feel the warmth of his hand on my hip and almost moan. It's as if his touch prompts memories from our night together, making me feel flushed.

"Mommy, can we have movie night tonight? Since we worked hard to clean everything up," Ruby pleads with her hands steepled together.

"Yeah, and maybe Luigi's for dinner?" Seth adds.

"I think we need to clear out some of the food from yesterday first, bud."

"Yeah. I guess so."

"I don't think there's an inch of space left in there. Where would we put the Luigi's leftovers?" I tease. "We never finish what we get from there."

"Huggie, are you staying?" Ruby asks.

"Hmmm. I'll stay if we can make a deal."

"What?" Seth and Ruby ask simultaneously.

"First, does anyone have homework?"

All heads rotate to Seth, who starts to laugh. "No. She said it wouldn't get done anyway, so she'll really pile it on after the holiday."

"Okay, good. So the three of us will use the leftovers to make dinner so your mom can have a break. She cooked all day yesterday and cleaned all day today. If we can do that, I'll stay and have a movie night."

"Deal!"

Now I can't help it. Turning to look at this sweet man, I place my hand over my heart. "Thank you." Lord, I'd probably kiss him if the kids weren't here. But that's not what this is. He agreed to one night. I can't take advantage of him. Even if I'd welcome a repeat performance.

Dinner is over, the dishes are put away, and now we're watching an Avengers movie. Thank goodness we started the evening early, as the kids still have a few days of school before Thanksgiving break. I'm fading in and out of this movie, exhaustion from the last several days catching up with me.

"Here," Huggie says, handing me a blanket. "I'll wake you if you fall asleep." He winks.

Just that simple gesture has my heart rate picking up. I've known this man for over half of my life. How is he suddenly affecting me this way? I lean my head back against the cushions of the sofa and try to focus on the movie. That is until I feel my feet being pulled toward Huggie's lap. I nearly groan out my pleasure as he skillfully massages them under the blanket while watching the television. I open my eyes long enough to see Thor on the screen. The last thought I have before succumbing to sleep is that Thor has nothing on the superhero next to me.

HUGGIE

Nate, Jamie, and I trudge into the firehouse, exhausted after the last several hours of working a car fire. The car accident required us to extricate the driver and help EMS get him to the trauma center. Then we had to act quickly to take care of the vehicle after it burst into flames.

"What are the odds I can make it in and out of the shower without the alarm going off?" Nate asks.

"The way today has gone, not good. But if you don't chance it, I will." I say.

"Okay. This is going to be the quickest shower in history."

Nate heads for the bathroom, and I grab my toiletry bag, hoping I can manage one myself before we receive another call.

"I'm starving," Jamie says.

"Man, do you eat twenty-four-seven?"

"It takes a lot of calories to keep this body churning."

"Well, I'm hitting the shower after Nate is out, and then maybe we can feed your tapeworm."

"Okay, Huggie, you're up," Nate belts out.

"That was fast. Be right back." I head to the shower and practically whistle. I should be exhausted, but I have to fight to keep the constant grin off of my face, or someone will surely think something's up.

I admit I haven't slept well since Saturday night. And not for the reasons sleep has evaded me in the past. I'm not stressed or nervous about Mel. I cannot stop replaying that glorious night. Sure, I broke almost every ground rule I set. It was supposed to be all about Melanie that night. Ha! Who was I kidding? I've been longing for her for so long. I enjoyed every second. And it was supposed to be one night. Yet I couldn't get enough. I was so certain one time wouldn't be enough that I snuck out to a twenty-four-hour convenience store for condoms.

I tried to separate my feelings. Only focus on the physical. And oh, how I loved being physical. But it took incredible effort not to blurt exactly how I felt about her. At least I managed to keep two rules. I didn't come inside her, and no one knows but us.

I quickly towel off and grab my clothes. The last thing I need is for an emergency call to come in, and I'm holding up the works trying to get dressed.

"Okay, I'm done," I announce to no one in particular. I sit on the edge of my bunk and put my shoes on, knowing it's only a matter of time before we leave. Whether in response to a call, or Jamie's stomach is left to be seen. I lie back with my arms crossed behind my head, waiting for the memories from the other night to dance across my mind's eye and smile.

"You didn't?"

My eyes flick open, and I find Nate standing above me.

"Didn't what?"

"You slept with her."

I bolt upright, looking around. "Who? What are you talking about?" I whisper.

"Cut the crap, man. I've known you forever. When we get back from a call like that, you're the first to grumble about it until you can distract yourself with your phone or the television."

"And?" I prod.

"You're lying on your back, no phone, no TV, grinning like a Cheshire cat." He bends, so he's right in my face. "Unless you met someone since Saturday, my bet is the turkey wasn't the only thing getting stuffed that night."

"Come on, Nate." I fall back onto the bed, disgusted. Both by his statement and the fact I must be the most transparent guy on the planet. Guess that's rule number four down.

"Are you two—"

"No. "It's only physical, Nate. There's nothing more."

"Who are you kidding? You've been in love with her for years. That's the very definition of more." He's quiet for a moment. "You know this is bad, right?"

"What? Spending any time with you? Yes." I mock.

There's a brief period of silence, and I start to second-guess everything. Why did I let things go this far?

"No wonder you chose this profession. You like playing with fire." Nate mutters.

Part of me wants to sit up and give him what for. But the thing is, he's right. There's no doubt when this is all over I'm going to end up burned.

"Hello?"

"Hi, Huggie. It's Seth."

"Hey, buddy. What's up?"

"I need your help with something."

"Shoot." I get up from my chair in the TV room and walk to where it's quieter in the bunk room.

"Well, Mom just got a call from Aunt Morgan. Grandpa had to go to the hospital."

"Is everything okay?"

"I think so. Mom said it sounded like they were keeping him to run some tests. But she told Aunt Morgan she didn't know how she could come without pulling us out of school."

"Well, it is Thanksgiving. Maybe she wants you guys to spend it with her parents."

"I know. You're right. But I have an assignment I need to do over break. It's not due until the week after we get back, but I'm worried I won't be able to get it done if I'm away. And I don't want to worry Mom about it once we get back."

"How can I help?"

"If I send you the information on the project, can you help me get the supplies and maybe work on it with me when I get back home? I know Mom will have to go back to work, and I don't want to stress her out."

"You're a good kid, Seth. I'm happy to help. Just keep me up to date on everything."

"I will. Thanks, Huggie."

~

A few hours go by without calls to distract me, and I have to wonder why Melanie hasn't reached out about her dad. I don't want to let the cat out of the bag that Seth called, so I can't bring it up.

I try to stay focused on the game or, like Nate, on mindless social media. But I'm worried about her. Is she downplaying her dad's health to protect Seth? If not, is he seriously ill?

~

Dinner is over, and the kitchen is clean. After the car fire, we've only had one other call, which barely counted as it was a frequent flier who we secretly think is lonely. She often calls for chest or abdominal pain, but by the time we arrive and check her out, she frequently decides to forego transport to the hospital.

The silence is deafening. I can't take it anymore. Retrieving my phone, I begin to send a message to Melanie, asking how things are going, when my phone buzzes.

Melanie
7:45 p.m.
Mel: Hey, wanted to let you know we're at the airport. Dad's had what they think is a mini-stroke. They want to keep him in the hospital for a few days to make sure. I'm taking the kids out of school for the week. If all goes well, he'll be discharged home for Thanksgiving. So I'll plan to spend it here with Mom and Morgan and her family.

7:49 p.m.
Huggie: I'll say a prayer for your dad. Hope he's okay. I start to type *I'll miss you guys* **but think better of it. I don't need her having any thoughts of me here alone for Thanksgiving.**

Melanie
7:52 p.m.
Mel: Guess you're off the hook from babysitting us for a week and can have your old life back.

Reading this makes me edgy. Am I being dismissed? What if I don't want my old life back yet? I stop to consider. Is this trip as necessary as she would like me to believe? Or after the other night, is she simply trying to put distance between us?

CHAPTER TWENTY

MELANIE

"Lean on me, Grandpa," Seth says as he walks alongside Dad.

"Thanks, Seth. I'm getting stronger every day, but I appreciate you being here."

"You gave us quite a scare, Henry," my mother scolds.

"Yeah, well, I'm sure I won't hear the end of how I could've avoided all of this if I'd only eaten what you told me and walked every day."

I turn to look at Mom, biting the inside of my cheek so I don't laugh at the scowl she's giving him. I'm sure he'll get an earful once there aren't little ears around.

"Melanie, come sit down. I'll put on a pot of coffee," my mother encourages.

"I'm fine. Please don't fuss over me. I came here to help you."

"You just being here is all the help I need." She grins and comes over to give me a big squeeze.

Walking over to her kitchen cabinets, I open the door that houses the cookbooks and retrieve one of the older ones I remember from childhood. Sitting at the kitchen table, I start to flip through the pages. "Any idea what you want to make for Thanksgiving?" I ask.

"Oh, we usually have the same thing every year. You're the fancy one, dear."

"I'm not fancy. I just enjoy trying new things. I feel bad we haven't come for the holidays in so long. With—"

"It's okay, Melanie. We understand."

"No, I want to explain. I wanted to come the last few years, but Jake was always working. And I wanted to spend the day with him. So the kids and I would make a meal and bring it to the hospital. We were usually only lucky enough to have about twenty minutes to eat with him before he had to return to the ER. But we were all together. And we were thankful."

Mom hands me a cup of hot coffee and creamer and sits down at the table by my side.

"It's taken me a long time, but I think I'm at a much better place than I've been since he died. But I really wanted to thank you and Morgan. You two did so much to help me back then."

"I wish we could've done more. It's hard when the ones you love live far away." She takes a small sip of her coffee, steam billowing from the cup. "Morgan should be by later. Then we can figure out our dinner plans for Thursday."

We finish our coffees, catching up on my job and the kids' school and soccer happenings. It's been a long time since I've had one-on-one time with her.

"Thank you for picking up dinner, Morgan. This was great." And it was. The pizza and Italian take-out she'd brought almost rivaled Luigi's. Almost. I thought she'd bought too much, but between her husband, two kids, my kids, and my parents, there was barely enough for me.

"So Mom says you guys have the same dinner menu every Thanksgiving. Fill me in on what to get at the grocery store and if anyone is interested in trying something new." I laugh.

"I think it's Dad that has caused us to have the same food year after year. And after this mini-stroke business, I bet she'll be trying to get him to eat healthier. So he'll be trying something new whether he likes it or not."

We pour over cookbooks and internet searches for healthy Turkey Day alternatives to build a menu and develop a grocery list. I haven't spent much time with my sister in recent years. Morgan and I were very close growing up, but when she married and his job required them to move, my parents moved with them to help look out for the kids. It made sense. I'd mostly volunteered or worked very part-time. It was easy enough to find childcare for the few times I needed it. But I know full-time daycare is expensive. It was the right thing for my parents to do. But I often felt orphaned when my whole family was states away. Thank heaven I have Kat. She's as close as any sister could be.

"I'm surprised Huggie didn't come with you," Morgan says.

"What? Why would you say that?"

She gives me a blank stare.

"What? He's just a friend."

"Melanie, that man is more than a friend. I'm married and practically fell in love with him when Mom and I were staying at your place. He was so devoted to looking out for you and the kids."

"He was Jake's best friend. I think he feels obligated," I admit. I often wonder when he'll feel like he's done his due diligence and move on from us. I mean, he has his own life to lead. I had no right asking him to stay. Much less push the boundaries of our friendship the way I have.

"You have to think it has to be more, Mel. The way he looked at you."

"It was sympathy. I'm not sure how much of it still is. He's been in our lives forever. I feel bad we packed up and left right before Thanksgiving. He has come to our house every year for as long as I can remember. He's an only child and lost his mother when he was still a teenager. He's estranged from his dad. We've practically thought of him as a member of the family all of these years."

Morgan stops flipping through cookbook pages and looks directly at me. "So, since Jake's been gone, has there been anyone?"

"No. I don't think I was ready before."

She shifts so she's sitting taller in her seat. "So does that mean you are now?"

A small smile lifts the corner of my mouth at her questioning. "I don't know. Maybe. I've only ever been with Jake." As I finish the sentence, my mind immediately harkens back to the other night with Huggie, and I feel my cheeks heat.

"Oh, my gosh. You're blushing. Who? I need all of the details. Is it your boss?"

"No, no. I'd never do that."

"Then, it is Huggie."

Covering my face with my hands, I can't believe I'm sharing this with her. I can't tell Kat. She'd be watching us every second afterward. But Morgan lives far enough away, and I'm sure she can keep this to herself.

"I practically threw myself at him," I tell her.

"What? No way! You little harlot."

"Ugh." I groan.

"So, skip to the good part. Did you do the deed?"

My face is on fire now.

Giggling erupts from my sister, and I don't need to answer. "Oh, my god. I'm so excited for you."

"It was just one time, and we made a pact that it wouldn't change anything between us."

"Then why are you here, and he's there?"

"He works for the fire department. He has responsibilities. He can't just take off to come here with me."

Morgan stares at me, looking as if she's waited for this moment for ages. "Let me get this straight. You slept with one of the hottest firefighters on the planet, and you don't feel anything for him?"

"I never said that. I just didn't expect to, that's all. This has all caught me by surprise. I mean, we've been friends forever."

"Was the sex not good?"

I look at her deadpan.

"Holy shit. Really?"

"Morgan, I didn't know it could be like that."

Now my sister is blushing. Maybe that's enough of this talk. "If you're both consenting adults, what's the problem?"

"Well, there are multiple. I don't think Huggie thinks of me that way. I think he was a typical horny male who just took me up on my offer. He's a self-proclaimed bachelor for life. He's told me he has no interest in a long-term relationship on multiple occasions. And lastly, there are the kids. They adore him. They could get hurt if we tried to turn this into something it isn't."

I sit quietly, thinking about all I've said. I really put Huggie in a bad position by propositioning him. If I bring any of this up, it'll put him in a worse spot if he's forced to tell me he's not interested in more. So, as much as I'd like a repeat performance, I need to manage without him for a while. So we can get our friendship back on sound footing.

~

Thanksgiving Day arrives, and it's a flurry of kids, food, and Mom getting after Dad.

"You better keep an eye on them after we leave. She's libel to give him a full-fledged stroke with the way she's on him every second."

"I know. I'm going to have my hands full."

We watch the Macy's Day parade, Ruby helps me make a pie 'like Huggie would do it,' and we attempt to eat around football games. My mind is miles away, wondering how his day is going. I hope Nate or someone invited him to dinner. My heart hurts thinking of him alone.

"Watcha thinking about?" Morgan asks.

"Nothing."

"I bet that nothing is tall, blond, and handsome."

My smile instantly betrays me.

"Go call him."

I grab my phone and head out onto the back deck. I don't know why I'm so nervous. Has sex really changed that much between us?

I feel my teeth chatter as I listen to the phone ringing, awaiting him to pick up. He could be sitting down to eat. I'll just leave him a—

"Hey! How are you? How's your dad?"

Oh, the sound of his voice. It instantly relaxes me. "We're all good. They think he had a mini-stroke and placed him on some medications to prevent any future occurrences. He had some initial weakness in the left arm, but that completely resolved."

"Wow, it sounds like he got pretty lucky."

"Yeah. He did." The line goes quiet for a moment. I hate the awkward silence, so I blurt, "Where are you? I hope you aren't at your place alone." Well, I hope he's not at his place with someone, either.

"I'm at the station. I figured I'd offer to cover for someone with a family."

My heart feels like someone has stabbed me with an ice pick. We were his family.

"Plus, someone had to feed Jamie." He laughs.

"So, are you guys all cooking together? Even the ones who are off?"

"Yeah. It's not bad. Football is on, and we get a nice meal together..."

I sit, soothed by the sound of his voice, wondering what else he is going to say.

"Mel?"

"Yeah?"

"Thanksgiving isn't the same without you guys. The guys are great. I'm lucky to have them. But..."

"But, what?"

"Is it okay to say I miss you?"

CHAPTER TWENTY-ONE

HUGGIE

"Huggie!" Ruby squeals and runs full steam as I stand in the kitchen, waiting for them to get off of the bus.

My smile must spread from ear to ear. God, how I've missed them. "Awe, hi, Rubs. It feels like forever since you've nearly knocked me over." I chuckle and look for Seth to come through the door.

"What's all this?" she asks.

"It's your brother's turn. He said he had a project to do and wouldn't be able to carry it back on the plane. It's due next week. So we've got some work to do."

"Huggie!" Seth says and actually runs over to where I'm standing. I don't know if it's the relief of knowing he won't let down Homework Hildegard or if it's me he's excited to see.

"I missed you," he says, looking up at me with a big grin.

"I missed you, too, buddy. Both of you guys." There's a definite lump in my throat. It's clear I need to find a way to distance myself from these two. After sleeping with their mother, things already feel more awkward than I'd anticipated. There's no way I can let anything happen to the two of them if things become strained with her. They've lost so much. But through the holidays, I hope I can be a shoulder to lean on if they feel sad about missing their dad.

"I'm sorry we didn't do Turkey Day with you this year," Ruby says. "Grandpa got sick."

"I heard. He better now?"

"Much. Can you tell us what all this stuff is now?"

I laugh and look at Seth. "Well, this is your project, my man. Why don't you get your assignment out and direct us on what you need us to do." I no sooner finish my sentence, and I'm handing the kids a pair of science goggles. I probably should put on a pair myself, the way things go around here. Let's hope we can manage not to destroy the kitchen before Mel comes home from work like the last two projects we attempted in here.

Seth retrieves his assignment and stands between Ruby and me. "Okay, I have to build a volcano. It has to erupt and everything."

Of course, it does, Hildegard. I secretly wonder if this woman takes great joy in creating these projects. I mean, she doesn't have to do anything but sit back and judge the time and effort put into these by parents, or me, who could otherwise be enjoying a football game. I bet she enjoys exerting her power over—

"Huggie! Pay attention!" Ruby yells. I look over to Seth, who's trying to hand me the ingredients we need to create the salt dough to form the volcano.

"Sorry, man. I'm slippin.'"

I glance at Ruby, who's shaking her head at my inability to keep up.

"Okay, as I was saying, I want you and Ruby to help try and mold the volcano out of clay. I'm going to start preparing the ingredients for the test eruption. Then once we know it will work, we can put a second one in the clay volcano you guys are making to erupt at school tomorrow."

"Ah, good plan. So, other than torturing me with this project, what does Hilde hope to accomplish by making you guys spend Thanksgiving creating volcanos?"

Seth looks at me, irritated.

"Sorry. What's she trying to teach with this project?"

"It's an introduction to chemistry. She said a chemical reaction occurs when you mix an acid and a base. That's what causes the volcano to explode."

Shit. Hildegard knows her stuff. "Seth?"

"Yeah?"

"Are you in some type of advanced learning class?"

"Yeah. Why?"

It's all getting clearer—this kid. Bending down so I'm closer to eye level, I try to find the right words. "Seth. There will come a day when I can't help you with these projects anymore."

His eyes grow wide.

"Why?" Ruby interjects, sounding nervous.

"Because you two are smarter than me."

The two of them begin to cackle, their relief evident.

Ruby and I construct the best-looking volcano I've ever seen. We stand back, arms crossed over our chests, proud as peacocks.

"When do we get to do the test experiment, Seth?" Ruby asks excitedly.

"Well, this clay needs to dry until tomorrow. So let's put it over there and get out the soda bottle we will use to mix the vinegar and baking soda."

Seth diligently reviews his instructions and tells Ruby that since he gets to do the experiment at school, he will let her explode the volcano here. She's so thrilled you'd think he told her she's getting a pony.

"This isn't going to do anything that'll get me in trouble with your mom, is it?"

"Nah. Ms. Hooker wouldn't let us do an experiment where anyone got hurt or into trouble."

He's right. But I think I'll have them put on the goggles, just in case. "Okay, Ruby, you have to pour the baking soda into the vinegar. I put the vinegar in the bottle while you two were molding the clay."

In true Ruby style, she grabs the can of baking soda, and instead of using the small measuring spoon Seth has placed next to it, she enthusiastically pours a large dollop of the white powder into the funnel at the top of the soda bottle.

"Oh, no," Seth says, pulling the funnel from the bottle.

"What do you mean, oh—"

Before I can finish my question, a white foamy substance burps from the bottle several times before the bottle tips over and sprays all over us and the kitchen.

I barely have time to take in the mess when the front door swings open. "Uh oh."

"Hi, Mommy," Ruby greets, sounding nervous. I can barely see Ruby's eyes for all of the foam. The two of them look like Minions standing here.

"Sorry, Mel."

MELANIE

"Um, what happened here?" I'd laugh, but I spent days cleaning up this kitchen the last time I was home. This wasn't on the agenda tonight.

"I think we used too much baking soda," Seth says, his face and silly goggles covered in white foam.

"I'm sorry, Mommy." Her voice sounds remorseful, but I can't see if Ruby appears sad. I can't find her face.

"We should've done this outside, Mel. I'm sorry."

Placing my things on the bench, I notice a white foamy substance covering the island, the floor, and the three anxious-looking people standing before me. A dollop is covering the front of Huggie's pants, making me blush.

"Can someone fill me in on what happened?" Have they decided to play mad scientist to pass the time?

"Huggie's helping me with my science project for school."

I watch as Huggie leans toward Seth and mutters, "Thanks for throwing me under the bus, man."

"Ms. Hooker gave me the assignment right before we had to leave. And I knew I couldn't take it on the plane." Seth points behind him at the makeshift volcano. "And you had to take care of Grandpa. It's due tomorrow. So I asked Huggie if he'd help."

My poor sweet kids. They're trying to get things done despite their circumstances and my inability to keep up. My eyes meet Huggie's. He looks nervous. This guy. He moves heaven and earth to help us. So why am I so worried after my talk with Morgan?

"Well, thank you for trying to finish your project without worrying me." I want to say more but decide to wait until I can speak with the kids privately. I don't want to hurt Huggie's feelings for trying to help. "Let's clean you two up. And then we'll get the rest of this."

"I've got this, Mel. You take the kids."

I look up at him, and my heart skips a beat. I've missed him too.

When he said he missed us, I knew the holiday weighed heavily on him. As it had for me. I love my parents, and that was where we needed to be.

But we'd managed to get accustomed to *a new normal,* as Huggie had put it. Holidays without Jake still feel hollow, but when the three of us are home, and Huggie is here, I can almost feel Jake's presence. And it's comforting not having to listen to people bring him up. Having Thanksgiving outside of our home, without Jake or Huggie, just felt off.

I walk with the kids to the upstairs bathroom and run the shower so we can rinse all the foam off them. My heart feels heavy thinking of Seth reaching out to Huggie for help.

After the kids are clean and dressed in fresh pajamas, I'm about to tell them we'll order pizza for dinner when I decide to address the elephant in the room. Squatting down to their eye level, I make sure I have their attention. "First, you aren't in any trouble. I think it was sweet of you to call Huggie because you knew I was stressed over Grandpa. But I'm your mom. I want to know what's happening. I'm glad Huggie could help, but don't leave me out."

"I'm sorry, Mom. I thought it would upset you, knowing there was another project that had to get done."

"I know, baby. But we're in this together. There are times I'll have to reach out for help because I can't manage everything like I used to. We're blessed to have good friends who can help us. Yet when it comes right down to it, it's about the three of us. We're a team. Okay?"

The two of them come in for a hug. They're both squeezing me so hard I nearly topple over. I start to laugh until I see Huggie at the top of the steps, looking dejected.

"I just came up to change my clothes," he says quietly. "The kitchen is back to normal."

"Thank you."

"Mom's ordering pizza. You want pepperonis?" Ruby asks.

"I think I'm going to pass, Rubs. Thanks anyway."

"But we just got back," she pleads.

"I'm meeting Nate and the guys," he says.

I have the distinct feeling this is the first time Huggie has lied to my children. But this is on me. I haven't exactly given him a warm reception since we've been back. I'm so confused about my feelings right now. Is this transference like Dr. Miller warned? And if it is, continuing to let my kids turn to him can cause a lot of harm down the road.

Part of me wants to go to Huggie. Hold him tight and tell him I'm falling for him, and I'm scared. The other part wants to protect myself and run. I've been through enough in the last few years. And so have my children.

"You guys head on down. I'm going to change my clothes and order the pizza."

"Okay," they both answer.

I step toward my room, simply needing some space, when I hear him.

"Mellie?"

Turning toward him, I feel my hands start to shake. I don't understand what's happening. I'm so overwhelmed.

"Is everything okay?"

I promise to always be honest with him. He's my friend, and I love him.

"I think I've made a mistake."

CHAPTER TWENTY-TWO

HUGGIE

"What's going on, Mel? What mistake?"

She looks up at me like I'm supposed to understand. This isn't about the kitchen. Unless...

"Do you want me to go back to my place?"

"No," she blurts.

Well, that's reassuring. "Then what is it?" I try to step closer, but she instantly backs away. My stomach lurches. Something is horribly wrong. I knew this would happen eventually, but it's barely been two weeks. I'm not ready for this to fall apart yet.

"I think sleeping with you has put us in a weird position."

"I'd be happy to try a few more if that's what you need," I say, trying to add some levity to this conversation. Yet the minute the words have left my mouth, I regret them. Melanie looks miserable.

"I'm feeling overwhelmed. It could be getting back home, worrying about my dad, and managing to get back into my work routine. Plus, the holidays are officially on me. Trying to juggle the day-to-day things are hard enough, then add in playing Santa, and it's a challenge. On top of that, I've got the memories of Christmas past taunting me."

She's right. That'd be a lot for anyone. I feel like a fish out of water since we slept together. As amazing as that night was, I question everything. And Melanie's got so many new things to contend with. I'm damn sure not going to let her start regressing because of me.

Holidays are complicated. Even more so for anyone who's lost someone they care about. The years following my mother's death were brutal. I simply wanted to skip all of them. There was nothing worth celebrating. And Thanksgiving was the worst of all. How are you supposed to be thankful when the only true family you've had is gone?

But I can't lose Melanie. She's been the center of my universe for years. I understand why it could never work between us. How would I get past the guilt of taking Jake's place?

"I don't want to do anything that causes you stress, Mel. I'm sorry if my being here is upsetting."

She looks down at her hands, and I can practically feel the heaviness from across the hall. "No, no. You've only ever tried to give me what I asked for. I feel terrible saying these things. I don't understand how I'm feeling." She glances up, and it's all I can do not to pull her into me. "For the first time, I realize I want more. I just don't want to hurt the kids trying to figure out what that looks like."

Melanie's right. This isn't simply about the two of us and how sex may or may not have thrown a wrench into our relationship. These kids are attached to me as I am to them. We need to take a step back before there's collateral damage.

"Look. I'm going to go. Call if you need anything. But I think we both need some space."

"Please don't be upset with me," she pleads.

Walking over to her, I place my hands on her shoulders and look into her eyes. "I'm your friend to the bitter end, Mellie. I'm following your lead. You only have to tell me what you need." I place a chaste kiss on her temple and walk away before I consider begging her to give me a chance.

∼

"Hey, thanks for calling me. How'd you know I needed a cold one?" Nate clinks his amber bottle with mine.

"Just a feeling, I guess," I mutter.

"Fuck. You sound worse than you did over the phone. What gives?"

"Man, you were right. It's only been a few weeks, and things are imploding."

"Shit, what happened?"

"I don't know. I can't stop thinking about her and that night, and she's doing everything she can to keep her distance."

Nate grows quiet as if giving serious consideration to my plight. "You must suck in the sack, bro."

I practically spit out my drink. "What the hell? There's no way it's that."

"How would you know? Have you even slept with the same girl twice?"

Part of me wants to share how popular I am at The Rox. Then I remember I'm using his name when I'm there. Hell, he knows enough about my private life already. "There've been a few." I sneer.

"Come on. You know I'm ribbing you. Give her some time. She's finally allowing herself to live again, and she's having a tough time adjusting. That's all."

"I can't help thinking I should've said no." There's always a transition guy. That poor sap that gets used until they recover and move on to the one they really want. Maybe if she'd gotten it out of her system with Derek, she would've been ready for me. The thought of her sleeping with her boss makes me want to hit something.

"Let's be real. There was no way you were saying no to her. Not possible."

He's right. "So why did you need a beer?"

"It's the whole marriage thing. Never thought it'd actually happen, and now that it has, it's a pain in the ass."

"What do you mean?"

"I mean, I don't want to worry about details. The day should be about us, not what color napkins we're using."

I put my beer down and look at him in shock. "Adam's into that shit?"

"No. I think it's coming from his parents. I mean, fuck, he has two sisters. Wait for them."

I chuckle and finish off my beer. "Won't ever have that problem."

"We'll see."

~

Carefully closing the door behind me, I make my way to the guestroom. Once inside, I kick off my shoes and slump onto the bed. This sucks. The thoughts of my night with Melanie are incredible and painful in equal measure. The happiest night of my life and a reminder of what I'll never have.

The stench of cigar smoke from baring my soul to Nate in the VIP section of The Zone earlier is more prominent in this clean room. I grab a change of clothes and head to the bathroom for a quick shower.

I adjust the showerhead to allow deeper pressure and relax as the scalding water pounds into my tense muscles. How is it they get more of a workout from stress than working as a firefighter? Maybe I need to put in more time at the gym.

Toweling off, I give myself a virtual pat on the back. Not only did I manage to get through that shower without wanking off, but I also kept thoughts of Melanie at bay while I was in there. It's bad enough I'll likely stare at the ceiling all night, wishing... Hell, I don't even know what to wish for anymore.

Padding down the hall, I reach my room and turn off the light. Crossing to the bed, I climb in and pray the beer from earlier will hasten sleep so my current predicament doesn't torture me.

As expected, I close my eyes and picture Melanie spooned in front of me. The way she fit snuggled against my chest, her warmth, her softness. And that watermelon scent that drives me crazy.

I start to drift to sleep until I feel the bed shift. My eyes fly open until I smell that fresh, fruity aroma as she lies her head down on my chest. Wrapping her in my arms, I don't even want to question why she's here. I'm merely glad she is.

"I'm scared."

Me too, Mellie. Me too.

CHAPTER TWENTY-THREE

HUGGIE

"Thanks for splitting the shift with me, Huggie. My son's travel league has a big tournament out of town this weekend. Their practice was mandatory, and no one else could get him there," Jeff says.

"No problem." I've been picking up whole shifts on set to cover fall sports for most of the guys with a family. Half a shift is a walk in the park. "It's been a beautiful day. Paxton and I have barely moved a muscle." I laugh.

The crew has moved to a plantation in James City to film. The leaves have turned brilliant shades of red, orange, and purple. It's perfect sweater weather, and I've enjoyed more than my fair share of cider and coffee while reading a new spy novel.

"You got plans tonight?" Paxton asks.

"Nah. I work at the station in the morning. I'll probably head to bed and read another chapter," I say, waving my book at him.

"See you."

∼

I head to Mel's place, not knowing what I'll find. Melanie and I haven't spoken much since she crawled into bed with me the other night. I can tell this has weighed heavily on her, so I'm giving her space. Why does life have to be so complicated?

There's no real reason for me to stay there over the weekend unless she's on-call. I'm working at the station tomorrow and may head to my place on Sunday. Given how turbulent things have gotten since we slept together, I need to limit how much time I'm spending there. If nothing more than to put some distance between the kids and me.

I walk to the door and stop as Nick and Kat are blocking the doorway.

"Hey, Huggie."

Kat is holding Grace, who's two now. "Hey, Super G."

Grace was born prematurely, but she's a fighter. Her birth mother was a patient Kat had taken care of on multiple occasions in the ER. When she determined she could no longer provide for her daughter, she entered into an open adoption with Nick and Kat.

"Bye, Huggie," Ruby says as she marches out with her soccer and overnight totes.

"Where's the bag lady going?" I ask.

"We're going to Nick and Kat's house so they can take us to soccer in the morning. Mom has a big meeting tomorrow."

I look questioningly at Mel. What big meeting could she have on a Saturday?

"See you at the game, Mel," Kat says as she and Grace wave goodbye.

I stand by the door momentarily, but Melanie doesn't speak. "Have you had dinner?"

"No. But I'm not hungry. I think I'll probably head to bed early."

Dropping my head in disappointment, I walk past her to the stairs. "Okay. I'm going to get cleaned up."

Showered and dressed for bed, I decide to make it an early Friday. My shift starts at 6:00 a.m., so it'd do me well to get some shut-eye.

Knock, knock.

My heart rate picks up, knowing who's on the other side of the door. Yet I tell myself to knock that shit off because Melanie's behavior of late has been so aloof. There's no sense getting my hopes up.

Opening the door, Melanie stands before me appearing nervous. She's wearing those tiny sleep shorts and the top I was glued to recently. The one clinging to her beautiful rack so deliciously. I stay silent, trying to keep my eyes on her face.

"Can I come in?"

"It's your house," I tease. It probably comes off as irritable. But maybe I'm tired of hiding everything. I leave the door ajar so light can enter the space. I'm sure she won't be here long, so there's no point turning the lamp back on.

As I turn to look at her, I notice her fidget from foot to foot. Before I can take in what's happening, she takes several steps toward me and wraps her arms around my neck. Within moments, she has her sweet lips on mine, and my hands fly up to cup her cheeks. Tilting her face to get a better angle, I plunge my tongue deeper into her mouth and take my fill of her. It's like getting a hit off of an addictive substance. That immediate high I feel with her.

The kiss stops, and I try to calm my breathing and follow her lead. But there's nothing collected about my body's reaction when she drops to her knees.

"Mellie. You—"

"Please? I want to."

She pulls my boxer briefs down, and a look of shock crosses her face. She may have wrapped her hand around me last time, but I think Mel's reassessing whether she's sure she wants to do this. My dick is a blessing and a curse. Ninety-five percent blessing. But as much as I'd love to feel her lips wrapped around me, I don't want her to be anxious.

"You're so big," she says. From this angle, it appears she's speaking directly to my cock.

"Mel, you really don't—"

"But I want to. I'm just worried you won't—"

"You can put aside any worries about me not liking *anything* you do to me," I tell her. Reaching out to her, I rub the pad of my thumb over her plump lower lip and can feel my dick jumping at the thought of this happening in real life. There have been more than enough fantasies of this moment. Years of fantasies.

She tentatively sticks out her tongue, and I have to fight to keep from groaning as she teases the head of my cock with the tip. Too much of that, and I'll lose my mind. *Maybe that's her plan.*

Gliding her warm, wet tongue down my length, I feel her wrap her fingers around the base to steady me before gliding her hand up and down.

I have to spread my legs a little wider to steady myself. Yet nothing prepares me for the sensation of having her sweet lips engulfing me.

"Oh, fuck, Mel."

She lets out a little moan that vibrates over my steely length, and I start to pant. Up and down, she glides her firm hand as she licks and sucks. Once in a while, she attempts more than is comfortable and starts to gag.

Petting her hair, I try to reassure her. "It feels so good, Mellie. You don't have to take me so deep." Yet, that only spurs her on. Her eyes shine with tears as she tries to swallow more of me. Seeing her mouth full of my cock, big brown eyes staring up at me... it's enough to make me come right now. But no way is that happening.

"Baby, I need to be inside you."

She pulls back from me with a pop. "Are you sure I—"

"I don't want to come in your mouth. And if you keep worrying about whether you satisfy me, I really will take that glorious ass over my knee."

Her eyes fly wide in surprise. Reaching my hand out, I encourage her to stand and walk over to the bed.

I kiss her hard and deep, squeezing her sweet ass as she strokes my dick that's now pressed against her stomach. "Will you do something for me?"

She nods, those sparkling violet orbs still wide.

"I want you to ride me," I say, giving the seam of her swollen mouth a lick. "I want to suck on your pretty tits while you're on top of me."

Her head is instantly nodding like a bobblehead doll. I have to try not to laugh. I push my shorts the rest of the way down and remove my shirt, hoping it's dark enough that she won't pay that much attention to my tattoo. I don't want anything to wreck this moment.

As I center myself on the bed, I watch in eager anticipation as she removes my favorite shirt and those tiny shorts. "Can you grab a condom from the drawer?" I ask, pointing to the bedside table. Yes, it was only supposed to be one night. But I'm allowed to hope.

She hands the foil packet to me, and I quickly open it and sheath myself, just imagining her body wrapped around me. As she lines herself up, I can tell she's nervous.

"Take your time. I don't want to hurt you."

She rocks her hips from side to side as she lowers herself, biting her lip as she adjusts to me.

I reach out to stroke her pussy and see the moment she relaxes enough to take all of me. Fuck. She feels so good.

Propped up on pillows, I don't have to lean far to suck a nipple into my mouth. I'm literally in heaven as she rides me with my face buried between her breasts.

"Oh." She moans.

I continue rubbing tiny circles over her bundle of nerves with the pad of my thumb as she rocks back and forth on top of me. "Fuck. I love seeing your tight pussy stretched around my cock."

"Oh. God," she whimpers.

Suddenly, she picks up speed, alternating between rocking her hips back and forth with gliding up and down on my shaft. A familiar sensation builds at the base of my spine. Flipping her over, I slide between her thighs to fuck her hard before I come. Her moaning is getting me to the finish line quicker than I'd hoped. *Shit. I need her to come.*

"Mellie." I pant and start to pull out when she digs her nails into my ass.

"No."

"Mel."

"I want you to come inside me."

MELANIE

Suddenly, Huggie's eyes go from a silvery blue to stormy gray. He looks like a man possessed as he lifts my thighs, so they're wrapped around him. Leaning on his forearms, he fucks me like a porn star. *Yeah, I've watched. And they have nothing on this man.*

"Oh, you greedy girl. It's not enough to have my dick in your mouth, then your pussy. Now you want me to fill you full of come?"

"Yes," I shout. I'm afraid I might draw blood the way my fingernails are buried in his ass.

He pounds into me relentlessly. "Fuck. Fuck."

"Oh, god." I'm barely hanging on.

"That's it, take it. Take all I have to give you. And next time you want to suck my cock, you better do it while that sweet pussy is sitting on my face."

I'm no match for his dirty talk. My orgasm hits me like a tidal wave. The feeling of him above me, his masculine scent surrounding me, and the way his hand is wrapped around my throat. I'm drowning in sensation. In him. I never knew I'd like it like this, so primal. It's euphoric.

"Yes. That's it." He stills, and I can almost feel him pulsing inside of me. It's the last thing I remember before—

"Mellie! Mellie!"

What? I fight against the exhilaration I feel to lift my lids and see a frantic Huggie on top of me. He appears panic stricken.

Suddenly he jumps from the bed and darts over toward his clothes. *What the heck is happening?*

I struggle to speak. "Wait? Where are you going?"

"Fuck, Mel. I could've hurt you. You were out cold."

"What are you doing?"

He stops abruptly, standing up straight. "I need to go."

"Why?"

"I could've hurt you, Melanie."

"The only way you'll hurt me is if you walk out that door!" I cry.

Turning back to me, his expression changes to concern as he sees I'm becoming distraught. I don't have any control over my emotions right now. I went from the most incredible sex of my life to watching him almost storm out in mere minutes.

He rushes back to me, fully dressed, and takes me in his strong arms. "Shhh. I'm sorry."

"Don't leave. Please don't leave."

"I'd die if I hurt you. I looked down, and my hand was wrapped around your throat, and you were out cold."

Pushing away from him, I need him to see me. Really see me. "I loved every second of it. It was so good I must've blacked out for a minute. I don't hurt anywhere." I stop to check to make sure he hears what I'm saying. "Honestly, until the last minute, I didn't know your hand was there... but I liked it. All of it. I like everything you do to me."

His gaze is intense. I can't read it.

"I had no idea it could be like this," I tell him.

His shoulders appear to relax a bit, so I push forward.

"Please talk to me."

With that, he pulls me back into his chest as we recline against the pillows. I finally feel like I can exhale.

"Is that the way you always are?"

"What do you mean?"

"In bed? Wild and rough?" I can feel him stiffen around me again. "I told you. I liked it. But..."

"But, what?" he asks hesitantly.

"It's just so different from the man I know." Maybe that's what I like most. How he's this incredible friend, looks and acts like the boy next door, and then the lights go out, and BAM! "Huggie?"

"Yeah?"

"Will you please be truthful with me?"

He's silent for long minutes before answering, his voice low, "Yes. Always."

"Where do you meet women? There's no way someone with your skills in the bedroom is a monk."

"Mel."

That's all I get? You promised.

"I meet them in a few places. But it's nothing but a hookup."

I contemplate his words. Not that he shared much. "How do you find women who like it... well, like you do? Do you ask them that up front?"

He lets out a little groan of irritation, and I know I need to stop this conversation. Yet, he has to remember I've only been with one man before him. I just don't get how it works. "I'm not some sexual deviant, Melanie. I like what I like. With the right person, I think I'd enjoy every type of connection. Rough, dirty, sweet."

With the right person. The words cut through me. I don't know what I was expecting to feel. I mean, I asked him to have sex with me. Told him it was only physical. And then, after getting confused, I threw myself at him again. I should be grateful he was willing to give me this, no questions asked.

"I bet someone out there could give you all of that," I tell him. I'm starting to discover I want that person to be me. There's no transference about it.

But ultimately, this man deserves to be happy. And if our devotion to Jake can't allow for us to be together, he needs to know he's worthy of it with someone else.

"Mel. I know what I want, and I don't think that's possible for me. But thank you." He kisses my head, and that familiar ache in my chest returns. Why can't I still be basking in the glow of all that happened here?

Sitting up, I pull the sheets over my breasts and look at him. There has to be a reason he's chosen this. Is it his family situation? Knowing I'll likely never get this chance again, I'm taking it. "Why wouldn't it be possible for you? You have to know, any woman would be lucky to have you."

His face turns red. I worry I've pushed too far. But he's my friend. He cares so much for me that he'd risk our friendship to be intimate with me. Yet he can't talk about this? I almost feel offended.

"Why won't you talk to me?" I feel myself becoming upset and try to take a breath. "I'm closer to you than anyone. We've risked our friendship by doing this. And you can't even tell me why—"

"Because I'm no good for anyone! I go to sex clubs to get off because I can't get what I want any other way. Don't worry, I'm clean. I don't go often and get checked regularly." He pulls away and gets out of bed. He walks into the closet, and I practically feel the anger emanating toward me that I pushed him into divulging this.

God, was it worth it? I should've left well enough alone. None of this was any of my business. But it's like I can't stop myself.

He emerges, and I blurt out, "But why would you think that? That you're no good for anyone? You're one of the best men I've ever known."

Stopping at the foot of the bed, I see he's fully dressed and carrying his duffel bag. My heart sinks. "I'm going to the station. I'll need to be there in a few hours anyway." He starts toward the door and then stops before leaving. "What is this big meeting you have on a Saturday anyway?"

"I'm going to a group therapy session with Derek."

And with that, he walks away without another word.

CHAPTER TWENTY-FOUR

HUGGIE

"Hey, what are you doing here already? Bad night?"

"You could say that."

"Fuck, Huggie. You seemed like you were in a better mood when you left the club. What happened?"

"I don't want to talk about it."

"Mel?"

I just glare at him. I really don't want to rehash this. What would it solve? And I can't tell him everything, given that I snapped and told Melanie about going to The Rox when I'd hit my breaking point.

"Let's just say things are getting worse instead of better."

"Did you sleep with her again?"

"Yeah." I huff.

He gives me a confused look. "Was it that bad? Jeez, man. You finally sleep with this girl after all of these years. You'd think that alone would be enough to make you happy."

"Oh, trust me. Sleeping with Melanie is the opposite of bad. It's just all the baggage that comes with it."

Nate comes over and sits on the bunk next to mine. "Look. You're a grown man. Just tell her."

I look at him, alarmed. "Tell her what?"

"Everything. That you're in love with her. That you've always loved her. That the four of you belong together."

I shake my head in utter disbelief. "Have you lost your mind? I can't move in on my best friend's family. It's disrespectful. No, it's just plain wrong."

Nate moves to his bunk, where he lies back, crossing his arms behind his head. "Well, if you think your life sucks now when you're finally sleeping with the woman you love... just wait."

"Wait for what?"

"'Wait 'til someone else is."

My stomach drops. The thought of her with someone else is bad enough. Imagining their hands all over her is even worse.

"I think this is only physical for her. She's worried we've messed up our friendship, allowing this to happen. But, hell. I'm worried that's going to happen anyway if I see her with another man after years of feeling trapped." I picture her sitting beside the hot widower in group therapy. "I can't take it, Nate."

"Then what do you have to lose? Pull on your bootstraps and face this like any challenge on the job. Tell her how you feel. You can't live like this anymore."

We both lie still. The only sound is the loud clicking of the second hand on the cheap plastic clock on the wall.

I try to absorb what he's saying as if for the first time. Because I know we're reaching a pinnacle with how things have been lately. I need to decide once and for all.

Am I going to risk everything or walk away like a coward?

∼

"Hey, you guys hitting The Zone Friday?" Jamie asks as we sit in Waffle House, eating unidentifiable protein that's 'smothered and covered' with gravy.

"What's Friday?" I ask.

"The Manning brothers organized a Christmas Party. No one wants to clean up at their house behind a bunch of us, so some of the guys pitched in and reserved the VIP space for the night."

"Man, that's great," Nate says around a bite of food. "I'm in."

I continue to eat this unappealing food. I'm not interested in anything *party related.*

"What about you?" Nate nudges.

"I don't know. I'm not really in the mood. Between work and the movie set, I'm exhausted. Thinking about getting away for the weekend."

"Well, do that Saturday. Hang with us for the night Friday, and then go," Nate says.

"Trevor Laurence moved to Sycamore Mountain. Zach told me he went for a visit and loved the place. Said it's God's country down there. Maybe he can hook you up?" Jamie says.

What is in that breakfast? That's the most words I think I've ever heard Jamie string together in one sitting. Inspecting him closer, he seems different.

"What?"

"What's up with you, man?"

"I'm hungry." He chuckles. *Chuckles.* That fucker is getting laid. I'm sure of it.

"Jamie, call Zach and get Huggie the details. He's coming out with us Friday before he goes to get right with nature," Nate says.

"What the fuck? When did you become my personal secretary?" I ask him.

Nate looks down at his phone and then turns it to me so I can see the schedule for the movie shoot. "You're free and clear."

"Man, this place is packed," Nate yells over his beer. I have to admit that I'm glad I came. Just seeing him and Adam together here makes it worth it.

"Here," Tate says, handing me another cold one.

"Thanks."

There are tons of people on the dance floor and mingling around the dark, smoky edges of the club. The strobe lights and fog are working overtime. I'm too old for this shit, but I don't mind hanging in the VIP section with my crew. It feels as if this area is a separate entity, and I can just relax, even if the music is not my style and is *way* too loud.

My eyes scan the room. There are dozens and dozens of hot girls with barely-there holiday wear on. Lots of skin-tight dresses adorned with flashing lights and sparkling jewelry. Why can't I just focus on one of them?

It's as if a genie has sprung from a bottle when my eyes land on one particular female—a tall, dark-haired female with a tight red dress and legs that go for miles. I'd be shocked at letting myself enjoy anyone but Melanie if I didn't already know from looking at this woman's shapely ass...

It is Melanie.

Sitting up in my seat, I consider whether she came here with Derek until I see Kat standing by her side. My eyes dart around the space. He could still be here.

My eyes refocus on where she's standing when I notice Kat pointing directly at me. Melanie turns, and I immediately lick my lips. She's a goddess. Her bright red lips match her dress, and all I can think about is the way they looked wrapped around my dick the other night. What the hell is wrong with me?

Mel gives me a bright smile from across the room. It's so glorious I have to force myself to continue breathing. We haven't spoken since I left her home. I only assumed she'd be upset with my behavior. But my chest warms that this beauty is standing there, smiling directly at me in all of her glory.

I take another swig of my beer and lean back in my chair, watching her. I'm too tired to care if anyone notices. My biggest challenge right now is keeping my dick concealed. There's going to be a lot of jerking off to thoughts of her taking that little red number off, especially now that I know what lies beneath.

She glides about the room on her four-inch black stilettos as if she owns the place. Kat exudes a similar confidence, but her's is more playful. Where Mellie always has that pose-ready expression. Like a pin-up girl.

My fucking pin-up girl.

Some random guy approaches and has the balls to lay his hand on her lower back, and I almost shoot up from my chair.

"Calm down, killer. Just give it a minute."

I look at Nate, wondering what he's talking about before returning my angry glare toward the newcomer. I witness a silent conversation between them before the guy walks off, and Melanie turns to Kat.

Leaning back into my chair, my eyes land on Nate. "How'd you know?"

"Shit, man. That girl dressed up and came here for you."

Stunned at his reply, my eyes land back on her. She has her incredible back to me but looks over her shoulder in my direction, and I instantly know he's right. Adjusting in my seat, I feel taller, a sense of hopeful anticipation squeezing into every ounce of my being.

I find it odd they haven't come over. Nate's practically Kat's best friend, and Adam is here. Am I getting ahead of myself, believing Nate? Or is she playing coy? It dawns on me I haven't exactly been displaying a come hither expression since I got here.

I try to look elsewhere to get this damn boner under control when I feel her near me.

"Hey, guys," Kat says, leaning in to kiss Nate and Adam.

My eyes instantly connect with Melanie's, and I feel a crackle of electricity between us. Shit. Is it going to be like this every time we're together now? Am I going to want to sleep with her every time I bump into her in the freezer section? Or fuck her against the car if I pull up at the gas station and she's filling up?

"Hi, Huggie," Mel says.

"Hi," I answer. This is awkward as hell. I'm sitting here among my colleagues and friends, trying to pretend this girl is nothing more to me than a pal. Yet, I have a raging hard-on about to rip through my slacks. "You look nice."

"Thanks." She turns to Nate and Adam. "You guys want to come dance with us?"

"Sure," they tell her as they eagerly stand from their chairs. The four start to walk toward the dance floor, but not before Nate smacks me against the back of the head.

I order one last beer from a passing server and wonder if I shouldn't go to the men's room and splash some water on my face versus sitting here and torturing myself. Because there's no doubt if she's swaying that sensational ass about the dance floor, that's exactly where my eyes will be. And this stiff dick will be evident to everyone within a fifty-foot radius.

Placing my bottle on the table, I decide to get some air—clear my head. *I'm making myself fucking crazy.* I head for the back hallway, knowing I can dart out without being detected. It's a doorway I've noticed staff stepping out of to have a smoke.

As the cool night air hits my face, I instantly feel better. It was getting overwhelming in there—too many eyes on us. Too many dirty thoughts I should tamp down. We've let this get far enough. My life was a mess before, but I spend every waking moment obsessing over her now.

As if my thoughts have conjured the one thing I want most, I turn to find Melanie at my side.

"What are you doing here?"

"Dancing," she answers, almost defensively.

"I meant—"

"Do you not want me here?" she asks.

I want you everywhere. Can't you see?

She comes to stand directly in front of me, wrapping her arms around my neck and laying a soft kiss on my adam's apple.

"Mellie? What are we doing? Someone could see."

Her dark, violet eyes stare into me with an almost frightening intensity. I have the distinct impression we're approaching a precipice, which can only go one of two ways.

Her hand drops to cup my engorged cock and squeezes. "I need you."

I have to gulp down my shock. She needs *me*? Me? I don't let another second pass. Lifting her into my arms, I turn so her back is to the wall.

"You need me to fuck you right here?"

"Yes."

Rotating my head from side to side, I ensure we're alone. "This is risky, Mel. Someone could see."

"I know."

"Is that what you want? You want someone to come down the alley and see me railing you?" I pant as I bite into her neck.

She shakes her head, and I stop, worrying I've gone too far. "I don't want that. I just want you. Please?" Her pelvis grinds into my needy cock, and I groan.

Reaching underneath her skirt, I rip her tiny thong before attempting to lower my zipper. I jump when I hear something until I realize one of her shoes has tumbled to the ground.

"We have to be quick."

"Yes."

"Are you ready for me, Mellie?" I dip my finger into her pussy and moan. I have my dick in my hand in a flash, lining it up with her entrance. Her heat guides me, and I growl as the head of my cock slips in.

"Oh, god. It's so good," she whimpers into my ear. Her words and her eagerness are driving me to the brink.

"Fuck, your pussy is so wet." I groan. "How'd you get so turned on, Mellie? Were you thinking about riding my dick?" I breathe heavily. "Or is it the thought of my face between your thighs that gets you wet?"

"All of it." Planting her mouth over mine, we try to kiss, but it's tough to maintain a connection when I'm plowing into her like this.

I hold her against the wall, drilling into her, growling against her collarbone as I chase my orgasm. *This fucking woman.* No one will ever do it for me but her. "Ahhhh!" I groan out, feeling the impending force of this climax barreling toward me.

"I'm coming. I'm coming."

"Fuck." I press my full weight into her, crushing her against the bricks as I empty my load. I'm shaking from the force of it, burying my face in her throat.

As my breathing calms, and I finally withdraw from her, it hits me. *Shit!*

"Mel—"

"It's okay. I got on the pill."

"You did?"

"Yeah. I felt like it was the smart thing to do. It should be ready to go."

Should?

"I'm more worried about how I'm going to go back in there with no panties."

What the fuck was I thinking? "Follow me back in, and we'll head to the bathroom." But she's definitely not staying here without panties. That's for damn sure.

I reach for the shoe that had fallen onto the ground. As I help her to step inside, I see my seed dripping down her leg and almost roar. I've avoided marking her in this way. Knowing I'd replay the sight. But there's no sense avoiding this. Whether she's wearing my spunk or not, she's mine.

She'll always be mine.

CHAPTER TWENTY-FIVE

HUGGIE

Gazing at the clouds as I lie by this pond, I smile at the memory of the other night. We excused ourselves, saying Melanie had a stomach ache, and drove home with our hands entwined. It was probably unwise to leave together, but I'm quickly approaching the point that I don't give a shit anymore. So long as it doesn't affect her.

I know I need to make some tough decisions. I almost canceled yesterday morning and stayed at the house, wanting to be near her. But we've done this dance long enough. And this place promised to have Mother Nature's energy, a peaceful setting to clear my thoughts under this art gallery of white cirrus clouds dancing on a bright blue sky.

There's nothing I want more than a life with Melanie and her children. It seems ridiculous to keep suffering because of this guilt. Jake was a good man. He loved Melanie and wanted her to be happy. And I know he felt the same about me.

I think he always knew I was in love with his wife. He just never let on. He'd never want to embarrass me in that way. I hope he respected what I gave up for our friendship. Not that she had eyes for anyone but her husband.

I think back to Nate and Adam at the club the other night. How brave Nate's been to go all in, despite the fears of how his brotherhood would welcome his partner. Then add the struggle of planning a wedding and a future while shunned by his family. I'm simply a chicken shit for not going after what I want and letting fears of what other people think get in the way. Jake would forgive me. Hell, there are times I think he'd want me to be with her.

The night he died has replayed on autopilot more times than I can count. It was obvious he and Melanie were arguing. It's not like him to look so pensive. And when she arrived at the bar, she kept her distance from him until right before she left. I got the feeling harsh words were exchanged from his demeanor.

But it was what he said to me later that's plagued me.

"Do you want another beer?" I'd asked.

"No, I need to get home and fix this."

"That bad?"

"Yeah. She deserves better than me." He looked at me as if he was trying to relay some morse code as he stood before heading for the door. *"She deserves the best. Someone like you."*

I breathe in a lung full of crisp mountain air. There are times my mind plays tricks on me. It's as if he knew what was coming and was giving me permission. I'm sure this is only morbid wishful thinking. This whole scenario is ludicrous.

Staring at the clouds, I chuckle. "Why can't you just send me a sign? Something concrete to know you're okay with this? Couldn't one of those billowy white masses turn into a thumbs-up or something? That you understand." But the landscape doesn't change. The clouds above me don't alter their shape.

I need to pack up soon. It's not a far drive, but I'd prefer to get home at a decent hour, get a bite to eat, and have a good hard sleep before work tomorrow. I've decided to stay at my place for the time being. I told Melanie this week I'd be tied up between this trip out of town, working every other day at the firehouse, and the shifts at the movie set. Oh, and that campout.

Our group, with the permission of the production crew, has held a family campout every year. The kids look forward to it. We find a safe area amongst the set and allow the family members of our team to join us in popping up tents and sleeping under the stars. It's become so popular we've actually had a few of the *stars* join us. Several years ago, we were hired to assist with the production of a new indie movie in Petersburg. A few principal actors were so happy with how the filming had been going that they flew their families out to join us.

Financially, I don't need to work so much. Honestly, I could quit one of these jobs. I've invested well. So long as the stock market continues to go my way, I don't need to work. But it keeps my mind focused on something other than my ridiculous life.

∽

"Hey, how was your weekend?" Nate asks.

"Good. I needed it. Thanks."

"So? Were you able to make any decisions about how to handle things?"

"I haven't completely decided," I answer honestly. I want to just go over there and tell her how I feel. But after all of this time, I need to be one hundred percent sure before I risk ruining our friendship.

∽

Honk. Honk. Honk. Honk.

The loud overhead tones barrel down on us, and we instinctively head toward the engine. It's not until we've pulled out, lights and sirens blazing, that the dispatcher shares that the call is for a motor vehicle accident along the highway—an accident involving an EMS unit.

Nate and Jamie look at me in alarm, all of us remaining silent as we race down the highway to the location of the accident.

We arrive on scene and jump from the engine. Each of us runs full speed toward the vehicles involved. There's a car on the shoulder, an ambulance parked behind it, and another vehicle along the grassy edge in the distance. One of the drivers waves us to them frantically.

"What happened?" Nate asks as we notice Henry, a volunteer EMS provider we've known for years, lying on the ground.

"They arrived to help me. I was having chest pain and got scared and called 911," the elderly woman states. *Hell, how many patients do we have here?* "I didn't want to leave my car on the side of the highway, but they insisted I come with them to get evaluated. I didn't want a stretcher, so I followed them down here when this car veered into us."

I drop to one knee, attempting to assess Henry, and notice a state trooper with the driver who slammed into Henry. But there's no time to worry about that right now.

"Henry, bud, what hurts?"

"It's his leg," a junior squad member states. I don't recognize this kid, but he couldn't be more than twenty and looks like he's in shock. Fuck, I would be too. In all the years I volunteered, I never had to endure anything like this. All three of them could've been killed.

"I tried to splint it, but he's in too much pain."

"Are you allowed to give meds?" I ask, knowing a lot of the new EMTs do not have the qualifications to start IVs or give medication.

"No."

"Jamie, grab the drug box!" I yell.

"Hang in there, Henry. We're going to get you some medicine and then splint this leg." I notice the bleeding on his trousers is on the lower leg. Pointing to it, I ask, "Is this where it hurts?"

"Yeah." He breathes out.

Thank God. A femur fracture could be much worse.

"Anything else hurt? Your hips or your back?"

"No." He grunts. "I didn't hit my head or lose consciousness. It's just the leg."

We get Henry medicated, splinted, and loaded onto the ambulance. The Hammer volunteers to drive to the hospital, and I ride in the back with Sam, the EMT-basic, after he obtains an EKG from the original patient. I'm trying to keep an eye on him after everything he's been through, but keeping him occupied may help keep his mind from wandering to 'what if's.'

"Meet you at the hospital," Nate yells.

As we close the doors and head down the highway, Henry asks, "Think they'll let me go home tonight?"

"I seriously doubt it," I tell him.

"Damn. It's my wedding anniversary. I've never spent one away from my wife."

"I think she'll understand." I chuckle. "Can she come to the hospital to be with you?" Henry is probably in his sixties. I don't want to assume I know his wife's situation.

"Yeah." He grows quiet. "It just throws a wrench into my plans."

"A broken leg can do that," I tell him. "How long have you two been married?"

"Five years," he answers, surprising me. At his age, I guess I was expecting a lot longer. "She was my childhood sweetheart. But life got in the way back then. We didn't find our way back to one another until five years ago." He stops, and I'm unsure if the pain is coming back. "So much time wasted."

I try to stay focused on taking his vitals and writing my report to prepare for arrival at the ER. But his familiar story is pulling at my heart.

"Huggie?"

"Yeah?"

"Would you mind calling my son for me? Let him know what happened so he can drive her to me?"

"Of course."

We arrive at the hospital and Jamie runs over to help Sam and me lower the stretcher from the back of the ambulance. As the ER doors open, I search for a nurse to guide us to the bed he's been assigned. I see someone on a phone mouth, 'number five,' and we head in that direction and carefully slide Henry from our gurney to the larger stretcher sitting in the center of the room. I'm about to turn when I feel Henry's hand upon my arm.

"Hey, these red roses are Mellie's favorite," he comments looking at the ink on my upper arm.

I freeze. What did he say?

"Who?"

"Melinda. My wife." My head is practically spinning at the remark. "Oh, and let me get my cell phone for my son's number. I don't know anyone's by heart anymore. They're all trapped in my phone."

"I get it. I'm the same way."

"Here it is." He holds his phone out to me, and I take it so I can copy the number down for the nurses as well as myself.

After scribbling down the number, I go to write his name and laugh. "Should I call him Scooter?"

"Ha." He laughs. "No. His name is Jake."

The week passes quickly amongst the two jobs. The days at both have been busier than those of late. Primarily minor injuries and small brush fires, but it's occupied my mind. But not busy enough to ignore how I feel.

I'm all in. It's just a matter of timing now.

I throw my toiletry bag into my knapsack and head for the door. This campout should be fun. I haven't seen much of Ruby and Seth in the last few weeks, and the weather is supposed to be beautiful but cold. We knew it would be chilly camping out in December, but they are letting us sleep in the little log cabins that were built for the movie. Some have working fireplaces, and a few others have built-in space heaters. The thing they don't have is inside plumbing.

Pulling up to Melanie's place, I see the kids peeking out of the front window. Yeah. They're not excited.

"Huggie!" Ruby yells.

"Hi, Rubs." I clutch her to me as she collides with my chest. "You guys all set?"

Seth grins. "Yeah, I'll put our stuff in the back of your truck."

"It's going to be cold. Did you pack enough to stay warm?" I ask Ruby.

"Mom made me pack long underwear."

I laugh. "Well, that was smart."

"Long underwear makes me itch."

"Well, you'll appreciate it when you have to go outside in the middle of the night."

"Why would I do that?"

"To go to the bathroom," I tell her.

Her mouth drops open. "There's no bathroom in the cabin?"

"Nope, not even a sink."

We arrive on set and immediately see that the guys have constructed a bonfire. It's still fairly early, but the sky has already grown dark. The kids are excited. Ruby's face is practically pinned to the window. I place my hand over Melanie's and give it a squeeze. She looks back at me with a broad smile, and I know if I get cold, that's all I'll need to keep me warm.

I park, and we gather our things from the back of the truck before heading toward the crew.

"Hey, Huggie. You guys are staying in that cabin." Jeff points. After the kids and Melanie have sped up in that direction, I hear behind me. "We heard it was haunted."

I twist back around to look at him.

"You guys are the last ones here." He shrugs his shoulders like this is common sense. The owner of this business, where these guys are generously compensated, gets the haunted house for the night.

I enter the small space to find Seth and Ruby constructing a makeshift fort in the corner from the sparse furnishings here. "Don't you think you'll need those later when it gets cold?"

"Nah, our sleeping bags are warm," Seth says.

I turn to find Melanie laying out her sleeping bag on the floor with a pillow at the top.

"You too?"

"What?"

"You have some sort of thermal sleeping bag?"

"As a matter of fact, I do." She giggles.

I take in the meager setup I've brought along and wonder if I'll make it through the night without frostbite.

We enjoy an evening among friends, singing campfire songs, roasting hot dogs and marshmallows, and a few of the guys inventing ghost stories for the kids. Luckily, the tales remain tame. Particularly after the whole, *it's haunted* routine.

Everyone says their goodnights, and we move our way toward the cabin. The kids look tired after chasing each other through the open field in the cold. Seth and Ruby take a small battery-charged lantern and a bag of popcorn into their fort after wishing us good night.

Melanie and I go to our respective sleeping bags and try to settle in. She's been quiet much of the night. Has something happened? Is she upset after we lost control outside the club the other night? Or could it be because I've practically ghosted her since then?

"How has your week been?" I ask. "I missed you and the kids."

A small smile turns the corners of her lips, and I instantly feel better.

"It was good. Busy. But for the first time, I'm starting to think I can manage all of this."

Wait? Does that mean she doesn't need me there anymore? I mean, I'm proud of her. I am. But I don't want to go back home. Not now, when I'm trying to get the nerve to tell her I'm all in.

"That's great," I say, lying on my side facing her. She's not looking in my direction but staring at the ceiling.

Suddenly, the door flies open, and the two of us sit up from where we're lying. A burst of cold air flies into the room. Scrambling out of my sleep sack, I rush over, look to make sure no one's trying to come in, and quickly close the door until I hear it click into place.

I dart back over, seeking refuge in the thin sack as my nuts shrivel to the size of peanuts. "I think it's dropped twenty degrees since we came in here."

Melanie lies back down, and I shiver, pulling a wool blanket from my knapsack to try to add another layer of warmth. *Why couldn't we get the cabin with the fireplace?*

Moments later, I hear a creaking noise, and the cabin walls begin to rattle. Inching my sleeping bag closer to Melanie's, I whisper, "What the hell is that?"

"I think it's the wind." She laughs. Her sweet sound soothes my nerves a bit.

I lie back down and try to rub my hands up and down my arms when I notice something odd in the window. It's small and round and gray in appearance. The plastic window panes in the cabins are frosted for shooting indoor scenes. Is someone looking in here?

"Mellie?" I whisper as I scoot closer to her bag.

"Yeah?"

"What is that?"

"What?"

"In the window?"

She rolls in my direction, our faces practically touching before she looks over to where the object was taunting me moments ago. "I don't see anything."

I look back over my shoulder and realize it's gone. *I'm losing it.*

A wolf howls in the distance, and I continue to inchworm over to her inside my sleeping bag. The kids must be asleep, as I haven't heard a peep.

"What's wrong now?" Melanie teases.

"You didn't hear that?"

"Hear what?"

"It was like a wolf or something."

"Huggie. We're in Richmond, not the wild."

"Whatever." I reach over and slowly unzip her bag until I can lift up the top layer enough to curl up next to her.

"What are you doing?"

"I'm cold," I say. *Sounds better than scared.*

Reaching back for my blanket, I again notice the light gray orb in the window. What the hell is that? I curl even closer to Melanie as if she can protect me.

"We shouldn't be doing this with the kids here," she says quietly.

"I'm just protecting you."

"Sure you are. From what, exactly?" She laughs.

I try to come up with an answer when I hear the sound of something scratching behind me. Rolling over, the orb is there with an odd light shimmering behind it. "Hey, where did we leave the flashlight?"

"It's by the door. Where are you going?"

"I think my beer caught up with me." I refrain from telling her I'm afraid I'll pee in my pants if any other weird shit happens.

"Okay. Be careful." *That's it. No offer to come with me?*

I get up from the floor and look through the dark for my coat and the flashlight. Braving it to the bathroom located in a large portable unit about fifty feet away, I shine the light all around the front of the cabin to see if anything resembling the gray blob is there. Nothing. Well, except there's a large clump of brown and orange poop near the steps. What the hell dumped that there? I shine the light all around to no avail.

Walking swiftly to the porta-bathrooms, I swing my light back and forth along the way in case I spot any of the wildlife that could've made the sounds I heard earlier. Again, nothing.

Once inside, I notice the lid is closed, so I put the flashlight down, lift it up, and empty my bladder. Reaching down to retrieve the flashlight, I go to stand and—

"Holy shit!"

I take off running, trying to hold my pants up as I sprint to the cabin. That was the biggest snake I've ever seen. I'm lucky he didn't bite my pecker when I peed all over it curled up inside the commode. I'm about twenty feet from the cabin when I hear that wolf thing howling again.

"Jesus," I yell as I try to run faster while not losing my pants completely.

Just as I reach the steps, multiple flashlights come on, and I see Jeff and Paxton holding a grey balloon and laughing hysterically. Two others come around the cabin, doubled over in laughter.

"Ha Ha. Keep it down, will ya," I bark just as Jeff bends down to scrape the poop off the ground with his bare hand. "What the—" I can almost taste the bile rising up my throat as he puts it in his mouth. "The fuck?"

"Never let a good Reese's cup go to waste."

"I'm going to kill every one of you fuckers."

They all bust up laughing, and I stomp past them into the cabin. I shine the light briefly toward Seth and Ruby's fort. By some miracle, it appears they slept through all of that. When I return the light in the direction of my sleeping bag, I see Melanie sitting upright.

"Awe, Mel. I'm sorry if I woke you."

"No, it wasn't you. I swear I heard a little girl screaming."

Fuck me. "Go on back to bed. I apologize in advance if my chattering teeth keep you up."

"Is it that cold out there?" she asks, snuggling back into her sack.

"I'm shivering like a mobster in a tax office."

I can feel her back rumble against my chest in laughter. "What?"

"You never heard that one? How about, it's so cold I farted snowflakes," I whisper.

"Oh, my god."

I fold my frigid body around her toasty one and bury my face in her hair. "It's so cold, Miley Cyrus got stuck on her wrecking ball."

"Please stop." She laughs.

I wrap my arm around her. "What are you doing? Your arm feels like a frozen slab of beef."

"I'll show you a slab of beef," I tell her as I push my hips into her. Trust me, there's nothing hard going on down there. My junk is completely frozen, but with her lying next to me, it'll only take minutes to heat things up.

Melanie rolls over, facing me, and rubs her warm hands up and down my arms. My teeth are still chattering. Raising her hands, she cups my cheeks. "They're so cold." She leans in closer, rubbing her warm nose over my frozen one, then drags her hot, wet tongue over my lips and kisses me. Yep, it took mere minutes for my cock to thaw and stiffen.

I'm shocked when Melanie slides her toasty palm down my belly and into my pants. She grabs ahold of my growing erection and skillfully strokes it.

"Ohhh." I groan. "I'd offer to repay the favor, but I'm not sure you want my frozen fingers in your hot little—

"Shhh."

"Should you be doing this?" I ask, desperately hoping she doesn't stop.

"Probably not. But if the kids come out, we're clothed and covered."

"You're such a good mom, Mellie." I chuckle. "But I meant, should you be doing this because if I come all over your hand, it'll freeze on the way to the porta-potty."

"Oh, my god."

"Shhh. Keep rubbing. The frostbite is almost gone."

I feel her giggle against my throat again.

We lie there, kissing as she continues to give me the best hand job of my life. She nibbles on my lips, unaffected by my heavy breathing.

"Mellie, I'm getting close." I groan quietly.

Reaching behind her, she brings back her tiny sleep shirt.

I'm shocked to see it, as cold as it is. She wraps it around her hand and continues to tug on my cock. The image of her beautiful, full breasts pressed against that top cause me to close my eyes and visualize fucking them. "Mel." I moan into her neck as I squeeze her ass. "Mel." My balls draw up, and I have to bite down on my lip to prevent groaning too loud when the first spurts of come shoot into her shirt-covered hand.

I'm trembling for a whole different reason now. It's on the tip of my tongue. I want to tell her how I feel. But I can't blurt that out here.

"Mommy," I hear in the darkness.

Shit. I roll back toward my sleep sack and make sure everything is tucked into place.

"Yeah, baby?"

"I have to go to the bathroom," Ruby says with a yawn.

"Me too. Let's get bundled up, okay?"

"You need me to come with you?" I ask them.

"No. I wouldn't want to feel responsible for waking up any other campers if you saw something that made you squeal again."

CHAPTER TWENTY-SIX

MELANIE

"Hey, how are you?" I greet Kat on the soccer field.

"We're good," she says as she comes over for a hug. Grace is bundled in multiple layers and tries to run about but only makes a few steps before falling. It seems so long ago that my two were learning how to walk.

Nick is coaching Seth and Ruby's team in preparation for their first indoor soccer league. This league allows both of their age groups on the same team, which helps single parents tremendously. They only get to compete indoors, so practices are limited to the arctic afternoon and evenings on their regular field or a local park, whichever is available.

"How's the hospital?" I ask her.

"Busy. The usual. It really doesn't change much." She shakes her head. "How's Dr. McHotty?"

I roll my eyes. "Kat. Nothing is happening there. He's sweet. And he's a dream to work for."

"And he's hot as hell," she says, looking to ensure little ears aren't nearby. "You aren't the least bit attracted?"

"Well, I wouldn't go that far." It's about that time I spot Huggie walking over toward Nick. When did he get here? I refocus my attention on Kat, who's noticed and follows where my gaze has been trained. "I actually went to a group therapy meeting with him not long ago."

Her head snaps back to me with a look of shock. "You did?"

"Yeah. It wasn't as intimidating as I thought it'd be."

"Was it helpful?"

"Yeah, I think. It was nice hearing other people's perspectives on their grieving process. Made me feel better about how long it's taken for me to get to this point."

Kat reaches a hand out to stroke my arm. "Oh, Mel. You've done amazing. Don't ever doubt that."

"You're right. Nothing about this has been easy. I'm still struggling a little with how I neglected my kids, but otherwise, I'm so far from where I started."

She pulls me in for a hug, and I try not to get too emotional. "I'm actually meeting with Munish in a few days. I'm going to tell him I'm not interested in any more updates or pursuing a civil case against Mark."

"Wow. Really?"

"It wouldn't solve anything. I'm still mad. But I think continuing to feed that negativity will only hold me back. I'm ready to put that awful time behind me."

A whistle blows in the distance, and I turn to see the kids' scrimmage has begun. I refrain from cheering them on, as they've been put into teams playing against one another. But Huggie has no problem shouting their names proudly as they chase the ball as if it were a tournament.

His eyes connect with mine as if he's heard my inner dialogue, and the most beautiful smile takes over his handsome face. The warmth from my blush instantly heats my cheeks. This is bad. I can't stop thinking about him.

"Holy shit."

I turn to Kat, worried Grace has fallen, and see her staring at me with her mouth hanging open.

"What?"

"You're sleeping with him."

"What?" My voice doesn't sound as forceful as it should if I'm going to challenge this.

She steps up close enough that a puff of frosty air hits me in the face. "You. Are. Sleeping. With. Him."

I'm so stunned that I open my mouth and immediately close it again. A huge lump in my throat makes it hard to breathe until Kat's megawatt smile takes over her face. The relief is instant.

"How long has this been going on?" she asks, flicking her eyes between her toddler and me.

"Nothing is going on," I try to clarify. "I basically asked him to make me feel alive again." I stop, unable to believe I'm sharing this with anyone. "And he did."

Kat starts dancing in place, and I panic.

"Please. Don't. We don't want anyone getting ideas."

She instantly looks perplexed. "Ideas about what? You two are perfect for each other."

"Kat," I scold. "He's not into relationships. You know that. And, well, I don't know what I'm ready for."

Kat grabs my hands, giving me a look of sincerity that almost makes me tear up. "Mel. It's been years. Don't do this to yourself."

"Do what? Other than you, he's my best friend. What if this doesn't work? I can't lose him too."

Realizing this isn't just some fling, her face becomes more serious. "You're right. But—"

"Plus, there are the kids to think about. They'd be devastated if we tried dating, and it wasn't in the cards for us."

She grows quiet, tilting her head as if questioning me. "How do things stand now? I mean, if you aren't interested in pursuing this with him. I don't think he caught the memo."

Looking over my shoulder, I see Nick and Huggie speaking to one another, but Huggie's eyes are locked on me.

"I'm not sure. I want to see Dr. Miller again to talk about all of this. But..."

"But, what?"

Turning back to him, I can almost see his silvery blue eyes smiling down at me. "Kat, I think I'm willing to risk it."

∽

"Mel, it's good to see you."

"Hi, Munish. It's good to see you too."

"You said you needed to speak with me about Jake's case, so I wanted to fit you in before the holidays. To hopefully give you closure, regardless of the direction you're headed."

"Thank you. I appreciate that." I pick at the hem of my sweater, which I hadn't realized was unraveling. How had that happened? And this is my favorite sweater. I grimace.

"You okay?" Munish asks.

"Oh, I'm sorry. My mind wandered. Funny how things can sneak up on you right under your nose." He remains quiet, and I put all of my cards on the table. "I've decided to close this chapter, Munish. I want to move forward with my life. Christmas seems like the right time to do that. Start fresh, and do what's best for my family."

Leaning forward in his chair, he places his forearms on the desk in front of him. "So, we're discontinuing pursuing any charges against Mark."

"Yes."

"I think that's wise, Melanie. It's not to say we couldn't win if we attempted it, but it wouldn't be easy. And the cost to you and your children by rehashing all of the dirty details in public might be painful."

Is he referring to emotional damage? I mean, Jake's gone. Other than staying trapped in that horrible time, reliving it, what other cost is there?

I sit a little taller, suddenly feeling immensely proud of how far I've come. "I'm not sure I understand. What dirty details?"

He gives me a blank expression, and my mood shifts from pride to utter dread.

HUGGIE

"Hi. Could I have a dozen deep red roses, please?"

"Hi, Mr. Hughes," Tuesday greets. She's been working at Cynature

Blooms for several years now. I've come to count on her whenever I need something special. "Would you like them in a vase or wrapped in pretty paper?"

"Paper is fine."

"Any card?" Her green eyes twinkle, awaiting my response.

"No. I'm hand delivering these."

The pretty young lady scurries off to prepare my flowers, and I roam nervously about the shop. A variety of floral arrangements are on display. Some are bright and colorful, and others are monochromatic. All of them rival the flowers I've seen prepared in other floral shops. Guess that's why I keep coming back.

"How are these?" she asks from behind me.

Her arms are extended with a dozen brilliant, long-stemmed scarlet red roses.

"They're perfect." I smile back at her. She has dark blonde hair with streaks of auburn. Obviously, not my type, but there's something about this young woman that is enchanting.

"Okay, I'll be right back." With that, she darts around the corner to a hidden shop area where I assume all of the magic happens.

I put my hands in my pant pockets to calm my nerves. I can't believe I'm doing this. I've never been more uneasy about anything in my life. Starting my business, graduating from the fire academy, and even making arrangements for Jake's funeral. Nothing can touch the anxiety I'm feeling about telling Melanie I love her.

"Thank you for waiting," Tuesday says, making me jump. "Oh, I'm sorry. I didn't mean to startle you."

"Ah. Saw that, did you?"

She giggles, and it reminds me of my girl. "Must be an extraordinary person receiving these." She beams.

Extraordinary. "Yes. Yes, she is."

~

I approach the porch steps and have to take a few deep breaths. *Holy fuck. Is this really happening?* I'm physically shaking. Apparently, rehearsing what I'm going to say over and over in the car has done nothing for my nerves.

Get yourself together, George. Why would she say no? You two are great together. She has to see that. If there are issues regarding Jake, we'll talk them out because I've never felt more certain of anything. I feel it in my bones that I have his blessing here.

I ring the bell and wait for her to answer. I confirmed she'd be home this afternoon before I came. I wanted a few child-free hours to do this. And this is a big fucking deal. No way I can waltz into her home like I own the place.

Looking around, I see the mailman down the street and start to feel ridiculous. Should I just go in instead of standing here looking like a tool? Fortunately, I don't have to second guess this long as the door opens and Melanie comes into view.

Standing here, dressed in dark suit pants, a white button-down, and my peacoat, holding out these flowers like some sappy Hallmark Christmas movie, I immediately know I've made a mistake. Melanie's eyes are bloodshot, and her face is stained with tearful trails of mascara.

"Mellie, what—"

"Don't Mellie me."

What the...? I have to take a step back. Alarm bells are going off in my head. "Melanie, what's going on?"

"Let's see. I saw Munish this morning."

I stare blankly at her. Is that supposed to mean something?

"I told him I wanted to discontinue any more discussions about pursuing a civil case against Mark." I decide to remain quiet since I have no idea where this is going. "He told me it was probably a good thing. Given all of Jake's dirty laundry."

Shit.

"Turns out he hadn't mentioned it before because he assumed I knew." My pulse is pounding in my ears. "He'd confirmed after the accident that Jake's alcohol was below the legal limit. As was Mark's."

I feel as if I'm standing in front of a judge myself right now. And nothing about this scenario is going to end well.

"But the fact Jake was still driving under a restricted license, given his two convictions for drinking under the influence, would make it very difficult to prove Mark caused this accident," she seethes. Her anger is palpable.

I can feel all of the color drain from my face. Jesus, what do I do?

"And it appears you knew all about this, given you posted bail both times and were the one driving him to appointments with Munish."

"Mel—"

"Don't! There's nothing you can say that will justify keeping this from me. Nothing! Beyond the fact I trusted you. My children were getting in the car with him. My children, George."

Fuck.

"I didn't know what to do, Melanie. He asked me for help. I was between a rock and a hard place."

"Well, I see who won. Where your allegiance was, and it wasn't to the three innocent bystanders in this equation."

I drop my head in shame. I've wanted to tell her so many times. Tried to get Jake to admit it. He'd gone to alcoholics anonymous and turned things around. He was limiting the sleeping pills, or so he said. But she's right. I should've given him an ultimatum. That either he told her or I would. She deserved to know.

Yet, I didn't want anything coming out that could tarnish his reputation once he died. He couldn't defend himself. He was a good man who made mistakes but tried to turn things around.

As I raise my gaze from my feet to plead with her to forgive me, I catch a glimpse of something near the doorway. My bags. She's packed my bags. I'm suddenly filled with panic.

"Mel, please?"

"Please, what? What could you possibly say that would make this all right?" she cries out. "He had my children in the car with him, Huggie. What if something had happened to them?"

I'm at a loss for words. Nothing I practiced on the way here prepared me for this.

"You two. All this time, I thought he'd been tirelessly working in the ER day after day. They were always so short staffed." She sneers. "Never considering he'd served time in the county jail."

Fuck. It just keeps getting worse. What had I been thinking? He was my friend. My only focus was protecting him. Melanie belonged to him. As much as I wanted to tell her the truth, it wasn't my place.

"And if he couldn't drive, guess who was getting him to work? How many months did that happen before he got his license back, Huggie?"

"Four," I mutter.

"Four months. Four. You two must have had this operation down to a science so I wouldn't find out."

What do I do? There has to be something. I step forward, hoping I can get her to listen. "Melanie, I'm begging you—"

"Please, just take your things and go." She pauses for a moment. I can feel my heart about to pound right through my chest. "And to think I was struggling with—" She stops, turning her head to look away from me. She's either deciding not to share any more with me or simply composing herself as a solitary tear tumbles down her cheek.

I feel like I'm going to be sick. "I'm sorry." Placing the roses on the floor, I reach for my bag and try like hell to keep my shit together.

When all I really want to do is tell her I love her and beg her to forgive me.

CHAPTER TWENTY-SEVEN

MELANIE

"Mommy," Ruby yells from downstairs. "Where are you?"

Dabbing a little more concealer under my eyes, I prepare for one of the hardest conversations of my life.

"When are we leaving?" Ruby asks as she busts into my bathroom.

"What?"

"You said we'd go get a Christmas tree today. You wanted to wait until Huggie was off so he could help us get it in the house."

My heart. How do I do this to them? "Ruby, I—"

"Hi, Mom," Seth says as he knocks on the door.

"She's decent," Ruby yells.

My incredibly smart son comes into view, and I see the exact moment he knows something is wrong. I'm not sure how I managed to get this past Ruby, to be honest.

"Ruby, Huggie's not going to be able to help us with the tree." I'm going to have to save the part where he's not staying here any longer until I'm better composed. I turn and grab her hands. "So, we have two options. We either wait for someone who can help us get a real one, or we pull out the artificial tree and start decorating." I know I could probably manage getting a real tree on my own, but I'm already so overwhelmed by everything that's happened I don't want to push my luck right now. Seth and I can attempt that next year.

"Yes. Yes. Can we do it tonight?"

The last thing I'm interested in doing tonight is decorating a Christmas tree. But I'm done letting my children down. "If Seth can help me set it up, we can start tonight."

"Yay!" Ruby jumps up and down, completely oblivious to the two other people in the room who look like their dog died.

"We can't do the whole tree tonight, but we can start. But only after your homework is done."

"Okay," Ruby squeals. "I'll start right now." She runs from the room full of holiday cheer. Seth, on the other hand...

"Mom?" His voice sounds broken, much like my heart feels right now.

I reach for his hand and pull him closer. "Seth. I don't tell you enough how proud I am of you. Of the young man you've become. You've helped me pull through since..." As much as I try to fight it, a sob breaks through. "I appreciate everything you do around the house to help me. As well as looking out for Ruby."

"Mom?"

"And I'm going to need your help even more now." I wipe my nose and take a fortifying breath. "Huggie won't be staying here any longer."

"But why?"

"I wish I could explain, but it's a private matter between Huggie and me. The three of us can manage. We just need to be strong. Because Ruby might not understand."

"Mom, I don't understand," he cries. A tear rolls down my sweet boy's face, and it takes all the strength I have not to crumble.

"I'm not sure that I can explain it other than to say the two of us had a disagreement regarding your dad. One I'm not sure we can get passed."

His head drops at my reply, and so does my heart. This brave boy has endured so much.

"Please, help me keep Ruby from being upset when she finds out.

Tonight let's focus on the tree and figuring out how to start new traditions around here. Okay?"

"Okay." He sniffles. It's not often I see him show his emotions. He's tried to shield that from me. But I expect the next few months are going to be really hard on the three of us.

We manage to get through the evening. About thirty ornaments adorn the artificial tree, all in the same general spot. Why do children tend to place every ornament they pick up within arm's length of where they're standing? Every year I wait until they're in bed and move them around, so their weight doesn't topple the tree.

Luckily, Ruby doesn't ask any more questions about Huggie, and Seth, while quiet, appears to be managing. I wish the same could be said for me.

The kids are in bed, and I sit balled up in mine. My heart hurts. When Munish first shared the missing pieces of the puzzle with me, the heartache felt like one of betrayal. But now it's like another death. I feel empty. As if everything I knew was a lie and the people I counted on most didn't think I was worthy of the truth.

The man I married had integrity. He loved me with his whole heart. I've never had any doubt. I understand if he was scared the news could get leaked and his reputation would be questioned. But why wouldn't he tell me?

The first incident had apparently occurred over ten years ago. Seth would've been a baby at the time. Was he worried I couldn't handle the stress? Munish said Jake was able to get by the first time with community service, which I, again, knew nothing about. I recall him saying he wanted to help out at the rescue squad, and we'd argued about how he'd find time to do that around a stressful ER job and the baby. But was it simply a requirement for keeping his license?

Although my curiosity wants to continue playing connect the dots, it's only fueling my anger. I lie down and look at the clock. It's only 9:00 p.m. How am I ever going to get to sleep?

Sitting up, I reach for my phone.

"Hello?"

"Kat. It's not too late, is it?"

"No. Of course not. I was going to call you, but... well, I didn't know if you needed time with the kids."

"You know?"

"Yeah. Nate called me. Mel, I'm so sorry."

"Kat? Did you know about all of this?"

"No. But honestly, I don't know what all of *this* is. Nate said Huggie was beside himself. He's called out of work for tomorrow. Only said that the two of you had a falling out and that Huggie wasn't taking it well."

"It's a little more than a falling out, Kat." Over the next twenty minutes, Kat listens silently as I share all I learned in Munish's office today and Huggie's response to it. At times the phone line was so quiet I wondered if she was still there until a gasp in reaction to something I said would reassure me.

"Kat, I don't feel like I know what's real and what isn't anymore." The phone is again silent, and I wonder if she's considering what to say next. "Kat?"

"Sorry. It's... well, it's a lot to take in. How are the kids holding up?"

"I've only told Seth so far. Tried to explain that Huggie and I had a disagreement about his dad that I wasn't sure we could get past." Thinking about my brave boy, the lump in my throat from earlier returns. "He's taking it pretty hard, Kat."

"You sound like you're handling this pretty well, Mel. Better than expected, given everything that's been happening between the two of you lately."

"I'm trying to do better by my kids than I have in the past. I hope it doesn't all catch up to me. I'm more angry than hurt right now. I guess I'll have to see what tomorrow brings. The timing sure stinks, though."

"Yeah. This is bad enough without throwing Christmas into the mix."

"I may ask the kids if we can keep decorating to a minimum and plan to stay with my parents for the holidays."

"Mel?"

"Yeah?"

"You don't think there's any way you could forgive him?"

This was big. I don't want to think about this being the end of our friendship, but he's lied to me for years. And this could have hurt my children.

"I don't know, Kat."

HUGGIE

Lying in my bed feels odd. I'd grown to love that guest room. Knowing all of the people I loved most in the world were right outside the door. I've lived more in that house in the last few months than I have in the last twenty years. Before Melanie asked me to stay with them, I was merely getting by. Work, friends, sex with nameless, random women... all just to pass the time.

If there was any doubt about how much I loved Melanie, the last few months have proved it. Being with her and her children was everything I ever wanted and more. Her children... my heart feels like it's being torn in two. I promised them I'd always be there. And then I betrayed their mother. It's bad enough I kept my feelings for her secret, but now this.

I have no one to blame but myself. Sure, Jake should've never put me in that position. But I was a grown man. I knew better. The first time it happened, I was in my early twenties. I felt loyal to Jake and would've done anything to protect him. It was a mistake, and he had a bright future ahead of him. He insisted Melanie had enough on her plate worrying about Seth. Getting up half the night to check on him as many new mothers do. He didn't want to add to that stress. And he promised he was putting the sleeping pills away and limiting his alcohol.

I honestly thought it was just a mixture of early twenties partying and an erratic schedule requiring the use of those stupid sleeping pills that led to his arrest. But it became more evident that he had an issue with alcohol the older we got. Whenever I mentioned it, he'd rein it in. But that second driving under the influence charge could've cost him everything. And he knew it. He wouldn't be able to tell Melanie about one without explaining the other. He had to go to the medical review board to work out an arrangement to keep his license and work. There was the issue of serving his sentence every weekend for a month. The only thing he had in his favor was the timing between the two. Had they been closer together, he would've served serious time in jail.

But the guilt I feel knowing Melanie was right. I couldn't police his activities all the time. I posted bail and went along with the charade to protect my friend, knowing his actions could've gotten someone killed. And that someone could've been one of the three people I love more than life itself.

Knock, knock.

I spring from my bed, praying she's come to tell me she forgives me, even if it's just for the kids. Running down the steps, I have to slow down when my socks cause me to slip. I don't want to end up with a broken hip, for real, this time. *Although, if I thought it would cause her to take me back in until I healed...* Yeah, not even that's going to work.

As I fling open the front door, I find Nate holding two six-packs, and my face falls. "Hey."

"Hey, man. Sorry. It's just me and some backup," he says, lifting the beer. "Can I come in?"

I turn and trudge into my den, knowing he'll follow.

"Any word?"

"No. But I don't expect any. I don't know why I came running. Thought maybe the prayers for a miracle might've come true."

Nate slaps me on the leg and pops the top of a lager.

"I can't stop thinking about the kids, Nate. I never wanted to hurt them."

"I know, man. I think they'll know too. Kids are smarter than we give them credit for."

We both take long sips from our bottles in an otherwise still room. At times I wonder if he can hear my heart breaking. From the inside, it feels like an iceberg calving. At any moment, I expect to hear the sound emanating in the room as each shard splinters off.

"It's really over. I had a few short months of pretending it could be real, and that was it."

Nate turns to me, true sorrow in his gaze. "Man, did you ever get a chance to tell her how you felt about her?"

I chuckle sarcastically. "Nah, man. That was the best part. She handed me my bags and my broken heart while I stood on her porch holding a dozen roses."

"Fuck."

"You can say that again."

~

The next few weeks are a blur. I spend the holidays voluntarily taking shifts from my brothers at the station so they can enjoy the time with their family, and I can have a better chance of remaining distracted.

Christmas came and went. I received a text message from Seth wishing me Merry Christmas. That fucking ripped my heart out. Otherwise, it was turkey at the station, trying to pretend everything was fine. I guess I should look at the bright side. If the guys didn't all jump at the chance to trade their holiday shifts, I could've been stuck at the house alone.

~

"Hey, you coming with us Friday?" Nate asks.

"What's Friday?"

"It's sort of a combination New Year slash retirement party. For Wilson."

"Ah. I don't know, Nate—"

"Don't try telling me you're all partied out. You've practically lived at the station."

"I'm not in the partying mood," I say, enunciating the words clearly for him.

"C'mon. We're only going to Luigi's. It's just the guys. No significant others. Just wishing each other well and giving him a good send-off."

I consider this and have to admit, Wilson's been a stand-up guy all of these years. It's not his damn fault I got sucker punched in the heart. "Yeah, okay. I probably won't stay long."

"That's the spirit," Nate says, giving me jazz hands.

Oh, for fucks sake.

~

"To Wilson," Zach toasts.

"To Wilson," everyone chimes in with their drinks held high.

"Thanks, guys. I'd say I'm going to miss you, but I've seen enough of you to last a lifetime."

Everyone chuckles, and I try to imagine what it'll be like when I leave these guys. Little do they know, I've started putting out feelers to other counties. I'm worried I won't be able to live like this much longer. I'm tired of looking over my shoulder, worrying I'll see her with someone or bump into the kids and not be able to contain my emotions.

If things aren't going to turn around, I need to consider a fresh start after all of these years. My bitter heart has already started to turn to ice once again. It'll be a glacier once I walk away from her for good. Hell, I've had years of practice to prepare me for this.

Nate can take over the day-to-day operations of the side business. He's worked alongside me for years, and I trust him. I can still manage administrative tasks long distance. But watching Wilson saying goodbye to the guys has me melancholy before I even have another job.

When the pretty waitress comes to my side and asks what I'll have, my eyes land on the front of the restaurant. The front of the restaurant where Melanie and Derek are standing together. Dressed in a black cocktail dress and heels, the sight of her would cause what's left of my heart to calve if I wasn't seeing fucking red.

"That's okay. I'm not staying," I tell her.

Nate immediately becomes alarmed. "C'mon man, you said you were leaving early, but before dinner?"

Unable to keep my eyes off of the two of them, Nate picks up on my ogling. Grabbing my jacket, I stand.

"Don't do it, Huggie," he says from behind me. But it's too late.

Walking up beside her, I catch her unaware when I bend down so my mouth is beside her ear.

"He can't give you what I can. No one can." Placing my hands in my pants pockets, I avoid making eye contact, even when I hear her gasp, and stroll out the door to my truck.

I'm getting this woman out of my system, once and for all.

CHAPTER TWENTY-EIGHT

MELANIE

Days turn into weeks, and soon weeks will turn into months. Time ticks by so slowly that it feels like it's going in reverse. But it couldn't be. Because it wasn't that long ago, I was happier than I'd been in years.

Looking back, I don't know how I managed to get through the holidays without falling apart. I tried to stay focused on my kids and my dad—anyone who might need me. I saved my heartache until I was alone. The shower and my bed were my sanctuaries. A reprieve to let out all of the tears I hid from my children. I refused to put them through that again.

It took Ruby more than a few tears to get over Huggie moving out. I think she may have been even more attached than Seth or me. But with time, she doesn't bring him up as often. Now it's merely every other day.

I've taken some time off of work now that Christmas is over. Once the distractions of shopping, baking, and wrapping were gone, I had nothing preventing me from slipping into an overwhelming sadness. I thought work might prevent me from going there, but it's been nonstop with the kids and my parents. So I asked Derek if I could have some time to get myself together.

He's proven to be a good friend. I worried he might be interested in more, but he seems to have shut himself off to the idea of another woman. In hindsight, I think that would've been wise. Maybe if I hadn't let myself develop feelings for Huggie, I could've handled this better.

"Mel, you here?" Kat's voice travels up the stairs to my room.

"Yeah. My room."

I'm still wearing my flannel pajamas. After getting the kids on the bus, I haven't been motivated to dress and be a productive member of society.

Kat enters the room and notices me lying on my side and comes to sit beside me. She curls her arms around me and wraps me up, instantly bringing tears to my eyes.

"Mel?"

"Yeah?"

"You okay?"

"No."

We lie there in silence, and it takes all of my willpower not to lose it in front of her.

"I might need your help, Kat. I'm struggling. I did so well during the holidays, but I'm starting to slip. Maybe it's seasonal affective disorder—the lack of sunlight and warmth. I'm so emotional. I just want to sleep and cry." It really feels like depression is pulling me back under. I've tried to manage this for too long on my own. I probably need an emergency session with Dr. Miller before the train comes off of the tracks.

"Mel, come on. It's me. What's this really about?"

Unable to come up with a logical explanation, I just continue to lie there and wipe the stray tears that fall.

"Are you still upset because Jake put Huggie in a no-win position? If you're going to be upset with anyone, it should be Jake, not Huggie."

"But I can't be mad at him. Not after..."

I stop myself. I can't go there. I've come so far, and I won't let myself succumb to that guilt again.

"Mel, talk to me. Not after what?"

"Kat, I gave Jake an ultimatum the day he died. I told him if he couldn't make our family a priority, maybe he shouldn't come home." I cry. "And then he didn't."

"Oh, Melanie." Kat holds me tighter, stroking my hair. I pray she doesn't try to tell me that it wasn't my fault. I know that. But how can I stay mad at him after what I said?

"I understand more than you know. Being married to someone who's dedicated to their profession is hard. Add to it insomnia and the side effects of the sleeping pills... well, been there, done that."

All of a sudden, it hits me that Kat would understand what Jake was dealing with better than most. She dealt with similar demons, minus the alcohol.

"But, let's look at it this way. Your husband loved you. He was flawed, but there's no doubt he was devoted. And I think it'd break his heart to know that you've lost someone who cares deeply for you and the kids because of his actions."

I've never really thought of it that way. So mired in anger and heartbreak.

She continues to run her hands through my hair, comforting me as only Kat can. "Melanie, Huggie had to have felt trapped between a rock and a hard place to even consider doing what he did. There's no doubt in my mind that Huggie asked Jake on multiple occasions to tell you everything. He would've never willingly kept anything from you."

An unattractive sniffle sneaks out, betraying me. "Kat, I'm so mad. At both of them."

"I know. I get it. I really do."

"But I miss them." I lie here, trying to calm my breathing and stop crying before I lie in a pool of snot. "At least I can still go talk to Jake when I need to."

Kat continues to rub my back, soothing my nerves.

"But I miss Huggie. Talking to him. Laughing with him. Having both of them gone is too much."

I can feel Kat adjusting herself in the bed right before a brush drags through my unruly strands. It's nice. Feeling cared for. The act brings back memories of lying catatonic following Jake's death when she did the same.

"Thank you," I tell her.

"For what?"

"For this. It's one of the few things I remember from that awful time after Jake died. When I could barely function, and you'd do this for me. It made me feel cared for in a safe way. Without the pitiful glances and the sympathy cards. No awkward conversation. Just showing me you cared with that simple act."

She stops brushing, and the room grows quiet. Well, heck, if I thought bringing it up would make her stop, I wouldn't have said anything.

"Mel?"

"Yeah?"

"That wasn't me."

CHAPTER TWENTY-NINE

MELANIE

I spring up from where I'm lying and swiftly turn to face her. "What do you mean that wasn't you?"

"Melanie..."

"Then who?"

"Mel, that was Huggie."

"No. You're confused." I try to scan through the recesses of my mind to that awful time, but I admit much of it is a blank. What little I was conscious of, I quickly tuned out. "I know I was out of it for a long while. I even doubted my sanity at times, thinking Jake was curled up around me when I was at my lowest." Turning back to face her, I notice when her eyes flick down to her hands.

"What?"

She doesn't answer with words, but I instantly know.

"It was him?"

She simply nods.

"But I don't understand."

Kat stands from where she's been seated beside me and starts to pace. I'm glued to her every movement, trying to make heads or tails of this. When she starts nibbling at her fingernail, I start to come unglued.

"Kat. Is there something else you aren't telling me? Because I'm tired of people withholding things. People who claim to care about me."

She stops in her tracks and turns to me. Looking as guilty as Huggie did when I confronted him on the porch that day.

"Melanie. I'm pretty sure Huggie's in love with you."

"What? No. He's my friend." *Was my friend.*

She continues to look at me deadpan.

I have to admit that I was falling for him too. I questioned the depth of my feelings, confused by our transition from friendship to physical. "When? You mean after we started sleeping together?" How would she know this? I mean, she barely figured it out before I asked him to leave.

"Melanie." She exhales, and I can't tell if she's frustrated with me or upset about this conversation. "I think he's always loved you."

It feels like she's speaking in code. The four of us have been tight since we met at the rescue squad. It's not often you meet such amazing people that, years later, you still think so highly of them. I frequently considered Jake to be the glue that held us all together. But looking back, we each contributed in some way to this little pact. While Jake and I were romantically linked, Kat and I developed a close, almost sisterly bond, and Jake and Huggie were as close as any brothers I've seen.

I try to calm my racing thoughts and speak rationally to her. Because I'm starting to feel this conversation is going in circles. "Kat, we've all been close. There's a bond between the four of us that most people will never be lucky enough to experience. I love all of you."

Kat walks over to me, takes my hands in hers, and looks at me more intensely than I can ever recall from her. And that's saying a lot for all we've been through. She's lost a child and later her fertility. I've lost a husband and now a friend. What else could possibly cause this solemn expression?

"I need to clarify this by saying I've never actually spoken with him about this directly. But I've had my suspicions for years. I planned to take it to my grave with the exception of one conversation with Nate."

"You're speaking in morse code again, Kat. I'm not following you."

"Huggie's been in love with you since the day you met."

The room suddenly feels as if it's spinning, and I have to drop down onto the bed to steady myself. Kat comes to my side, rubbing my back. "That man adores you, Mel. I started putting two and two together when I'd catch the way he'd look at you when we were on duty. He's never spoken of it to anyone but Nate."

Looking at her, it's like I need some physical confirmation her lips are moving to prove this conversation is really happening. "Nate told you that Huggie said he loves me?"

"Again, I've never asked him specifically whether Huggie said love, but that was the impression I got. And I've suspected the same for years." She stops for a minute as if trying to gather her thoughts. "You know Huggie. He's quiet and unassuming when he's in a group. It's not until you really get to know him that you realize what a clown he is."

This actually causes the corners of my mouth to curl. I'd forgotten what a genuine smile felt like. Because Kat's exactly right. Huggie's an introvert until he's safe to let his true self emerge.

"I think he's always kicked himself that he didn't ask you out before Jake. But once he swept you off your feet, there was nothing Huggie could do."

Listening to this is surreal. It's like she's talking about two different people. I know once I lie down each night, I'll be flipping back through all of my memories of those times, looking at them through a different lens.

"The problem is, he couldn't get passed it."

"What do you mean?"

"Well, that's why I spoke to Nate about it initially. It was your rehearsal dinner."

I study her face, hanging on her every word.

"I told Nate it looked like the best man was having a hard time."

My hand flies to my chest as if to soothe the ache of thinking of him that way.

"And Nate agreed." Kat looks forlorn, remembering the occasion. "Everyone else was happy, dancing the night away. But Huggie spent most of the night watching you from a distance. I think he tried to move on that night. But from what Nate says, he's never been able to let go."

Covering my face with my hands, I try to prevent bawling. How is this real? She said herself, she's never confirmed any of this. Maybe this is Kat being dramatic. I mean, it wouldn't be the first time.

Raising my chin, I force a few cleansing breaths. I'm not sure what to do with this. It's too much to absorb at one time.

"Melanie. If the last few weeks have been this hard on you, think of the impact it's had on him. Huggie's had to deal with the guilt of loving his best friend's wife, finally becoming physical with you after all of these years, worried about what that could do to your friendship, just to have it all ripped out from under him when you found out about Jake's past."

"Stop. Please," I cry. "I can't handle this anymore." I literally feel like I could be sick.

"Oh, honey, I'm sorry. I shouldn't have pushed. I just hate seeing everyone hurting."

I look at my watch. It's almost noon. The kids will be home in a few hours, so there's no chance of reaching out to him. And this conversation has to happen in person.

"Kat, I'm going to try and lie down and get myself together before the kids get home. I don't feel well."

"Melanie, I feel terrible. I shouldn't have said anything."

"No. Someone should have said something years ago. I feel like I've spent the last twenty years in the dark. Is there anything else I need to know?"

She looks down at her feet, and I panic. "No. I think that's it."

I've taken a shower and tried to take a nap to clear my head, but it's useless. I'm sure my kids will come in wondering why I look like I did years ago. And I couldn't possibly explain it to them. I don't believe any of this myself.

I need to talk to Huggie. I want to know what is real and what is a figment of Kat's melodramatic imagination. And he owes it to me to tell it to me straight. But I think there's someone else I need to see first.

"Dr. Miller, I can't thank you enough for seeing me on such short notice."

"Melanie, I'm glad we could fit you in. I hate to hear you're struggling."

"Thank you." I immediately look for the box of tissues that is usually at the ready. When I can't find them, he stands to retrieve the box from where it's sitting by the window.

Returning to his desk, he encourages me to continue. "So has something happened, or do you think the recent holidays have put you into a tailspin?

"Both, I think." That didn't take long. I'm already sniffling."Okay where to start..." I look across the desk to where he's sitting patiently. His expression is neutral, just giving me the platform to proceed. "So, first, I need to talk to you about what you mentioned when I was previously here."

He adjusts in his seat, giving me a questioning look.

"You warned me about having my friend move in. Thought I could be at risk of transference."

"Have you developed feelings for him?"

"That's the thing. I've been friends with Huggie for twenty years. We're incredibly close. I trust him—" I pause to consider my words, but that part of the conversation needs to happen later. "I've trusted and loved him as a friend for a long time." I reach for another tissue. "But over the last few months, I've developed very different feelings. I thought it was just my mind testing me after you mentioned transference. But they persisted and... well, we acted on them."

"How did that go?"

"I was nervous. Worried I was crossing a line. I didn't want to risk our friendship by taking it to another level. But I was incredibly happy. We both seemed to be."

"Seemed?"

I bend my head down, trying to figure out how to put this whole mess together so he'll understand. "I recently found out some information from my attorney about my husband. I decided I didn't want to pursue a civil case. I'm ready to move on from that time in my life."

"That's good. I think that's a positive step."

I try to find the best way to explain. "My attorney shared information about my husband that I was unaware of. It appears he'd struggled with alcohol and, I believe, the use of sleeping pills. He had been convicted of driving under the influence. Not once, but twice. He'd managed to hide all of this. The jail time, the community service, and even the restricted license until Munish told me."

I stop to take a breath before looking at Dr. Miller.

"That's a lot to learn. It must have broadsided you."

"Yes. Exactly." He always knows the right thing to say. "I was shaken to the core. I felt like everything I knew about my husband was wrong." I expect him to challenge me on this, but he sits quietly to let me proceed. "It turns out Huggie was the one helping him to get around and keep things from me."

Dr. Miller changes positions but continues to sit silently.

"I confronted him about it..." I stop, feeling the tears starting to pour. "I told him he needed to leave." I rethink this statement. I mean, I'm here to get help. I should tell the whole truth. "Well, I packed his bags and told him to get out." Sniffle. "He tried to apologize, but I was just so angry. I mean, between the lies and the fact we were riding with Jake having no idea this was an issue." I dab my eyes. "What if one of us had gotten hurt?"

Silence. Still only silence.

"He was struggling with alcohol and had these huge things happen, and he couldn't trust me enough to let me in," I cry. "What kind of wife was I that he'd go to those lengths to hide this from me?" Another sniffle. I dab my eyes and nose and reach for another tissue. "At first, I was so angry with Huggie. I couldn't see straight. But he would've done anything for Jake." My tears start to slow a bit.

"Have you spoken with him since you asked him to leave your home?"

I jump in my seat, his voice startling me. I'd been rambling as if I was talking to myself. "No. That's the other piece of this puzzle."

"What do you mean?"

"I haven't heard from him since he left. I'm a bit surprised he wouldn't have tried harder to reach out. But I was so upset with him.

I..." Has he been afraid to reach out, or is he giving me space? The memory of him standing there, pleading with me to listen to him, holding those beautiful flowers taunts me. If only I could take the whole thing back and handle it differently.

"My best friend came over. I told her everything. While she was there, the enormity of all of this really hit me. I think somewhere along the line, I fell in love with Huggie."

My gaze connects with Dr. Miller's calming, deep blue eyes, and I try to compose myself. "When I shared this with Kat, she said that she thought Huggie had been in love with me for years. Throughout my marriage. I was floored. Not only because he could've felt this way, but that it was one more thing I was completely blind to."

I can't sit in this uncomfortable chair any longer. Needing to pace, I stand and walk to the window. "I'm a mess. I don't seem to know what's real anymore."

"I understand. I'd question things as well."

Turning to look at him, I give Dr. Miller an appreciative smile. If nothing else, it's nice to feel validated.

"So, from what you're telling me, it sounds as if he and your husband had to be incredibly close."

I just nod. Unsure where he's going with this.

"For him to have remained in such a close relationship with him, while secretly being in love with you, his wife, there had to be a powerful bond between them."

"Yes."

"Powerful enough, he would've likely done anything to protect him."

"Yes. I think Jake put him in a terrible position. I couldn't see that before."

Dr. Miller leans forward in his chair, resting his forearms upon the desk. "I think you were transferring the anger you felt at what your husband did onto him. Don't get me wrong, I'm not condoning what he did. A lie is a lie is a lie."

I must be feeling a bit better. Dr. Miller almost sounded like one of Matthew McConaughey's characters with that statement.

"Do you think you can forgive him?"

"I'm pretty sure I already have." I walk back over to the green chair and have a seat. My tears have all but dried up now, but I grab another tissue just in case.

"This doesn't sound like transference, Melanie. This man has genuine feelings for you. And by all accounts, you fought yours for a while. Probably wanting to be sure you were doing the right thing. For you, your friendship, and your children."

"Yes. That's why this is so hard. I didn't know if I could trust my feelings after all this. And I was so angry."

"As anyone might've been."

"I'm not sure what to do. My kids are heartbroken. They adore him. If I reach out to him and we do this, I don't want to hurt them again if it doesn't work out."

Leaning back in his chair, I can see the corner of his mouth turn up, and I know things are going to be okay. "That's a risk anyone with kids would have to take. But you're ahead of most. You two have a long history. And it sounds like you were happy until this information about your husband came out."

He's right. And we were happy. I think back on that crazy campout on the movie set. The four of us were happier than we'd been since we lost Jake. It felt like a turning point.

"We were."

"Then be open with him. It sounds like the two of you have a lot to discuss."

A hopeful smile actually emerges. I never expected this.

"But, Melanie."

"Yes."

"He's been hurt too. If what you say is true, he's spent years suppressing his feelings, only to be turned away when he tried to act on them."

Turned away? That's a nice way of putting it. I was a raving lunatic.

"You two have a lot to talk about. But he may need some space too."

It's been several days since my appointment with Dr. Miller. My first inclination was to run to Huggie, but after all that's happened, I want to do this the right way. I considered calling, but I knew I wouldn't be able to hear his voice and not blurt out everything right then and there. I considered driving to his home, but what if he wasn't alone? That would kill me.

The safest thing feels like meeting him at the firehouse. If nothing more than to see his face. To ask if we can talk when it works for both of us. Yes. That's it. But how do I know when—

The calendar.

Bolting down the stairs, I reach the kitchen in record time. Pulling the makeshift calendar from the side of the refrigerator, I try to flip to the current month, but realize it stops at December. I start to feel defeated and think I'll be at the mercy of a text message when it dawns on me.

They work a steady rotation, ten shifts per month.

I flip back through the last few months and figure out the way the shifts roll out. It's predictable—every three weeks like clockwork. I flick back to December, look at where his shifts end, and count forward. He's working tomorrow. That's it. I'll go to the station tomorrow and ask if we can meet. Somewhere neutral. So we can talk.

My heart rate picks up for the first time in months. Until it dawns on me. What if he's finally moved on? What if, after all of these years, I've pushed him over the edge?

I think I really am going to be sick.

You can do this, Melanie. I've been sitting in my car at the station for almost thirty minutes, trying to get the nerve to go in there. I know all of these guys. This should be a safe space. But between knowing there will be a crowd of onlookers and unsure what to expect from Huggie after all this time, I'm basically a hot mess.

I open the car door, inhale the crisp January air, and make my way to the door. I've been here dozens of times over the years. And have never needed to knock or ring a bell. These guys are professionals regarding how much they cut up. I certainly don't need to stand here waiting now.

I timidly enter the building and walk toward the kitchen and main room of the station.

"Hi. Can I help you?"

Startled by the unfamiliar voice, I turn to find a handsome, dark-haired young man. He stands about six foot two and has big brown eyes and a welcoming smile.

"Hi. I don't think we've met. I'm Melanie."

"Alex. Nice to meet you."

"Mel. What are you doing here," Nate greets and comes in for a hug.

I have to admit, the familiar face has definitely helped my nerves.

"I see you met our newest recruit, Alex."

"Yes," I answer, feeling awkward. Coming here to speak to Huggie is stressful enough without dealing with newcomers. I stop talking and look at Alex, hoping he'll get the hint that Nate can handle this.

"Well, it was nice meeting you, Melanie. I'm going to finish up in the bay."

"Good. Oh, make sure to put some extra oxygen masks in the ambulance while you're out there. We looked low on the last call."

"Got it," Alex yells as he walks away.

Nate takes my hand and leads me into the kitchen. "So, how've you been? It feels like forever since I saw you last."

"Busy. You know. The holidays with kids. It was a lot. But they're back in school now and hopefully getting back to a routine."

"How about you?" I ask. I love Nate, but I'm not really interested in his answer. I'm only making small talk until I can get the nerve to ask him where Huggie is.

"Same, minus the kids." He laughs. "I was actually going to call you. You stopping by is perfect timing."

"Oh?" I look around, surprised Huggie hasn't come out to see me. Maybe Kat had this all wrong. Or else he's so pissed off at me that he's keeping his distance. The thought makes my stomach roil again.

Unable to hold back any longer, I decide to go all in. "Is Huggie here?"

Nate looks shocked. Maybe after Huggie shared how bad our last conversation went, he's shocked that I'd even ask.

"No, Mel. Huggie's not here."

"Oh." I can't pretend to hide my disappointment. I'd managed to get through the last twenty-four hours, sure that he'd be here, and I could at least see his face and those beautiful silver eyes until we could talk. "Did he have off today?" I was sure I counted out the days right.

"No. He doesn't work here anymore."

CHAPTER THIRTY

MELANIE

"I'm sorry, what?"

"He doesn't work here anymore."

"Did he get transferred to another station?"

"No, Mel. He moved out of state."

I stand there, dumbfounded. How did this happen? "When?"

"Last week. I think he started looking for another job sometime between Christmas and New Years."

"Where did he go?"

Nate looks guarded. What's happening here?

"I'm sorry, Melanie. I'm not allowed to say."

Walking over to the table, I take a seat. "I don't understand."

"He said he wanted a fresh start. He asked if I'd promise not to share his whereabouts. And I'm honoring my commitment."

Looking down at my hands, I wonder how I let this get so far. I've known Huggie for so long, and now I feel like I don't know him at all.

"Are you okay?"

"What?

"You don't look too well."

"I'm just tired. I haven't slept well." I think the last good night's sleep I had was in that cabin with Huggie.

"I'm glad you're here. I was going to call you. Adam and I would love your help planning our wedding."

"I'm sorry. What did you say?" I need to get out of here. I feel like the walls are closing in on me.

"I said, Adam and I would love for you to help us with our wedding." Nate is beaming. Bless this sweet man. He deserves this.

"Sure. I'd love to help."

"Oh, thank you. I loved everything you did to help Nick plan Kat's wedding. We want something elegant but not ridiculous. His parents have been trying to take over. At first, I thought, if they're paying, go for it. But it's gotten so over the top I'd almost prefer to elope."

"Well, call me and fill me in on all the details, and I'll start working on whatever you need." A project like this will at least keep my mind busy, even if the last thing I want to work on is a wedding.

HUGGIE

"Hey, man. A few of us are going out Friday. You want to come?"

"Thanks, Parker. I'll probably catch up with you guys next time. Still getting settled and all that."

"Sure. I get it," he says. "Moving to a new home sucks."

I've been in Maryland for only a few weeks, and nothing about this place feels like home. I'm renting a small brownstone at the moment. I found one that was furnished, so I didn't have to bring much beyond my clothes. I'm still in denial this has happened. But I can't put it off any longer.

Seeing Melanie with Derek at Luigi's was a wake-up call. I've loved that woman since she was practically a girl. Watching her create a family with my best friend had been brutal, but I loved them both and decided it was either endure it or face a life without them. The second simply didn't seem like an option. But I never imagined I'd be stuck in that vicious cycle for twenty years. Every day wondering if I'd had enough and wanted a family of my own or stay to preserve the relationships with the people who meant most to me.

I assumed as time passed, the reality of the situation would give me the push to move on. But try as I might, there was no one else that could make me feel the way she did—having her in my life in any way I could meant more than looking for that in some other woman.

Maybe there's something wrong with me. I tried. I went out. But after years of uncomfortable first dates that always left me frustrated, why continue to put yourself through that? I just accepted my lot in life and moved on the best I knew how. But when all that shit went down after Jake's first arrest, I knew I was digging a hole I'd never climb out of. Friend or no friend, what he was asking me to do was wrong. And now, I'm paying the piper.

~

"Hey, Parker, it's George. I got your number from one of the guys at the station. You guys still headed out tonight?"

"Yeah. Needed a break from unpacking?"

"Something like that. Just out of these four walls."

"We're all meeting around ten. I'll text you the address of the club."

"Thanks."

~

I arrive at the Cigar Bar and find it's a step up from what I'm used to. The place has a classy aesthetic: dark wood and burgundy furnishings throughout. There's no loud dance music or strobe lights. Just small clusters of tables and chairs scattered around a gorgeous oak bar. In the back corner, there's an open area where patrons can dance on the parquet floor to the jazz tunes playing.

Spotting my new crew, I head in their direction.

"George, glad you could make it," Parker greets. It's taking some getting used to, going by my given name.

"Thanks for including me. This town is a big place to learn on my own."

"Stick with us. We'll show you all the best spots," Andrew adds.

"Well, this place is fantastic," I say as I take a seat.

"Cigar, sir?" I glance up to see a stunning, light-skinned Black woman with beautiful eyes and long, dark hair leaning over my chair. Her tits are practically spilling out of that little white top. I recognize the tight black mini skirt completing her ensemble matches those of the other servers I passed on the way to the table.

"Thank you," I tell her and look over the selection. "Could I have a two-finger pour of Macallan? Is this real?" I ask, stunned at the sight of the Cuban Cohiba on display. "It's not Dominican?"

"No, sir. It's Cuban."

Wow, this night just got better. I don't smoke cigars often. The last I had was with some stinking rich producer who took Jamie and me out for drinks one night after a near miss on set.

I'd had a Cohiba that night and discovered shortly thereafter it's very difficult to find given the politics with Cuba. No goods from Cuba can be purchased legally in the United States, so when someone has an authentic one, they probably have connections to get it through somehow.

"What the hell were they paying you in Hanover?" Parker asks.

Shit. I didn't even think about this. The guys at my old station had been with me as my wealth accumulated. We all enjoyed the finer things in life on occasion but never took ourselves too seriously. It wasn't pretention. Just enjoying the fruits of our labor.

"Nah. I ran a side hustle that did well and invested, which did better. So every now and then, I splurge a little. Felt like after this move, I deserved it."

"Well, hook a brother up with your side hustle," James says, raising his glass.

"Here, here," a few more add.

The night goes surprisingly well. The guys are very different from who I'm accustomed to. Their mannerisms, their accent. I still feel like the odd man out, but I have to start somewhere. They all seem like decent guys.

And this club is incredible. I'd love to replicate this back home.

Home.

I have to stop thinking that way. I'd left my home as is when I rented this one. I still have ties to Hanover. My other business is there. There's no need to jump the gun by putting my place on the market. But I have to stop treating it like a safety blanket. I can't go back there.

When I told Nate I didn't want anyone to know where I'd gone, it was for a number of reasons. I needed to cut ties with my old life if I was going to have a chance at starting a new one. I didn't need any temptations to bring me back. I'd purchased a new phone and given the old one to Nate, knowing he'd contact me if there was anything urgent there. It had to be done. I've wasted too much of my life wanting something I can't have.

"Can I get you anything else, sir?"

I can think of a few things.

I'm surprised at my thoughts. I haven't had any interest in pussy since the fallout with Melanie. Thinking of women, in general, just pissed me off. But it feels like forever since I spent the night in the cabin with her. And at least a month since I saw her with *him*.

There's no sense lying. Seeing her with the hot widower did something to me. I could handle staying in the friend zone with her when she was with Jake. But I was kidding myself if I thought I could remain friends with her if she began dating again. And it had nothing to do with the fact we'd been sleeping together. That only put another layer of shit on top of the torment I was feeling.

I left Luigi's that night wanting to find someone. Anyone who could make me forget. But there's no one on the planet who could do that for me. So instead, I visited my best friend. I've been doing a lot of that lately. Guess it helps when you're screaming at someone you love, knowing they can't talk back.

I've had to be careful when I visit Jake's grave. I'm aware now that Melanie frequents there as well. This isn't new for me. I've paid my respects many times over. But I hadn't started having conversations with him until recently.

Maybe I knew what lay ahead of me. That I'd be leaving all of the friends I could share my thoughts with behind and have to find someone else who'd listen when things got bad enough. I know Nate is always a phone call away, but he's about to get married. He doesn't need me raining on his parade.

Suddenly, I realize the beautiful server is still beside me, waiting on my answer. "No. I'm good. Thank you."

Is it the scotch, this woman, or her tiny outfit that has me interested in things I'd put off until now?

Perhaps it's the way she keeps saying 'sir.'

This thought brings me back to a time when I questioned someone's submissive past. She may not have said 'sir' with her voice, but she did it with her actions. I never considered this was something I was into. I'm certainly not into BDSM as one would read about, but asserting my influence over a situation is a definite turn-on. And why wouldn't it be? I've had little control over anything in my life.

I wish the guys well and tell them I'll see them for duty on Monday. Hopefully, the heavy pours of scotch will allow me to relax enough so I can sleep tonight.

My car arrives, and I climb inside. It took me a while to arrange, as I haven't learned my address yet. As we head in the direction of my new digs, my mind keeps drifting back. The hot waitress, the submissive woman from The Rox, my anger at knowing I've had to move here and start over while Melanie is probably entering a relationship with another doctor...

I grab my phone and look for one of the few contact numbers I entered when I handed off my old one.

"Hi, is Annalise available?"

"Yes, sir. May I ask who's calling?"

"It's Nathan Mars."

I sit silently, wondering what the hell I'm doing. I can still hang up the phone. But if she tried to call back, Nate could answer.

"Mr. Mars. It's a pleasure. I'd wondered if you'd changed your mind about us after all."

It's been a long while since I've frequented The Rox. I'd paid through the end of the year and was hopeful I was done with needing this in my life. Boy, was I wrong.

"It's been a busy time. I'm actually in the area and wondered if the woman I spent time with the last time I was there was available?" I can't believe I'm doing this. But I need to move on. Get Melanie out of my system.

"No. I'm sorry. She's no longer working here."

I should take this as a sign. Say thank you, go home, and jerk one off in the shower like I've done for years. Wait until I can find someone new. Someone worth taking a chance on. Even if there's no possibility in forever with anyone but Melanie, I could at least try getting laid on a regular basis.

But I don't do anything the easy way.

"Annalise?"

"Yes, sir?" *And there it is.*

"Is your offer still good?"

CHAPTER THIRTY-ONE

MELANIE

"Do you have your gloves, Ruby?"

"Yes. Wearing them!" she shouts, following Seth out the front door to the bus stop. They've been home for almost five days between the weekend and the school closures for the weather. This is the second time since Christmas we've had a sizeable snowfall. The last few years were mild.

"Be careful. There are still some slick spots!" I yell. Thank goodness we are lucky enough to have the bus stop close enough to the house that they can make it there by the time we see it stop down the road.

Every day I find new challenges to being a single parent. In the beginning, I was so overwhelmed with it all I didn't pay attention to the random things that would pop up. Like household maintenance, changing out fire alarm batteries or A/C filters. Things I took for granted when Jake was here. And I have to admit, I called on Huggie to help with a lot of these tasks too.

I'm trying to look at the bright side. I no longer have days where I worry I can't handle it. I've acquired new skills and have done more for my little family in the last two years than I would've ever thought possible. I've developed resources. People I can turn to if there's a challenge I feel ill-equipped to meet. And then the next time, I'm better prepared.

I've grown so much in the last few months. More so since Huggie left. He did me a favor by moving away. At least, that's what I keep telling myself. His not being here forced me to step up to the plate and take care of things on my own. Sure, I still lean on Nick and Kat from time to time. And will continue to do so. But I'm proud of how I've managed.

The day I went to the fire station to talk to him nearly sent me spiraling backward. I was so distraught that he would not only have left, but made it clear he didn't want to be found. But over the next few days, it became clear after everything Kat had shared that he probably felt he had no other choice.

I'm sure if I begged Nate, he would've reached out to Huggie for me. But I knew I still had a lot of healing to do. Not only was I recovering from all that Jake and Huggie had kept from me, but I was also dealing with the fact everyone knew of Huggie's feelings for me... except me.

I'd returned to Dr. Miller weekly following that heart-wrenching day. I lay my worries and my sadness at his feet and don't look back when my session is over. This is something I should've embraced years ago. Making it a habit of sharing my feelings with a trained professional has built my confidence. But there are still days I struggle and wish things were different.

Derek has become such a great friend. He's tried to allow more flexibility with my schedule once I shared how I was feeling completely exhausted by managing full-time work and the kids. He's aware I don't need to work full-time to support my family, and I've told him I wouldn't be offended if he needed to hire someone who could support him better. But, for now, he's working with me. Maybe it'll be easier after Nate's wedding is behind me and warmer days return. That's what life is all about, right? Finding a way to be happy despite the challenges.

Bzzz. Bzzz.

I reach for my phone and notice Nate's picture. "Hi. You getting nervous?"

"No." His laugh carries through the receiver. "I've got you. I don't need to worry about a thing."

I'd accept the compliment if I didn't already know it was a little white lie. He's let it slip that he's bothered by the fact Adam's extended family is planning to come to the wedding, yet he has no one.

"Well, things are coming together. I'm so glad the two of you agreed on The Manor House. It's gorgeous and doesn't require a lot of decorating. And given the time of year, you can choose to have your pictures done inside or out. The gardens are beautiful, even if covered in snow." I try to assure him. "And the ceremony space is perfect for a smaller wedding. It'll accommodate Adam's family and yours."

"Mel, I told you—"

"We are your family, Nate. Don't ever forget it."

The line grows quiet, and I worry I've upset him.

"Thank you. I needed that." His voice sounds heavy. It breaks my heart that such a joyous occasion is fraught with such pain. Given Nate's situation, he and Adam had decided against using groomsmen or any of the usual bridal attendants. They told their loved ones they were trying to keep the event from getting out of hand and wanted the focus on the two of them. But I knew the truth.

"I wanted to let you know. My sister could potentially be coming."

"Oh, Nate. That's wonderful."

"I'll believe it when I see it. But it was nice of her to reach out, despite my parent's opinion."

"Is she playing any type of role in the service?"

"No. I'll just be thrilled if she supports me. I'm not sure why I even told you. It's not like we're having some big sit-down affair with place cards or anything."

"Well, I'm personally very glad you shared it. I think it's great news."

I can hear a commotion in the background and suspect he's calling from work. "Sorry, Mel. Have to run. Duty calls."

"Bye, Nate. Be safe out there."

≈

I've taken a shower, tried to eat a little something, and still, I'm feeling restless and a little more depressed than normal. I don't see Dr. Miller again for several more days, but this feels different. Could it be all of this work on Nate and Adam's wedding is starting to get to me? Realizing I had two beautiful men in my life who cared for me, and now they're both gone.

Enough of this, Melanie. I head to the closet and grab my gym bag. I need to get out of this house, even if it's simply to get some fresh air.

After a quick change into some workout clothes, I open the front door and welcome the frigid air as it hits my face. Whatever will wake me up and get me going. I take the short drive to the gym carefully, knowing there could be black ice on the roads. Plus, the realization I can't just call Jake or Huggie if I get stuck as I have in the past hits me square in the chest.

I drive for about ten more minutes before realizing I've zoned out, have driven past the gym, and am headed for the cemetery. Turning into the desolate parking area, I sit and take in the snow-covered space. I wrap my scarf and coat tighter around me as I step out of the car and make my way to see Jake.

I'm not sure why I'm even here. But I've found over the last few years that often, the universe leads me where I need to go. Fighting it is futile.

As I trudge the path to Jake's gravesite, I notice the snow isn't as deep as I'd expected. With each step, the light crunch of a top layer of ice is the only sound present, just as I prefer it when I come here. Peaceful solitude.

It's a little more difficult to locate his headstone when they're all covered in snow. They all look so much alike. But as I get closer, I recognize a tree that stands off in the distance, as well as some artificial red and white flowers at the marker next to his.

Squatting down, I swipe the snow from the granite marker until his name appears. Whenever I see it, that familiar lump in my throat returns. But the mass has gotten smaller, barely recognizable now.

"Hi," I tell him. "I've missed you. Sorry I haven't been by in a while. The kids, and work, and Nate... well, it's a lot to keep up with. But you'd be proud of me. I'm doing so well, Jake. I've been doing all of this on my own, and—"

Tears start to form, startling me. I don't have to question this long. This isn't about Jake. It's the fact that I don't want to be doing this on my own. When Huggie was near, everything was better.

"I'm still so mad at you," I cry. "I didn't feel like I was allowed to say that before. Because of the way I treated you. But you had no right to do this. Keeping things from me and putting our family in harm's way without letting me in. Sure, I would've been upset. But we could have figured out a way together. We were a team."

I swipe away my tears with my snow-covered gloves, only to smear more moisture over my face and nose. Reaching into my pocket, I quickly determine there's no tissue. How had I thought I'd healed enough that I've stopped putting tissues everywhere?

"And because of this. Because you put Huggie in this awful position, now I've lost him too," I shout. I begin smacking the headstone as if Jake can feel my wrath, snow flying about until I collapse onto the ground. I must look like I've lost my mind. Do they have cameras here? I'll probably show up on the news later when some passerby catches this on their phone.

I start to cover my face, overwhelmed that I've finally let Jake have it, then stop when I realize there's even more icy snow on my gloves. Looking up at the sky, I wail, "Why?"

The chill is starting to settle into my bones. I can feel my body starting to tremble. But it could just as well be that I'm finally getting this out.

"I was falling in love with him, Jake," I splutter. "Maybe it was too soon, and I wasn't ready. Maybe it wouldn't have worked. Maybe Kat was all wrong, and he never felt the way she thought he did. I don't know what to believe anymore."

The tears fall a little heavier now. I don't even care if they turn into icicles. "But I was happy." Sniffle. "I was starting to think I could be happy again."

Sniveling into the cold air, I instinctively wipe away more snow from the top of the dark granite. My breath comes out in frigid clouds as I lean down to clear the frosty slush from the base. It feels like a mission to remove each flake. Maybe because I know it'll likely be even longer before I'm back now that I've gotten this off of my chest.

Sitting back on my heels, I notice something poking out of a small mound of snow by his gravestone. I try to wipe the debris away and determine what it is before grabbing at it. But as I see the deep scarlet color, I gasp.

My head instantly snaps to the gravestone from across the path where I'd seen these roses before. I hadn't noticed, given they were covered in snow and ice, but I can tell the roses are there now. How is it possible that a stem has landed in this spot every time I come here? There's no way the wind's trajectory causes a stray rose to make its way to this spot every time.

I gently slide the stem out of the slush and examine it. It's beautiful, just like the others. I'm surprised it's so unmarred by the icy weather.

Leaning on the cold, harsh granite, I push myself to stand on shaky legs. The snow has soaked through my workout pants, causing me to shake. But my curiosity is winning this war, so I carefully make my way to the roses that match the one I'm carrying.

Bending down, I carefully swat away the bright white snow from the tops of the flowers. They're brilliant red, with no visible thorns. I place the stem I'm holding in the metal vase attached to the granite marker and step back. "There. Back where you belong," I tell it. A small smile curls my lips before I consider I'm losing my mind.

I begin to walk away, but can't help the need to clear away the ice and snow from this marker as I had Jake's. I feel a strange connection to this spot, knowing the flowers always find their way to my husband.

As I dust off the snow with the back of my hand, I gasp. My heart rate begins to escalate, and I lean forward, using both hands to remove any remaining snow.

Evelyn George Hughes

This has to be Huggie's mother. It has to be. Confirming the year of her death matches when he would've ridden at the rescue squad with me, I slump down into the snow in shock. It dawns on me, Huggie made all of the funeral arrangements. So it shouldn't be surprising that he found a spot near her.

I reach out to touch the flowers, feeling so close to Huggie all of a sudden. As I trace the furled edges of the rose petals with my fingertip, my mind flashes back to a similar time. I picture my nail detailing the thorny vine of his tattoo as it crept up his arm. The barbed wire intermingled like a helix. My eyes had been focused on his incredible body. All I could make out plainly in the dark was his toned abs and chest.

Until the night I came to his room and ended up on top of him. I'd caught a glimpse of the ink along his upper body. I never fully took in the details but saw little snippets each time I opened my eyes. My focus was clouded by lust, but I remember seeing enough of it in the dim light.

I've seen his arm enough times to know there weren't many roses on that vine. It was primarily thorns. The flowers would sporadically appear higher up his arm. From what I can recall, the vine crossed behind his neck and came back down over his other shoulder onto his chest. There were multiple vibrant roses all clustered over his left pec.

With one solo red rose entrapped next to his heart in a gilded cage.

Suddenly, I begin to shake, and I'm certain it's not from the cold. I close my eyes and rub my hands up and down my arms, trying to steady myself. My mind is playing tricks on me. I'm sure of it. Random pictures flip behind my closed lids as if I'm looking through one of the kids' old View-Master toys.

Click. Click. Click.

One after the other, I take them in. The beautiful flowers he brought to my house the day I turned him away. Huggie smiling at me as I stock the ambulance with supplies. The multiple bouquets of red roses in my room following Jake's death. The look on Huggie's face I didn't understand as he stood next to Jake on our wedding day. Finding the roses, I assumed Jake left for me. The same roses artfully inked onto his skin. Ones that are now replaced by thorns and barbed wire.

"Oh, god!" I yell. The enormity of this is too much.

What have I done?

CHAPTER THIRTY-TWO

MELANIE

"Come on, guys," I shout. We're so late. We should've been at The Manor House by now.

"I thought the wedding was at six? Why do we have to be there so early?" Ruby whines.

"I want to meet with the caterer and make sure everything is all set," I tell her as I wave her toward the front door.

"Can I have the first piece of cake then?" she asks with her hands steepled together.

Bending down to her eye level, I ask her, "Don't you think Nate and Adam should get that?"

"Oh, all right." Even her antics can't get to me today. She looks like a princess in her deep navy taffeta dress, white faux fur stole, and the little silver tiara I found. Her dark locks bounce against the back of her dress as she walks. It compliments my deep navy dress and heels.

Seth is standing by the door. He's not a fan of dressing up, and it shows.

"Thank you for being such a good sport," I tell him.

"I still don't understand why I have to wear this thing. I mean, couldn't I just have worn khakis and a white shirt?"

I squeeze his cheeks. "Make your mom happy, please? We never dress up anymore, and I want pictures."

Seth groans as he closes the door behind me. The cool night air hits me, giving me a chill. It's colder tonight than they predicted. I hope we don't get more snow. It'd be a beautiful backdrop for the wedding ceremony, but who wants to worry about the roads and potentially their guests all deciding to leave before the cake is cut?

We make it to the venue in record time. I'd been here all afternoon but wanted to come home and relieve Stacy and shower and change before returning. "You two have your electronics? Try to stay out of the way if you can. There are a few quiet rooms upstairs you can hang out in until guests start to arrive."

"Can I help with anything?" Ruby asks.

"Yes. Once guests arrive, you can help them to sign the cards."

"What cards?"

"At some weddings, people sign a guest book. So the couple can look back and remember who attended. It's going to be a busy evening, and in all of the commotion, sometimes they miss who was there." This shouldn't be too much of an issue for them, as there aren't that many people attending. "I thought it might be nice to have people write down wishes for their future instead."

"Do I get to do one?"

"Nate would love that."

We pull up to the stately brick colonial mansion to find multiple vehicles parked unloading supplies for the big event. The florist is here, along with the caterer. The photographer should be arriving soon to take pictures of the two of them before the service gets underway.

We walk into the space to see beautiful Magnolias all along the dark stained banister leading to the second floor. "You two head on upstairs and out of the way. I'll get you when guests start to appear. Okay?"

I scurry to the kitchen prep area to check in with the caterer. "Hey, everything good?" I ask.

"Yeah, we're all set. The bartender is setting up over there," she says, pointing to the area behind me.

"Oh, that's perfect."

"Justin is going to stand at the door and hand everyone their choice of either a glass of champagne or a hot apple cider, just as you requested."

"Thank you. Everything looks and smells perfect."

I miss the days when I could be in the kitchen preparing the food myself. But it was more than I could manage with work and the kids.

"Melanie."

I turn to find Nate dressed in his tux. This man is breathtaking in a pair of Bermuda shorts and a T-shirt. So in a tuxedo, there are no words. "Nate, you look amazing."

"I know, right?"

We both laugh.

"I can't tell you how grateful I am for all you've done. Everything I've seen so far is perfection."

"I didn't do much. Is Adam here?"

"No, he's coming soon. With his family." Nate makes a worried expression, but I know it's all in fun. He looks happier than I've ever seen him.

"I'm so happy for you, Nate. Please, take a few moments tonight to take it all in. It'll fly by, and I want you to remember how you felt when you look at your pictures later."

"I will." I expect to see a grateful smile or an expression of joy, but the look on his face makes me uneasy.

"What's the matter?"

"I'm trying to find the way to tell you. There's been a change in plans."

Um, what? If the last few years have taught me nothing, it's to roll with the punches. But the last thing a Mistress of Ceremonies wants to hear is that there's been a change in plans. "Do you have more people coming you hadn't planned on?"

"Yes," he answers with a look of nervousness.

"How many are we talking?"

"Oh, just one."

"Whew," I answer dramatically. "You had me worried. I didn't want to have to ration the guests' food. One we can handle."

"And we've changed our minds on groomsmen."

Wait a minute. I stare blankly at him.

"Adam really wanted his brother to stand up for him."

I exhale. "Oh, of course. That shouldn't be—"

"And Huggie is mine."

My stomach drops. I'm in no way prepared for this. The last thing I want is any type of emotional confrontation on Nate and Adam's big day. I admit I'd secretly wondered if he'd invited him. But didn't have the nerve to ask.

"You okay?" he asks.

"Of course. Why wouldn't I be? It's your big day. He should be here," I say, knowing all of this to be true but secretly wishing I could go crawl into a closet until this thing is over. I consider asking Nate if Huggie is bringing a date, but what would that matter? I don't need that in my head over the next few hours.

I knew there was the distinct possibility he'd be here. But with his absence and refusal to let anyone know where he was, I mistakenly thought he might avoid returning. When Nate never mentioned him, I tried to ignore the elephant in the room.

"I asked him to come early so we can get a few photos with him."

"Okay," I say, still trying to wrap my head around this. "I'm going to go check on the kids." I walk briskly up the stairs, my mind a flurry of emotion. Once I reach the top, I head for the changing rooms. I know they're unoccupied as Nate's downstairs, and Adam is on the way with his family.

Stepping inside, I close the door behind me and try to take a few breaths. *You can do this, Melanie.* My pep talk seems to be working until I hear Kat's voice from months ago in my head.

"Melanie. If the last few weeks have been this hard on you, think of the impact it's had on him."

∾

"Mom!" Seth shouts. I'm immediately alarmed because that child never yells.

"Mommy, it's Huggie," Ruby squeals.

I walk briskly over to the window and look out. My heart is in my throat. Huggie's wearing a black tuxedo that matches Nate's. I can practically see his silver eyes from here. Clutching my hand to my chest, I try to prevent the tears from falling. I've missed him so much. I'm hoping my smile doesn't blind him from up here, I giggle to myself. I turn to run downstairs until I catch him opening the passenger door out of the corner of my eye. As I look back through the window, I see a stunning woman with long dark hair take his hand as she steps out.

"Oh, god."

I stay upstairs, off to the side as they enter, and Huggie engulfs Nate in his arms. The two look so happy to be back together. His date smiles brightly at their exchange. She's absolutely gorgeous. I can't handle this right now.

I leave my perch to go find a bathroom and splash some water on my face. The photographer is here. They can manage this without me. Looking at my watch, I only have to make it another twenty minutes before guests should be arriving. Once Nate and Huggie are occupied with the photographer, I'll give Seth and Ruby their instructions and let them know I'll probably be busy in the kitchen or something. I'm not ready to see him up close until the reception. At least then, I can escape if I need to.

I exit the bathroom and hear Adam and his family enter downstairs. Nate approaches, makes introductions, and then they all head to the back of the home to take pictures.

"Mommy, did you see? Huggie's here."

"Yes, Ruby. I did. Did you say hi to him?"

"Yes. And told him how much I missed him." My heart. How am I supposed to make it through this night?

"Well, I'm glad you got to see him. Now I need your help. Guests will be arriving soon. Can you go down and explain the little cards we talked about as they enter?"

"Yes. I'm excited."

"I'll probably be in the kitchen if you need me."

Ruby runs downstairs to man her station, and Seth walks over. "You okay, Mom?"

"Yeah, honey. Why?"

"Because he came here with a girl." Seth looks upset. Why would this bother him?

"Honey. Why would you say that? He's allowed to bring a date." Seth grows quiet. This isn't like him. I take his hand and lead him over to the chair by the mirror. "What's going on?"

"He's supposed to be with you." Seth drops his head, appearing dejected.

"Seth." I'm not sure what to say to him. I wish he was right. But we've learned painfully that life doesn't always give you what you want.

"Don't you love him?" he asks.

"Well, of course, I do, but—"

"But nothing. If you love him, you need to tell him." He's getting so worked up it's making it hard for me to remain calm.

I squat down in front of him and take his hands. "Seth, I made a mistake. I was angry with Huggie and didn't handle it well. I'm going to try to apologize to him and see if we can remain friends. But if that makes his girlfriend uncomfortable, we'll have to be okay with that."

He looks miserable. Great, now there are two of us. "Seth, you are one of the most mature young men I know. And I'm not saying that because you're my son. It's the truth. You've stepped up to the plate for your sister and me more times than I can count. Now I need you to help me."

He looks up from his hands until our eyes connect, and I'm instantly comforted he'll do just that.

"This is an important day for Nate and Adam. I don't want anything to take away from their celebration. I'll try to talk to Huggie at the reception. I'll even ask if he can meet us for dinner one night. But I need your help to keep our focus on Nate. Okay?"

"Yes, ma'am."

I lean in to give him a hug and pray we can both make it through this night unscathed.

The violinist begins playing Pachelbel Canon in D, and I enter the small hallway outside the room where the ceremony is being held. Standing off to the side, I cue Adam's brother to make his way to the front of the room and then turn. As my eyes land on Huggie's silver-blue orbs, it takes my breath away. It's all I can do not to go to him.

His expression is unreadable. But there's no time to figure that out now. I extend my arm toward the ceremony space, giving him the signal that it's his turn. Without another glance, he turns and walks away. As my gaze follows him toward the officiant, I notice Nick, Kat, and Grace sitting in the second to last row. Kat turns to look at me with a bright smile, reminding me of the joy of this moment. We're here to celebrate our dear friend, Nate, all of us. Nothing else matters right now.

Adam and Nate take their turns walking into the ceremony, large smiles evident on everyone's faces. Each person gathered here, happy to witness these two committing themselves to one another. My eyes roam over the room. Friends, big burly firefighters, and Adam's family are all gathered together to wish them well. That's what I need to focus on.

Ruby and Seth stand by my side as the officiant begins the process of uniting the two in matrimony. Wrapping my arms around them, I focus on the words.

"I, Nathan Mars, take you, Adam Bostworth, to be my husband. I promise to be true to you in good times and bad, in sickness and in health. I will love you and honor you all the days of my life."

I tear up, thinking of my own vows. We weren't always good to each other. We made mistakes, but I honored and cherished Jake. And despite his faults, he did the same for me.

Wiping away a stray tear, I look up to see Huggie's eyes locked on me. Or is it the three of us? God, I miss him. Why didn't I beg Nate to tell me where he was all those weeks ago? Maybe, if he really felt for me as Kat said, all of this heartache could've been avoided.

I squeeze my kids closer to my sides, regret shaking me to the core. Seth was right. He's supposed to be with me.

The ceremony comes to a close as Nate and Adam are pronounced married. There is clapping from their guests and whooping and hollering by the boys at his station. Even Jamie is all smiles.

The three of us move off to the side so that the wedding party can exit the small space. I advise the kids I'm going to let the caterers know that we'll be showing guests to the buffet station soon. But as I start to walk away, I notice Huggie stops next to where his date has been sitting, gives her a radiant smile, and holds out his hand for her.

My heart breaks a little, seeing them together. But he deserves to be happy. And I love him enough to do the right thing.

Dropping my hand to my belly, I hold my head up high. I can do this, with or without him. But before he returns to wherever he's living now, I need to tell the man I love that I'm carrying his baby.

CHAPTER THIRTY-THREE

MELANIE

This wedding venue can easily accommodate twice the guests that are in attendance today. Yet, with the weight of Huggie's presence, and his date, it feels claustrophobic in here.

As the well-dressed guests follow the wedding party out to the dining room to find local favorites of Fried Green Tomatoes, and Adam's favorite, Beef Wellington, I step back to make room. *Okay, I try to hide.*

I'd set aside plates of Seth and Ruby's favorites and decide to go in search of them to make sure they eat something besides cake. I find them laughing with Nate and Adam and point to the table I'll be bringing their food to. Before I can step away, Nate pulls me in for a hug.

"Thank you. Everything looks amazing."

"You're so welcome. It was fun. I'd love to do more of this kind of thing. I miss it. I'll be back. Just getting Seth and Ruby's dinners."

I turn and practically collide with Jamie. I'm glad neither of us was carrying anything.

"Hey, big guy. Can I get you anything? I'm headed to the kitchen."

"No. Everything looks great. Just waiting for the buffet line to go down."

"Well, you're in luck. I've got an in with the chef. I'll get you some of everything. Do me a favor?"

"Sure?"

"If you can carry the kids' food out to them, I'll bring yours out right after."

I dart into the kitchen and grab the two plates I've kept in the warmer. "Hey, Gail. Can you make a couple of plates with everything on it? Make mine small, and the other plate, think giant." I laugh.

"Sure, Melanie. Coming right up."

I'm so glad I chose this caterer. Gail's been so easy to work with. I'd secretly like to pick her brain and see if I could work as an apprentice for a while. See if I could do something like this on my own.

I hand off the kids' plates to Jamie and return to the kitchen. The constant flurry of activity is almost soothing. It keeps my mind focused on my tasks, tuning out the chaos behind me, especially when part of that chaos is here with another woman.

"Mel, here you go," Gail shouts.

Reaching for the plates, they both contain a large amount of calorie-laden food, but one is piled notably higher than the other. I make my way out to the tables and stop as the metallic clinking of utensils against glass stops me in my tracks and makes me grin from ear to ear. I haven't been to a wedding in ages. I'd almost forgotten this tradition until I see Nate's broad smile as he turns to kiss his husband. Such a simple thing. But when someone starts to clink their glass with their spoon, soon the other guests follow, egging on the newlyweds to seal it with a kiss.

Lots of awes and ohs follow before everyone returns to their meal. It takes me a minute to realize I'm standing here like the bronze lady statue that stands in the gardens of this venue.

"Here you go, Jamie. And if you're still hungry, help yourself to some of mine." I laugh. "'Cause I'll never eat all of that."

"Thanks, Mel."

"Do you two need punch?" I ask the kids.

They both nod like bobblehead dolls, enjoying the decadent food. It makes my heart happy to see them like this, despite the last few months.

They'd finally recovered from losing their dad, just to have to endure Huggie going away. It had to be incredibly confusing for them. I mean, until I met with Dr. Miller, I didn't understand. But after weeks of quiet time and a startling surprise, I've grown stronger than I thought possible.

I love Huggie. I've never been more sure of anything in my life. But I've already had a great marriage, faults and all. If it's not in the cards for us after everything that's happened, I'll live with that. My priorities are my three children. But, for now, I just need to get through this evening.

HUGGIE

Standing here with Nate, I'm trying to pay attention to him and Adam, but I cannot keep my eyes off of Melanie. She's practically glowing.

I'm happy for her. She seems to have gotten along fine in my absence. The kids look like they're doing great. That's all that matters. It was never in the cards for us anyway.

"Did you meet Adam's family?" Nate asks.

"Yeah. His brother introduced them earlier when we were taking pictures."

"Oh, good. Everything's happened so fast tonight. It's hard to keep up."

I stop to take him in. This man I've known for so long. He's beaming. "I'm happy for you, Nate."

"Now it's your turn," he says.

"What are you talking about?"

He puts his hand on my shoulder, and I watch as the broad smile is replaced with a serious expression. "If you don't go over and talk to her, then I'm going to make a scene when I announce that you two are having the first dance instead of Adam and me."

What the...

"This has gone on long enough. You two are killing each other."

"From where I'm standing, she looks like she's doing just fine. She hasn't spoken a word. Acts like I'm not even here." I shrug.

I admit, as happy as I am to see her, I'm irritated. I've tried to move on. Yet time and distance have done nothing to sate my ache for her. Hell, I made it all the way to the front door of The Rox before I had to call a second Uber to take me home. It was hard enough trying to be physical with someone that wasn't Melanie before. It's going to be a very long time before I can consider sleeping with anyone but her.

"Do it! The first dance is supposed to start any minute. Don't test me."

Hell. He looks serious. Looking about the room, I come up short until I see her standing in the corridor that leads to the kitchen, speaking animatedly with a short, redheaded older woman. I need another drink for this.

Walking to the bar, I ask for a Jack and Coke just as Melanie walks in my direction. I practically stare her down, hoping she'll turn my way. When her shining eyes connect with mine, she stops in her tracks, and I almost think I hear a gasp.

Walking over to her, I can't put this off any longer. "Hi."

"Hi." Her voice seems so timid. Has she always had those little freckles on her cheeks? I've loved this woman for twenty years. How had I not noticed it before?

"You look beautiful."

"Thank you."

This conversation is awkward as hell. Jesus, what's happened to us? "Can I get you a drink?"

"No," she answers abruptly. Is she dismissing me?

I nervously look back to the bartender, who has my drink in hand.

"Thank you," I tell him, dropping a few dollars in the tip jar. Turning to Melanie, I let out a sigh of relief that she didn't ditch me while my back was turned. "Can we go somewhere and talk?"

"I can't," she says. Again it sounds curt. "They're about to have the first dance and then cut the cake."

I lean in, the warmth radiating from her and her familiar watermelon scent enveloping me. "I have it on good authority from the groom that he won't mind."

Melanie scans the room and finds Nate standing with his arm around Adam, looking in our direction. He's not smiling but looks hopeful.

"I wouldn't feel comfortable stepping away now, but maybe over there." She points to a little alcove where we're out of the way of guests who'd like to dance but not so removed she couldn't intervene if needed.

I follow her the short walk to the area, taking slow breaths in and out so I don't hyperventilate if this goes all wrong. She turns to look at me, and all I can do is stand there, staring into her big brown eyes.

"Mellie—"

I'm cut short as she turns to look about the room. Is she looking for the kids?

"I feel bad monopolizing you like this," she whispers.

"What are you talking about?" I mimic her tone, using our hushed voices as an excuse to inch forward.

"Where's your date?"

"My what?" I look about the room until my eyes land on Nate, who's standing with his sister. She must've seen us arrive together.

"I don't have a date." I wait until her eyes reconnect with mine. "Nate's sister, Lyla, was anxious about coming here alone. So I offered to drive her."

Melanie's shoulders visibly drop, and her expression relaxes. It gives me the in I'm looking for.

"The only woman I'm interested in here is you."

This time I'm sure I hear it. That little gasp that makes my heart sing.

"Melanie, I—"

"I'm so sorry."

"What?"

"I should've never acted that way." She sounds as if she's pleading with me.

I'm stunned. This is the last thing I was expecting. "Please, let me say this." I reach for her hands, hoping she won't reject me. "I had no right to lie to you. None. What we did was wrong. I have no excuse other than I felt so bad for him. I was trying to lessen the impact on both of you however I could. At least that's how I tried to justify it."

"I understand," she says simply. "He had no right to put you in that position."

"But, Melanie, I can't put all of this on Jake. I'm a grown man. I could've told him no." I rub the pad of my thumb back and forth over her soft skin. God, I've missed this. As uncomfortable as this is, I'm just happy to be near her.

She takes a step closer, and I think I may have gasped this time. Is it the time away? How is she even more beautiful than when I left?

"Can you ever forgive me?"

"I did long ago," she answers. The sincerity in her eyes is undeniable.

The hope that springs through my body causes me to stand a little taller. But I can't assume anything. We've been through too much.

"Is it my turn now?" she questions.

"Oh, yes."

"I'm really sorry for the way I handled everything. I was just so upset. Mostly by the deceit." I drop my head in shame.

"It took me a while to realize I was transferring my anger from Jake to you. But, Huggie, I've come a long way. Now that I'm facing life on my own, I need to have all the cards on the table." She pauses for a moment, and I try to give her the space she needs to say everything that's on her heart. "It's hard to manage when you find out things that've been kept from you."

I know she says she's already forgiven me. But why do I have the sense there's more?

"Huggie?" she asks, stepping even closer.

My heart is in my damn throat. "Yes?" My fucking hands are probably sweating all over her.

"Do you love me?"

Unable to stop, I pull her against me and cup her cheeks. "More than any man should."

Her smile could light up the whole room.

"Melanie, I love you more than all the stars in the sky. I love you more than eggs and bacons on a Saturday," I pronounce. She giggles and I suddenly feel like I'm the groom at this wedding. "I love you more than Sponge Bob loves jellyfish. More than Michael Jordan loves basketball." Her cheeks are pink as she smiles back at me. "I love you more than Jamie likes to eat!"

Our conversation is cut short as I hear the familiar clinking of spoons against glassware, encouraging the newlyweds to kiss. Melanie and I simultaneously turn our heads to look for Nate and Adam when we realize they're on their feet, clinking their glasses... for us, with Nick and Kat beside them smiling wide.

Looking down at this beautiful woman, I plant my mouth over hers and kiss her hard. I give everything to her in this moment. As if sealing *my* vow to be true to her all the days of my life.

I'm so engrossed in the kiss I barely notice the uproarious claps and whistling coming from my firefighter brothers behind me. I pull back, rubbing the pad of my thumb over her lower lip just as Seth and Ruby wrap their arms around us.

"Does this mean you're coming home?" Seth asks. The hope in his eyes almost brings a tear to mine.

I look to Melanie. I don't dare say anything without checking with her. Even though I'm praying she says—

"Yes."

"Mommy?"

I notice Ruby looks concerned. God, what've we put these poor kids through?

"Yeah, baby?"

"Can we have cake first?"

∾

The night comes to an end, and I wish Nate and Adam well before looking for his sister, Lyla. I'd give anything if I could stay the night, but I knew this was going to be a painful turnaround for me.

"Melanie, I want you to meet Lyla, Nate's sister," I introduce.

"Oh, it's so nice to meet you. I think the world of your brother."

"He tells me you helped pull all of this together." She gives Mel an appreciative smile.

"I tried. I love entertaining. But it's even more fun when you're celebrating someone you care about."

Lyla reaches for Melanie's arm and gives it a squeeze. "Thank you. I'm so glad he has friends like you."

"Do you live nearby?" Melanie asks.

"No. I live in Spotsylvania. I still can't believe how nice Huggie was to drive me here. I was a little intimated being the only family member here in a sea of strangers."

"Well, you're no longer a stranger. We're thrilled you were here. I hope we get to see more of you," Melanie tells her, and I can tell it's sincere.

Leaning down next to her ear, I whisper, "I'd give anything if I could stay. But I need to take her home, and I have work tomorrow."

As I stand to my full height, she looks perplexed. "I transferred to a fire station in Maryland."

"Oh." Hell. More I've kept from her.

"I'm off on Tuesday. Can I see you after you get off work, so we can talk? I want to fill in any missing pieces. I'm never keeping anything from you again."

Her eyes twinkle mischievously. "Anything?"

I swallow hard, worried about what she has in mind to ask.

"I'm teasing." She laughs. "Yes. I think it's about time we get everything out in the open."

I go to look for Seth and Ruby, telling them I'll see them in a couple of days. They look as happy as I feel.

Returning to Melanie's side, I pull her back into me. "Please, tell me I'm not dreaming? That I'm really going to get to see you Tuesday afternoon."

My sweet girl wraps her arms around my neck and pulls me in for a kiss. "Will you have to leave early the day you visit? To get back for work the next day?"

"No, ma'am." I kiss her on the nose. It feels surreal doing this in public after all of these years. "It's the first day of my ten-day break." Kiss. "I hope to see a lot of you." I wink.

"Please, drive safely, Huggie." The impact of her words isn't lost on me. Not just because of the distance but the worry she may have as I drive up and down the busy highways that separate us. The sooner we can figure out if we're making this official, and I can return home to Hanover, the better we'll be.

CHAPTER THIRTY-FOUR

HUGGIE

Man, I95 sucks. We had a busy night at the station, so I went straight home to take a power nap before braving the interstate back to Hanover. The trip from Maryland through Washington D.C. is like driving through spaghetti junction. The highways interloop each other like long overlapping strings of pasta. Thank god for GPS.

I've made the trek from Hanover to and from The Rox enough times directions shouldn't be an issue. However, there've been multiple road delays due to construction and accidents. I've had to pay close attention every time I get off or on the highway. It's easily doubled my commute today. Three hours is doable. Six, not so much.

But I'm keeping my eye on the prize. I get to see my favorite girl and the two best kids around. I'd hoped Melanie and I could talk today, but that'll likely have to wait until tomorrow as the kids will be home by the time I manage to get there. I'll ask if she wants to place a takeout order for Luigi's, and I'll bring it to the house with me. That way, I won't lose any time away from her as we try to organize dinner.

It'll feel odd sleeping in my bed tonight. I haven't been there in so long. Given my commute, many of the guys I covered for during fall sports have stepped up to the plate on the movie set. Between inclement weather and my work schedule, they've tried to do their part as the production wrapped up so I wouldn't have to make the drive.

Sure, it's tempting to ask if I can stay with Melanie and the kids for the night. But it doesn't feel right until we can work all of this out. The kids have been through enough. We need to be one hundred percent sure of what we're doing before we drag them into any more drama.

Bzzz. Bzzz.

Looking at the name on my phone eases all of the strife related to this ridiculous commute. "Hi."

"Hi," she answers. "I would've thought you'd be here by now."

"What? Are you anxious to see me?"

"No," she answers in a huff. "I'm hungry."

I chuckle. "You waited to have lunch with me?"

"Yes. Now you've taken so long to get here, dinner better come quick."

"Well, as it so happens, I was going to call and see if you wanted to place an order with Luigi. I can pick it up on the way there."

"You and Luigi's? Our cup runneth over." She laughs. "How's the traffic been?"

"A bear. But I'm being extra careful."

The line grows quiet. Should I have said that? After all of these years—

"Huggie?"

"Yeah?"

"I know we'll need to talk later. There's a lot to say. But can we focus on the four of us tonight? We've missed you so much, and the kids..." It's suddenly so quiet, I have to look at my phone to see if I lost the connection somehow.

"Mel?"

"I'm sorry. These kids think you hang the stars in the sky, Huggie. Can we eat dinner, enjoy being together tonight, and save the heavy stuff for tomorrow?"

She's getting me a little emotional now. "Yeah, of course." The GPS directs me to return to the highway from where I've bypassed the last accident, and I try to focus on the road. I hit my brakes as I come down the onramp, and a police car whizzes by.

"Huggie?"

"Hey, I'm here. It's just typical I95 traffic. Mel?"

"Yeah?"

"I'm going to go. But I should be at Luigi's in a little over an hour. I'm going to have dinner and watch a movie with you guys, then head to my place afterward. But what is your schedule like this week? Is there any chance of having any alone time with you in the next few days?" Before I left, she was working practically Monday through Friday. I don't know if I'll make it 'til the weekend.

"I've taken the day off tomorrow. So the day is yours until the kids are home."

Things are looking better by the minute. "Good. Just didn't want to have to beg after they went to bed."

Her sweet laughter tickles my ears. "Okay, drive carefully, and I'll see you soon."

"Huggie!" Ruby yells as I step out of my Suburban. God, I've missed that sound.

She hurtles into me, nearly knocking me into the side of my car. Has she grown that much since I've been gone, or is it merely her excitement to see me? I look down at her, and the joy written on her face answers that question for me.

Seth jogs over, giving me a hug as well. I don't tend to get many of these from him. He's had to mature so much over the last two years, and I feel like I missed when those days ended.

"How've you been, bud?"

"Okay. Better now."

My heart squeezes at his statement. Me too, buddy. Me too.

I look up to see Melanie grinning at me from the front porch, and I feel like I've hit the lottery.

"Please, tell me you have pasta in that car."

"Mom's hungry." Seth laughs.

"Well, think how I feel. I had to smell it the whole way here?"

The kids help me carry everything into the house, and I stop to give Melanie a chaste kiss before heading inside. It's nice being able to show her affection openly. I've waited twenty years to lay one on her in front of everyone.

The night goes by way too fast. It was hard to stay focused on the movie. I just wanted to stare at the three of them. When did I turn into such a sap?

We say our goodnights to the kids, and I attempt to clean up the kitchen as she tucks them into bed. In some ways, it feels like nothing has changed. Then I see artwork drawn while I was away and a stray Christmas ornament, and I realize how much I've missed.

As Melanie comes around the corner from the steps, I can see she looks exhausted. Keeping up with the kids and working has really taken a toll on her. I'm sure the holidays were even harder. A wave of guilt washes over me that she was handling that alone.

"Thank you," she says, noticing the kitchen is tidy.

"You're welcome." I take her in my arms and bury my face in her hair. "How early can I come by tomorrow?"

"Well, I'll be up to get the kids on the bus. So how early would you like?" She giggles.

"I'll be here at eight."

The night goes by way too fast. It was hard to stay focused on the movie. I just wanted to stare at the three of them. When did I turn into such a sap?

"Huggie!" Ruby yells as I walk through the front door. She races over to me, gives me a side hug, then takes the box of donuts I'm carrying and runs back to the island.

"So, was it me you were excited to see or the donuts?"

"Bof!" she announces with a mouth full of chocolate pastry frosted with sprinkles.

"Hey, Seth."

"Hi. Will you be here this afternoon?" he asks.

"I plan on it. Why? Have you got some project Hilde needs you to turn in?"

"No. She's been out." Seth's expression seems flat.

"Everything okay?" I prod.

"She got married," Ruby answers, mouth still full.

Poor kid.

"You two need to head out, or you're going to miss the bus," Melanie says as she comes around the corner. The kids both look at the clock over the oven and scurry.

"Sorry, Mom," Seth says, grabbing his coat.

They rush for the door and make it down the driveway just as the flashing lights from the bus come into view.

"Whew, that was close," Melanie says.

We stand in the doorway together, watching the kids drive away. As we step inside, all thought of waiting until we talk is gone. I grab her, thrusting her against the wall and kissing her hard. She doesn't appear to mind, giving it back as good as she's getting it. The two of us groping, licking, and grinding against each other like horny teenagers.

"God, I've missed you." I pant.

"I couldn't sleep last night, knowing you were so close."

"Melanie, I know we have a lot to talk about, but I'm not going to be able to think straight until—"

"I know. There's so much we need to—"

I immediately scoop her up under that beautiful ass that's taunted me in my dreams and carry her up the stairs. Every two steps, I have to stop and kiss her. At this rate, the kids will be home before I get her undressed.

I start to remove her robe and stop. "Is this okay?"

Melanie gives me a look that says, "duh," and rips it off her shoulders before stopping abruptly. "Huggie?"

"Yeah?" I need to be inside her. We need all this small talk over with.

"I need to see you."

"What?" I look down at my junk that's pressed squarely against my gray sweatpants, leaving nothing to the imagination. I mean, hell, she can practically see me now.

"No," she corrects. Stepping forward, she lifts my shirt over my head and tosses it to the side. There's no more hiding anything from her. I'm all in. I watch as she traces her fingernail along the barren vines of my arm and continues until she reaches my neck. Without removing her finger, she walks around to stand behind me, seeing the trail continue across my back to my other shoulder.

Turning my head in an attempt to read her expression, I have to swallow down this boulder lodged in my throat. The morning light casts shadows across her face as she painstakingly takes in every detail. I've imagined this moment for years, how I'd explain.

As she returns to stand in front of me, I see the sorrowful expression as she places her finger over the gilded cage, my broken heart trapped within it. It's easy to miss. It's buried within layers of ornate red roses of the same hue.

"Is this because of me?" She looks pained.

"No. It's because of me." I take a breath. "You did nothing wrong. You're beautiful and smart, funny, and confident. It's not your fault you're... everything."

"All those years, Huggie. I—"

"Don't. You were happy. And that made me happy."

Tears start to tumble down her sweet face.

"Please, don't cry, Mellie. I wouldn't trade any of it. I loved Jake. And your kids..." I have to stop and collect myself before I start bawling like a baby. "Things happened as they were meant to. I'd give anything if Jake was still here. He was the best man I ever knew."

Melanie wraps her arms around me and squeezes me to her. I can feel her tears against my chest. But I know they aren't tears of loss. This is a new beginning for both of us. I've never been more certain of anything.

Growing impatient, I slide my hands to the straps of her gown and slide it down her arms. My dick jumps at the sight of her beautiful breasts. They seem fuller than the last time I saw them, but I'm sure it's my mind playing tricks on me. Everything about reuniting with her is more than I hoped it would be. Bending down, I suck her nipple into my mouth and toy with the other, stopping briefly to push my face between them. I can't contain the moans.

Picking her up once more, I carry her over to the bed. God. Who'd think anyone would love a guest room bed so much? Placing her down, I slide her panties off and then start to remove my sweatpants when she stops me.

MELANIE

"Huggie, the other women..."

"Don't."

"No. I want to—"

"Don't go there, Mel."

"I just know you... have needs. There are things you like. I want to give you what they did."

He gives me a stern look. I'm not sure I can recall him ever giving me such an expression. Is it annoyance that I brought it up? His penchant for being rough or the other women? Or possibly anger that he has to be put in the awkward position of telling me I can't give him what they could?

"You can't."

And there it is. Disappointment sits on my chest like an anchor. I'm not sure I'll ever be what he needs in the bedroom. How will I ever be able to put it—

"They were nothing to me. They gave me nothing. I took what I wanted. But ended up with nothing."

His words are raw and full of emotion. But I don't truly understand what he's saying. There's an urgency in his tone. Staring up at him, I try to decipher what he's saying. It's as if he's talking in riddles.

His voice drops an octave, and a touch of the sweet man I've known most of my life returns. "They weren't you. All I ever wanted was you."

Standing from the bed, I pull his face down and kiss him hard. Cupping his cheeks, I slide my tongue inside and try to share just how much his words mean to me. As I pull back, I'm surprised at his expression. It's not of love or lust. He looks scared.

"What's the matter?"

"I'm nervous."

"Why?"

"I've never made love to anyone before."

I have to blink several times to contain my emotion, or I'll start to cry again. This man. Our prior encounters, while loving, were raw and powerful. I think we've been afraid to let our guards down to enjoy tenderness.

"You aren't sending away the hot, dirty-talking bad boy for good, are you?" *Gah. I'd miss him.*

He reaches for my breasts and bends back down to suckle, his mischievous blue eyes teasing me. "I don't think that's possible with you." Moving up to grasp my face, he trails his tongue along the seam of my lips before plunging in.

I can't wait any longer. Reaching forward, my face still held captive, I start to slide his pants down. He knew exactly what he was doing wearing those sweatpants here this morning. I have no doubt. As they slide down his legs, the head of his cock is visible over the hem of his boxers. I instantly begin to salivate.

He slides them down and steps out, and I marvel at him. This man is perfection, inside and out. He wraps his hand around his thick shaft and strokes, and I can't contain my moan. I've never seen a more erotic sight in my life. This lean, muscular man, covered in beautiful ink, standing before me as he strokes his heavy cock. Knowing it's all for me.

Sitting on the edge of the bed, I slide my hands around his backside and squeeze as I lean forward and take him into my mouth. The groans above me match mine. Gliding my hands up and down the velvety skin, I enjoy the taste and feel of him.

"Mellie, you feel so good. But I'm never going to last like that. I need you."

I pull back and look up at him. He reaches out to stroke my swollen lips with his thumb, and the mixture of reverence and lust takes my breath away. I scoot back, centering myself on the bed, and watch as he climbs over me.

All of a sudden, he sits back on his heels and gives me an earnest glance. "Mellie, I don't have anything with me. In my head, I thought my condoms were in the nightstand, but I completely blacked out everything that's happened..." he says, shaking his head in disbelief.

I'd planned to tell him this morning about the baby, but things changed gears so quickly. The need for condoms hadn't crossed my mind, given my current state.

"I haven't been with anyone. Only you," he declares earnestly.

My eyes flick up to his, I'm sure reflecting my relief.

"I haven't so much as touched another woman." He leans down closer, and I reach up to stroke his cheeks. I could drown in those sparkling silver eyes every day for the rest of my life.

"Me either," I assure him. I'm surprised at how his expression softens. Had he thought I'd been with someone... Derek? "Only you."

Huggie lies down, engulfing me with his body. The hard planes and warm skin combined with his masculine scent are intoxicating. And if I can't drink for the next six months, I'll gladly substitute.

He lifts my legs, draping them around his hips as he nudges my opening with the head of his cock. I'm getting tearful, knowing I almost lost this. Lost him.

As he gradually glides the rest of the way in, he pulls back and stops. "Baby, what's wrong? I should've made sure you—"

"No, no. I'm okay."

He doesn't move. His imploring eyes wait on me to proceed.

"I'm so in love with you," I cry.

"Mellie." He breathes. "Mellie." He trails kisses along my neck, down to my collarbone, as he adjusts the angle of his pelvis. Hastening his strokes in and out of me, he hits my sweet spot, pushing me closer to the edge. The combination of the heavy drag of his cock as he takes me and his tongue along my skin is causing sensory overload.

"I've missed this. Burying my face in your watermelon hair, the taste of your sweet skin..." Kiss. "The feel of your hot, snug pussy." Lick. "I want to make love to you Monday through Friday..." Kiss. "and fuck you every weekend." He continues to make love to me as only he can. Mixing the dirty with the sweet.

His pace is becoming frantic, and I can feel my thighs tighten as my climax nears.

"Are you close?" He grunts.

"Yes."

"I need you to do something for me." I can hear the gravity of his question hanging heavy in the air around us as he thrusts in and out of me.

"Anything."

"I need you to scream my name when you come. My name!" He growls.

I sink my fingers deep into his backside and hold on for dear life as he pummels forcefully into me. All the years of want. All of his torment.

"Hugs!" I yell as my orgasm starts to crash. "Huggie!" I feel as if I'd float away if I didn't hold on. But I can't let that happen again. This man deserves to have everything, without any fear.

"Oh, fuck!" He's coming undone. The pounding is relentless. "I love you." He breathes into my ear as he starts to quake above me. "I love you."

"Huggie," I cry. I'm so overwhelmed but, for the first time, it's in a good way.

His breathing slows, and I run my hands through his damp hair as he lies above me, resting on his forearms as he buries his face in my neck. It takes a moment to realize he's crying.

"Baby." I stroke his hair and try to comfort him. As overpowering as my reaction was moments ago, I'm sure this had to be twenty years worth of emotion crashing into him. I turn my head, trying to kiss his temple when he looks up—those silver-blue orbs conveying all of his feelings.

"Maybe I should stick to fucking."

"What?"

"If that's what happens when I make love to you."

I giggle, continuing to play with his still-damp curls.

"Promise you won't leave me if I cry every time I make love to you," he teases.

"Well, there's no need to worry about that." He drops his head back down into my neck. "I could barely keep up with two kids without your help. I know I can't handle three."

CHAPTER THIRTY-FIVE

HUGGIE

Wait, what? My head pops up to make sure I'm awake. I'd had my suspicions this was a dream until she caught me weeping like an overcome child. Searching her eyes for some acknowledgment of what I just heard, I'm met with a look of pure joy. "Three?"

She simply nods.

Pulling back to sit on my heels, I rub my hands down my face. As my vision clears, I can see she's now pensive. "You're sure?"

"Yes," she answers hesitantly. "But I'm fully prepared to do it on my own if this isn't something you—"

"Ahhhhhhhh!" I roar. Roar. I can't contain my emotions right now. "We're having a baby?" I ask, the tears starting to build again. *Fuck, she's going to change her mind about me if I keep this up.*

"Yes," she answers, covering her mouth with her hands. I can't tell if she's happy or worried right now.

Pulling them away from her face, I bend down and kiss her. The love of my life and the mother of my child. "Mellie?"

"Yes?"

"You want me, right? You love me and want to be with me?"

"I thought I made that clear already." She laughs.

"You don't feel obligated. Because—"

"I knew I was in love with you before I ever realized I was pregnant. I tried to tell you, and you were gone."

I turn my head away from her, not wanting her to see my anguish at my decision to run.

"It's okay. I understand. As painful as it was, we both needed some clarity."

I lie down by her side and cup her cheek. "Marry me?"

"You've loved me for decades, and that's all I get?" She giggles.

"You know I'll propose for real. But I wanted one try where I wasn't bawling, so you weren't worried about what you were getting into." I reach over and stroke her belly lightly. The amazement of her news is going to take a while to sink in. Not only does this woman love me, but she's having my baby. I shake my head.

"It's a lot, huh?"

I nod. "When can we get married?"

She sits up and takes a deep breath. "I don't want to rush it."

The fuck? "Mel. I've been waiting for twenty years. I think that's the opposite of rushing it."

"No. I mean, now that we've found our way back and know that it's real. I need to do the right thing by the kids. They've been hurt enough." She looks down at her hands for a moment. She has to know I'm not leaving again. "Let them get used to you being back in their lives for a bit. I mean, you live in a different state right now."

She's right. They've had to take on a lot more than two kids should in the last few years. "Do they know?"

"About the baby? No. Although Seth is smarter than I give him credit for most days."

"You aren't going to be able to hide this too long."

"I know. I was prepared to tell them it was going to be the four of us." The statement hits me in the chest like an anvil. "I think we should take things slow for the next few weeks. Hopefully, you can spend more time with us around your schedule, and we can find the right way to tell them."

"You're right." I can't help feeling a little dejected. She never said yes, and I asked twice. But I'm still happy, just impatient.

I feel her hand on my chin as she turns my face toward her. "Yes."

"What?" I ask hopefully.

"Have no doubt, George Hughes. I will marry you."

I crush her in my arms until I remember. "Oh, shit. Did I hurt you earlier?"

"Huggie? How long have you been a paramedic? You have to know I'm okay."

"Hell, Mellie. It's different when it's your baby." I reach for her again, placing a kiss on the top of her head. "And your girl." The smile that crosses my face is nearly painful.

My girl.

~

The next few weeks are busy with trips back and forth from Maryland to Hanover, but I wouldn't have it any other way. The kids are gearing up for spring soccer, and I'm hard at work trying to get back to Hanover Fire. I'm not certain I'll be able to return to my home station, but just returning to my county's jurisdiction will make me feel like I'm home.

Melanie has cut back to three days a week at the cardiology office. If it were up to me, she'd leave entirely. But I have no need to worry. I know she loves me. I'm not afraid of the hot widower.

With extra time on her hands, she's managed to connect with Gail, a caterer she worked with on Nate's wedding. Melanie's always been a hostess at heart. She's happiest when she's spreading her sweet spirit to those around her. And I'm the lucky bastard who she's going to come home to every night. Well, at least, I hope so.

I've been biding my time, but she's starting to show. I'm shocked the kids haven't caught on, but we are sharing the news this weekend. We sat down last weekend and explained I'd be moving back in, and they were thrilled. For now, I'm back in the guest room. We haven't shared our plans to marry just yet. But we've started working on a vision to update the house and will need to let them in on what's happening.

Melanie and I have had Jake's study transformed into a first-floor master bedroom. I reached out to some of my firefighter brothers who work in home renovation, and they quickly drew up plans to change it dramatically. We still need to make some minor adjustments, but it already feels like our space.

There's no way Melanie or I would feel comfortable staying in the original master. That space will be divided into two connected rooms, a guest room, and a nursery. The old guest room will be a multipurpose office for Melanie, myself, and a quiet space for the kids to tackle tough assignments from any future Homework Hildegards they acquire.

"You ready," I ask Melanie, anxious to head out.

"Yeah. Just wanted to check in with Kat to see how the kids did today." Mel helped Gail at a wedding today, and I was 'busy' on set. Sure, the latest filming wrapped up a week ago, but she doesn't need to know that. Kat took the kids for the day and offered to let us have a date night.

I'm trying not to pace. I have so much nervous energy, but I don't want to give too much away. She already reads me like a book.

"Okay. They're great. They're eating pizza and playing with Grace."

"Awe." My mind instantly pictures the two of them playing with their sister or brother, and I can't hide the grin. "Training practice."

She giggles. "Where are we going?"

"They're having an event at the set. They're closing things up and invited our crew to come by."

"Oh, Seth and Ruby will be sad they missed it."

"This is more for the grown-ups. Dinner under the stars kinda thing."

"Wow. That sounds great."

We head out, and I find I'm probably giving myself away. I can't stop kissing her hand in the car and looking at her like she's waving this dog a bone.

We park the car and head over to where my friends have placed rental tables and chairs, dressed with white tablecloths and lanterns in the grassy area near the cabins we used the last time we were here. They've even set up a few heat lamps in the perimeter I hadn't thought to ask for.

"Huggie, this is beautiful. It's so romantic."

We're off to a good start. I point to Nate and Adam, who see us and stand from their table. "Hey, man. How are you?"

"Good. When are you getting your ass back to the station?"

"Working on it. Hey, Adam. How've you been?"

"Great. Hey, Mel. It's great to see you."

Melanie clutches her coat around her, more to hide her growing belly than from the cold, and leans in to offer each of them a kiss hello. We've both tried hard to tamp down our excitement about our new arrival until we can share the news with Seth and Ruby.

"Well, I hate to cut and run, but I'm starving," I tell Nate.

"Enjoy. We'll catch up later."

I escort Melanie over to the table closest to the cabin and hold out her chair. It's a little chilly, but the warmth from the heat lamp is helping.

"Can I offer you champagne or a cocktail?" the hired server asks.

"Oh, no. Just water, please," Melanie answers.

"Same." I take her hand and rub it with my thumb. "You cold?"

"No. It's perfect." She smiles at me. I notice a few more freckles around her cheeks that I'm sure were not there before this pregnancy. I didn't think it was possible for her to be more beautiful.

We enjoy the meal, catered by our favorite Italian restaurant, and I try not to let the fact that my leg is shaking under the table give away my plans. I'd scold myself for being so nervous if this weren't decades in the making. I think it's the awareness this is real more than the act of proposing.

"Can I interest you in dessert or a cup of coffee?"

I look to Melanie, who shakes her head, and I exhale. I'm not sure I could sit through another course.

She stands from her chair, and I walk over to let her slide her arm through mine. The ground is uneven, and— oh hell, holding on to her is keeping me from shaking out of my shoes.

"Hey, any chance I can sneak a kiss in the cabin for old times' sake before we leave?"

Melanie smiles up at me suspiciously, and I feel my balloon burst. I'm so transparent. Leaning in closer, she says, "If memory serves, it wasn't a kiss I gave you last time." Her laugh soothes my nerves. She's right. But I'm not asking for a hand job this time. As much as I wouldn't argue with giving her one.

As we walk up to the door, I take a step back, letting her enter first.

"Oh, Huggie." She gasps.

The small cabin is covered in deep red roses: long stems and clusters of red roses in planters. There are rose petals on the floor with small flickering lanterns scattered about the space. Nate did good. Not that I had any doubt.

"Huggie, I—"

I manage to drop to one knee before she turns and hope I can keep it together. "Mellie, I think I fell in love with you that first day we met. You said hello, and I was a goner. I'd made peace with the fact that loving you from afar was enough." Stopping for a moment, I have to turn away from her so I can keep going. But this incredible woman kneels down in front of me and clutches my hands, silently encouraging me with her loving smile. "But you, Seth, and Ruby are more than I ever dreamt possible. Add this baby, and I could never want for anything more." I open the ring box housing the platinum cushion cut diamond resting inside.

"Oh, Huggie. It's breathtaking."

"Then you're a matching set." I slide the ring on her shaky hand and try to warm it with mine. "Will you marry me?"

"Yes. I can't wait to be your wife."

I stand and pull her into me, so I can wrap my arms around my soon-to-be wife and child and kiss her. "I love you. I promise to be good to you."

"You already have," she says, looking adoringly at me. "Now it's my turn."

"I can't believe you're letting us help you paint," Ruby says.

Given how much of a mess I've gotten myself into with these two before, she's probably right. "I trust you. Besides, there is tarp covering everything but the wall. And we can repaint the wall."

"So, what are we doing with the guest room?" Seth asks, appearing a bit concerned.

My eyes connect with Melanie's, and she comes closer. "Well, we're doing a little redecorating."

"This room is going to be an office for all of us," she explains. That's why we packed up the things from downstairs. To move them up here.

"But where is Huggie going to sleep?"

Melanie looks at me nervously. Her kids are smart. I can't imagine they aren't already a step ahead of us.

"I'm moving into the new bedroom with your mom."

Seth surprises me by smiling from ear to ear. I expected him to be disgusted by the idea.

"So, it's official?" he asks.

Melanie twists her engagement ring around her finger to demonstrate how very real it is, and Ruby jumps up and down, screeching as only a preteen girl can. *Or a guy frightened by a plastic snake in a porta-potty.* But she looks excited for a good reason.

"Can I be your flower girl?" she asks.

"You can be whatever you like. Flower girl, junior bridesmaid. I just want the two of you by my side when I say I do."

I come closer and wrap an arm around her.

"When are you getting married?" Seth asks.

Melanie looks to me.

"How about May?" I ask him. "We were thinking of asking Nick and Kat if we could do it at the lake.

"Wow. That fast?" he asks. "I figured with the way Mom plans parties, it wouldn't be for a while. So everything is just right." Seth uses his fingers to demonstrate quotation marks around the *just right.*

"Well, I think it's going to be just right no matter what we decide to do," she tells Seth as she pulls him in, wrapping her arm around his neck playfully.

"We need to get cracking on painting this room so we can get to the other one?"

"What other one?" Ruby asks.

"The one down the hall. We don't have a lot of time," I say, winking at Melanie.

Seth looks to me and then back at his mother, who's smiling at him, and he instantly bolts for the door. *Shit. This was all going so well.* I rush after him, Melanie hot on my heels, worried this is too much for him, when we see he's made it to the old master bedroom.

We slowly approach the doorway when Ruby pushes passed us. Seth has his hands over his face, and Ruby's back is to us as they take in the crib and rocking chair draped in clear tarp. I turn to Melanie, worried we've gone about this all wrong. This may be more change than they're ready for.

"Mom?" Seth asks, tears coming down his face. *I feel horrible.* What were we thinking?

He rushes over to hug Melanie before looking up at her. "Are you?"

Ruby turns to look at us.

"Think we have room for Huggie *and* a little brother or sister?" she asks quietly.

Ruby collides with Seth and Melanie, and I try to hold it together as the three of them cry together.

Seth looks up at me, his eyes swollen. "I love you."

CHAPTER THIRTY-SIX

HUGGIE

"I still can't wrap my head around this," I say as I look in the mirror at the man reflected back at me. I'm wearing a light gray linen suit, preparing to marry the love of my life.

"What? You look very dapper, my friend," Nate answers.

"Not the suit, man."

Nate walks up behind me, joining me as we look at each other through the reflection. "I know." He drops his arm around me, patting me on the shoulder. "This has been a long time coming."

I smile.

"Don't fuck it up."

We both laugh as a knock hits the door behind us. We turn to see Nick and Seth in the doorway.

"Can we come in?" Nick asks

"It's your house," I tell him. "Seth, you ready?"

"Yes, sir." He's wearing similar attire to my and Nate's suit, and his smile may rival mine.

"You have the rings?"

He simply pats the inside pocket of his jacket and grins.

I'd planned to ask Nate to be my best man when I purchased Melanie's engagement ring, hoping he'd return the favor as I'd done for him. But once we shared the news with the kids, and Seth told me he loved me, there was no doubt.

Nate acted offended that he was merely a groomsman, yet still made arrangements for my bachelor party, finding a cigar bar similar to the one in Maryland where all of my friends could come together.

"I'll leave you guys to it," Nick says. "I need to go grab Grace from Kat so she can help Melanie."

"Thanks, Nick. For everything."

"I'm honored you guys chose to have your wedding here. I'm really happy for both of you." He smiles before walking away.

Melanie was right when she said no gifts. With friends like ours, we have all we need.

"You nervous?" Nate asks.

"No. Just excited." I wrap my arm around Seth and pull him in for a side hug. "Besides, all I had to do was show up. You think Kat and Melanie were going to let me plan anything?"

"You didn't get to pick anything?" Nate laughs.

"I told her I wanted red roses and to pick the song we dance to. I think knowing she was getting her way with all the rest sealed the deal."

"She let me and Ruby pick the cake flavors," Seth says.

"Are we having a chocolate cake with chocolate icing?" I ask.

"No." Seth laughs. "But just be glad Ruby didn't have her way, or your wedding cake would've been covered in sprinkles."

We make our way down to the ceremony site by the dock, and I start to feel my nerves getting riled up. We decided to keep the ceremony small —only family and friends who are closest to us. Melanie's family have come to town for the weekend. My brotherhood are here. Between them and Melanie and the kids, that's all the family I need.

Because the wedding party is small and the ceremony and reception will be informal, we elected to take pictures after we're pronounced husband and wife. Melanie said that was traditional, but I secretly think she knows the ceremony wouldn't start on time if I saw her beforehand.

"Huggie!" Ruby yells as she runs down toward me from the lake house.

"Be careful, Rubs. I don't want to fish you out of the water in that dress."

"I can't believe I get to be the flower girl and a bridesmaid," she shrieks, holding her basket of deep red rose petals.

Melanie had told me Kat and Morgan would be her official bridesmaids, but she wanted Ruby to feel extra special today. Ruby's in that undecided stage between remaining a young girl and becoming a young lady. But to me, she'll always be sweet, overzealous Ruby.

Looking around, I notice a small tent set up to the left of the chairs and archway where the ceremony will take place. Within the tent are tables dressed in white tablecloths and light gray linens, with an area for dancing in the center. Red roses and candles decorate the space beautifully.

Nate and Seth come to my side, and I glance down at my watch to confirm it's almost time.

"Preach is here." Nate laughs.

Turning around, I stand in shock. I thought he was joking at first. I wouldn't have believed it in a million years if someone had told me Jamie 'The Hammer' Sherman would be our officiant.

He'd announced at my bachelor party he was getting ordained as his gift to us. I thought he was drunk. But several days later, he confirmed with Melanie that he was serious.

Reaching out my hand to him, I'm almost at a loss for words. "Thanks, man. Really."

"Just say your lines, and don't mess me up," he says sternly. "I don't need any screwups on my watch." He puts down his backpack and pulls out a small cooler. *What the hell?* Before I can ask if he's packed a snack, he retrieves a small notebook from his back pocket. It looks like he's about to take our order.

"Oh, lord," Nate bellows.

Seth could get motion sickness the way his gaze ping-pongs between the three of us.

Nate leans toward Seth. "Something tells me we're in for an adventure."

The thought barely has time to settle before music begins playing in the distance, and the guests start coming down to find their seats. My nerves are really dancing now.

As Melanie's mother takes her seat up front, I know it's showtime. Ruby practically skips down the grassy area, between the two sets of white wooden chairs, tossing rose petals everywhere until she reaches us. Happiness radiates from her. She gives me a thumbs-up right before she takes her place next to Morgan.

Turning away from Ruby, I glance back down the aisle and freeze. Melanie stands with her dad, her hair down in ringlets, with her long white dress flowing about her. The sight of this woman, belly swollen with my child, floating toward me like an angel has me coming undone.

I feel a nudge at my side and look to see Seth holding a handkerchief.

"Thanks, buddy." There's no sense pretending. I'm sure everyone here knows my story. Hopefully, they'll give me a pass for one day after all of these years.

Melanie comes to stand before me, handing her brilliant bouquet of red roses to Ruby, who clutches them to her chest. The sight of her like this is beyond surreal. She reaches over to wipe a tear from my cheek, and I grab her hand, kissing her palm.

"Uh, hmm."

We both turn to Jamie.

"We're not ready for all that yet."

Everyone laughs. But him.

Looking at his little notebook, he begins. "I'm happy you could all make it." He pauses. "To show your love and support for these two. And to enjoy all of the free food and drinks."

Again, snickers come from around me, and I simply shake my head.

"We've all seen that life isn't easy. But it's clear these two belong together." The Hammer flips the page in his little notebook, and I feel a little better about this ceremony than I did when he started.

"They're like peanut butter and jelly, beer and pretzels, donuts and sprinkles..."

I spoke too soon.

I look at Ruby, who's smiling from ear to ear.

"They're like milk and chocolate sauce. Once you bring them together, there's no taking them apart." He bends down to the cooler and retrieves a small container of milk and a bottle of chocolate sauce.

What the?

He hands the milk to Melanie and gives me the bottle of syrup. Reaching back into the cooler, he pulls out a large glass and asks Seth to hold it for us.

"Melanie, if you'll pour the milk," he directs.

She giggles as she opens the top and pours it into the glass.

"Huggie, if you'll pour the chocolate," he says dryly. Who is this guy?

I chuckle and squeeze some syrup into the glass. Clearly, he isn't happy with my pour as he motions with his hands for more, and the guests behind me laugh.

Turning, he reaches back into the cooler, extends a long teaspoon to Ruby, who tosses Melanie's bouquet to Morgan like it's on fire, and darts over to where the three of us are standing around this glass of milk.

"Ruby?"

"Yes?"

"Will you blend this family?" he asks, pointing to the glass.

She beams at him before turning that contagious smile on Melanie and me. With more care than I thought she possessed, she delicately places the spoon in the glass and begins to stir. Holy hell, why am I crying over a glass of chocolate milk?

Jamie places two straws in the glass and motions for the two of us to drink up. Melanie and I lean forward, our heads touching as we sip from the glass. We both stand tall, smiling at one another. Then The Hammer goes one better and hands straws to Seth and Ruby.

Shit, I just stopped crying.

"Good, huh?" Jamie asks them. The guests chuckle as the kids' nod.

Then he looks meaningfully at Melanie and turns to me. "It's good."

"You hold onto that. In case you get thirsty," he tells Ruby, encouraging her and Seth to return to their places. "Do we have rings?"

Seth reaches into his pocket and hands them to Jamie, who hands Melanie's to me.

"Do you, Melanie, take George to be your lawfully wedded husband, to have and to hold, for better or for worse, for now and for always?"

"I do," she says as I slide her wedding band onto her finger. The sight of it putting a lump in my throat.

Jamie hands Melanie my band and repeats the question. "Do you, George, Huggie, Hughes, take Melanie to be your lawfully wedded wife, to have and to hold, for better or for worse, for now and for always?"

Melanie nimbly slides the ring onto my trembling finger, gazing up at me with tears in her beautiful violet eyes.

"I didn't think we were going to have trouble with this part," The Hammer goads, and the guests all erupt with laughter.

"Oh. Yes. A million times, yes!" I shout.

"All right, then. The two of you, repeat after me. I give you this ring as a promise to love you today, tomorrow, and always."

Melanie and I repeat the statement, not letting go of each other's hands.

"No take-backs," The Hammer adds.

"No take-backs." We laugh.

"By the power vested in me." The Hammer stops reading and looks out at the guests and grins with pride.

"We've created a monster," Nate whispers to Seth.

Jamie gives him a curt glare before returning to his notebook. "By the power vested in me by the state of Virginia, I pronounce the two of you married."

The guests all clap, and Melanie and I beam at one another.

"What are you waiting for? Kiss her already!"

We laugh. I guess he stopped writing in that thing before he got to the 'you may kiss the bride' part.

I step forward, holding my bride's face in my hands, and kiss her lovingly. 'Cause people are watching.

As everyone stops clapping, Jamie adds, "Let's eat!"

We take pictures, spend time with our loved ones, and enjoy Gail's food. I have to remind Melanie she's a guest at this party each time she heads over to where Gail is standing.

The sunset is the perfect décor for this amazing celebration. My heart is so full. It isn't until I hear the music stop playing that I realize Nate has our first dance music geared up. Looking over to him, he just shakes his head, and I laugh.

Walking over to Melanie, who is standing with Nick and Kat, I place my hand on her elbow to get her attention. "It's our dance."

She grins at me and takes my hand just as Tom Jones starts singing, "She's a Lady." She stops in her tracks. "What on earth?"

Tom belts out, "She's all you'd ever want," and my smile feels as if it will crack my face in two. The lyrics continue to play, the crowd laughing at my choice, and my wife glowing as she sways with me on the dance floor.

I can't help but sing the last line of the chorus with gusto.

"And the lady is mine!"

EPILOGUE

"Seth, stick with her," Melanie yells.

"He's fine, Mel." I sit in the Adirondack chair, watching Seth chase our two-year-old through the grass, her red ringlets all the brighter as they dance in the summer sun.

We hadn't settled on a name until we saw her fair skin and the strawberry tufts of hair on her little head. Then we knew. Georgia bore such a resemblance to my mother. While I have no baby pictures, there's no mistaking the similarity.

George was my mother's maiden name. Ruby has already nicknamed her Georgie. I just call her beautiful.

We waited until she was six months old to have our honeymoon. Sure, we snuck off to the Hot Springs resort for a long, child-free weekend the week after we were married. Our gift from Nick and Kat. But our growing family needed a little more time before we could risk boarding a cruise. So we waited until last year for the Disney ship Melanie and the kids had been dreaming of.

My life is so full I can barely wrap my head around it. I'd been able to move back to Hanover with the fire department but never managed to return to station ten. The new crew was great, but it wasn't the same. I only needed five more years before I could claim retirement benefits.

Yet, I've done well for myself and decided that my quality of life with my family was worth more.

So I took a chance. I left the fire department and embraced working with the production studios full-time. I set up satellite offices in major filming areas along the east coast and recruited firefighters and EMS providers to work at each location. If there wasn't a movie being shot in the surrounding area, I'd oversee one in progress somewhere else. However, I've committed to never being away from home for more than a few days.

It's been so successful that producers have approached me to set up crews in other areas of the country. For those without family, it's an opportunity to travel and make more money. But for guys like me with the old ball and chain...

Not a good example. I chuckle to myself. I'd shackle myself back to her if she ever tried using the key.

"What are you laughing at?" she asks suspiciously.

"Trust me. You don't want to know."

She gives me a side eye before returning her attention to Seth and Georgia.

"Ruby still finishing her homework?"

"No. She's done," Ruby says as she runs past to join her sister and brother. "But you have a phone call inside, Mom."

Melanie springs from her chair. "Duty calls."

Melanie has hung up her stethoscope for now. She occasionally volunteers and remains involved enough to keep her license, but she no longer works in cardiology. I'm sure Derek was sad to see her go, but his loss is my gain.

My wife renewed her passion for entertaining, working alongside Gail. She's in her element when she helps people celebrate a special moment together. Trying to juggle that, along with the medical practice and the kids, was too much. I'm glad she followed her heart.

"I have another private party booked," she says before lowering into her chair.

"Before long, you're going to have to hire more staff. Want me to ask the guys at the station if anyone's interested?"

"No!" She laughs.

We both turn to the sound of squealing and fits of laughter from our three playing in the yard. Life is good.

"Hugs?"

"Yeah?" I ask, picking up her hand to kiss her palm.

"How long have we known each other?"

I stop with her hand in midair. "About twenty-two years. Why?"

"I've never gotten the feeling it was an area you wanted to talk about. But what happened with your dad?"

So much for life is good.

I'm stunned it's taken so long for this conversation to come up. Jake knew. I always assumed he shared the details with her, and she was being respectful in not bringing it up. And after my mother's death affected me the way it did, it was apparent to those closest to me I wasn't inviting conversation about my family.

"He's the devil, Mel. Be glad you never met him."

She sits quietly. I'm sure she's afraid to push. But she's entitled to know.

"He used to beat my mother."

I hear a gasp before her hand cradles my ink-laden arm.

"He came at me too, for a while. But I got big enough that he was afraid to mess with me. I tried to convince her to leave. But he had her under his thumb. She wouldn't go."

My mind drifts back to that awful time, and I can feel my heart squeeze. I'd buried my head in my books and tried to find any outlet to keep me busy enough that I didn't have to return to the house. The rescue squad was perfect. I could spend days at school or the library and every night away from the memories of growing up there if I needed. "He was never around much. I have no idea what he did for a living, but I doubt it was legal."

Her warm hand slides up and down mine. I assumed my life would be like my mother's. Cold and alone. That we simply weren't cut out for people to love us.

"I begged her to divorce him. Each time he'd come to the house, it was just long enough to take what he wanted and leave her battered and bruised." I pause, trying to block out the memory.

"Oh, ." I can hear her sniffling, but I have to get through this. I don't ever want to come back to this conversation again once we're done.

"I don't know if she just gave up the will to live or if her body was so marred down by what he'd done to her... she got really sick, and then all of her organs just shut down."

I look up to the sky, wondering if she can see my beautiful family.

"We used to live next door to this sweet old lady. In the early years, I'd hang out in her backyard when things got bad. Because I was scared." I pause. "She had these beautiful red rose bushes. One day she asked if I wanted to take some home to my mother. I'm sure she didn't know what was happening to her. We hid that really well for a very long time."

Glancing at Melanie, I notice her eyes are red-rimmed. I finish the kiss on her hand that had been interrupted earlier. "The first time I brought the flowers, my mother smiled. It was so rare to see that from her. I was proud." The memory of that moment is permanently etched in my mind. "So proud I'd done something to make her happy. So whenever I was at Mrs. Peabody's house, I asked if I could have more."

"," Melanie cries.

"Baby. Please, don't cry. It's been years. I didn't mean to upset you. I just don't ever want to talk about this again."

"I understand. I knew it had to be bad for us to be so close, and you never speak a word of it."

"Mom, I'm hungry. Can we get dinner soon?" Ruby yells.

"I think they may have worked up an appetite chasing Georgia around. I'll go get things started, and I'll see you inside."

MELANIE

Dinner is done, the kitchen is clean, and the kids are down for bed. I want to check in with my husband to ensure the earlier conversation isn't wearing on him.

Walking through the house, I'm surprised when I can't find him. I thought he might've taken a shower or called it an early day. I almost give up when I notice a little flicker glow outside the sliding doors.

Walking closer, I watch what appears to be an ember move. I'm shocked because 's not a smoker.

Carefully sliding open the glass door, I poke my head out. "Is it okay if I join you?"

"I'm not good company," he says. This also startles me, as he's never come close to turning me away. He starts to put out his cigar when I stop him.

"You don't have to put that out because of me."

His eyes connect with mine, and I recognize a look about him I haven't seen in a long time. This may not be a smart move, but I decide to go for it.

"When's the last time you smoked one?"

"My bachelor party," he's quick to reply. He sounds testy.

"How about before that?"

His stormy eyes look back in my direction. "Where are you going with this, Melanie?"

"Tell me," I push back.

His face wrinkles in irritation. I already know. He smoked these with a scotch at the sex club. I'm sure of it. It's the only thing besides his father he keeps from me.

I stand and walk behind his Adirondack chair, so I can whisper in his ear before retreating to our room. "They can't give you what I can. No one can."

I've showered and changed into 's favorite sleep shorts and T-shirt set. I discovered their effect on him very early and have to admit to using them to my advantage on several occasions.

It isn't long before he comes into the room. He's still wearing a button-up and khakis from earlier. He had a few meetings today, but nothing stressful. Not until that conversation about his dad. But I'm hoping I may have incited the need to work off his stress in other ways.

He comes into the room looking distant, almost prickly. When I say this isn't a side of him he lets me see. I'm not exaggerating.

He walks toward me, unfastening the remaining buttons of his starched white shirt until the artful skin beneath is visible. He walks over, scoops me up, and carries me over to the plush chair in the corner of the room. Placing me down on shaky legs, so I'm facing the mirror in front of us, he removes my top and then bends to gingerly slide my shorts down my legs.

I stand naked before him, staring into this full-length mirror as he runs his hands gently down my sides. My nipples are already at attention, but now he has the rest of me feeling electric.

He whispers into my hair, "I want you to sit in my lap and let me fuck you. Is that okay?" He bends down to kiss my shoulder, and I simply nod for him. "I'm going to slowly lower you down onto my cock."

I'm a little confused as to what he has in mind. I've had sex on top of him scores of times.

He sinks into the chair, his hands caressing the backs of my thighs before I hear him unzip his pants. His fingers curl around my waist, and he gradually brings me down on him while facing the mirror.

"Grab ahold of my thighs, beautiful girl."

He lines his erect cock up with my entrance and eases my descent. The moment he nudges my entrance, I feel my heart rate start to pick up. Once I'm fully seated on top of him, he spreads my thighs wide and reaches around to tease my pussy with his fingertips.

The sight of him fingering me while I'm mounted on him is the most erotic thing I've ever experienced. As he continues to play with my wet, swollen flesh with one hand, the other massages my breasts.

"Ride me," he demands. "I need you to ride me."

I grind myself on him until I'm teetering on the edge. Tilting my head back, I buck my hips on top of him while his masterful fingers thrum over my wet flesh. I try to control the moans.

All of a sudden, he lifts my hips until he withdraws and brings me to my feet. "Come with me." Taking my hand, he leads me to the bed. "I need you on all fours, right on the edge."

I comply, nervous but excited. He gives my bottom a tender stroke right before he plunges into me.

"Oh, Hugs," I cry out. He wastes no time rutting into me. I have to dig my nails into the sheets for leverage. His pace quickens, and the telltale sign of my orgasm begins.

"Oh, fuck." he groans. "Fuck. I'm going to come. Come with me, Mellie." He smacks my ass hard, and I hover so close, but not quite there.

"I want you to come all over me." He pants, bucking wildly into me. He reaches around as if knowing exactly what I need, lying his fingertips over my mound, allowing the repeated friction from his pounding to help bring me over the edge.

"I'm ready to fill this hot pussy full of come, but not until you—"

"Ahhh!" My body starts to shake as my climax detonates.

Three, four, five more thrusts, and I hear him growl as his body stiffens, and he empties into me.

We remain in this position for several moments before I feel him brush my hair away from my face and place a kiss on my ear.

"Thank you."

Rolling over, he hovers over top of me, appearing sated and relaxed —his release like a salve to his soul. "You're right. Only you can make me feel this way, Mrs. Hughes. Only you."

"You ready?" asks.

"Yes. Just let me grab my bag."

"Okay, we'll meet you out there. The kids are already in the car."

The short drive is quiet. This is surprising anytime there are three kids in the car. But they know how nervous I am. I think even little Georgia knows something is going on.

I've been helping manage parties and catering for almost a year now. But this will be the first time we've held a private party in our new space. A restaurant and party location where the tagline reads, "Let us be the life of your party."

We arrive at the restaurant and park in the back. The place is a flurry of movement and sound as the catering team I've worked with gets used to their new digs. As they spot us, they all begin to clap. Which in turn makes Georgia clap, causing everyone to laugh and smile.

I touch base with everyone to ensure they have what they need for the big day before going to look for my husband. I see him through the front glass, sitting on a bench in front of the restaurant while the kids happily explore. When I reach him, I wrap my arms around him and give him a big kiss. This dream could've never happened without him.

"What was that for?"

"For being the best," I say, nuzzling his neck.

"Nah. Someone else holds that title." He looks up at the sign above the door.

Jake's Place.

"I'm happy to settle for Mr. Second Best."

The End

THANK YOU FOR READING

I hope you've enjoyed reading Mr. Second Best. If you'd like to read the spicy little novella where this book began, check out Possessed: https://dl.bookfunnel.com/b9d4l2szjr

If you haven't read The Deprivation Trilogy, it's where all of the standalone spin-offs originate. Keep reading for an excerpt from chapter one. Amazon universal link: https://geni.us/qVoIg6

I enjoy celebrating stories based on true life experience. While I alter the information for privacy, I find real life is beautiful. If you have a story you'd like to share, medical or otherwise, please send it to authorlmfox@gmail.com or mail it to:
LM FOX P.O. Box 143 New Kent, VA 23124

And keep turning for a bonus excerpt from The Bitter Rival. The epilogue to The Bitter Rival, Sweet Surrender, is due in the spring of 2023. Preorder link: https://geni.us/4ESALE

Many of the characters in my books will make appearances in future books or headline in their own.

To obtain more information on my books, upcoming work, and signed editions, please visit my webpage: www.authorlmfox.com

While you're there, subscribe to my newsletter to receive the latest information on releases, promotions, and giveaways straight to your mailbox.

And be sure to visit me on Facebook at AuthorLMFox and my readers' group, Layla's Fox Den, as well as on Instagram, Twitter, and TikTok @authorlmfox

PLAY LIST

The Sound of Silence, Disturbed
Dirty Little Secret, The All-American Rejects
I Found, Amber Run
Watermelon Sugar, Harry Styles
Unstoppable, Sia
I Am Invincible, Cassadee Pope
Lost Without You, Freya Ridings
The Last Word, Frances
Love Someone, Lucas Graham
Someday We'll Know, New Radicals
Beautiful, Bazzi
Wild Ones, Flo Rida
If Our Love is Wrong, Calum Scott
Rise Up, Just Sam
Friends, Marshmellow & Anne-Marie
Bad Habits, Ed Sheerin
Before You Go, Lewis Capaldi
Love Me Now, John Legend
She's a Lady, Tom Jones
I've Been Waiting, Lil Peep & iLOVEMakonnen
Say Something, A Great Big World & Christina Aguilera

ACKNOWLEDGMENTS

Thank you to my team! I would not have been able to complete this book without the help of my amazing editor, Kelly, my proofreader, Cheree, and my ever-patient formatter, Shari. Thanks to Hang, Michelle, and Wander, I'm in complete awe of my cover. God bless Stephanie who keeps me from losing my mind on the daily. Thank you to Jo and the gang at GMB for continually getting my books in front of new readers. And to Linda and the entire Foreword team, I don't know what I'd do without your tireless support.

I'm so grateful to TL Swan for starting me on this journey. You're not only my favorite Author but one of the most genuinely kind and selfless people I know. I intend to continue to pay it forward in honor of all you've done for me and so many others.

Thank you to my dear friend, Logan, for generously sharing your wisdom. Your friendship means the world to me. I hope you know how much inspiration and motivation you've given me.

Thank you so much to my alpha & beta readers! You're all so patient and encouraging. I cannot thank you enough, Denise, Siri, Taylor, Susan, Laura, Stephanie, Emma, Kate, Rita, and Kelly. All of you help shape my story into the finished product. I love and respect each and every one of you for taking the time out of your busy lives to do it. **Thank you to my ARC/Street Team members.** Your constant support means more than you could ever know. I'm so grateful for the shares, the graphics, and the reviews. You all lift me up and keep me going every day!

Thank you to the Fox Cubs in Layla's Fox Den and all of the members of my Facebook, Instagram, Twitter, and TikTok

Author pages. I love engaging with you there. It's like having girls' night, except you have to pour your own margaritas.

Ultimately, I would have never completed this book had it not been for my husband and my kids' endless love, patience, and support. Working full-time in the emergency room kept me distant much too often. I love you all so much!

AN EXCERPT

Check out The Deprivation Trilogy to find out where this story began.
Deprivation, Book One in The Deprivation Trilogy

———

Present Day
Kat

Rolling away from the harsh sunlight, I squint at the clock. It's 6:29 a.m. Bolting upright, I realize my day is once again starting with a bang. I rarely sleep well. When I do manage to get some shuteye, it's usually short-lived as I frequently awaken from nightmares. Occasionally, I'm able to get back to sleep. However, this time, I've slept through my alarm. I need to brush my teeth, take a four-minute shower, braid my hair, and make it to work within the next thirty minutes.

Running into the bathroom, I jump as my toasty feet hit the harsh, cold tiles. My awakening is nearly complete as I turn on the water and my tepid skin meets the frigid spray. *Holy crap!* I dart through the shower, running shampoo and body wash onto me like it's a cheap car wash, then quickly jump out to dry off and don my scrubs for work. *Ugh, no time for coffee. Please let this shift go better than the last.*

As I drive the fifteen-minute commute to work, I reflect on my chaotic morning. Rubbing my eyes of any remaining debris Mr. Sandman left behind, I try to recall anything specific about my most recent nightmare. *Nope, not a thing.* After a while, they all run together. I can't remember the last time I've gotten more than three to four hours of sleep.

It isn't like I have PTSD. No one's ever attacked or abused me physically. How have I developed constant nightmares and insomnia from years of bad boyfriends? I'm sure something's wrong with me. I know I should find a therapist, but how would I explain my reason for being there? "Hi. I'm Katarina Kelly and I'm having nightmares from the ghosts of my past relationships?" Granted, I could win an award for worst dating life ever, but enough to cause years of this? There's a reason I've avoided dating over the last three years. Quickly, I do the mental math and realize it's probably closer to four. Oh well, three or four, it doesn't matter, Gabe was the last and biggest dickwad in a string of many and I'm not going there again. Lonely or not, I'm better off this way.

As I pull into the physicians' parking lot with mere moments to spare before the start of my shift, I spot one remaining open space. Knowing I need to grab my bag and run once this car is in park, I quickly turn toward my destination. I make a harsh left into the parking spot, throw my gear shift into park, and open the door like I'm a contestant on *The Amazing Race*. Grabbing my work bag, I pull it swiftly from the back seat, close my door, and look up to see a car idling behind mine. As if everything else in the world has ceased to exist, I watch as the driver's window rolls down and the operator of the vehicle leans out.

My mouth goes dry, and I stop breathing momentarily as I take him in. *Jeez, this guy is like something out of a Hollywood movie.* He has gorgeous, tousled dark blond hair worthy of a photo shoot, movie star aviators sitting atop his straight nose, and the sexiest stubble covering his firm, square jaw. I watch as a sneer becomes evident despite the sunglasses.

"Nice. You almost took me out trying to steal that spot out from under me, Mario Andretti," he says, the angry timbre of his voice breaking through my stupor.

What? There wasn't another car waiting for this spot. I instantly feel my cheeks turn pink in embarrassment. Realizing I don't have time for this, I decide to avoid a car lot confrontation, return his menacing glare, and abruptly sprint for the ER doors.

~

"Hey, Kat, you ready to sew up Mrs. Barker?" I hear Jessica call. Jessica Rush is one of my favorite ER nurses, and I'm relieved to be working alongside her today. It's been nonstop in this busy emergency room for almost six hours now, and although I'm worn out, I still have six more to go. Working with people you adore can make all the difference in a stressful environment.

"Sure. You got an extra set of hands? Mildred can throw a mean left hook." I've taken care of this elderly patient before. "Dementia is no joke," I reply, sitting at my usual spot in my favorite hallway. Working as a physician assistant in a demanding ER keeps me hopping. Trying to gather my thoughts to type appropriate notes is much easier in this narrow breezeway next to the supply room. Sitting in the main work area is like trying to work at the bar at TGI Fridays. With the endless interruptions, who can get anything done? For the most part, this little alcove of three computers in this busy forty-five bed ER is my sanctuary.

"Is this seat taken?" a deep voice floats in my direction, interrupting my thoughts. I look up to see a strikingly handsome, dark-haired physician with piercing blue eyes beaming at me. He has bright white teeth which match his lab coat, a stethoscope is peeking out of the left pocket. He points to the chair and computer monitor closest to me, knowing full well there's an identical spot one seat over that's empty. *Heck, come on over. I don't mind a little eye candy sitting next to me for a while.*

It dawns on me that my mouth might be hanging open. He continues to smile down at me while I sit wordlessly, staring at him. "Um, it's all yours," I manage to reply. I notice he isn't wearing a ring on his left ring finger. Why I've looked is anyone's guess, as I haven't had so much as a blind date in three years. Oh, yeah, almost four. But if I was going to start socializing with men, well, he would be quite the—

"Kat, you ready? Mrs. Barker has been driving us crazy. The nursing home says she has sundowners. You know what that means. The later it gets, the more confused and agitated she'll become. If you don't sew up that cut on her forehead soon, she's going to let you have it with both hooks," Jessica says, halting my musing.

"Yeah, I'm coming." I stand, preparing for battle. "Get Wyatt to help hold her still. He can sweet talk the pants off of any confused elderly patient," I laugh. I take off my pristine, starched lab coat and hang it over the back of my chair for fear sewing a laceration on this spirited, unusually strong, Alzheimer's patient would have my white coat resembling a butcher's apron.

I glance over to see my appealing companion is again smiling in my direction. There's one deep, sexy dimple present in his right cheek.

"Go get 'em, Kat," he says playfully.

Feeling a flush creep from my chest toward my face, I quickly exit and head for my awaiting patient.

Thirty minutes later, exhausted from the workout Mildred gave the three of us, I return to my seat to chart my impressive accomplishment. After wiping my brow, I drain nearly half a bottle of water. Let's face it, that's probably the only nourishment I'm getting this shift. To think it required the assistance of two able-bodied professionals, one of whom is our best senior sweet-talker, in order to place five simple stitches in an eighty-two-year-old lady who weighs about ninety-five pounds. I shake my head as I review the computer to see which patients are waiting to be seen. I only have about two hours left in my shift, so I try to choose wisely. Ah, there are three quick turnaround patients waiting. I might actually leave on time today.

As I'm assigning my name to the awaiting patients, I sense an ominous presence to my left. Feeling my skin prickle and my heartrate begin to hasten, this aura is unlike the feel of Dr. Divine who graced this hallway earlier. Slowly peering to my left, I observe no dreamy white smile, no flirty dimple, no warmth or pleasant banter. The brooding, chiseled face of a dark blond god is all I see as he grabs the back of the chair furthest from me and slowly sits down. Again, my mouth is agape. Quickly clamping it shut I notice he's dressed similarly to the carefree doctor who sat in the chair adjacent a short while ago, but the rest of this encounter is the polar opposite. There's no witty engagement, just the briefest of intense eye contact before he jolts his view from me, as if he's witnessed an unpleasant stain.

I'm unable to look away, despite his off-putting demeanor. He's a tall, incredibly attractive man with honey blond stubble covering his jawline. Unconsciously, I rub my fingertips over my chin, longing to stroke the golden strands. Feeling parts of me awaken I've kept dormant way too long, I sit transfixed as he attacks the keyboard in front of him like it's committed a personal affront.

I practically jump in my seat as Jessica shouts from around the corner, "Kat, you ready to go downtown? I have Ms. Simmons in room four, ready to roll."

"Sure, Jess. Let's end my day with one more pelvic exam." I think this might be my sixth one today, which is sadly still not a record for me. "I'm starting to feel like I work at an OB/GYN's office," I mutter.

"Well, we don't want to deliver any babies in here. I'll meet you there in a sec. I just have to grab some peppermint oil." Jessica snorts with a lopsided grimace, her strawberry blonde locks in her hand as she refastens her hair in a messy bun above her head.

"Oh my god, Jess, is it that bad?" I whisper, knowing we tolerate a lot of unpleasant smells in the ER, but we save the peppermint oil for some of the worst.

"Nah, it's for the guy in the room next to her. You really don't want to go in there." I hear her voice trail off as she walks away.

Glad to know I dodged that bullet. I remove my lab coat again in the hope one of us will make it out alive today. Walking past the glowering male perfection banging on his keyboard near the doorway, I ponder what it is about him that seems so familiar. Turning the corner toward my patient's exam room, I hear him utter, "Nice" under his breath. *Wait, where have... Holy heck, he's the angry guy from the car. But what does nice mean? Nice what? Nice face? Nice ass?* I'm sure he's being sarcastic. He is hot, I'll give him that, but *nice* is the last word I'd use to describe this interloper.

Fifty minutes later, I return to my computer after evaluating my last three patients. I finish the bottle of water I've accepted to be a clear substitute for dinner and momentarily place my head down on the desktop in front of me. Hoping to clear my thoughts so I can generate discharge instructions for my last three patients, I feel someone place their hand on my left shoulder. Cautiously I peer up to see one of my least favorite ER attendings, Dr. Silver.

I believe Dr. Silver completed a fellowship at the University of How to Pick Patients I Can See in Less Than Ten Minutes and Have the PA Spend Nearly Ten Times as Long Completing Their Care. If it was just completing a procedure for him so he could focus on more complex patients, it'd be different. But this arrogant son of a gun has made an art of picking up a patient requiring a complicated procedure, knowing he has no intention of completing said procedure. He'll claim he saw the individual and leave work on time while I stay an hour late taking care of his patient. I'm already so tired I can barely keep my eyes open and my shift is scheduled to be over in forty minutes.

"Hey, Kat. Could you put a sugar tong splint on the young lady in room eleven? She has a distal radius and ulna fracture. Thanks," he states, walking away without waiting for my reply.

I try to pick my work battles carefully, so in spite of sheer exhaustion, I silently agree to place the splint on a young lady who appears to have severe developmental delays. *So much for leaving on time. Again.* Ultimately, it's about giving patients the best care possible and I realize Dr. Silver is often *not* the best care. As I see him walk past me near the main physicians' work space, probably to grab his things and head home early, I mutter, "ass wipe" under my breath, just as I almost collide with a tall, broad chest. As if drawn to him like a magnet, I lean in as I inhale the pheromones which now surround me. *God, he smells good.* Ignoring the sizzle that has again crept into my loins, I hesitantly gaze up into the eyes of Dr. Broody.

"Nice," he remarks, sneering down at me with an air of superiority, shaking his head in disgust.

Wincing, I walk around him. I feel my blood pressure rise, knowing he's either heard my degrading comment or simply finds my presence distasteful. Either way, I try to shake it off. What do I care if he heard? He may be hot as hell and smell like sin on a cracker, but I don't need some condescending asshole making me feel stupid. If I wanted that, I'd call one of my ex-boyfriends.

Returning to my work station, fifty minutes past the end of my scheduled shift, I slump in my seat to complete my procedure note on the splint I've just applied. The sweet girl required sedation in order to immobilize her broken arm because her developmental delay didn't allow her to grasp what we were doing. I try to remind myself of a medical professional's call to serve so as not to want to drive to Dr. Silver's home and wring his neck while his trophy wife serves him dinner. I manage to complete the rest of my documentation in record time, now that interruptions are at a minimum and the smoldering but pompous Dr. Broody is no longer distracting me. *God, what was that cologne he was wearing? I'm sure that's what got my motor running, not him.*

Fatigue has taken over, and I find it's too much effort to pay attention to my growling stomach. I grab my bag and head for the door. I just need a hot bath, a glass of wine, my EarPods, and hopefully a few restful hours of sleep.

Heading down the hallway leading to the physicians' parking area, I see Jessica Main and Meghan Rush. I've worked with them since I started at St. Luke's, and quite honestly, every shift is better when they're here. These two nurses are crazy girls and get me through the toughest of nights with laughter instead of tears. "Finally grabbing some grub?" I ask, peering at their yummy plates of grilled cheese and fries. *Oh, there's that growl again. I knew you didn't go far.*

"Yeah, I could eat a horse," Jessica utters with a mouth full of French fry. This makes me chuckle because she literally eats all of the time and never gains a pound. She's a thin, fit, five foot seven, freckle-faced, blonde that one would describe as the quintessential girl next door. You can't help but instantly love her. Every time I see her in the department, she's snacking on goldfish crackers, M&Ms, or Skittles. "I saw you were pretty cozy with Dr. Lee earlier. You better watch that one, Kat. He's a real lady killer," she warns.

"Which one was Dr. Lee?" It dawns on me her description could apply to either of my earlier unnamed companions, particularly if said women were into arrogant dickwads. "I was surprised when they joined me in my little sanctuary. I don't get a lot of strangers in there. They usually prefer the open area with the docs."

"Which one? How many hot men were you entertaining in your lair today, Kat?" Meghan laughs. Meghan, is a sharp-witted brunette with curly hair and an endearing smile. Her humor is infectious and keeps me in stitches.

"Two, actually," I bat my eyes, teasingly. "But of course, I'm so skilled in the art of men I made a complete fool of myself with both of them." I reach over and steal a fry off of Meghan's plate. I'm quite honestly afraid to touch Jessica's, for fear she might bite off my finger. "The first one was nice enough. Heck, I think I might've drooled a little before I could get words out of my mouth when he started talking," I laugh in embarrassment.

"Oh, god," Jessica giggles. "Well, Dr. Lee is super dreamy. He has a smile that could melt lead. And that dimple, uh," she moans. "But rumors travel fast in this place, and he's definitely a playboy. He's hot and he knows it. He's a love 'em and leave 'em kind of guy, and as much as I'd like to get all up on that, I don't know that I want to be standing in the grill line looking at the nurse on either side of me wondering who had him last."

"Yeah, not my scene, either," I say, scrunching my face up. I'm done with playboys. "He is smooth, though. It was nice to know all my parts are still functioning as they kicked into overdrive when he spoke. I think I started sweating a little before I even laid eyes on him. That voice, it's like ear porn."

Jess and Meghan laugh with Meghan almost choking on her fries.

"How have I not heard of this guy?" I ask.

"You don't hang in the rumor circle, Kat. That's Dr. Sebastian Lee. He's a reconstructive hand specialist who primarily works out of Mary Immaculate. He'll occasionally come to our ER when it's something hand or wrist related or if the on-call orthopod is a hip guy... or if his bank account is low that week, ha. Like that ever happens." Jessica takes a bite of her grilled cheese, trailing a string of warm gooey goodness from her sandwich to her mouth.

Before the bite is completely gone, she smirks. "He's probably made his mark on plenty of nurses at both hospitals." She stops to ponder for a minute. "I think in a moment of weakness, like if I saw him in a bar and could blame my actions on one too many cosmos, I'd do him." Jessica continues to bite into her toasty, cheesy sandwich as she looks at my shocked expression. "What? He's hot. When can you ever say you were able to sleep with a guy like that? It's just not possible that he could look like that, hook up with that many women, and be bad in bed."

"Well, what if he ruined all future sex for you? Hmmm?" Meghan inquires sarcastically. She turns back to me and covers her plate of remaining fries with her hand. "So who was your other suitor, Madam?"

"Heck if I know, but quite honestly, I'm not really interested in another interaction with that one. He was ridiculously hot, but that attitude. So rude! And he kept muttering things under his breath. He was very judgy. Dr. Broody can take his sexy hazel eyes and glowering stare somewhere else."

Meghan and Jessica chuckle until Jess looks down at her watch. "We need to get back or we won't have time to finish eating. I'm not leaving my food in the nurses' lounge or someone will steal it for sure." They say goodbye and wave as they head back to the ER to end their shift. Continuing toward the parking lot, I inwardly laugh at their antics while my stomach growls and visions of melty cheese and greasy fries dance in my head.

Amazon universal order link https://geni.us/qVoIg6

THE BITTER RIVAL

***Sweet Surrender*, the epilogue to *The Bitter Rival*, is coming *spring 2023*. Here's a sneak peek if you haven't met Sebastian and Isabella.**

The Bitter Rival

An excerpt

"Thank you," I utter quietly in the direction of the gorgeous man. He's wearing an expensive gray suit and crisp white shirt. The top buttons are undone, revealing tantalizing bronzed skin and just a hint of dark chest hair.

"Don't thank me," he replies. "I'm kicking myself for letting that guy slither over before I could get the nerve to talk to you."

Unable to help myself, I roll my eyes at this statement. Like this guy would ever need to 'get the nerve' to talk to anyone. I hope he doesn't think I'm falling for that line.

"Awe, come on. You need to dance with me, at least. To keep up the rouse." He winks.

Craning my neck toward the bar, I notice the man in question has already found a new source of entertainment. "I don't think that's necessary." I point a finger in the gentleman's direction, making my point he's completely forgotten about me. I rotate slightly and realize Bailey has slipped back to our table. "Thanks again," I acknowledge before heading in her direction.

"Really? Not even one dance?"

I stop in my tracks, trying to come up with some clever anecdote when it dawns on me. *Why am I in such a hurry to distance myself from the hottest man I've ever encountered?* Everything about this attractive man screams 'Run.' But it's just one dance. I spin on my heel and look up at him. *God, he's one tall drink of water.* "Okay, one dance then."

His expression shifts from a seductive smirk to a warm grin. His bright blue eyes twinkle in my direction, like constellations painted across a clear, dark sky. They could easily hypnotize me if I wasn't distracted by that flirty dimple sending me morse code. Not wasting any time, he steps forward and wraps his strong arms around my back, pulling me into him. An immediate hum begins to stir in my belly. *Just one dance, Bella.*

Shocked at his invasion into my personal space, as well as my reaction to it, I attempt to retreat a step until the warmth of his strong hand caresses my lower back. I instantly feel goosebumps pimple my flesh and try to take a cleansing breath to calm my nerves. This action has the opposite effect, as now I've inhaled the most intoxicating scent. I relent and place my palms flat upon his chest as we move in beat with the music, all the while trying to decipher the incredible notes of his cologne. There's a woody, floral scent with a strange touch of spice. I lean into him, continuing to draw in the heady aroma. I quickly determine I should discontinue this investigation before his scent completely inebriates me.

As I attempt to pull back, his strong arms pull me closer. I can feel him slide his body down the length of mine in time with the music, placing his pelvis entirely too close to mine. One firm rock against this incredibly well-built man, and I might start entertaining ways to satisfy my much overdue craving for some hot and dirty sex.

Taking an opportunity to change positions during a transition in the chorus, I twist to dance with my back to him. His hands move to position themselves, not on my hips, but my lower abdomen. As he rocks my body back against his, I can feel his steely erection against my back. *Good lord, is that his arm or his dick?*

The song comes to an end, and I seize the opportunity to make my exit. As tempting as it might be to consider a one-night stand with this man, he's way out of my league. Truth be told, I think I'd be nervous considering anything with the likes of this one. He seems a little too hot for me to handle.

"Thank you," I blurt before offering a smile that feels forced. Before he can offer a reply, I make haste to my table to find Bailey. Dropping into my chair, I grab the remains of my margarita and chug it down. *Hell, who am I kidding? I'm going to need an ice bath to cool down after that hot piece of—*

"Uh, Bella? Why on earth would you come back here with me when you could keep dancing with tall, dark, and *fuck me, is he sexy?* Jeez, he's the hottest man I think I've ever seen. I almost had an orgasm watching him move his hands all over you. That look on his face. Gah," she utters, fanning herself.

I can't possibly find an answer that will appease her, so I simply shrug my shoulders.

She gives me a blank stare, mimicking my ridiculous motion by drawing her shoulders up toward her ears in question. "What is wrong with you? That man is beautiful."

"Yeah, a little too beautiful."

"Huh?"

"The way he was looking at me, Bailey, and touching me... I was starting to feel like shark bait," I reply as I swiftly look toward the bar for a waiter. I need another drink.

"Well hell, Bella. I'd let him bite me," she scolds, waggling her brows in my direction.

"Bailes, something tells me if a guy like that takes a bite out of you, you won't recover."

Amazon universal order link: https://geni.us/7rP7VrA

ADDITIONAL TITLES

BY LM FOX

The Deprivation Trilogy, Book One: Deprivation

The Deprivation Trilogy, Book Two: Fractured

The Deprivation Trilogy, Book Three: Stronger

The Deprivation Trilogy, The Epilogue

The Bitter Rival (the first interconnected stand-alone spin-off from the series)

Moonshot (the stand-alone prequel to The Deprivation Trilogy)

Naughty & Nice: A Man of the Month Club Novella: Sycamore Mountain series

Upcoming Titles:

Sweet Surrender, The Epilogue to The Bitter Rival
(due spring, 2023)

Luca, the first standalone in the Bianchi Brothers series, (due 2023)

Sunflowers and Surrender:
A Wild Blooms series Novella, (due June 2023)

ABOUT THE AUTHOR

Born and raised in Virginia, LM Fox currently lives in a suburb of Richmond with her husband, three kids, and a chocolate lab.

Her pastimes are traveling to new and favorite places, trying new foods, a swoony book with either a good cup of tea or coffee, margaritas on special occasions, and watching her kids participate in a variety of sports.

She has spent the majority of her adult life working in emergency medicine and her books are written in this setting. Her main characters are typically in the medical field, EMS, fire, and/or law enforcement. She enjoys writing angsty, contemporary romance starring headstrong, independent heroines you can't help but love and the hot alpha men who fall hard for them. www.authorlmfox.com

Printed in Great Britain
by Amazon

16791971R00219